Iona Grey has a degree in English Literature and Language from Manchester University, an obsession with history and an enduring fascination with the lives of women in the twentieth century. She lives in rural Cheshire with her husband and three daughters. She tweets @iona_grey

Praise for *Letters to the Lost*:

'An epic story of love and loss that will break your heart'
Santa Montefiore

'A beautiful, tender story from a naturally gifted storyteller. A wonderful debut novel and a real weepy!'
Lucinda Riley

'I fell completely in love with this novel. *Letters to the Lost* is extraordinary – vivid, compelling and beautifully told. It will stay with me for a long time'
Miranda Dickinson

'A beautifully woven tale of love and loss that breaks your heart and rebuilds it. I couldn't put it down. It was a big juicy read that reminded me of books that I loved in the past that wrapped you up, held you tight and didn't put you down until you were left devastated that the book had ended yet totally satisfied'
Liz Fenwick

Letters to the Lost

IONA GREY

SIMON &
SCHUSTER

London · New York · Sydney · Toronto · New Delhi

A CBS COMPANY

First published in Great Britain by Simon & Schuster UK Ltd, 2015
A CBS COMPANY

1 3 5 7 9 10 8 6 4 2

Simon & Schuster UK Ltd
1st Floor
222 Gray's Inn Road
London WC1X 8HB

www.simonandschuster.co.uk

Simon & Schuster Australia, Sydney
Simon & Schuster India, New Delhi

A CIP catalogue record for this book
is available from the British Library

TPB ISBN: 978-1-47113-983-3
PB ISBN: 978-1-47113-982-6
EBOOK ISBN: 978-1-47113-984-0

Typeset by M Rules
Printed and bound by CPI Group (UK) Ltd, Croydon, CR0 4YY

To my daughters

Prologue

Maine, February 2011

The house is at its most beautiful in the mornings.

He designed it to be that way, with wide, wide windows which stretch from floor to ceiling, to bring in the sand and the ocean and the wide, wide sky. In the mornings the beach is empty and clean, a page on which the day is yet to be written. And the sunrise over the Atlantic is a daily miracle he always feels honoured to witness.

He never forgets how different it could have been.

There are no curtains in the house, nothing to shut out the view. The walls are white and they take on the tint of the light; pearly pale, or pink as the inside of a seashell, or the rich, warm gold of maple syrup. He sleeps little these days and mostly he is awake to see the slow spread of dawn on the horizon. Sometimes he comes to suddenly, feeling that familiar touch on his shoulder.

Lieutenant, it's 4.30 a.m. and you're flying today . . .

A circle is closing. The finger tracing it on the misted glass

1

is slowly coming around to the top again, to the point where it all began. The memories are with him almost constantly now, their colours fresh, voices vivid. Dawns of long ago. The smell of oil and hot metal. The plaintive, primitive thrum of engines on the flight line and a red ribbon on a map.

Today gentlemen, your target is . . .

It is such a long time ago. Almost a lifetime. It is the past, but it doesn't feel like it's over. The ribbon is stretching across the ocean outside his window, beyond the distant horizon, to England.

The letter lies amid the bottles of pills and sterile needle packs on the nightstand beside him, its familiar address as evocative as a poem. A love song. He has waited too long to write it. For years he has tried to reconcile himself to how things are and to forget how they should have been, but as the days dwindle and the strength ebbs out of him he sees that this is impossible.

The things that are left behind are the things that matter, like rocks exposed by the retreating tide. And so he has written, and now he is impatient for the letter to begin its journey, into the past.

1

London, February 2011

It was a nice part of London. Respectable. Affluent. The shops that lined the street in the villagey centre were closed and shuttered but you could tell they were posh, and there were restaurants – so many restaurants – their windows lit up like wide-screen TVs showing the people inside. People who were too well-mannered to turn and gawp at the girl running past on the street outside.

Not running for fitness, wearing lycra and headphones and a focused expression, but messily, desperately, with her short skirt riding up to her knickers and her unshod feet splashing through the greasy puddles on the pavement. She'd kicked off her stupid shoes as she left the pub, knowing she wouldn't get far wearing them. Platform stilettos; the twenty-first-century equivalent of a ball and chain.

At the corner she hesitated, chest heaving. Across the road was a row of shops with an alleyway at the side; behind, the pounding echo of feet. She ran again, seeking out the dark.

There was a backyard with bins. A security light exploded above her, glittering on broken glass and ragged bushes beyond a high wooden gate. She let herself through, wincing and whimpering as the ground beneath her feet changed from hard tarmac to oozing earth that seeped through her sodden tights. Up ahead there was the glimmer of a streetlight. It gave her something to head towards; she pushed aside branches and emerged into a narrow lane.

It was flanked on one side by garages and the backs of houses, and by a row of plain terraced cottages on the other. She swung round, her heart battering against her ribs. If he followed her down here there would be nowhere to hide. No one to see. The windows of the houses glowed behind closed curtains, like slumbering eyes. Briefly she considered knocking on the door of one of the small cottages and throwing herself on the mercy of the people inside, but realizing how she must look in her clinging dress and stage make-up she dismissed the idea and stumbled on.

The last house in the little terrace was in darkness. As she got closer she could see that its front garden was overgrown and neglected, with weeds growing halfway up the peeling front door and a forest of shrubbery encroaching upon it from the side. The windows were blank and black. They swallowed up her reflection in their filth-furred glass.

She heard it again, the beat of running feet, coming closer. What if he'd got the others to look for her too? What if they came from the opposite direction, surrounding her and leaving no escape? For a moment she froze, and then adrenaline squirted, hot and stinging, galvanizing her into movement. With nowhere else to go she slipped along the side of the end house, between the wall and the tangle of foliage. Panic made her push forward, tripping over branches, gagging on the feral, unfamiliar stink. Something shot out from beneath the hedge at her feet, so close that she felt rough fur brush briefly against her shin. Recoiling, she tripped. Her ankle was wrenched round and a hot shaft of pain shot up her leg.

She sat on the damp ground and gripped her ankle hard, as if she could squash the pain back in to where it had come from. Tears sprang to her eyes, but at that moment she heard footsteps and a single angry shout from the front of the house. She clenched her teeth, picturing Dodge beneath the streetlamp, hands on his hips as he swung around searching for her, his face wearing that particular belligerent expression – jaw jutting, eyes narrowed – that it did when he was thwarted.

Holding her breath she strained to listen. The seconds stretched and quivered with tension, until at last she picked up the sound of his receding feet. The air rushed from her lungs and she collapsed forward, limp with relief.

The money crackled inside her pocket. Fifty pounds – she'd only taken her share, not what was due to the rest of the band, but he wouldn't like it: he made the bookings, he took the money. She slid a hand into her pocket to touch the waxy, well-used notes, and a tiny ember of triumph glowed in her heart.

*

She'd never broken into a house before. It was surprisingly easy.

The hardest part was crawling through the hedge, and beating through thorny ropes of brambles and spires of stinging nettles in the garden as her ankle throbbed and burned. The glass in the back door was as brittle and easy to break as the crust of ice on top of a puddle, and the key was still in the lock on the other side.

The kitchen was small, low-ceilinged. It smelled musty, as if it had been shut up for a long time. She turned around slowly, her eyes raking the gloom for signs of life. The plant on the windowsill had shrivelled to a twist of dry leaves set in shrunken soil but there was a kettle on the gas stove and cups hanging from a row of hooks beneath the shelf on the wall, as if the occupant might come in at any moment to make a cup of tea. She shuddered, the hairs on the back of her neck rising.

'Hello?'

She spoke loudly, with a confidence she didn't feel. Her voice sounded peculiar; flat and almost comically Northern. 'Hello – is anyone there?'

The quiet engulfed her. In a sudden flash of inspiration she fumbled to find the pocket of her jacket and pulled out a cheap plastic lighter. The circle of gold cast by the flame was small, but enough to show cream tiled walls, a calendar bearing a picture of a castle above the date July 2009, a kind-of vintage cupboard unit with glass-fronted doors at the top. She moved forward awkwardly, reaching out to support herself on the doorframe as pain sank its teeth deeper into her leg. In the next room the glow of the tiny flame outlined a table by the window and a sideboard on which china ladies curtseyed and pirouetted to an invisible audience. The stairs rose from a narrow passageway. She paused at the foot of them. Staring up into the darkness she spoke again, softly this time, as if calling to a friend.

'Hello? Anyone home?'

Silence greeted her, and the faintest breath of some old-fashioned perfume drifted down, as if she'd disturbed air that had been still for a long time. She should go up to check that there was no one there, but her aching ankle and the sense of absolute stillness deterred her.

In the room at the front she let the flame go out, not wanting to risk its glow being spotted from outside. Drooping curtains were half pulled across the window, but the light from the streetlamp filtering through the gap was enough to show a sagging and lumpy settee pushed against one wall, with a blanket made up of crocheted squares in clashing colours covering its back. Cautiously she peered out, looking for Dodge, but the pool of light around the streetlamp was still and unbroken. She sagged against an armchair and breathed a little easier.

It had been an old person's house, that much was obvious. The television was huge and comically outdated, and an electric bar fire stood in front of the boarded-up grate. Against the front door a pile of mail had gathered like a drift of autumn leaves.

She limped back into the kitchen and turned on the tap

above the sink, letting the water run through the clanking pipes for a few moments before cupping her hands beneath it and drinking. She wondered who owned it and what had happened to them; whether they'd gone into a home, or died. When someone died their house got cleared out, surely? That's what had happened to Gran's, anyway. Within a week of the funeral all the clothes and pictures and plates and pans, as well as Gran's vast collection of china pigs and the fragments of Jess's shattered childhood had been packed up and dispersed so the council could get the house ready for the new tenant.

The darkness felt mossy and damp against her skin. Goosebumps stood on her arms beneath her fake-leather jacket. Maybe the owner had died and not actually been discovered? Some masochistic instinct brought out by the dark and the quiet made her picture a body decaying in the bed upstairs. She dismissed it briskly, reasserting common sense. What harm could the dead do to you anyway? A corpse couldn't split your lip or steal your money, or close its fingers round your neck until stars danced behind your eyes.

Suddenly she felt bone tired, the pulse of pain in her ankle radiating outwards so that her whole body throbbed with exhaustion. She made her way haltingly back to the front room and sank onto the sofa, dropping her head into her hands as the enormity of the events of the last hour overwhelmed her.

Shit. She'd broken into a house. An empty and neglected one maybe, but even so. Breaking and entering wasn't like nicking a packet of crisps from the corner shop because you didn't want to be called a skank for having a free school dinner. It was a whole different level of wrong.

On the upside, she had escaped. She wasn't on her way back to the flat in Elephant and Castle with Dodge. She wouldn't have to endure the lust that afflicted him after a beery evening watching her sing in the slapper's gear he made her wear. Not tonight, not ever again. The first thing she'd do when her ankle was better was find a charity shop or something and spend a bit of the precious money on decent clothes. Warm clothes. Clothes that actually covered up her body, rather than displaying it like goods in the window of a cut-price shop.

Wincing, she lay back, resting her leg on the arm of the sofa and settling herself on the cigarette-scented cushions. She wondered where he was now; whether he'd given up looking and gone back to the flat to wait, confident that she'd come back eventually. She needed him, as he liked to tell her; needed his contacts and his bookings and his money, because without him what was she? Nothing. A Northern nobody with a voice like a thousand other wannabe stars. A voice that no one would ever hear if it wasn't for him.

She tugged the crocheted blanket down from the back of the sofa and pulled it over herself. In the wake of the adrenaline rush her body felt heavy and weak, and she found she didn't actually give a toss where he was, because for the first time in six months what he thought or felt or wanted was of no relevance to her whatsoever.

The unfamiliar house settled itself around her, absorbing her into its stillness. The noise of the city seemed far away here and the sound of cars on the wet street had receded to a muted sigh, like waves on a distant beach. She stared into the shadows and began to hum softly, to keep the silence at bay. The tune that came into her head was not one of the songs she had belted out on the stage in the pub earlier, but one from the past; a lullaby Gran used to sing to her when she was small. The words were half-forgotten, but the melody stroked her with soothing, familiar fingers, and she didn't feel quite so alone.

Light was filtering through the thin curtains when she woke, and the slice of sky visible in the gap between them was the bleached bone white of morning. She went to adjust her position and instantly pain flared in her ankle, as if someone had been waiting until she moved to hit it with a sledgehammer. She froze, waiting for the ripples of agony to subside.

Through the wall she could hear noises; the rise and fall of indistinct voices on the radio, then music and the hurried thud of feet on the stairs. She sat up, gritting her teeth as she put her foot to the floor. In the icy bathroom she sat on the loo and peeled off her shredded tights to look at her ankle. It was unrecognizable; puffy and purpling above a foot that was smeared with dirt.

The bathroom didn't boast anything as modern as a shower, only a deep cast-iron bath with rust stains beneath the taps and a basin in the corner. Above this there was a little mirrored cabinet, which she opened in the hope of finding something that might help. Inside the shelves were cluttered with boxes and bottles that wouldn't have looked out of place in a museum, their faded labels advertising the mysterious medicines of another time; Milk of Magnesia, Kaolin, Linctus. In amongst them, on the bottom shelf, there was a lipstick in a gold case.

She took it out, turning it around between her fingers for a moment before taking off the lid and twisting the base. It was red. Bright, vibrant scarlet: the colour of poppies and pillar-boxes and old-fashioned movie star glamour. An indentation had been worn into the top, where it had moulded to fit the shape of the lips of the user. She tried to imagine her, whoever she was, standing here in this bathroom with the black-and-white tiles and the mould-patterned walls; an old woman, painting on this brave daub of colour for a trip to the shops or an evening at the bingo, and she felt a burst of admiration and curiosity.

There was a roll of yellowing crepe bandage on the top shelf of the cupboard, and she took this and a packet of soluble aspirin into the kitchen. She unhooked a teacup and filled it with water, then dropped in two of the tablets. Waiting for them to dissolve she looked around. In the grimy morning light the place looked bleak, but there was something poignantly homely about the row of canisters on the shelf, labelled 'TEA', 'RICE', 'SUGAR', the scarred chopping board propped against the wall and the scorched oven gloves hanging from a hook beside the cooker. The cup in her hand was green, but sort of shiny; iridescent like the delicate rainbows in oily puddles. She rubbed her finger over it. She'd never seen anything like it before, and she liked it. It couldn't have been more different from the assortment of cheap stained mugs in the flat in Elephant and Castle.

She drank the aspirin mixture in two big grimacing gulps, her throat closing in protest at the salty-sweetness, then took the bandage into the front room where she applied herself to the task of binding up her ankle. Mid-way through she heard whistling outside, and stopped, her heart thudding. Footsteps came closer. Dropping the bandage she got to her feet, tensed for the knock on the door or, worse, a key turning—

With a rusty, reluctant creak the letterbox opened. A single, cream-coloured envelope landed on top of the heap of garish junk mail and takeaway menus.

Mrs S. Thorne
4 Greenfields Lane
Church End
London
UNITED KINGDOM.

It was written in black ink. Proper ink, not biro. The writing was bold and elegant but unmistakably shaky, as if the person who had written it was old or sick or in a rush. The paper was creamy, faintly ridged, like bone or ivory.

She turned it over. Spiked black capitals grabbed her attention.

PERSONAL and <u>URGENT</u>. If necessary and possible
<u>PLEASE FORWARD</u>.

She put it on the mantelpiece, propped against a chipped
jug bearing the slogan 'A Present from Margate'. Against the
faded furnishings the envelope looked clean and crisp and
opulent.

Outside the world got on with its weekday business, but in
the little house time faltered and the day dragged. The initial
euphoria of having got away from Dodge was quickly eroded
by hunger and the savage cold. In a cupboard in the kitchen
she discovered a little stash of supplies, amongst which was a
packet of fig rolls. They were almost two years past their sell
by date but she devoured half of them, and made herself save
the rest for later. She kept trying to think of where to go from
here, what to do next, but her thoughts went round in futile
circles, like a drowsy bluebottle bashing senselessly against a
closed window.

She slept again, deeply, only surfacing when the short
February day was fading and the shadows in the corners of
the room had thickened on the nets of cobwebs. The envelope on the mantelpiece seemed to have absorbed all the
remaining light. It gleamed palely, like the moon.

Mrs S. Thorne must have been the lady who had lived
here, but what did she need to know that was 'Personal and
Urgent'? With some effort she levered herself up from the
sofa and scooped up the landslide of mail from beneath the
letterbox. Wrapping the blanket around her shoulders she

began to go through it, looking for clues. Maybe there would be something there to hint at where she'd gone, this mysterious Mrs Thorne.

Most of it was anonymous junk offering free delivery on takeaway pizzas or bargain deals on replacement windows. She tried hard not to look at the takeaway menus, with their close-up photographs of glistening, luridly coloured pizzas, as big as bicycle wheels. In amongst them she found a newsletter from All Saints Church with 'Miss Price' scribbled at the top, and several flimsy mail order catalogues selling 'classic knitwear' and thermal nightwear addressed to Miss N. Price.

No mention of Mrs Thorne.

She tossed the church newsletter onto the junk pile and stretched her cramped spine. The idle curiosity that had prompted her to start the search had faded when it yielded no instant answer, and the pizza photographs made her feel irritable and on edge. Since she wasn't even supposed to be here it was hardly her responsibility to make sure the letter reached its destination, and it wasn't as if she didn't have enough of her own problems to sort out. She didn't need to take on anyone else's.

But still . . .

She got up and went over to the fireplace, sliding the letter out from behind the clock. 'Personal and Urgent' – what did that mean anyway? It was probably nothing. She knew from Gran that old people got in a state about all kinds of random things.

The paper was so thick it was almost like velvet. In the gathering dusk it was difficult to make out the postmark, but she risked taking a step towards the window to squint at the blurred stamp. Bloody hell – USA. She turned it over and read the message on the back again, running her fingers over the underlining where the ink had smudged slightly. Tilting it up to the dying light she could see the indentation in the paper where the pen had scored across it, pressing hope into the page.

Personal and Urgent.

If possible . . .

And before she knew what she was doing, before she had a chance to think about all the reasons why it was wrong, she was tearing open the envelope and sliding out the single sheet of paper inside.

The Beach House
Back Creek Road
Kennebunk, ME
22 January 2011

Darling girl
    It's been over seventy years and I still think of you like that. My darling. My girl. So much has changed in that time and the world is a different place to the one where we met, but every time I think of you I'm twenty-two years old again.
    I've been thinking a lot about those days. I haven't been

feeling so good and the meds the doctors have given me make me pretty tired. Not surprising at ninety years old, maybe. Some days it seems like I barely wake up and lying here, half sleeping, all those memories are so damned vivid I almost believe they're real and that I'm back there, in England, with 382 Squadron and you.

I promised to love you forever, in a time when I didn't know if I'd live to see the start of another week. Now it looks like forever is finally running out. I never stopped loving you. I tried, for the sake of my own sanity, but I never even got close, and I never stopped hoping either. The docs say I don't have much time left, but I still have that hope, and the feeling that I'm not done here. Not until I know what happened to you. Not until I've told you that what we started back then in those crazy days when the world was all upside-down has never really finished for me, and that those days − tough and terrifying though they were − were also the best of my life.

I don't know where you are. I don't know if the house on Greenfields Lane is still yours and if this letter will ever reach you. Hell, I don't know if you're still alive, except I have this crazy belief that I'd know if you weren't; I'd feel it and be ready to go too. I'm not afraid of Death − my old adversary from those flying days. I beat him back then so I'm easy about letting him win this time around, but I'd give in a hell of a lot more gracefully if I knew. And if I could say goodbye to you properly this time.

I guess that pretty soon none of this will matter, and our story will be history. But I'm not done hoping yet. Or wishing I

*could go back to the start and do it all again, and this time
make sure I never let you go.*

If you get this, please write.

My love

Dan

Oh.

Ohhhh . . .

She folded the letter in half again and shoved it hastily back
into the envelope. She shouldn't have touched it; would never
have done if she'd thought for a minute it would be so . . . *serious*. Life and death kind of serious. Personal and urgent.

But it was too late now. The letter had been torn open and
couldn't be resealed. The plea sent out from across the world
by a dying man had been heard, however inadvertently, by her
and no one else. And so now she had a choice: to ignore it, or
to make some attempt to find Mrs S. Thorne. Whoever she
might be.

2

London, August 1942

No one expected a wartime wedding to be lavish, but the parish ladies had done their Reverend proud.

The austere brick interior of St Crispin's was decked with dahlias, phlox and chrysanthemums garnered from tired August gardens, and across the road in the church hall a spread of bloater paste sandwiches, Spam rolls and Marjorie Walsh's inevitable scones had been lovingly laid out around the one-tier cake. King's Oak was a small suburb of North London, mostly made up of Victorian terraces with tiny brick-paved yards at the back, and neat pairs of semi-detached houses built after the last war. It certainly wasn't a rich parish, but no one could say it wasn't a generous one. Coupons had been swapped and rations pooled, and the resulting feast was a tribute to the resourcefulness of the St Crispin's parishioners, and the high regard in which they held their vicar.

He stood at the front of the church, not facing them as he

usually did, but with his head bent in private conversation with God. There was something vulnerable, Ada Broughton thought from her usual place in the third-row pew, about the pinkness of his neck above his collar, and something rather impressive about his solitary communion with the Lord. He wasn't a particularly young man – the difference in years between him and his bride had been much muttered about during meetings of the Mothers' Union and the Hospital Supplies Committee – but his bookish, undernourished appearance gave an impression of youth, and inspired in his lady parishioners (in the days before rationing, at least) an urge to bake him suet puddings and individual cottage pies with the leftovers from the Sunday roast.

They'd all had him down as a confirmed bachelor and his engagement to young Stella Holland had come as quite a surprise. In fact, as Marjorie Walsh sounded a strident chord on the organ announcing the arrival of the bride, Ada saw his head snap upwards and his eyes widen, as if he too had been caught off-guard by this turn of events. His expression, as he looked at his best man beside him, was almost one of panic, poor lamb.

Ah, but the bride was a picture. Looking over her shoulder, Ada felt her eyes prickle and her bosom swell beneath her best pre-war dress. Slender as a willow, her narrow shoulders held very straight, her face pale behind the mist of her veil, little Stella looked like Princess Elizabeth herself rather than a girl from the Poor School. The bridal gown was another collaborative effort, donated by Dot Wilkins (who'd worn it in

1919 when her Arthur had recovered enough from the gas to rasp 'I do') and altered by the Ladies' Sewing Circle. They'd stopped making field dressings for an entire month while they updated the style and took in all the seams to fit Stella's tiny frame, which was currently further dwarfed by the solid tweed-clad figure of Phyllis Birch walking beside her, in lieu of a father. But it was Stella who drew everyone's gaze. None of them had ever dreamed that the mouldy old lace dress could be transformed into this vision of loveliness. Ada dabbed a tear and allowed herself a moment of maternal pride. In the absence of the girl's mother she didn't feel she was overreaching herself too much.

Her expression soured a little as it came to rest on Nancy Price, walking behind the bride. Her dress was of ice blue satin, which had looked smashing on Ethel Collins's daughter when she'd been a bridesmaid in the summer of '39, but less so on Nancy. The colour went well with her bottle-blonde hair, but she inhabited the demure garment with an attitude of secret amusement, as if the puff-sleeves and modest sweetheart neckline were somehow ridiculous. Even doing something as simple as walking down the aisle, Nancy managed to make herself look faintly unrespectable. The two girls really were chalk and cheese – it was a wonder they were such good friends, though maybe having no family and being brought up in one of those places made you cling to whatever comfort you could find. Ada hoped that now Stella was going to be Mrs Charles Thorne and a vicar's wife, she'd grow out of the unsuitable friendship.

Marjorie speeded up the tempo of the wedding march as the bride approached her waiting groom. Shafts of sunlight poured over their bent heads, filled with dust motes like fine, golden celestial confetti. Ada put aside all other thoughts and settled down to enjoy the vows.

Charles's first name was actually Maurice; until she heard the vicar saying it, Stella hadn't known that. Maurice Charles Thorne. It seemed so strange and so funny that she couldn't focus on anything else as she repeated her vows, and afterwards she had no recollection at all of promising to love and honour and obey. She supposed she must have done, because there was the shiny gold band on her finger – just a thin one, which was all they could get – and people were kissing her on the cheek and slapping Charles on the back and congratulating them both on being husband and wife.

Wife. Standing outside the church, her arm tucked through Charles's as Fred Collins adjusted his camera, she hugged the word to herself and felt something expand and glow inside her chest, like an ember unfurling. Wife meant security; a proper home filled with your own things, not a narrow strip in a dormitory surrounded by the snifflings and mutterings of twenty other girls. She thought of the wedding presents displayed on the dining-room table in the Vicarage – a china tea set patterned with roses from an aunt of Charles's, a crystal rose bowl from Miss Birch and an embroidered dressing-table set from the girls at Woodhill School – and her smile widened, just as the flashbulb exploded.

The church hall looked lovely. The damp-stained corners were hidden by Union Jack bunting, hoarded since the armistice, which lent the drab green interior a holiday atmosphere. A banner, painted on a frayed bedsheet, hung over the buffet table, bearing the words 'The Happy Couple'.

And everyone had been so kind. Even Charles's parents, conspicuously smart and decked in brittle smiles, had kissed the air beside each of her cheeks and pronounced themselves delighted. It was no secret that they would have much preferred their son to marry a girl from the tennis club in Dorking, who could make up a four on Lillian's bridge afternoons and converse with her friends in the right sort of accent, but Stella was grateful to them for keeping up the pretence.

'Such a pretty dress!' Lillian Thorne exclaimed brightly, standing back to look Stella up and down. 'Did you make it yourself? It looks terribly professional.'

'It belonged to one of the ladies in the parish. The sewing circle altered it for me.'

'Really? Oh, gosh, you should have said – you could have had mine! It was a Hartnell: cost a small fortune, and now it's just squashed into a trunk in the attic. If I'd known you were in need of one I'd have dug it out.'

The offer would have been kind, but since it came about three months too late Stella wasn't sure how to respond. Unperturbed, Lillian ploughed airily on. 'What a sweet bouquet too – though it looks like it could do with a drink.'

Stella looked down at the roses wilting in her hand. Lillian was right. They were tea roses of the old-fashioned kind –

donated with great pride and ceremony by Alf Broughton from the one bush in his tiny patch of garden that he had refused to give up to rows of sprouts and potatoes – but they were already beginning to collapse. Stella remembered the roses in Lillian's garden in Dorking, which were as stiff and immaculate as she was, and realized that the compliment was as barbed as their stems.

'It's not the only one,' Roger Thorne muttered, looking irritably across the room to where Alf was cheerfully dispensing bottles of stout and glasses of lemonade from a makeshift bar by the kitchen hatch. Mr Thorne had somehow managed to lay his hands on a case of champagne, but it was still underneath the trestle. The people of King's Oak didn't go in much for fancy stuff like that, and Alf – a stout man in every sense – wasn't up to the engineering feat required to open a bottle.

Stella took a sip of her lemonade, aware of the dangers that lurked like Atlantic mines beneath the surface of the conversation. 'It's not you, it's me,' Charles had said curtly, staring out of the train window on the way home from their one visit to Dorking. They'd never understood him, he explained. They were baffled by his calling, and annoyed that he hadn't followed the path that had been prepared for him into Roger's accountancy firm. Stella had sensed a deep hurt, and her heart had ached for him. Family dynamics were a mystery to her, but once they were married they would build their own family and Charles, at its centre, would be healed by her understanding and the huge stores of love she had inside, just waiting to be given.

'Where is Charles?' Lillian asked testily, as if reading her mind. 'I've hardly spoken a word to him.'

That makes two of us, thought Stella, following Lillian's gaze as it roamed the hall. It was quite crowded now, with members of the St Crispin's parish who hadn't bothered coming to the church service slipping in to grab a free bite to eat. Stella barely knew most of them, but felt a beat of affection and relief at the sight of Nancy, incongruously dressed in blue satin and smoking a cigarette, like a film starlet captured in *Picture Post* relaxing backstage between scenes. There was no sign of Charles inside, but a movement in the yard outside caught her eye.

'He's out there, talking to Peter.'

Peter Underwood was Charles's best man. A friend from his days at theological college, he was now the vicar of a small parish in Dorset. It was the first time Stella had met him, though Charles talked about him a lot. From the tone of these comments Stella had expected someone altogether more charismatic than the slight, sallow-skinned, cynical young man whose eyes were owlish behind his spectacles.

'Well he shouldn't be,' Lillian snapped. 'He should be in here, talking to his guests with his new wife.'

That at least was something they could agree on.

'I'll go and have a word,' said Roger, excusing himself with a note of relief. 'The buffet has almost disappeared. Surely it must be time for the speeches?'

Miss Birch was the first person to climb the rickety steps to the small stage. As she cleared her throat in that emphatic way that demanded silence Stella had such a vivid sense of déjà-vu that she was surprised to look down and see Mrs Wilkins's white lace rather than her dark green school pinafore.

'It is my great pleasure and privilege to stand before you on this joyful occasion and say a few words on behalf of the new Mrs Thorne,' Miss Birch said in her Assembly Voice, and a ripple of applause went through the hall. 'Stella is one of the great successes of Woodhill School, and I had no hesitation in putting her forward for the position at the Vicarage when Reverend Thorne found himself in need of a housekeeper. Little did I suspect that I wasn't only helping fill a domestic breach,' (here her severe features took on a most uncharacteristically playful look) 'but playing cupid too. As the months progressed it was not only the Vicarage hearth that was warmed, but the heart of its incumbent too!'

Heads turned in Stella's direction and a collective 'ahh' echoed around the assembled crowd, as if they were watching a display of fireworks. Her face burned. 'The qualities that made her such a valuable member of Woodhill – her kindness and diligence, her cheerful outlook on life and her faithfulness and loyalty – will also make her a wonderful vicar's wife,' Miss Birch went on. Stella wished she still had the lace veil to hide behind. Or Charles, but he was standing with Peter Underwood beside the stage. Suddenly she glimpsed Nancy, who rolled her eyes and pulled a face, and she felt better.

'I wish the Reverend and Mrs Thorne every happiness in their life together. May it be long and full, unblighted by this blasted war, and blessed with the joy of children,' Miss Birch concluded, in the ringing tone she used when announcing the next hymn. 'Do please join me in a toast to the happy couple – the bride and groom!'

Mr Thorne's champagne was still in its box beneath the trestle, so the bride and groom were dutifully toasted in stout and lemonade, or – in the case of the groom's parents and Dr Walsh – with nothing at all. Charles mounted the steps to fill the place vacated by Miss Birch.

Stella loved to hear him speak. During the months of their engagement she had sat in a side pew at St Crispin's on Sunday mornings while he delivered his sermon and her blood had secretly thrilled. There was something remote and romantic about him then, standing before the altar in the cavernous church or reading from the vast Bible in the pulpit. However, it didn't quite translate to the church hall. The solemnity and passion with which he preached deserted him as he stood between the limp plush curtains and stammered his thanks to Miss Birch, then went on to deflate her claim that she had brought Stella and himself together, giving the credit to God instead.

'Many times I questioned Him about His purpose – a lovely young wife wasn't something I had expected to find in my ministry at St Crispin's – but it's not unusual for God to have to put things right in front of my nose before I notice them.' He smiled his shy, boyish smile and the ladies of his congregation sighed. 'That only left me with the task of convincing Stella!'

Everyone laughed indulgently, but Stella's face felt stiff with smiling. The halting progress of their awkward courtship was the last thing she wanted to be reminded of today, when at last they could start life properly as man and wife.

Secretly Stella wasn't entirely sure that she believed in God, but she had certainly felt His presence, like a disapproving chaperone, whenever she and Charles had been alone together since their engagement. Charles had kissed her for the first time on the evening he'd asked her to marry him, but it had been a hurried, dry thing that carried with it a sense of relief rather than longing, and a far cry from the lingering, melting kisses she and Nancy witnessed in the Picture House on a Saturday afternoon (both on the screen and in the back row). Stella always left the cinema with a sense of restless yearning, weighted down with all the love she longed to give. Now that there was no extra-marital sin to police, she hoped God might leave them in peace to get on with it.

On the stage Charles rather stiffly thanked the bridesmaid, and Nancy gave a cheeky little mock curtsey, which he pretended not to notice. Peter Underwood made his creaking way up the steps.

Heat was gathering beneath the rafters now. The men had taken off their jackets and rolled back their shirtsleeves and the children could be heard shrieking and whooping in the yard outside. Everyone was getting restless. In the kitchen the ladies doing the washing up had forgotten to whisper and, as the best man's speech stretched from five minutes to ten, most people tuned out his thin, sardonic drawl and listened instead to the far more interesting conversation drifting through the kitchen hatch, about Ethel Collins's sister who'd been bombed out of her home in Enfield and had moved in with her son and daughter-in-law in Bromley.

'And it was in the summer of '31 that Charles and I embarked on our memorable fishing trip to North Wales. Just as Jesus our Lord found himself on Jordan's banks with five loaves and a few small fishes, so Charles and I found ourselves stranded in the middle of Lake Bala with only a meagre cheese sandwich between us . . .'

Stella's attention wandered away from the wilds of North Wales to the kitchen, where Ethel Collins's voice rose indignantly above the groan and hiss of the tea urn. 'They've got an inside lav, but Joan's not allowed to use it. She's handed over her ration book, but there's barely a scrap of food, and that woman swiped all her coupons and used them for a new dress for herself . . .'

Guiltily Stella retuned her mental wireless back to Peter Underwood. The hearty, outdoor Charles emerging in his speech bore little resemblance to the man Stella knew. Or didn't know. She might learn something if she listened.

When Peter finally turned the last page of the sheaf of papers in his hand, there was a relieved ripple of applause, then Miss Birch bustled forward clapping her hands and announcing that it was time for the bride and groom to cut the cake. Fred Collins was dragged back from the yard and ordered to put down his stout and pick up his camera. Stella found herself standing beneath the banner beside Charles, once more smiling into the lens. On the photographs it would look like they'd been at each other's side all day, though the reality had been rather different. His hand covered hers on the cake knife and her chest clenched. He had such lovely hands – long fingered and elegant. She thought of later on, in the hotel in Brighton, and how those fingers would undo the buttons of her nightdress and move across her skin . . .

'We'll have to do that one again,' Fred Collins guffawed. 'You had your eyes closed, Mrs Thorne!'

The Vicarage was a solid Victorian house with its own particular scent of boiled vegetables, damp tweed and masculinity that Stella hoped would somehow alter when she was properly in residence, as a wife rather than a housekeeper. Carrying her cardboard suitcase she led the way upstairs, with Nancy following behind, peering into rooms as they passed.

'Big old place, isn't it? Just fancy – all these rooms are yours now.'

'Not really. The house belongs to the church, not Charles, but I know what you mean. I'm very lucky.'

'I wouldn't go that far,' Nancy muttered as she followed her into the bedroom that from now on was to be Stella's. The high wooden bed was covered by a mustard-coloured counterpane and there was a wooden cross bearing a carved figure of the tortured Christ hanging on the green-painted wall above it. Everything in the Vicarage seemed to be painted green; the same shade as the church hall, and the pavilion on the playing field, come to think of it. 'Anyway, it's not luck,'

Nancy went on. 'You deserve all of this and more. He's the lucky one, marrying a gorgeous girl like you.'

'I don't think his family see it that way. I'll always be the girl from the Poor School to them.'

'That shows what they know.' Brusqueness, in Nancy's case, was a sign of sincerity. The bed creaked as she collapsed back onto it, hitching up Betty Collins's blue bridesmaid satin to reveal a packet of cigarettes tucked into her stocking top. 'You're a cut above the lot of 'em. Daughter of a Duke, that's who you are.'

Perching on the stool in front of the squat chest of drawers that did service as a dressing table, Stella smiled. All she knew about the mother who had given her up was that she'd been in service in a big house in Belgravia. Her father's identity was a mystery, but Nancy's theory was that he was from 'upstairs', which explained what she called Stella's 'ladylike ways'.

'Well, it doesn't matter whose daughter I am now, does it?' she said softly, beginning to pull out the pins securing her veil. 'I'm Charles's wife. That's all that matters to me.'

'If you say so.'

'I do. I know you think I'm mad, but it's all I've ever wanted: a house to keep and a husband to love. A tea set with roses on it. You know that.'

Looking out of the window, Nancy exhaled a sighful of smoke. There was a long pause, in which the only sound was the hiss of the brush through Stella's hair and the distant sounds of children shouting in the street. 'I'll miss you,' Nancy said, suddenly sombre.

'Oh, Nance – I'm only going to Brighton for four days.'

'I don't mean that, and you know it. Things are bound to change. You can't go out dancing and eat chips on the bus on the way home now you're a vicar's wife, can you? You'll have to cook his tea and be there to hand round biscuits at all those evening prayer meetings he has.'

'It won't be so bad. We'll still see each other.' Stella supposed Nancy was right about the dancing, but she wasn't sure she'd miss it that much. It seemed a small thing to forgo in exchange for all that she would be gaining. 'Here, help me out of this dress would you? We can meet up on Saturdays for the pictures or a look in the shops, and you can come round here whenever you like.'

Heaving herself up off the bed, Nancy gave a humourless laugh. 'I don't think Charles would be too happy about that.'

'Well, he'll just have to get used to it. We're as good as sisters, you and I; he knows that. You're the closest I've got to family.'

'Except Miss Birch. I reckon she thinks of herself as family now – can you believe what she was like today?' Cigarette wedged into the corner of her mouth, Nancy smirked and said in her best Miss Birch voice, '*Stella is one of the great successes of Woodhill School . . .*'

A volley of Miss Birch impressions followed, accompanied by much giggling, as Stella dressed in the powder-blue suit Ada Broughton had snaffled from the donations for refugees and Nancy re-did her hair, pinning up her curls in one of the styles she had learned in the salon where she worked, and which she had assured Stella was the height of sophistication. When she'd finished she settled a little powder-blue hat on it, tilting at a daring angle.

Stella looked at the finished result uneasily, turning her head this way and that. 'I look very . . . grown up.'

'You look gorgeous. You'll knock his socks off. Talking of which . . .' Nancy turned away and picked up her handbag from the bed. Out of it she produced a small, brown-paper-wrapped package. 'Wedding present. Or, honeymoon present, more like.'

She watched as Stella opened it and, laughing, held up the slippery sliver of pale pink satin.

'Nance, it's beautiful! What is it?'

'It's to wear in bed, silly. On your wedding night.'

Stella's cheeks glowed, and there was a peculiar tingling in the pit of her stomach. 'I couldn't! There's nothing of it – I'll freeze!'

'Don't be daft – you'll be burning up with passion. Charles won't know what to do with himself. He'll have so much to praise the Almighty for he won't know where to start.'

Everyone came out of the hall to wave them off. Fred Collins made them stand beside the open door of the taxi for a final snapshot, Charles's arm stiffly around her, his expression tense because he was aware of the meter ticking away. And then she was kissing Nancy again, and Ada and Ethel, and even, awkwardly, Roger and Lillian. She was about to get into the taxi, hurried up by Charles, when Nancy shouted, 'Your bouquet!'

'Oh!'

She ascertained where Nancy was standing, then turned her back to the crush of well-wishers. But as she threw the bouquet upwards, the roses' thorny stems snagged on her gloves and its trajectory was altered, so that it sailed over her head in a confetti of velvety petals, straight into the hands of Peter Underwood.

Stella craned her head to look through the rear window of the taxi as they drove away. Everyone had crowded into the road and was waving frantically, except for Peter who was standing quite still holding the bouquet.

'It was supposed to be Nancy who caught it,' Stella muttered, anguished.

'Peter always was rather a marvel in the slips,' Charles said, admiringly.

The taxi turned the corner at the bottom of Church Road and everyone was lost from view. Settling back on the seat, Stella felt sudden, inexplicable tears prickle her eyes. Looking down she saw that her glove was torn and the pristine whiteness stained with blood.

3

2011

The short days bled into each other, through endless stretches of night.

The best way, the only way, to cope with the darkness and the cold and the hunger was to sleep. In the absence of electric light, television, regular mealtimes, her body clock reset itself to some more primitive rhythm and she did this with astonishing ease, like an animal hibernating, so that chunks of time were simply swallowed up by oblivion.

When she was awake, the silence boomed and echoed in her head and she felt her voice shrivel and harden in her throat, like the Little Mermaid's. It made her realize how much she wanted – needed – to sing; how, in spite of Dodge and her soured dreams, it was still part of who she was. Slipping soundlessly through the shadowy house she felt like she'd ceased to exist. Like a ghost.

The world shrank to fit within the damp walls and the narrow slice of street visible through the gap in the curtains.

Because the lane in front of the house was a dead end, traffic along it was limited and she became familiar with the regular passers-by. The house next door belonged to a young woman in her twenties, with either a job or a boyfriend that took her away from home overnight sometimes. She watched her leaving early in the morning, her heels clicking hurriedly up the front path, her ponytail swishing silkily, and envied her efficiency, her purpose, her cleanliness.

The house at the other end of the row was lived in by two middle-aged men, who left together in the morning, bundled up in bright, knitted scarves, and returned separately at night, one of them weighed down with bulging carrier bags from a posh supermarket. She hadn't seen the resident of the remaining house, but guessed it was an old person. Cars pulled up outside it three times a day, from which blue-uniformed women emerged. Carers, she assumed. Their visits were timed to coincide with mealtimes, and reminded her of her own hunger.

The meagre stash of supplies in the kitchen cupboard had dwindled to almost nothing. She had finished the fig rolls, as well as a tin of rice pudding, one of peaches and a box of soft, stale Ritz crackers. All that remained was another tin of peaches and a jar of meat paste. Just looking at it made her feel ill; she would only resort to eating that in the direst emergency.

The hunger was worse than the darkness or the cold because it didn't just affect her body but her mind too. When she wasn't asleep she found it increasingly hard to find the energy to move from the sofa, where she huddled beneath the blanket and gazed glassily out of the window as her thoughts scrolled, never finding focus. For months – since the night when Dodge had hurt her properly, frighteningly, for the first time – she had thought of nothing else but getting away from him. Most of the time it had felt like a hopeless ambition, but now she had achieved it she was like someone who had quite literally emerged from a dark tunnel into dazzling light. She had escaped, but couldn't see where to go next.

In the end it was the immediate need to eat that forced her to act. During her three days (was it three? . . . she'd lost track) on the sofa the pain in her ankle had eased until she was able to put weight on it and walk. She had the money in her jacket pocket . . . But she also had filthy hair, no shoes and the kind of dress that was likely to result in hypothermia and unfortunate assumptions. Wearily she mustered her remaining energy and applied it to the task of overcoming these obstacles.

She started with the hair.

There were scissors in the drawer in the kitchen; big ones, with long, rusty blades. Standing in the bathroom, she tipped her head upside down and, gathering her hair into a ponytail, attempted to cut it off. The blunt jaws of the scissors gnawed on it, like a dog chewing on a piece of tough meat, but eventually a heap of dark, lank hair lay at her feet. There was no shampoo, so she put her head under the tap, gritting her teeth as her scalp constricted beneath the icy water.

Afterwards she felt lightheaded from the cold, the inversion of gravity and the absence of her long, heavy hair. She rubbed her head vigorously with the scratchy towel, then stood in front of the mirrored cabinet to examine the results of her handiwork.

Oh God, she looked like a Victorian orphan, or someone from the chorus in *Les Misérables*. Her eyes and mouth were suddenly too big for her face, which was tiny and pinched beneath her new ragged hair. Her nose was bright red with the cold. But she felt cleaner. Lighter. Shivering, she wrapped her arms around herself and went towards the stairs.

The downstairs of the little house had become so familiar it almost felt like her own home, but so far something had stopped her from going upstairs. It felt intrusive, somehow; disrespectful. Her harsh laugh bounced off the walls of the narrow stairwell. She'd broken in, stolen food from the cupboards, opened mail that wasn't addressed to her. She was up to her neck in 'intrusive'.

At the top of the stairs there was a tiny square landing, with a door on either side. The one to the left was closed, but the other was half open, letting in light and revealing a bedroom too small to contain much more than a double bed and dressing table, and an old-fashioned wardrobe made of flimsy dark wood.

The bed was covered with a quilted counterpane in salmon-pink polyester, and though the dressing table was bare, on closer inspection it still bore the traces of spilled powder and the sticky rings left by bottles and jars on its polished surface.

Feeling like she was being watched, she went over to the wardrobe. The door stuck for a second before swinging back, so that the wire coat hangers inside gave off a silvery murmur. Most of them were empty, but pushed to the far end there were garments hanging; things from another era, another world, where women dressed like ladies in tailored suits and button-through dresses, and wore high heels and hats. In the darkness right at the back she saw the soft gleam of fur, the glitter of teeth and glassy eyes. Unnerved, she unhooked the nearest hanger, which held a beige trench coat. That would do to cover up the dress and provide a bit of warmth without making her look like the Granny in *Red Riding Hood*, or the Wolf.

At the bottom of the wardrobe shoeboxes were stacked in haphazard piles of two or three. The labels on their ends showed sketches of the contents. The ones on top were sturdy and unlovely, the type of shoe designed to cushion bunions and accommodate swollen ankles. Probably just what she needed, yet her gaze flickered over them to the bottom of the pile, where the boxes were older and more fragile, showing yellowed line drawings of elegant slippers with pointy toes and high heels. She slid out a box.

The shoes inside were of soft black leather, covered with a furring of mould like the bloom on a plum. She buffed it off with the edge of the pink bedspread and slipped them on. The heels were no more than an inch high, but they were narrow and she wobbled precariously as she took a couple of experimental steps. They were a bit big, but since the alternative was going barefoot she'd just have to manage.

A whisper of perfume wreathed itself around her as she slid her arms into the coat. It reached to the knee, fastening with big horn buttons and a fabric belt with a buckle. After a moment's hesitation she rejected the buckle and, dredging up some long-buried image from an old black-and-white movie or something, knotted it tightly instead.

Outside the light was already dying. She studied her headless reflection in the dressing-table mirror and saw nothing that she recognized. She looked smart, sophisticated; a woman of the world instead of a girl from the roughest estate in Leeds. And then she bent her knees and saw her face, ghostly in the gloom, her asylum hair, and the effect was shattered.

With a grimace she straightened up and left the room. At the top of the stairs she paused and looked at the closed door. The encroaching dusk cloaked everything in veils of grey, blurring boundaries and giving her a sudden sense of unease. She twisted the handle, rattling it this way and that, but the door remained closed. Locked.

She withdrew her hand sharply and backed away, then hurried down the stairs, ignoring the pain in her ankle, forgetting the need to be quiet, wanting only to get out of the shadowy house with its locked doors and mysteries and secrets and back into the world of lights and people and normality.

Will Holt stopped the car in front of a row of garages at the end of the road and slumped back against the seat. Greenfields Lane. At sodding last; next to Platform nine-and-three-quarters and the Lost City of Atlantis it had to be the most difficult place on earth to find, especially in rush-hour traffic.

Not that you could tell it was rush hour from down here, tucked away from the car-clogged roads. Greenfields Lane might not be as rural as its name suggested, but by London standards there was a fair amount of shrubbery – most of it growing around number four. According to the manageress of St Jude's Nursing Home, Nancy Price had only left her house two years ago, but in the early February dusk Will could see that undergrowth had almost engulfed it already.

It was pretty, though – or could be, if it was as well-kept as the others. The terrace was older than the houses around it, and consisted of four simple little red-brick cottages, probably built for workers of some kind when this part of London was no more than a village, separated from the city by fields where cows grazed. He wondered what it had been like here before the bigger Victorian and Edwardian villas had encroached, their backs turned like boorish guests at a party. Before the garages and the double yellow lines and the rows of wheelie bins.

He twisted uncomfortably and stretched, as far as he could in the tiny car. A 1975 Triumph Spitfire was a thing of beauty, but it was not, unfortunately, a thing of comfort, economy or practicality. Outside it was raining half-heartedly, and in the hour and ten minutes since he'd left St Jude's the erratic heater had finally got up a pleasant fug, making the prospect of getting out extremely unappealing.

Plunging his hand into the crumpled M&Ms packet on the

passenger seat he felt a stab of guilt when he found that it was empty. On the radio the pips sounded the hour. At least he could go straight home after this; there were no new leads and surely even Ansell the Arse couldn't come up with anything more that could be done on this case today. And that would be another Thursday over.

God, he thought, scrubbing the heels of his hands into his tired eyes, what am I doing, wishing my life away like this? Getting fat and embittered working for the biggest twat in London in a job that was only one step up from selling dodgy life insurance or grave robbing? *A Mickey Mouse job*, as his father had once sneeringly called it.

And just like that, at the exact moment when he thought of his father, the radio presenter announced that he would soon be talking to 'top historian and Professor at St John's College Oxford, Dr Fergus Holt' about his 'epic new TV series', conjuring him out of Will's head so that his face hung in the frigid air before him like the genie from Aladdin's lamp.

He switched the radio off quickly. The day was bad enough already without being forced to confront his father's stellar success, as well as his notable lack of it. Reaching for his faux-leather salesman's briefcase he got out of the car into the cold, wet afternoon.

He started with the house at the opposite end of the terrace to Nancy Price's. The front door was painted the sort of indeterminate greyish-blue-green that denoted Good Taste, and there were herbs growing in the window box beneath the front window. After a minute the door was opened by a man wearing a striped butcher's apron, wiping his hands on a tea towel. Music – something classical Will recognized but couldn't name – was playing in the background.

'Yes?' He peered at Will over square, black-framed glasses, his natural good manners not quite masking his irritation at being disturbed.

'Hi, I'm so sorry to disturb you. I'm Will Holt, from a firm called Ansell Blake, Probate Researchers. We're looking into the estate of a lady called Nancy Price, who we believe used to live in the house at the end there, and I wondered if you might be able to help fill in some details?'

Experience had taught Will that he needed to get through this little speech quickly. If he managed to get that far without having the door shut in his face, he was halfway there. Mike Ansell would always round it off with the suggestion that he 'come in for a quick chat', at which point he'd step forward, giving the hapless homeowner a choice between moving aside or forcibly ejecting him. 'And since nobody wants that kind of unpleasantness in their own home, you're in.' Will knew a little bit more of his soul would die if he ever resorted to tactics like that to get his commission.

The man dragged a hand through his sparse hair, distracted. From the kitchen behind him the smell of toasting spices wafted, redolent of warmth and comfort. In spite of the M&Ms Will's stomach rumbled.

'I'm not sure I can help you. My partner and I bought this place just over a year ago and the house at the end was empty then. To be honest, it's a bit of a problem, looking so run down – it brings the area down, if you see what I mean. If you can get something done about it that would be extremely good news.'

'Well, if it does turn out to have belonged to Miss Price, it would be sold and the proceeds of the sale distributed amongst any heirs. You don't happen to know anything about her, do you? If she had any relatives?'

Before Will had finished speaking the man was shaking his head, eager to get back to his cooking and his music and his ordered evening. 'Sorry, I've no idea. The old guy next door will know, though; Mr Greaves. Good luck with the search.'

'Thanks,' Will said to the greenish-greyish-blue door.

Mr Greaves's door was unequivocally red, though the paint had dulled and the cast iron knocker had been nibbled by rust. Will knocked, and waited, turning his back against the rain and bowing his head. Jesus, it was cold. The path beneath his feet had once been well-kept, but now weeds sprouted through the cracks between the paving stones. He knocked again. Before he'd got his hand back into his pocket the door was yanked open.

'Hi – sorry to disturb you—'

'Whaddayawant?'

Will's speech stalled. The woman who'd answered the door was Chinese, and tiny. Through the narrow gap she'd left between door and frame he could see that she was wearing a blue tunic with white piping on the sleeves and collar, and a ferocious scowl.

'I wondered if I might speak with Mr Greaves?' Even to his own ears his voice sounded stupidly posh, uncomfortably close to the mocking impression Ansell was fond of doing in the office.

'No. Mr Greaves have his tea now. He no see visitors.' Her accent was a curious mix of the Far East and the East End.

'I can wait? Or come back in half an hour? I'm from Ansell—'

'No. After tea I get him ready for bed. No visitors today. You come back tomorrow.'

And that was that. The door shut with such force that the knocker rattled and Will was left standing in the dark and rain, both of which were getting heavier. He sighed. The house next door – the third in the row – was in darkness, but he trudged dutifully up the path anyway and knocked, without hope or enthusiasm, then counted silently to twenty before turning away.

He'd got back into the car and was just about to start the engine when he noticed a figure coming up the lane, head down, walking slightly unevenly. In the darkness it was just a silhouette against the bright lights of the street beyond, but there was no doubt that it was a woman; a woman in shoes that seemed to be causing her some discomfort. She was carrying a bulging shopping bag, and as she got closer, into the circle of light cast by the streetlamp, he could see that her face was pale, her jaw set, her dark hair beaded with rain. She seemed to be heading towards the row of cottages – towards the house at which he'd just knocked, he guessed.

44

Wearily he opened the door and braced himself against the wet.

'Hi! Hello? Hi there—'

She started visibly, her white face a mask of alarm. God, I'm such an oaf, Will thought as he broke into a sort of half-jog towards her. What woman wouldn't be terrified at being approached by a bloke in a car down a dark backstreet? He tried to produce an encouraging, sensitive smile.

'Sorry . . . Sorry, I didn't mean to . . .' Seeing the stricken expression on her face he stopped a few feet away from her. 'Sorry. I knocked on your door, but you weren't in. Obviously.' Oh God. 'I'm from a firm called Ansell Blake—'

She was shaking her head, shrinking away, as if she wanted to run. 'I don't know anything about it. You've got the wrong person.'

And he'd actually thought the day couldn't get much worse. 'I'm so sorry, I thought you lived here. Do excuse me. I was looking for someone who might be able to help me find out about an elderly lady who used to live in the empty house there and I just assumed . . .' He was babbling, and he stopped himself. 'Sorry.'

Just for a moment, no more than a split second, her pinched face showed a glimmer of interest. And then it was gone, extinguished by wariness.

'Sorry, I don't know.'

Head down, she walked away, as fast as she could in the troublesome shoes, struggling with the cumbersome bag of shopping. And he was left, standing in the rain and feeling not only foolish, but oddly guilty too, as if he'd scared her away.

He was watching her, she could feel it. She couldn't turn round and go back to the house now. There was nothing for it but to keep walking.

Reaching the garages she pushed through the undergrowth she'd come through the other night, trying to look as nonchalant as possible. Oh God, he must think she was a complete weirdo – if he didn't already know exactly who she was and what she was doing. She couldn't remember the name of the company he'd said he worked for, but they sounded like lawyers or something. What if someone had seen her and tipped them off about squatters?

Her mind raced. But he'd said he was trying to find out about an old lady, hadn't he? The old lady who'd lived in the house. Stumbling out from the bushes behind the bins she stopped for a moment to relieve the pressure on the blister that had formed on her heel. She should have played along, pretended she lived in the area, asked him the old lady's name. Maybe he was looking for Mrs Thorne too?

The idea gave her a weird tight feeling in her chest, which might have been excitement or unease. She wanted to find her; she owed her that much as repayment for the fig rolls and the rice pudding and the loan of the coat and shoes. She'd squared it with her conscience by promising herself that she'd do her best to trace Mrs Thorne and hand over the letter from her lost love. If there was someone else looking for her, that would probably double her chances of success, which was a good thing.

And yet, it felt strange. Like Mrs Thorne was hers, even though she knew nothing about her. Nothing ordinary, anyway, like her first name or what she looked like or even whether she was alive or dead; only that she had once been in love with an American airman called Dan, and that he had loved her too. And loved her still.

She had been walking mindlessly, not paying any attention to where she was going, thinking only of filling in time until it was safe to go back to the house, but now she noticed a church on the opposite side of the street. It was an old-fashioned kind of church with a big square tower of dirty grey stone, and a sign outside which said, '*All Saints Church. All Welcome*' above a list of times for services and Holy Communions. Remembering the newsletter she'd discovered in the heap of junk mail, she found herself crossing the road.

The porch floor was deep in drifts of leaves and crisp packets. Noticeboards lined the walls. Shaking the rain from her hair she peered through the gloom at these, to see if there was any mention of Miss Price on the flower arranging rota or list of Sunday School helpers. There wasn't. The door to the main body of the church was slightly ajar, and cautiously she looked through the gap.

The space was huge and completely still, dimly lit by great glass lanterns miles above the aisle. She pushed the door open enough to slip through and took a few tentative steps, which echoed around the high walls. Her breath hung faintly in front of her face, and above the smell of cold stone and furniture polish the enticing aroma of coffee reached her.

A little area behind the far row of pews had been claimed as a sort of domestic space, with a square of red carpet on the floor, two wicker chairs, a shelf of books and a yellow plastic box of toys. A length of kitchen worktop had been fitted against the wall, and on this there was a coffee machine. As she got closer, drawn by the smell, she saw the plate of biscuits beside it, and a notice on the wall above, written in flowing, churchy writing:

Please Help Yourself.

She put the carrier bag down on one of the wicker chairs and looked around. There was no one to be seen. She read the notice again, wondering if it was some kind of trick, but the lure of caffeine and sugar was too strong to resist. Cups and saucers were set out on the worktop. She took one and filled it with coffee, helped herself to one biscuit, then another. She was just reaching for a third when the sound of brisk footsteps made her drop it back onto the plate.

'Ahh, you found our refreshments. Good, good. I hope the coffee's still drinkable. I made it this afternoon, but if it sits too long it tastes like burnt mud.'

The most striking thing about the man who'd spoken was that he was wearing the most hideous jumper imaginable; oversized and hand-knitted in uneven, garishly coloured stripes. The second most striking thing was his smile, which was wide and white against his dark beard.

'N–no, it's fine. Thank you.'

'In that case, if you're not just being polite, do help yourself to another cup. There's no choir practice or anything on tonight, so I shall just be pouring it down the sink if you don't. I'm Tony, by the way. Tony Palmer.'

He leaned across and held out a hand. She shook it timidly, trying not to stare at the neck of the jumper to work out if that was a dog collar beneath it, or just an ordinary shirt. He seemed very friendly for a vicar. Very normal.

'Are you——?'

'The vicar here, that's right.' He stepped past her and poured himself a coffee, then balanced a biscuit on the saucer. 'Do you mind me asking your name? You don't have to tell me if you don't want to.'

She didn't particularly, but since she was drinking his coffee and eating his biscuits it seemed rude to say so. 'Jess,' she said. 'Jess Moran.'

'Nice to meet you, Jess, and welcome to All Saints. Although on a cold night like this I'd be the first to admit that it's not the most welcoming place.'

He shivered elaborately in his ugly jumper and smiled again. It was a nice smile, but she steeled herself against it. She didn't want him to mistake her for a churchgoer. She and Gran never used to miss an episode of *Songs of Praise* but they only watched it for the singing – joining in with the words at the bottom of the screen was how Jess had first discovered she had a voice. But the church itself was full of busybodies, Gran said; women with too much time on their hands and nothing better to do with it than arrange flowers and pass judgement on those who were just struggling to get on with things.

She shrugged. 'I'm not religious or anything. I was just . . . passing.'

'That's OK. People come in for all sorts of reasons, and they're all welcome. Except the ones that come in to nick the candlesticks – those ones I could do without – but everyone else is, whether they're after a chat or a sit down in the quiet, or a cup of not very nice coffee. Churches need people. When they're empty they're just buildings.' Tony Palmer took a sip of coffee and said ruefully, 'Mostly people don't feel like they need churches these days, which is why we have to work at keeping them going. Here we run toddler groups and a book club and an art class and a lunch club for the old people, all without mentioning the G word.' He looked heavenwards and mouthed, '*God.*'

Jess thawed a little. The old people's lunch club reminded her of why she'd come in. 'You don't know anyone round here called Miss Price, do you? An old lady. She might come to your lunch club?'

'Miss Price . . .' He considered it. 'The name sounds familiar, though I can't put a face to it. I don't think she comes to the lunch club, but I've only been here for eighteen months so she may have been previously. Is she a relative of yours?'

Jess put her cup down and shook her head. 'A friend of a friend, that's all. It doesn't matter.' She picked up her bag of shopping from the chair. 'Thanks for the coffee. And the biscuits.'

'Anytime.'

Aware of his eyes following her, she tried to walk as normally as the too-big shoes and her painful ankle would allow. She'd almost reached the door when he called out to her.

'Jess? Just a thought—'

She turned round. He came towards her, tapping a finger against his bottom lip. 'Look, I don't know how you're fixed with work or other commitments, but you'd be very welcome to come along to our lunch club – then you could ask some of the other members about your Miss Price. It's on Mondays and Thursdays, in the church hall.' He grinned sheepishly. 'Of course, when I say you'd be very welcome, what I really mean is it would be great to have some younger blood. It gives the older folk a real lift to see a fresh face. You'd get a free lunch, of course. Hot food, and plenty of it.' He patted the slight paunch beneath the jumper.

'OK . . . Thanks.'

She had been going to make some excuse, but she was so hungry that the prospect of a free hot lunch was simply too tempting to turn down. It was only as she walked away that it occurred to her that he'd known that. It was that, rather than anything to do with old folk or young blood, that had prompted him to ask her.

The thought was strangely unsettling.

4

1942

The autumn days were getting shorter. At five o'clock Stella gave up struggling to peer through the gloom and did the blackout. It seemed such a shame; the sky was still streaked with ribbons of pink, against which the church's terracotta roof tiles looked like a frill of black lace, but it was just another thing to add to the list of wartime privations she supposed. Oranges. Chocolate. Soap. Autumn sunsets.

She went into the hallway to knock on the study door and ask Charles if he'd like her to do his blackout too, but the thread of light beneath the door told her there was no need. The meeting had gone on for most of the afternoon. An hour ago she'd taken in a tray of tea and eggless sponge, made especially in honour of the bishop who enjoyed the status of a Hollywood matinee idol in Charles's eyes. They had stopped their conversation while she set it down on the table, and the bishop had said – in a particularly loud, hearty voice so that Reverend Stokes, who was elderly and deaf, would hear – 'So this is the lovely Mrs Thorne. With cake! Something of a water and wine miracle, given the circumstances. Well done, my dear!' She'd retreated, glowing at praise from such an elevated source, pleased as much on Charles's behalf as her own.

The kitchen was warm after the gusting draughts in the passageway, and deliciously scented with the beef she'd been cooking slowly all day. Brisket, stringy with sinew and unpromising in its paper wrapping, but Ada Broughton, queuing behind her in Fairacre's the butchers, had told her that done on a low heat for long enough it would make a nice stew. Stella hoped so, since it was their meat ration for the week. She'd decided Woolton pie and cheese bake would be worth suffering for one special Saturday night meal, and had gone to some effort to lay the table in the dining room and the fire in the sitting room.

In truth she'd suffer a lot more than Woolton pie and cheese bake to breach the wall that seemed to have sprung up around Charles. Since they'd returned from Brighton he had slipped further and further from her reach so that she felt that their relationship was even more like that of employer and housekeeper than it had been before the wedding. Perhaps a quiet dinner – something less depressing than their usual dreary fare – and then the concert on the wireless afterwards, by the light of the fire . . .

Perhaps . . .

She shoved her feet into her ugly utility lace-ups and slipped out into the damp indigo evening. The air was scented with earth and cold and smoke from chimneys as she picked up fallen apples from beneath the tree, holding her apron up like a basket to collect the good ones. There weren't many; the season was almost at an end, and the harvest had been shared. There was hardly a household in King's Oak that hadn't had an apple pie this autumn, though the apples were green and sour and devoured valuable sugar. Stella had been terribly mean with what she'd put in the sugar bowl on the tea tray earlier, so she'd have enough to make a good crumble, and custard. Charles was too thin. The hollows beneath his cheekbones had got deeper, the angle of his jaw sharper, which she couldn't help taking as direct evidence of her inadequacy as a wife.

Before going back inside she paused on the back step, gazing out towards the city. Saturday night. The sky had lost its pink tinge now and was a deep, soft purple, scattered with a few stars and a waxy yellow harvest moon. A Bombers' Moon they used to call it, though the nights of the raids seemed a long time ago now and everyone had become quite blasé about the possibility of them returning. She thought of Nancy, who would be dolling herself up for a night on the town with her friends from the salon. Several times she'd invited Stella to join them – 'you're a wife, not a prisoner, aren't you?' – but Stella always found an excuse. She remembered that crush of bodies, the measuring stares. It wouldn't seem right to be in that atmosphere now that she was a married woman.

She and Nancy had met up for the pictures last week

though; Clark Gable and Lana Turner in *Somewhere I'll Find You*. There had been a useful film before the main picture, featuring recipes for stale bread. When Stella had scribbled one of them down on the back of her ration book Nancy had laughed so hard that the woman behind had tapped her on the shoulder and hissed at her to shut up.

In the light of the kitchen she saw that the apples were bruised and worm-eaten. What was left after she'd cut out the unusable bits would only be enough for the smallest of crumbles, but at least it would use up less sugar. She left the fruit stewing on the stove and went to check that everything was ready in the dining room.

It gave her a little beat of pleasure to look at the table, spread with an old cloth she'd discovered in a drawer and embroidered with bunches of daisies to cover the scorch marks. She'd sensed Charles's disapproval of her spending three evenings on such a frivolous project when she could be knitting socks for sailors. She knitted too, but couldn't quite believe that the endless supply of scratchy socks she turned out would make any real difference to the war, while the embroidered daisies had an immediate and discernible effect on morale on the home front. Against them even the green Vicarage china looked nice, and Miss Birch's rose bowl made a lovely centrepiece, though it was filled with dying hydrangea heads instead of roses. In a moment of impulse Stella took down the two brass candlesticks from the mantelpiece and placed them on either side of the rose bowl, then went to the sideboard for candles.

Opening the drawer, she hesitated. Would Charles think she was trying too hard? A framed photograph from their wedding stood on top of the sideboard, the one Fred Collins had taken of them cutting the cake. Picking it up, looking at it, she was transported back to the moment, and felt the fine hairs rise on her arms as she remembered Charles's hand covering hers and the secret thrill of anticipation his touch had given her.

Anticipation that had come to nothing, as it turned out. She put the photograph carefully back in its place and took a step back, though she couldn't seem to drag her gaze away from it. The girl in white with the wide, dark eyes already seemed like a naïve stranger – what a lot she'd learned in two short months. Like how to launder a clerical collar and make a milk pudding from stale bread and water, and that a white wedding isn't necessarily the start of happy-ever-after, like it always was in the picture house.

That time she'd gone with Nancy she'd averted her eyes from the screen during the parts where Clark took Lana into his arms and kissed her thoroughly and passionately. Nancy had nudged her at one point and asked if she was all right and she'd nodded dumbly, glad that they were in the dark cinema with the cross woman behind them and that she couldn't answer properly. She had missed her chance at honesty now; it had come when they'd returned from Brighton and Nancy had been agog to find out how it had gone. How *'it'* had gone. Her curiosity had been so laden with expectation that Stella had found it impossible to tell her the truth; that the bedroom part had been a dismal failure and the blushing bride had returned from her honeymoon every bit as virginal as when they'd driven away from the wedding.

It sounded so hopeless. She could just imagine the pity (and scorn?) in Nancy's eyes as she tried to explain about the first night, when they were both tired from the wedding and the journey and a little overwhelmed at the strangeness of finding themselves alone together in the huge and rather bleak hotel room. Charles's parents had insisted on treating them to the honeymoon suite, and the landlady had showed them in with much lascivious smirking – off-putting in itself. It had been late, but Stella had disappeared to the bathroom next door and, shaking with nerves and a sort of excited trepidation, changed into the silk camisole. When she'd returned the bed was still empty and neat. Charles was sitting, fully dressed, at the table by the window, his head in his hands.

Such was his attitude of despair that she'd spoken his name and gone towards him, ready to put her arms around him and hold him. But as she approached and saw that his eyes were closed, his lips moving, she'd realized that he was praying. Nancy was her best friend; there was nothing they didn't know about each other, but Stella would never be able to tell her about what happened next. About the moment when she'd touched him and he'd opened his eyes and seen her, and recoiled in distaste.

'I'm sorry,' he said stiffly afterwards. 'It was unexpected, that's all. Seeing you dressed like . . . like *that.*'

Stella had been too miserable and humiliated to say anything, least of all that 'that' was exactly how she'd thought most husbands would expect their brides to dress on the wedding night.

The next day she had started her monthly, which had also been embarrassing but had at least taken the pressure off the remainder of the honeymoon, which they'd spent walking along the seafront, exploring Brighton's churches and – one afternoon – going to a tea dance in the hotel, for all the world like any newly married couple. At night they'd lain side by side in the bed like effigies on a tomb.

She jumped as the study door opened and voices spilled out into the hallway. 'Glad to have got it sorted, Charles. It seems like a satisfactory outcome all round, but let me know if there are any problems your end.'

The rich tones of the bishop. Hovering behind the dining-room door, Stella tugged at the bow of her apron. Should she go out? Surely a good clergy wife would be there to open the door, make gracious pleasantries. She racked her brain for a single gracious pleasantry, but was distracted by Charles's voice. 'Thank you for your time and understanding in this matter, Bishop. You've been very accommodating.'

'Not at all, not at all . . . These are difficult times and we must all serve in the way we best see fit. I know this isn't something you've undertaken lightly. Your courage is to be commended, Charles. My regards to Mrs Thorne.'

Stella went into the hallway just as the bishop went out, so all she saw of him was a flash of silvery hair before Charles shut the door. In the light from the study Stella saw that his face had lost some of the tension that had shadowed it for the last weeks. His expression was softer, more thoughtful ... until he looked up and saw her standing there, when it became suddenly wary.

'Good meeting?'

'Yes. Yes, I think so.'

'Supper won't be long. I've laid the table in the dining room. I thought we could—'

She stopped as Reverend Stokes appeared in the study doorway.

'Marvellous,' Charles said, in his hearty, public voice. 'I've invited Ernest to stay. I hope that's not a problem?'

In the kitchen Stella vented her frustration on the potatoes, mashing them into a pulp to stretch them as far as possible. As if any casually invited dinner guest wasn't a problem these days! The beef that would have fed two indulgently looked meagre when shared between three plates, but even more upsetting than the disruption to her menu was the ruination of her plans for the evening. Music and candles. Talking in the soft circle of firelight. They could still do that with Reverend Stokes there, but the conversation wouldn't be what she had in mind. It would be conducted at exhausting, ear-splitting volume for a start.

She could hear Charles's unnaturally raised voice as she carried the tray of plates through from the kitchen. He was talking about the parish. 'It's hardly prosperous, but the people here have enough to get by. They're decent, hard-working folk

59

who don't mind doing their bit. They don't go in much for prayer groups, but the Mothers' Union is well supported, and the W.I. And there's a very productive Ladies' Sewing Circle, isn't there, darling?'

Caught in the spotlight of his rather forced smile, she had no choice but to swallow her sulk and reply, which annoyed her further because there was nothing to say but 'yes'. She set the plates on the table, placing the smallest portion by far in her own place.

'This looks delicious, my dear,' Reverend Stokes said, rubbing his hands together. 'But are you not hungry?'

'Shall I say Grace?' Charles said, quickly. As they all bent their heads he caught her eye and gave her a grateful smile.

It nourished her more than any feast.

By the time she had served the crumble – in teacups, to disguise how little there was – Stella's head was throbbing, but the shared effort of maintaining conversation had forged a fragile bond between her and Charles. Escaping back to the kitchen to make coffee she leaned against the sink and closed her eyes, allowing herself a moment of hope. It hadn't been the intimate evening she'd imagined, but she felt closer to him than she had in a long time. Perhaps this was what marriage was about? Not melting movie kisses or silk nighties, but something more real and meaningful; shared endeavour, joint goals. Maybe when Reverend Stokes had finally gone they could laugh about the teacup puddings and the fact that he thought her name was Sheila, and tonight the space in the bed between them wouldn't seem like such an arctic waste-land.

Taking a deep breath she carried the coffee through to the sitting room, where Reverend Stokes was now ensconced in the most comfortable chair nearest the fire. Stella hoped that didn't mean he would be tempted to stay longer. Surely he must be getting bored with hearing about the minutiae of running St Crispin's by now?

'Of course, there's no evensong service now, because of the blackout,' Charles was saying, 'but the Sunday morning service is always well attended. People like the sermons to be short but uplifting.'

Stella settled into the corner of the sofa and sipped her coffee. Charles had struggled with 'uplifting' lately, often staying up into the early hours of Sunday morning to produce a sermon that struck the right note. At least that's what he told her he was doing. On those nights he came quietly up the stairs and passed her door on his way to the box room at the end of the landing and, lying beneath the smooth sheets of their marriage bed, she wondered whether avoiding her was also part of his plan.

After what seemed like an eternity, Reverend Stokes hauled himself creakily from the depths of his chair and announced that he must be on his way. As Charles went in search of his coat the Reverend's damp eyes rested on Stella.

'Thank you for a lovely evening and a splendid supper, my dear. The first of many, I hope.'

'Oh ... yes, I do hope so,' Stella stammered. Funny how

she seemed to lie far more often now she was a vicar's wife than she ever had before. 'You're very welcome any time.'

Charles returned, winding a scarf around his own neck too. He glanced uneasily at Stella before holding out the other man's coat. 'Here, Ernest. I'll walk you down to the bus stop. Make sure you don't get lost in the blackout.'

She was washing the dishes in the kitchen when he came back. She heard the front door shut and glanced at the clock above the cooker. Almost nine; if she was quick she could finish clearing up in time to listen to the news on the wireless with him. Sometimes she thought she'd rather not know about the misery unfolding across the world but she knew that Charles liked to stay informed of all the latest developments in the war, with so many boys in the parish and now Peter Underwood out there on active service. It seemed a small thing to do to listen to it with him. She ran water into the enamel casserole dish in which she'd cooked the beef; it would be best left to soak overnight.

'Thank you.'

She jumped as Charles's voice broke the sudden silence when the tap was turned off. He was standing in the kitchen doorway, watching her. Something about his expression made her heart lurch slightly.

'It's all right . . . At least, I hope it was. There wasn't much food.'

'My fault.' He came forward, pushing the lock of hair back from his forehead in a gesture she had come to recognize as nervousness. 'I should have given you more notice.'

He unhooked the tea towel and stood, holding it awkwardly as if he wasn't sure what to do with it. 'I need to talk to you. There's something else I should have given you more notice about.'

Stella's heart had begun to beat very hard; a warning drum, although against what danger she couldn't imagine. The word 'divorce' flashed into her head, but she instantly dismissed it. Charles would never countenance breaking asunder what God had put together.

'Sit down.'

She sat obediently, thinking of the fire burning in the other room – all that precious fuel – and the wireless, and the news. He remained standing, pacing across the small kitchen, twisting the tea towel between his hands.

'Charles, you're worrying me. What's the matter? Is it something about the meeting – you've been moved to a different parish—'

As the idea occurred it took root, so that she was already beginning to think through the implications, looking for possible reasons why he might be breaking it to her like it was bad news. Nancy, obviously; if it was somewhere far away – Scotland perhaps, or the wilds of Cornwall – it would be hard not being able to see her, but other than that . . .

'Not quite.' He sighed and sat down opposite, clasping his hands together and dropping his forehead down onto them for a moment. Then he looked at her, with a directness that was both resigned and slightly challenging.

'The thing is . . . I've joined up. I know that as a clergyman

I didn't have to, but I felt I couldn't not, you see.' He smiled sadly, imploring her with his eyes. 'You're looking at the Reverend Charles Thorne, Chaplain to the Forces, 4th Class. I'm to report for duty at Chester in ten days' time.'

He was waiting for her to say something, but her mind was blank with shock, echoing with silence as if in the aftermath of an explosion. Which, in a way, it was, she thought numbly.

A direct hit at the heart of her marriage.

'It has not been easy. I have searched my soul and spent many long nights questioning God about this path that He has set me on. I would not be being honest with you if I said that I was not afraid, was not unwilling, was not *desperate* for God to tell me that there was another way in which I could serve Him – here, in King's Oak, with those I care for . . .'

Sitting in her usual pew Stella was suddenly reminded of Chamberlain's speech on the wireless at the start of the war. She wondered if Charles was about to say, 'No such undertaking has been received,' and had to press her hand to her mouth to stifle the hideous threat of laughter. Since that night in the kitchen it was as if her emotional switchboard was being manned by an incompetent operator, who kept plugging in the wrong responses.

'But God's purpose is clear,' Charles concluded solemnly from the pulpit. 'I have heard His call, and I have answered it.'

His arms were braced against the pulpit's wooden rim, and as he finished speaking he dropped his head down, allowing the full impact of his words to sink into the stunned congregation. For once, no one shuffled impatiently or knitted or dozed. Glancing surreptitiously around, Stella could see that the news had taken them as much by surprise as it had her. Only Reverend Stokes, sitting beside her as Charles's successor, appeared unruffled. Possibly he was so deaf he hadn't heard a word.

It was a powerful sermon, well delivered. For a moment, looking at the shaft of autumn sunlight falling on Charles's bent head she was relieved to feel a glimmer of the pride and aching concern she knew were more appropriate feelings for a wife whose husband was going to war than the bewilderment, hurt and anger she'd been guiltily lugging around all week like a suitcase full of dirty laundry.

'Let us pray.'

There was a rustling and creaking as, like sleepwalkers stirring, everyone shuffled forward onto their knees. Stella folded her hands together but kept her eyes open, staring at the spots on her dress.

'Almighty and most merciful Father, who sees all things and knows the secrets of our hearts, we pray to you for those who must fight, even when to do so goes against that which they believe in and takes them far away from those they hold dear. We pray also for them – the people left behind – whose courage, faith, steadfastness and devotion are equally tested, and ask that you watch over them. Keep them safe in body, strong in spirit, sure in the knowledge of your love.'

It's not God's love I want to be sure in the knowledge of,

Stella thought bitterly as the white spots danced in front of her stinging eyes. It's my husband's.

That night he came to bed earlier than usual. Stella was still reading – a novel about a nurse and an airman that she'd got from St Crispin's informal lending library, which was a shifting population of tattered paperbacks on a shelf in the flower arranging cupboard – when she heard him come upstairs and go into the bathroom. She was instantly cata-pulted out of a drowsy dream-world halfway between waking and sleeping, where the airman (George) had just pulled the nurse (Marcia) against his hard chest and kissed her 'with unrestrained desire'.

She heard the WC flush, water running into the sink, then the bathroom door opened. This time his footsteps didn't pass her bedroom door. He came in, glancing at her uncertainly as he went round to his side of the bed.

'I'm awake.' She shut the book and put it, cover side down, on the bedside table. Charles had never said anything but she sensed his disapproval of her reading choices. Beside his pillow was a Bible, and a slim volume of poetry by Oscar Wilde, which Peter Underwood had given to them as a wedding pre-sent. It seemed an odd gift to Stella but she could tell that it meant a lot to Charles.

'I thought it was time I had an early night.'

In the light of the green-frilled bedside lamp his face was unreadable, but she detected a faintly questioning note in his voice. Beneath the heavy layers of sheets and blankets her body leapt to life, the blood quickening and fizzing in her veins, heat spreading across her skin so that her flannelette nightie felt like a straitjacket. Was this it? She wished she'd had a chance to prepare; to dab on some of the scent Nancy had given her for her birthday last year. But maybe she was reading too much into his words – after her error of judgement on their wedding night she didn't trust herself to read the signs. Maybe he was simply tired.

The bed rocked as he climbed in beside her. Stella lay perfectly still, not daring to look at him in case he read the longing in her eyes and despised her for it. She waited for him to pick up Oscar Wilde but he lay back on the pillows for a moment, then, almost reluctantly, turned and propped himself up on his elbow so that he was looking down into her face.

'You've been very good about all this, darling. I know it hasn't been easy, but I'm grateful. I wanted you to know that.'

'I just want you to be happy. I want to be a good wife to you, Charles.'

'You have been. You are.'

'But . . . why . . . ?'

He sighed again, and she sensed something in him withdrawing from her. 'I told you.'

It was true. That night in the kitchen he'd explained, with infinite patience, almost as if he was talking to a small child, that he could no longer align his conscience with a non-active role in the war; that he felt less of a man, as if he was hiding behind his Bible and his dog collar. That phrase, 'less of a man', had touched some resounding chord of pity and love deep inside her and made her long to reach out to him, to prove that in her eyes he was every bit a man.

Tentatively she touched his cheek then, growing bolder, raised herself up to brush her lips against his. She felt him stiffen and was about to pull away when he seemed to gather himself, resolve some inner conflict, and begin to kiss her back with sudden fervour.

His lips were hard on hers, and his tongue forced itself between her teeth. Her mind registered shock, revulsion even; there had been no mention of George doing such a thing to Marcia. And yet her body seemed to understand and to respond entirely instinctively. The feelings that had been squashed down swelled and surged. As he pressed her against the pillows her hips rose up to meet his, her fingers sliding through the short hair at the back of his neck, her mouth opening. The flannelette nightie twisted around her legs and she kicked and wriggled upwards, then – frustrated – broke away to pull it over her head.

Naked, she reached for him again, wanting to strip him of his striped pyjamas and feel his skin against hers, but he turned his head, deliberately averting his eyes from her body. He reached over to the lamp on the bedside table and fumbled for the switch. Stella saw the set expression on his face before darkness engulfed them.

Thanks to the blackout, it was total. She was left with only her hands and lips to explore this new territory. This time it was Charles who lay back while she unbuttoned his pyjama top and ran her fingers hesitantly along the pronounced ridges of his ribs, the sharp angle of his hip. Her courage failed when she encountered the top of his pyjama trousers and she lay down beside him again, seeking the reassurance of his mouth against hers.

It was like kissing a marble saint. For a heartbeat he was perfectly still and then he levered himself up and kissed her with the same sudden ferocity of a few moments ago, like he was trying to lose himself. His knee nudged her legs apart while his hands gripped her shoulders, pinning her against the bed. In a tiny part of herself Stella was alarmed, but the greater part of her thrilled at this new Charles, hungry and decisive; at being wanted, devoured by him. After months of drought, the hard crush of his mouth on hers, the push of his knee on her thigh was like water to a parched plant. Instinctively she groped for the cord of his pyjamas and tugged at the knot so she could slide them down his legs. They resisted, as if they were caught on something. Her heart lurched with fear and a sort of primitive thrill when she realized that something was . . . *him*.

Tentatively her fingers closed around the surprising length of it. Above her in the dark he gave a low, guttural moan that was somewhere between pleasure and despair. Flaming spears impaled her. Of their own volition her fingers tightened and she felt him thrust into her grip, his breathing rapid and ragged.

'Charles, please . . . I want you to . . .'

She lacked the vocabulary to tell him, but her body was an

open invitation. A pulse was beating like a second heart between her legs and she arched her hips and guided him towards it.

As his flesh touched hers she heard his sharp inward breath and he jerked away as if she'd burned him. In that split second something changed irrevocably, as if a thread had been cut. He shrank from her – quite literally and alarmingly – the heat and hardness beneath her fingers melting into something soft and damp that made her vividly picture a deflated balloon. In contrast, the rest of his body went rigid. Abruptly he rolled away from her with a muffled moan of anguish.

'Charles! Charles, darling . . . What is it?'

She wanted to switch the light on but didn't dare. In the darkness she felt for him, discovering with her hands that he was lying on his stomach with his face buried in the pillow. She slid her arms awkwardly around him and held him, murmuring and crooning senselessly as her mind reeled. Eventually she felt the tension ebb from his frame.

'I'm sorry,' he said in a low voice. 'I can't seem to . . .'

His voice cracked. She rushed to reassure him, to spare him the indignity of having to explain further, to spare them both the embarrassment of dwelling on their failure. He was curled up, foetus-like, and she tucked herself around his back, her cheek against his shoulder, her arms looped around his waist, holding him tight as if she could somehow keep him safe from the demons that plagued him.

Later, when she was just slipping beneath the warm waters of sleep, she felt him gently detach himself from her hold. The mattress dipped and cold air fanned her naked skin as the covers were lifted. He crossed the room on soft feet. A moment later the door at the end of the passageway closed quietly.

Alone in her marriage bed Stella wrapped her arms around her knees and tried to banish the spectre of her own inadequacy, and the shameful fizz of thwarted longing deep inside her.

5

2011

Will was woken, as always, by the alarm on his upstairs neighbour's mobile phone. At 6 a.m. exactly, its electronic musak
jingle, set at maximum volume, jerked him violently out of
sleep. Unfortunately it didn't have the same effect on Keely
upstairs who, in addition to a laugh that could shatter crystal,
was blessed with an ability to sleep like the dead and always
took at least fifteen minutes to turn it off. Consequently Will's
day started, as usual, in a rush of adrenaline and impotent fury.

It wasn't likely to improve much either, he thought, staring
up at the brown stain on the ceiling. (The stain looked like
spilled coffee, and he often found himself unwillingly imagining scenarios where coffee could be spilled on a ceiling.) At
least it was Friday. Not that he had anything to look forward
to at the weekend, but the good thing about Friday was that
it wasn't Thursday any more, and it would be almost a whole
week before Thursday rolled round again.

As the electro-jingle notched up a level in volume and

urgency he thought back to a time when Thursday had been just another day of the week. He could actually remember enjoying Thursdays at one point: in his second year at Oxford, when he'd taken Dr Rose's course on Nineteenth Century Ireland his weekly supervision had been on a Thursday. She was the only lecturer who never made any reference to the fact that he was the son of Fergus Holt, never made a comparison or a joke, never asked to be remembered to him because they'd once shared a lift at some European conference or other. She listened to Will's thoughts, challenged them, often exposed the flaws in their logic. Those had been good Thursdays.

In those days if anyone had mentioned the words 'Bona Vacantia' he probably would have thought it was some new tapas bar in town. At his interview for the job at Ansell Blake, Mike Ansell had said (in the swaggering, know-it-all way that was his hallmark), 'So, Bona Vacantia, Will. That's what we're all about here,' and Will had felt the spark of optimism that had been all but snuffed out by the dingy office, the fluorescent strip-lighting and Mike Ansell's overpowering aftershave, flicker bravely back to life. He'd thought he meant good holidays.

In fact the Bona Vacantia list was the government's register of unclaimed estates, published weekly. On Thursdays. It recorded the names of people who had died without leaving a will and whose money and assets would go to the Treasury if no living relatives came forward to claim them. Ansell Blake were one of a growing number of firms who circled like sharks, waiting to snatch the largest and juiciest estates, trace heirs and pocket a fat commission by uniting them with cash to which they didn't know they were entitled from relatives they'd never met.

The work, the scramble for heirs and commission, was keenly competitive, hence the feeding frenzy on Thursdays. That alone Will could have coped with; he actually enjoyed the process of sifting through the records, piecing together information and conjecture to put together a family tree and a picture of someone's life, but the cruel, combative streak it brought out in Ansell the Arse was harder to bear. It reminded Will uncomfortably of his father.

Upstairs the alarm was suddenly silenced. With a sigh Will levered himself upright and sat on the edge of the bed, rubbing a hand through his hair. At least this morning he didn't have to face The Arse straight away. This morning he had the solid twenty-four-carat, bona fide excuse of going to see Mr Greaves on Greenfields Lane to keep him out of the office and away from Ansell's blistering sarcasm for an hour or so.

Tonight, he thought. Tonight I'll go online and have a look to see what else is out there. Who knows, maybe I'll be dazzled by the world of opportunities available to a twenty-five-year-old History drop-out, whose CV boasts a year's work in probate research and, before that, six months in a psychiatric unit.

And with that cheering thought he went into the kitchen to make coffee.

*

Albert Greaves was a desiccated scrap of a man, his body dwarfed by the armchair in which he sat, his head dwarfed by his large spectacles and a pair of ears like jug handles. 'I don't sleep, you know,' he told Will, in aggrieved tones. 'Hardly a wink. Back in the war I was on Atlantic convoys and we went for days without closing our eyes. Dropping with exhaustion we was; we'd have given our last farthing for five minutes' kip. Now I got nothing to do but sleep and I can't seem to drop off. Don't seem right, does it?'

As he spoke his right hand tapped emphatically on the chair's threadbare arm, while his left lay inert at his side. A stroke, he'd explained when the carer first showed Will in. 'Like being struck by bleeding lightning.'

'Of course, the quack's given me pills for it,' he went on now, his glasses reflecting the square of light from the front window. '"You take these, Mr Greaves", 'e says, "you'll get a good night then", but I ain't daft. I might be old, but I'm not stupid. Once they start shovelling their pills into you, that's it. Done for, you are, sure as eggs. That's what happened to Nancy when she went into that home.' He gave a knowing laugh. 'Well, they call it a home but it ain't nothing like. One-way doors in them places. She only went in because she broke her hip. They was going to look after her until it was better, but look what happened. Never came out, did she?'

During this speech he'd been infused with energy, but when it was over he sank further into the depths of the arm-chair and into his own thoughts. Will waited a moment, and took a sip of his tea. It was cooling and had white flecks of milk on the surface. Setting it down he prompted gently: 'Were you close to Miss Price, Mr Greaves?'

'Mmm?' The old man turned his head, as if for a moment he'd forgotten Will was there. 'Who's that? Nancy, you mean? Oh yes, we was close all right, as much as anyone could be close to Nancy. Law unto herself, she was. Like a cat I had when I was a boy. It would come and sit on your knee and purr like a Spitfire when it was in the right mood, but if you tried to pick it up—' His right hand shot out, imitating the swipe of a cat's paw, and he chuckled. 'That was Nancy. I'll admit I got scratched like that a couple of times, but it was worth it. She was a smashing girl.'

Will smiled. Albert Greaves must be pushing ninety and Nancy Price had reached the ripe old age of eighty-seven when she died. But in his eyes she was, and always would be, a smashing girl. For some reason, Will found that encouraging.

'Was she married?'

'Not as I know of.'

'Any children?'

'Like I said – wasn't married, was she?'

Will wrote it down, not wanting to offend the old man by pointing out that the two things didn't necessarily go together.

'When did she move into number four?'

With some effort Albert Greaves raised himself up and picked up his teacup from the table beside him. The room was small and dark, and crammed with a lifetime of clutter. It reminded Will of the antique shop in the Cotswold village where his parents now lived, the one his mother called 'that funny little junk shop'. Greenfields Lane was a fantastic location though, and the house had tons of character. He tried to imagine how it would look without the violently patterned carpet and the pine cladding over the fireplace, and the ornaments and brasses and bad paintings, then felt ashamed.

'Another thing about that cat . . .' Albert Greaves was saying now in a far-off voice, 'I used to say it was mine, but it never was really. My mother said it was a stray, she didn't want it in the house at first – dirty, flea-ridden thing, she called it. But I don't think it was no stray. It had lots of homes, that cat. It used to come and go between them. One time it disappeared for nearly three weeks. I was heartbroken. But then it turned up again, just like it had never been away.'

Will cleared his throat, and was wondering how to steer the conversation back to the subject of Nancy Price when Mr Greaves said, 'It was the same with Nancy. Sometimes she was here, sometimes she weren't. My wife and I bought this place in '48, from an old boy who'd lived here during the war. Nancy was in the house on the end then.' He chuckled again, and the sound seemed remarkably deep and rich coming from such a brittle and dried-up source. 'A right stunner she was. My Dorothy didn't take to 'er at all. Back in them days everything was all drab and worn out and broken, but there she was with 'er blonde hair and 'er red lipstick and high-heeled shoes . . .'

'And so she owned the house as long ago as that?' Will forced his attention away from the vivid picture Mr Greaves was painting and back to the facts Ansell would demand. *1948* he scribbled on his notebook.

'I don't say she owned it. But she lived there, sure enough. Most of the time.'

'And where did she go when she wasn't there?'

'I don't know. Maybe she had a fancy man somewhere – a nice-looking girl like that, who could blame her? But if she did, she weren't likely to let on about it. We kept things to ourselves in them days – personal matters, like; not talking, talking, talking all the time, airing our dirty laundry in public like they do now on all these TV shows.' He waved a disdainful hand in the direction of the enormous glassy screen in the corner of the room. He seemed agitated now and looked at Will accusingly. 'We got on with things and we minded our own business. We didn't ask questions about things that was no concern of ours.'

Will shut his notebook. 'Sorry, Mr Greaves. It must seem like I'm being awfully nosy, it's just we need to find these things out, for Nancy's sake – remember? We need to work out who her closest relatives are. Then any money she left can go to them instead of the government.'

That last bit struck a chord. Mr Greaves's features lit up with indignation. 'That bloody lot. Cheats and charlatans the lot of them, only out to line their own pockets with the hard-earned cash of the working man.'

Sensing that the conversation was about to take a sharp

diversion, Will interjected quickly to nudge it back on track. 'Do you know if Nancy had any brothers and sisters, Mr Greaves? Did she ever talk about her family at all?'

'She never 'ad none, did she? A Poor School girl, she was, and not ashamed of it. Used to looking out for herself, she used to say.'

'Good for her,' Will said, whilst reflecting that it was far from good for Ansell Blake. If Nancy Price had been sent to what amounted to an orphanage, the likelihood was that her family records would be virtually non-existent, making the case much more difficult to work on. 'You don't happen to know if she made a will, do you? She's listed by the authorities as having died without one, but sometimes it turns out that the document simply hasn't been found. It could be that there's one in the house somewhere—'

Mr Greaves gave a crow of laughter. 'Not likely. She weren't one for official doings like that; she didn't bother with no banks or nothing. I got a key for the house though – needs sorting out, it does. I used to look after things for her – pick up the mail and keep an eye on the place – but then I had this stroke . . . Like being struck by lightning, it was—'

Will's phone rang. Muttering an apology he took it from his pocket and saw Ansell's name on the screen.

'Will Holt.'

'Is it indeed? The elusive Will Holt – wonders will never cease. I thought your phone was more likely to be answered by Shergar, or Lord Fucking Lucan. For fuck's sake, where are you?'

'I'm interviewing a neighbour of Miss Price's. I've found out—'

'Oh, I'm sorry – did I ask where you were? I do beg your pardon. What I really meant to say was getting your posh boy arse into that poncey car of yours and get back to this office while you still have a job here. Is that acceptable, old chap?'

Assuming a guffawing public school accent was Ansell's favourite method of mocking Will, who'd worked out that it was best to simply ignore this. 'No problem, if that's what you want, but Mr Greaves here was just saying—'

'I'll stop you right there, if I may, old bean. Because unless your Mr Greaves was just saying that Nancy Price was a first cousin of the Aga-bleeding-Khan, there isn't a brass farthing in this case. She doesn't own the house, and her family tree is as bare as a Scots Pine on Twelfth Night. So yes, call me old-fashioned, but you getting yourself back here and doing some actual proper work on a case that's likely to earn us some boring old money is *what I fucking want.*'

Will put his phone back into his pocket. Mr Greaves was staring out of the window, his glasses blank and bright. Will wondered how much of that unedifying little exchange he'd heard.

'That was my boss, Mr G. He wants me to get back to the office now, so I'd better . . .' He trailed off, shoving his note-book into his briefcase and fastening it with a snap, then getting to his feet. 'Thanks so much for all your time.'

From the depths of the armchair the old man gave an almost imperceptible lift of his right shoulder – the side not damaged by the lightning strike. 'That's all right. I ain't got much of it left, but I ain't got much to do with it neither. I miss 'er, you know – Nancy. She was a laugh. When she broke her hip and wound up in that care 'ome she thought it was just temporary like, while she got 'er strength up again. She always thought she was going to be coming back. I kept an eye on the place for her, I did, made sure none of them druggies or squatters broke in and took her things. Course, a lot of 'er things ended up going up the home with 'er, but there's still a lot there . . .' He turned his face up to Will, towering above him. 'You'll find out who it all belongs to now, won't you? Go through it properly, like. It needs sorting.'

Will was about to say that was no longer any concern of his, but the old man's face was so full of hope that he found he couldn't. 'I'll certainly do my best, Mr G.'

Oh bugger, he thought, sighing inwardly as he let himself out. What a stupid thing to say. What could he do about it?

As he walked to the car he looked back at the house on the end. In the damp grey morning it appeared more than ever to shrink into the encroaching foliage, but there was no doubt it was an absolute gem. He thought again of the impression he'd had in Albert Greaves's house of how it could look, with the floors sanded and waxed and the patterned wallpaper stripped off. White walls, right through . . .

There was no way he'd be able to afford it, even if no heirs were found and it did come on the market. A period cottage in such a prime location would be laughably out of his league on the meagre salary he earned at Ansell Blake, but somehow, without meaning to, he was walking towards it. The front gate was half hanging from its hinges and had to be lifted as it was opened. It had once been painted duck-egg blue, but now the wood was soft and wet, the paint peeling. Someone had walked up the path relatively recently, he could tell from the flattened dandelion stems, but whoever it was hadn't opened the front door. Moss grew in the cracks between door and frame, and the fleecy spires of willow herb were undisturbed, reaching almost to the level of the letterbox in the centre of the door.

'. . . Attractive cottage garden . . .' he muttered under his breath, imagining the estate agent's details as he stepped delicately over trailing brambles to reach the window. Nettles grew in a thick clump beneath it, but he kicked them down and stamped a flat patch on which he could stand to look in.

A thin green film of moss clouded the glass, like pondweed on the lake in the grounds of his parents' house. Slugs had cleared winding silvery pathways through it. He cupped his hands and peered through.

The curtains were half-drawn, so he had to shuffle sideways to get a view of the room. It took a few seconds for his eyes to adjust to the gloom and to be able to distinguish shapes through the opaque film of filth. A chair in front of a prehistoric TV set, a sofa on the wall opposite the window, some kind of brightly covered blanket placed in a heap on top of it.

He was just dropping his hands and turning away when something caught the corner of his eye. His heart lurched and he swung back, his gaze going straight to the black mouth of the doorway leading into the next room, searching for the figure he thought he'd seen.

There was nothing there.

Skin prickling with unease, he went back to the car.

Jess sank down onto the stairs, her whole body rigid, her legs weak.

It was him again, the good-looking posh guy with the apologetic smile, the one who was trying to find out about the old lady who used to live here. By some amazing stroke of luck, or trick of the light or something, it didn't look like he'd seen her, but how long would it be until he was back?

If he'd actually gone away. Maybe right now he was discovering the path she must have made through the undergrowth at the side of the house and following it, and any minute he'd emerge from the wilderness in the back garden. The thought had her leaping to her feet and scrambling up the remaining stairs. Going into the bedroom she slid along the wall and ducked down so that she could see out of the window without being observed.

Her breath escaped in a rush of relief. His car – quite a cool car; sporty but kind of vintage – was parked beside the garages opposite and he was just getting into it, glancing back at the house. The wind blew his dark hair across his forehead and he swept it back with his hand. He looked way too tall to fit into such a small car, but he lowered himself into the driver's seat and the engine started. She leaned against the wall, tipping her head back and closing her eyes, waiting for her heart rate to return to normal, the relief giving way to curious disappointment, as if she'd almost wished he'd seen her.

Which was beyond ridiculous. Hurriedly she went downstairs again and snatched up the borrowed coat. She'd spent too long shut up here alone; she needed to *do* something – like find a job, get herself out of this weird state of limbo, and forget all about fairy tales in which the princess gets rescued from her lonely exile by a handsome prince. And anyway, she had some rescuing of her own to do. The letter lay where she'd left it on the table beneath the window. She picked it up and stuffed it into her pocket.

Outside the air was cold and wet, but fresh. She was aware of the stale, mildewed smell that clung to the coat and infused her hair and skin. No one was around to notice as she ducked out from beneath the branches by the house and walked down the lane, but the main street was busy with morning shoppers and traffic. Builders shouted to each other from scaffolding shrouding a shop front and a man in a suit carrying an oversized cardboard cup of coffee almost charged into her as he talked loudly into his mobile phone. She stepped aside just in time.

Yesterday when she'd left the house she'd felt horribly exposed. Even though the light had been fading and it had been rush hour, when the attention of every single human being was focused solely on getting home; even though this was London where no one made eye contact with anyone else and nothing seemed weird, she'd felt conspicuous, like everyone was staring at her in her not-quite-stylish trench coat and badly fitting shoes.

But today, despite the daylight, it was different. She felt people's eyes sliding over her, looking through her, just as the guy had done when he'd stared in at the window. No one knew who she was. No one cared. She was in a city full of strangers, and she was invisible.

6

1943

Alf Broughton had got a pig.

Christmas had been a meagre affair, stripped of most of its traditional comforts by the tightening noose of rationing. So, when someone had put it about in the bar of The Albion that the pig club in Palmers Green had a litter of eight going begging, Alf had pictured a glistening ham as the centrepiece of next year's feast. Before Ada had finished listing objections he had turned the coal house into a sty and installed in it a small, velvety pink piglet called Blossom.

'Daft so-and-so,' Ada sighed, propping her generous bosom on the shelf of her arms. 'He's that soft she's more likely to be joining us for Christmas dinner than providing it.'

'She's very sweet,' Stella said, pulling her coat more tightly around herself as she watched Blossom bury her stubby snout in the pile of vegetable peelings she'd brought from the Vicarage kitchen.

'Well, let's hope her bacon is sweet and all. Thanks for the scraps, love. Here – let's go in out of the cold and I'll make you a cup of tea.'

It was mid-afternoon but the February day had given up trying to get light. The whole world had taken on the sordid dirty grey tinge of Reverend Stokes's vests. Stella knew she ought to refuse – tea was so precious now – but the prospect was too welcome, not just of a hot drink but of someone to talk to. With Reverend Stokes in residence the Vicarage no longer felt like the home she'd so looked forward to having. Ada's kitchen was warm and damp with meat-scented steam, which billowed out of a pan on the stove.

'Lamb bone,' Ada explained shutting the back door with a conspiratorial wink. 'Mr Fairacre found it under his counter. It'll give a bit of flavour to a soup, though not as much as you'd think from the smell. Let-Down Soup, Alf calls it.'

'He hasn't tried mine,' Stella said bleakly. She should make more effort to run the gauntlet of Mr Fairacre's suggestive remarks and bawdy jokes, but her cheeks were always flaming before she'd even managed to ask for what she wanted and it scarcely seemed worth the effort with only herself and Reverend Stokes to cook for. Used to boarding school fare he ate everything she put in front of him with neither complaint nor praise, though Stella was constantly dismayed by the quantity of food he consumed, as if the concept of rationing had passed him by.

'Give over,' Ada said comfortably, spooning precious new leaves onto the old ones in the stout brown teapot. 'It takes time to learn the tricks, that's all. Long before we'd all heard of Hitler I was trying to feed a family of five on a few shillings – there's not much I don't know about cooking with scraps.' Setting cups down on the table she shot Stella a glance. 'You eating all right? You look like you could do with a square meal inside you.'

'Couldn't we all?'

Ada smoothed her pinny over her wide hips. 'I'll say, but some of us have got a bit more padding to keep us going. That was a nasty bout of the 'flu you had; you need to build your strength up again.'

'I'm fine.'

Stella picked up the cup that Ada slid across the table and folded her hands around its warmth. The 'flu had hit her the day before New Year's Eve, and she'd spent the first two weeks of 1943 in bed, sweating and shivering and hallucinating, until she didn't know what was real and what her fevered brain had invented. Recovery had come slowly, but the feeling of unreality persisted.

Across the table Ada was looking at her shrewdly over the rim of her teacup. 'Well, you don't look fine. You look like a puff of wind could blow you away.'

It was a curiously accurate way of describing how she felt, Stella thought, sipping her tea. Like she was becoming transparent. Like she might disappear. Like the rest of the world was a movie in Glorious Technicolor and she was the only character in black and white; a two-dimensional cut-out, the girl from the wedding photograph with the fatuous smile.

While she'd been ill the things with which she filled her

days – helping out at the crèche in the church hall, the Red Cross Parcels, shopping and cooking for Reverend Stokes and doing his dismal laundry – were taken over by other people. When she went to pick up the reins again she found that the hands that had held them were more capable than hers, and wondered what her purpose was. She was supposed to be a housewife, but since she'd so transparently failed at keeping both house and husband, where did that leave her?

'It's the weather, I expect. And the war – the start of another year and no sign that we're any closer to the end. It seems to have been going on forever.' She placed the cup reluctantly back into its saucer and forced a smile. 'But listen to me moaning when I've got nothing to moan about. Not compared to most people.'

'I wouldn't say that, love. There might be plenty worse off, but it's not easy saying goodbye to your husband when you've only been married a few weeks. Have you heard anything?'

Stella shook her head, resisting the urge to point out that if she had, Ada would have heard it too. Charles's letters were always addressed to her, but written in the style of a parish newsletter with the words 'please share with all at St Crispin's' printed at the top. Stella wrote to him once or twice a week, which was about as often as she could, given the scarcity of interesting things she had to tell him. He rarely acknowledged her trivial bits of local gossip ('the Scouts have begun their own Spitfire fund and are collecting tin cans ... Marjorie Walsh has been busy making rhubarb and carrot jam and very kindly gave me two jars ...') which was understandable, but made their correspondence seem like a one-sided conversation held over a bad telephone line. It had been three weeks since his last letter.

'Oh well, it's the post. Nothing for weeks and then four letters fall on the doorstep at once, that's what happens with my Harry, and he's out in North Africa like Reverend Thorne.' Ada picked up the teapot and swilled it round before pouring them each another cup. 'It's the waiting that's the worst thing. You ought to keep busy – go down the pictures or have a day out up west, take your mind off it.'

'Nancy's invited me to the Opera House with her on Saturday, but I don't know . . .' Stella sighed. 'It seems such a long way to go in the blackout.'

Ada's eyebrows shot up to disappear beneath her floral turban. 'Covent Garden? Wouldn't have thought Nancy Price was much of a one for the opera.'

'It's not opera any more. They've taken the seats out to turn it into a dance hall. It's where she goes most Saturdays now with her friends from the salon.'

'Very nice, I'm sure. Well, if it's good enough for 'er, I don't see why you shouldn't go and have a look at it. At least then you can say that you've danced at the Royal Opera House.'

'I'd have to get Reverend Stokes's tea first.' Stella picked absently at a pulled thread on her coat. 'And then there's Charles . . .'

Ada rolled her eyes. 'Old Stokes didn't starve to death while you was poorly, did he? Far from it, given the amount he puts away, the crafty old devil. And as for the vicar . . . Well, he's not here, is he?'

'Exactly. I'm not sure what he'd think about me going out to have fun while he's stuck out there in the desert.'

Ada stood up and carried her cup over to the sink. Her lips were pressed together, as if she was struggling to stop something escaping them. Evidently the struggle became too much. Seizing the dishcloth she swiped it vigorously over the draining board and said, 'Well I know what I think. North Africa's a long way from King's Oak, and things are different now. We're all in this war, like it or not, and we've all got to manage as best we can. Even Mr Churchill says that morale on the home front is very important, and if that means putting on a bit of lipstick and a nice frock to go out dancing – well, so be it.'

Stella smiled wanly. 'I don't have lipstick. Or a nice frock.'

Ada snorted. 'Well, if that's all that's stopping you, we can soon sort that out. Let's go and have a root through the donations.'

'But they're for the refugees . . .'

Ada hitched an eyebrow. 'You never heard of the phrase "Charity begins at 'ome"? Come on Cinders, let's see what we can find.'

7

2011

Jess was no stranger to charity shops. Back home in Leeds, Gran had been a regular, working her way methodically all the way from Cancer Research to the Red Cross on her Friday morning trip to town, hardly ever returning home empty-handed. Jess's childhood had been spent in the bobbly cast-offs of other children, but she didn't mind. Gran's eye was good, and her finds often included the kind of popular, branded items that would otherwise have been beyond Jess's reach.

But the Rainbow House Hospice shop in Church End was in a whole different league to Yorkshire's cheerfully eclectic second-hand shops. At first glance it could easily have been mistaken for another artsy little boutique, with a window display featuring a vintage suitcase, brown leather brogues, a scattering of dried leaves and a faux-fur coat. A second glance, at the price tickets on the garments inside, did little to revise that impression. With increasing despondency Jess worked her way along the rails. Fifteen pounds for a pair of jeans? Twelve for an ordinary-looking grey jumper? Gran would be horrified.

Fifty pounds had seemed like a safe, solid amount of money, but it was dwindling alarmingly fast. She'd spent almost ten yesterday on bread and cheese, milk and cereal, a toothbrush and toothpaste and, in a rush of homesickness she couldn't resist, a Battenburg cake − Gran's favourite. She'd hoped that another ten would equip her with some wardrobe basics. Nothing fancy, just stuff that would increase her chances of finding a job by not looking like a total freak.

Much to her relief she managed to find a pair of unassuming black leggings and a slightly bobbled dark green jumper amongst the designer offerings. Both were in her size and at a price that didn't make her eyes water. She took them over to the cash desk, behind which a tiny lady with an immaculately sculpted head of silvery curls was reading a detective novel. She laid it hastily aside as Jess approached.

'Just those, was it, dear? Very good. Would you like a bag?'

'Yes please.' While she fumbled in her pocket for her money Jess put the sheaf of application forms she'd collected during the course of the morning down on the counter. 'Oh, I forgot − I wanted shoes too. Can I—?'

'You go ahead, dear, I'm not in a rush. We've been quiet this morning. What sort of shoes were you looking for? Something nice to go out dancing?'

Jess smothered a wry smile. 'Oh, no. Flat. You know − comfortable, for every day. Anything, really. Size five.'

The shop contained nothing as utilitarian as a rack of shoes; rather, they were displayed in artistic arrangements, positioned against scarves in toning colours or alone on shelves, like pieces of statement sculpture. Jess couldn't see anything that fitted the description of 'flat' and 'comfortable', but the lady came out from behind her counter and reached, with difficulty, to take down a pair of black suede ankle boots. She turned them over and peered at the size on the bottom, holding her glasses like binoculars.

'There, dear, I thought so – size five. And brand new, by the looks of it. Would you like to try them on?'

'How much are they?'

More squinting and peering. 'Let me see . . . My goodness, twenty-four pounds. That seems like quite a price, but I suppose it must be the make. *L.K. Bennett*,' she read out slowly. 'It means nothing to me, but Audrey – she's the manageress – she knows about these things. She does the prices.' She held them out. 'They're lovely and soft. Very nice quality.'

Jess shook her head quickly, her cheeks tingling with sudden heat. 'It's fine. I can't really . . . I mean, I'll just take the other things. Thanks.'

Mouse-like, the lady scurried back to her place behind the counter and rang the items through the till. As she folded them, with neat little paws, she noticed the application forms. With a sympathetic cluck she said, 'Looking for work? There's not much about at the moment, is there?'

'You don't happen to know of any jobs going, do you? Anything at all, I'm not fussy—'

The curls didn't move as the lady shook her head. 'I'm afraid I don't. My grandson's been trying to find something for months now – just to give him a bit of pocket money to go out with his friends and what have you. That's six pounds, please dear.'

Jess counted out coins and slid them across the counter. She didn't say that a job meant more than pocket money for her, or that her chances of finding one were vastly hampered by not having an address to put on the forms. She'd imagined finding work would be a case of going into shops and enquiring, then perhaps being referred to the right person. Application forms to be sent to head office were not part of the plan.

'Never mind. Thanks anyway.' She picked up the bag and tucked the forms into it, and as she turned to go her stomach gave a loud, echoing rumble. It sounded like an earthquake in the quiet shop. Face burning, she hurried to the door, but in her haste her foot slipped out of one of the too-big shoes and she had to turn back to put it on again.

'Oh, one moment dear – I've just had a thought—'

Jess stopped, her hand on the door, her chest tight with humiliation. She just wanted to get outside, to slip back into the stream of people and become invisible again, but the lady was coming back now, her face creased with compassion as she held out a carrier bag. It was one of the expensive kind, made from stiff cardboard with ropes for handles.

'The lady who brought in the boots came in with another bag today. She's having a clear out, she said, because her daughter's gone off to university. I think there are some more shoes in this one, but Audrey hasn't had a chance to go through it yet. What the eyes haven't seen, the heart won't grieve for. You take it and see if there's anything you can use.'

'But I can't . . .'

'Nonsense. Go on. We've enough in the back to sort through, and you can always bring back any bits you don't want.' She gave Jess's arm a little squeeze. 'I like a young lady who doesn't demand everything new. Some young people these days have far too much, in my opinion.' She cast a disparaging look at the glossy carrier bag. 'In my day there was a war on and we had to be clever with our clothing. Make do and mend, that's what we used to say. Once you've learned the habit you never quite get out of it. Very best of luck with the job hunting, dear.'

She bought a sausage roll, hot from a bakery ('Sorry, we've got no jobs at the moment but if you drop in your CV we'll keep it on file . . .'), and ate it on a bench outside the library, taking tiny bites to make it last as long as possible. The wind's teeth were sharp and its breath metallic but it felt good to be out. She leaned back against the bench and looked cautiously around.

A man threw a ball for an excitable little dog, which leapt up to catch it, twisting acrobatically in the air. A little boy in a green coat ran across the grass, his cheeks pink with cold, his pure, high shrieks streaming behind him in bright ribbons of sound. Ordinary people on an ordinary day; no one following her or watching from the undergrowth. The iron band around Jess's heart loosened a little and she looked down at the neat black ballet pumps she'd found at the bottom of the posh carrier bag and felt suffused with sudden optimism.

People were kind. She'd got too used to being treated like dirt, to living in an atmosphere of aggression and scorn. But that wasn't normal; the vicar in the terrible jumper yesterday, the lady in the shop just now had reminded her of that. She had taken a wrong turn, that was all, but she could get herself back on track.

Screwing up the greasy paper bag she shoved it into her pocket and felt the letter there. She took it out and looked at the name on the front. In the cold, clear, outdoor light the handwriting seemed more fragile and ghostly than it had inside the house, as if a breath of wind might blow the words away, like cobwebs and dust.

Mrs S. Thorne.

Jess got to her feet and picked up the smart carrier bag. She had spent enough time trying – fruitlessly it had to be said – to find a way out of her own problems. It would be good to give herself a break and focus on someone else's for a while.

Walking lightly in her new shoes, she headed for the library.

It took Will an hour and twenty minutes to get from the houses on Greenfields Lane to the offices of Ansell Blake in New Cross. They were situated above a kebab shop (or

Turkish restaurant, as Ansell preferred to call it) in a 1960s development that managed to be both hideously ugly and vastly impractical, being sweltering in summer and arctic in winter. But it came with car parking and was, as Ansell pointed out, handy for the A2, which roared or crawled right outside their poorly fitting windows, depending on the time of day. It was also, of course, cheap.

The stairwell smelled of greasy meat and stale oil. The blue carpet was worn and stained. Since probate research didn't rely on passing trade and most client interaction took place in the homes of potential heirs, Ansell claimed having a 'poncey office with potted plants and copies of *Country Fucking Life*' was an unnecessary extravagance. Will thought that having walls that had been repainted in the last ten years and didn't have a halo of dirt around every light switch was a matter of basic hygiene.

He could hear Ansell on the phone. The absence of expletives and the note of false sincerity in his voice told him it was to a client, but as Will reached the top of the stairs he heard him finish the conversation and hang up. Almost an hour and a half in London traffic had left Will short on patience for dealing with Ansell. He tried to slip past his half-open door unnoticed.

No such luck.

'Halle-fucking-lujah, the wanderer returns. Bex, go downstairs and get Ali to kill the fatted kebab, would you? And then tell Poshboy to get in here.'

Will's heart sank. Bex appeared in the doorway, grinning.

98

She was nineteen and dressed for the office like she was heading out on some extreme hen-party weekend, but she was essentially a sweet girl who took her role as Ansell's comedy sidekick in good part. She rolled her extravagantly lashed eyes and stood aside to let Will past.

'Ah, Posh, glad you could join us.' The happy synergy of Posh and Bex was a matter of perennial hilarity to Ansell, especially as it allowed him to paint Will as a pointless airhead and Bex as the serious talent. 'News just in. A case in the name of Grimwood, which has been a breeze to follow up. While you've been gazing at your navel and paying calls like some kind of fucking Victorian lady, Barry has printed out the family tree and contacted relatives. In Clacton, if you think that pedal car of yours can make it that far?'

That was a good question. The Triumph had been Will's twenty-first birthday present from his parents, intended only for leisurely weekend runs along open country roads in the life they had assumed he would have (which had obviously not involved anything as low-rent as driving around making cold calls). However, it was also a rhetorical question. Wearily Will leaned across and took the printed list of addresses.

'No worries. But what about Nancy Price? I know she doesn't own the house, but her neighbour mentioned that she'd lived there since the war at least, and that she was the kind of person who didn't believe in keeping money in the bank. I was thinking – it might be worth having a look in the house, if we could get permission. You know – wads of cash under the mattress, that sort of thing.'

While Will had been speaking Ansell had been studying his computer screen. Now he tapped out a few words on his keyboard and looked up with a distracted air.

'Oh, I'm sorry, are you still here? Only I thought I told you to bugger off to Clacton and do some actual proper work for a change? Bex – get Nigel on the phone would you?'

Will sighed. It was a slim chance, he knew that, but still – he'd hoped he could persuade Ansell to take it. Because now he was left high and dry with the problem of his promise to Albert Greaves.

He went into the office he shared with Barry, a harassed ex-policeman with two divorces and a battle with alcoholism behind him, and ahead of him too, some days. Beyond the wide, blank windows the city was painted entirely in shades of dirt.

'So it's a day at the seaside for you,' Barry remarked, not looking up from his screen. 'All right for some.'

Will switched on his computer. 'Lovely. Perfect weather for it too.'

'Better than being stuck in here.' Barry still had eight months left of a two-year ban for drink-driving. He stretched and leaned back in his chair, locking his hands together behind his head. 'You can bring me back a stick of candy floss and some nice signed agreements. I've lined up quite a few appointments for you.'

'Excellent.' Distractedly Will scrolled down his screen and clicked open files.

'That Nancy Price case came to nothing, then. Thank

Christ. Finding heirs on that one was turning out to be a proper nightmare. No money there, Mike reckons. Complete wild-goose job.' When Will didn't respond he said, 'Got anything nice planned for the weekend?'

Will remembered the summons to Sunday lunch at his parents' house. 'No,' he said bleakly. In the corner the printer whirred and spat out paper. 'What about you?'

'I got the kids on Saturday afternoon. I was going to take them down Chessington, but Kelly wants to go to Bluewater. Shopping.' He grimaced. 'Here, didn't Bex give you the paperwork for Grimwood? I've already printed it out.'

'Oh, yes — thanks for that. Just printing out a map.' He closed Nancy Price's file and collected the papers from the printer tray. 'I'll be off then. Have a good weekend.'

'Ha flaming ha,' said Barry.

The Local History room in the library was warm and quiet. The helpful library assistant who'd shown Jess to it had pointed out directories where she might look up the name of a particular person, and books and records relating to Church End around the time of World War Two. Internet access was free of charge, and she explained to Jess (in a hushed voice, even though there was no one else in the room) how to log on using the number on her library card. Jess thanked her politely, and couldn't bring herself to mention that she didn't have one. The librarian left, and she looked at the rows of spines, wondering where to start.

An hour later she had amassed a small pile of books on the

table in front of her, and found several references to the cottages on Greenfields Lane. They were, she discovered, amongst the oldest properties in Church End, built when it was still a rural hamlet, for 'artisan workers', whatever they were. There had been another row, facing the remaining one, which was pulled down to make way for the gardens of the big Victorian houses that were built with the arrival of the railway in Church End. In a little book entitled *Kelly's Directory*, which appeared to be a sort of yellow pages and telephone book but without the telephone bit, she discovered that number four Greenfields Lane had been lived in by a Mr and Mrs Mitchell in 1914. But of Mrs S. Thorne there was no mention.

Outside it had started to rain. The library was a modern building with wide plate glass windows, through which Jess had a good view of the darkening street. The pavements glistened with rain and shimmered with the lights from the shops and passing cars. The thought of going back to the house, to the dark and cold and damp and eerie silence, had never been more unappealing.

The library was open until seven, the helpful assistant had told her. Jess put back the books she'd been using and walked slowly along the shelves, until she reached a section called 'Military History'. Something stirred in the back of her mind and she took the letter from her pocket and unfolded it.

382 Squadron. What did that mean? She scanned down. *Death, my old adversary from my flying days* . . .

There were loads of books on World War Two. The war at

sea, in Africa, in Italy, in the East ... The Battle of Britain. The Holocaust. Code breaking. Special Operations ... Jess read the titles on their spines, and when they meant nothing to her, slid them out to look at their covers.

They'd learned about World War Two at primary school. Mrs Ainscough's class. She remembered a display on the wall about rationing and the blackout, and a story they'd had to write about evacuation. The thought of leaving Gran and going to a strange house in a strange town had filled her with horror: little had she known then that she'd be doing exactly that just a few years later, when Gran died. It had been her dad she'd gone to live with, not a complete stranger, but it amounted to the same thing. Before Gran's funeral she'd only met him a handful of times, when he came up from Manchester on rare duty visits, bringing chocolate bars and garage flowers as gifts. The chocolate was for her, and was always a kind she didn't like, with nuts in. The flowers were for Gran, gaudy crysanths wrapped in cellophane with the cut-price label badly torn off, to say thank you for relieving him of responsibility for his accidental daughter.

At least he came, Gran said, stiffly. It was one up on *Her*, which was the only name Gran ever gave to the woman who'd decided she wasn't cut out for motherhood and left when Jess was four months old.

She took down a book about the Home Front (a term she remembered from those far-off days in Mrs Ainscough's) and, noticing one entitled 'American Invasion', pulled that out too. The gap it left revealed a photograph of an enormous aeroplane on the cover of the next book along. A group of men crouched beneath its nose, on which there was a painting of a sexy blonde wearing hardly any clothes and an inviting smile. The book was called *Bombs and Bombshells: a History of the USAAF in Britain*. She added it to her armful.

A gust of wind hurled rain against the windowpane as she settled herself back at her table and opened the first book. A black-and-white world opened up before her, of men in uniform with slicked-down, gleaming hair, of girls who looked like the painting on the plane but with more clothes on, of couples dancing the old-fashioned way, hands clasped, gazes locked. There was something innocent about them, but something romantic too. Sexy, she thought with a beat of surprise.

She paused on a double page blow-up of a crowded dance floor. Young people, just like her, dancing. The photograph had been taken over seventy years ago, and yet as she pored over the details the colour seemed to bleed back into the scene, until she could almost feel the heat, smell the sweat and perfume, hear the blast of the music.

In Mrs Ainscough's class the war had been distant history, but as she looked at that photograph she understood in a way she hadn't before that it was real life. Dan Rosinski's letter was lying on the desk beside her, and her eye was drawn back to its spiky, urgent handwriting.

Real life. Real people. And it wasn't over yet.

8

1943

In the end Nancy had won, as she always did. Though Stella still felt far from comfortable with the idea of going out, Saturday evening saw her sitting obediently at the dressing table while Nancy twisted her hair into little pin curls on top of her head and, cigarette wedged into the corner of her mouth, chattered nineteen to the dozen.

She'd arranged to meet some other girls from the salon at the dance, she told Stella. 'You'll love them – a right laugh they are, and it'll do you the world of good to spend some time with people your own age for a change.' Stella's heart sank. She knew she ought to be glad that Nancy wanted to share her new friends, but the prospect of meeting them was enough to make her courage fail. Their names popped up regularly in Nancy's conversation, so that Stella already had an idea of the kind of girls they were. Confident girls, who chewed gum given to them by GIs and knew how to do all the latest dances. The kind of girls that would stop at nothing in their pursuit of a good time, and were bound to think that Stella was seven kinds of boring. Normal, attractive girls.

From his cross on the wall, Christ watched reproachfully as Nancy took a compact out of the little vanity case she'd brought with her and dusted powder over Stella's cheeks and nose.

'Now – close your eyes.'

'What for?'

'A bit of eyeshadow, that's all. And ... the finishing touch ...' There was a muted snap and Stella jumped as she felt something being dabbed against her mouth. 'Lipstick!'

Stella opened her eyes. She barely recognized the woman whose glittering eyes stared back at her from the dressing-table mirror. Tentative butterfly wings of excitement fluttered in the pit of her stomach.

'I don't know about the lipstick, Nance – it's very ... red.'

'Which, in case you hadn't noticed, is what everyone's wearing these days.'

'Not in King's Oak they're not.' Stella laughed nervously. She couldn't stop looking at the woman in the mirror. A stranger, in a stranger's clothes. 'I'm not sure it's quite ... me.'

'Don't you dare rub it off – haven't you heard? It's unpatriotic to waste anything these days, and that goes just as much for my precious lipstick as it does for stale bread.' Nancy slicked her own lips with scarlet and pressed them together, then dropped the lipstick back into her bag. 'Come on, let's get going.'

The woman in the glass stood up and stroked a hand down the silky fabric of her dress. Excitement fought with misgiving. In the ugly familiarity of the Vicarage bedroom she no longer looked like Charles's respectable, dutiful, failed wife. She remembered what Ada had said about Cinders. She had been transformed from insipid drudge into a sophisticated siren.

'Hurry up, Dolly Daydream.' Behind her, Nancy straightened up from checking her stocking seams. 'You know what they say . . . So many Yanks, so little time.'

As she spoke, Stella caught sight of the little silver and marcasite watch Roger and Lillian had given her for Christmas, lying in the trinket dish on the dressing table. She slipped it on and fastened the clasp. The metal felt cold and tight around her wrist, like the hard grip of icy fingers. There – now she could be sure not to stay past midnight. She looked at the bed, scene of her failure and humiliation, its mustard-coloured cover pulled smooth. Just a few hours, and she would be back between its chilly sheets, where she belonged.

But until then she could pretend to be someone different; the stranger who wore red lipstick and had pin curls and a skirt that caressed her legs when she walked.

'Coming,' she said, and switched off the light.

London might have been a city in blackout, but if the Luftwaffe had just leaned out of their cockpits Stella felt sure they could have been guided towards it by the noise. As soon as they got off the bus they could hear the sound of Glenn Miller drifting down the street, over the heads of the people huddled together against the cold in the queue for the Opera House.

'Looks like we might not get in,' Stella said, trying to keep the relief out of her voice. The sense of optimism and adventure she had felt in the bedroom had been slowly draining away during the bus journey, and at that moment an evening spent listening to the wireless with Reverend Stokes seemed rather appealing.

Nancy seized her arm. 'Don't you believe it,' she muttered. 'Just keep quiet and look pretty.'

She set off at a purposeful pace, her pelvis swaying so extravagantly that her hip nudged Stella's with every step, her eyes scanning the row of faces in the queue. At last, when they were almost at the front she let out a joyful yell, and hurled herself at a soldier in American uniform, dragging a horrified Stella with her.

'Johnny – oh, Johnny, there you are! I thought I'd never find you!'

Before the startled GI could protest she'd thrown her arms around his neck and fixed her mouth on his. The swell of muttering and grumbling from further back in the queue was drowned out by the chorus of whoops and cheers that went up from the other Americans in the group. Stiff with embarrassment, Stella found herself absorbed into it, sheltered from the belligerent buffeting of the people behind by towering giants who gave off a collective scent of aftershave and mint chewing gum. They seemed taller than British soldiers, or was that just the elegant cut of their uniforms? One of them –

dark-haired and olive-skinned – introduced himself as Frank, and his friends as Jimmy and Ron and Mitch, then he bent his head to whisper in her ear, 'And that's Eugene that your friend there is eating, though I guess for tonight at least we'd better call him Johnny.'

Nancy had always been a skilled flirt, but had clearly been honing the art further since Stella had last been out with her. Torn between irritation and amusement Stella watched as she detached herself from Eugene/Johnny.

'Sorry about that, boys, but needs must,' she smirked, with a singular lack of contrition. 'How else was we going to get in and have a chance to dance with you lovely lot? And the good news is . . .' She dropped her voice to a conspiratorial whisper and they all came in a bit closer to hear it, 'Inside I've got three more gorgeous friends who'll be delighted to show you boys a bit of good old London hospitality.'

In fact, the Americans were so nice and courteous – insisting on paying them into the dance hall, addressing them both as 'Miss' all the time, arguing good-naturedly over who was going to buy them drinks – that Stella felt her initial misgivings begin to melt away. Perhaps it was the heat; after the arctic air outside the dance hall was absolutely sweltering. Glenn Miller was deafening in here, and as she followed Nancy and Eugene/Johnny across to a table she could feel the wooden floor bouncing beneath her feet. There was plenty of space to sit on the velvet banquette because everyone was crowded on the dance floor, where *American Patrol* had just given way to *In the Mood*.

'This tune could have been written for me!' Nancy yelled, pulling Eugene away to dance.

'May I?' Frank offered her his hand with a quaint little mock bow. Stella shook her head quickly. She wanted to explain about being married and only coming along for a night out with Nancy, but the music was too loud and it seemed like she was being presumptuous, assuming that he fancied her when he was probably only being polite. He shrugged. 'Why don't you take a seat? I'll get us something to drink – what'll you have?'

'Oh . . . a lemonade would be nice, thank you.'

'I'll be right back. Don't go away.'

Just as he made to move away, one of the others appeared through the crowd on the dance floor delicately juggling several brimming glasses in his hands.

'Nice work, Mitch. Shame your hands aren't that steady when you're in the gun turret.'

'Take a hike, Franklin.' Mitch grinned and slid a glass over to Stella. It clearly wasn't lemonade, but she could hardly complain. She picked it up and took a sip. It tasted warm, sweet and faintly spicy. She took another cautious sip. She was thirsty and it wasn't quite as refreshing as she would have liked, but definitely not unpleasant.

'Thanks, it's delicious. What is it?'

A look of surprise flashed across Mitch's freckled face. 'Port and lemon. I thought that was what all the English girls drank.'

Nancy appeared, dragging two girls by the wrist, another following behind them. They were all flushed and smiling eagerly and, as they were introduced, looked at the Americans in the same slanting, sideways way that Nancy did, simultaneously shy and knowing.

'Irene, Doreen and Maureen – I kid you not,' Nancy was saying, while the girls giggled and batted their eyelashes. 'If you can't remember which is which, just call them all Renee. Now, let me get this right, girls . . .' Nancy pointed a cheeky finger at each of the Americans in turn, like a schoolteacher. 'Frank, Mitch, Ron and Jimmy. Oh, and this is Stella – the friend I told you about.'

It was added as an afterthought and, unsurprisingly given the circumstances, none of the three girls gave Stella more than a fleeting glance. Electric looks were flying across the table as conversations were struck up and invitations to dance extended. Stella took another mouthful of her drink. The sensation of disappearing returned as the table emptied. Only one of the GIs remained: Ron, the stocky, fair-haired one. Stella watched him light a cigarette and felt sorry for him being stuck with her. As the band started up a new tune he offered her the packet.

'Oh man, I love this song! Shall we?'

He was already on his feet, the cigarette dangling from his lips as he held out his hand.

Finishing the last of her drink, Stella gave a nervous laugh. 'Oh, I'm very out of practice . . . But really, you go.'

'Hey, anyone can dance to *Chattanooga Choo Choo*, and if you don't believe me you gotta let me prove it! C'mon – as a Tennessee boy born and bred it would be a capital offence not to dance to this one.'

Strictly speaking, it wasn't impossible to refuse but it would certainly have been awkward. He reminded Stella of the coalman's dog, a squat muscular thing who had a habit of rushing around in circles, teeth bared in a grin. Without waiting for her to answer he had pulled her to her feet and dragged her out into the middle of the dance floor. Stella was jostled from all sides by couples swinging around, dancing with a vigour that was so far removed from the polite waltzes and two-steps she'd done with Charles at the odd church fund-raising evening that it was scarcely recognizable as the same activity. For a moment she stood motionless and at a loss, but then Ron had seized her by the waist and was pulling her towards him, taking her hand, and her feet were moving of their own accord, her hips too, as if she'd known how to do this all along. He was a good dancer, his stocky frame surprisingly agile, his hands swift and assured as he twirled and guided her.

'See? Like I told you – it's easy!'

She laughed. The air was scented with sweat and aftershave and pressed down on them like a damp blanket. Her dress billowed out as Ron spun her round. Out of the corner of her eye she saw Nancy, dancing with someone different. They were so good that the dancers around them had cleared a little space for them and were watching as her partner lifted her up by the waist and she swung her legs to either side of him. The band began playing a faster-paced tune that Stella didn't recognize and the gap between couples seemed to shrink as more dancers crowded onto the floor. She had to duck out of the way to avoid being socked in the eye by an enthusiastically flung-out hand. Ron shoved the offending couple out of the way.

'Whaddya say we sit this one out?' he yelled above the music.

Stella nodded and followed him back to the table. Two of the Renees were there, perched on the knees of their Americans like ventriloquist's dummies. As Stella sank gratefully into her seat Frank appeared balancing aloft a tray of drinks. He set it down with a flourish so that beer slopped from the glasses onto Stella's dress. Ron leapt to mop at it with his handkerchief.

'Watch it, Frank, you klutz.'

'Sorry.' Frank handed her a glass with an apologetic grin.

'Doesn't matter. Thanks for the drink – I didn't realize dancing was such thirsty work.'

Ron winked and chimed his glass against hers. 'Well drink up, sugar, and let's get back out there and do it some more.'

After that the evening became a bit of a blur. Stella danced – not just with Ron, but with Frank and Eugene and at least two other GIs whose names she didn't catch above the screech of trumpets from the stage. Whenever she found herself back at the table a drink was pushed in her direction, but no matter how much she drank she only seemed to get thirstier. It was part of the strangeness of the evening, she decided hazily. The magic. For the first time in months the chill had left her bones and she felt warm through and through, right to the very core. And not in danger of disappearing any more. Swaying lazily against her as the band played *Moonlight Serenade* Ron had told her how beautiful she was, and while she knew that she ought to feel guilty and wicked, she didn't. She felt somehow vindicated, and relieved. And happy.

Escaping to the ladies' cloakroom she pushed her way through the crowd at the row of basins to run cold water over her wrists in an attempt to cool down. Shaking the water from her fingers she peered at her watch, but its tiny face refused to come into focus. In the mirror above the sink she saw that her cheeks were flushed, her eyes glittering, and the make-up Nancy had applied had formed dark smudges beneath them. She was hastily wiping them away when a familiar face appeared beside hers in the mirror.

'Look at you – the belle of the ball!' Nancy smirked as she uncapped her lipstick. 'I won't say I told you so, but . . .'

'I know, I admit it,' Stella sighed. 'I should have done this months ago. I'm having such a good time, I don't want tonight to end.'

'Well, no need to worry about that just yet; the night, as they say, is still young . . .' Nancy pressed her freshly crimsoned lips together and twisted the lipstick back into its case. 'Matter of fact, we was thinking about leaving here and going on somewhere else.'

'Somewhere else?' Dreamily Stella slid her hands into her hair and attempted to smooth it back into its earlier sophisticated submission. Beautiful, he'd called her . . . Just like Gene Tierney. Stella knew she was a Hollywood actress, but couldn't quite picture her face. He'd made it sound like a compliment though, and he wasn't bad looking. Not tall and gentlemanly like Charles ... but then maybe that was a good thing.

'Yes, somewhere quieter. It's getting very crowded here,' Nancy said pointedly, throwing a dirty look at a girl who was jostling for a space at the mirror. 'The Yanks want to walk down to the Savoy and take us for a drink in the American bar.'

She said this last bit loudly as she pushed through the crush. Stella hurried after, biting her lip to stop herself from laughing at the envious stares that followed them all the way to the door.

Outside the cold took her breath away. She stumbled, but Ron was beside her and slid an arm around her waist. His body felt completely solid and slightly damp as his sweat cooled in the night air. A bit like a sandbag, she thought hazily. They walked down The Strand. The pavements were almost as crowded as on a weekday afternoon, in spite of the fact that it was dark, which added to the surreal feeling of the evening. Up ahead Nancy was twined around Eugene – or was it Johnny? Stella couldn't remember – and one of the Renees, the plump one with the loud laugh – had kicked off her shoes and was being given a piggyback ride by Mitch. Her pencilled-on stocking seams were smeared across the backs of her legs. Unsurprisingly they were all turned away from the Savoy by a supercilious uniformed doorman, and spilled out onto The Strand again. The Americans were belligerent and vociferous.

'Jeez, we're risking our necks for you guys – he coulda let us in for one goddamn drink!' 'Yeah – in the American bar, what with us being Americans and all.'

Stella leaned against the wall of Ron's body. She felt suddenly very tired, and her feet hurt from dancing. She was almost tempted to sit down on the pavement and take her shoes off like Irene, or Doreen, or – what was the other one called? She wasn't sure she'd like a piggyback though, especially not the way that Mitch was swinging Irene or Doreen or whoever around, which was making Stella feel queasy even to watch. They were walking without purpose, the evening's magic souring.

'Hey – look at this! It's a church!'

It was Frank's voice. He was no longer walking ahead of them, Stella saw, but had disappeared inside a bombed-out building to their left.

'Careful – it might not be safe!' one of the girls called, but the other GIs were already following him through the gaping doorway, stumbling over loose bricks and picking their way past piles of rubble.

'*Was* a church – Jeez, not much left of it now.'

'Good job by some Nazi bombardier. Ripped the whole of the inside out.'

'Musta been in the Blitz I guess – '40, '41?'

Ron moved away, as if following some herd instinct. Left alone Stella looked around for somewhere to sit and sank down on a slab of fallen masonry at the top of some shallow steps. It was peaceful in here, enclosed by thick walls, cut off from the rest of the city. She tipped her head back to take a deep breath, hoping it would clear the nauseous feeling that had been insidiously creeping up on her since they left the dance hall. High above the jagged, ruined walls, the moon floated on her back, beyond the reach of the searchlight beams that raked the darkness.

'I don't like it in 'ere,' whined the disembodied voice of one of the salon girls. 'It's spooky, and dark.'

'Hey, there's nothing wrong with dark,' came the husky reply. 'In fact, dark has a lot going for it . . .'

There was a shriek, which was immediately followed by a giggle, trailing off into a muffled moan. In the thin moonlight Stella could just make out two figures locked together against the wall. She looked away quickly, but once her eyes adjusted she became aware of another couple, the girl propped against the ledge of a glassless window, her legs wrapped around the man's khaki back. From the pale gleam of her hair Stella could tell that it was Nancy. Stella stood up, a peculiar feeling churning in the pit of her stomach. She jumped and gave a little cry of alarm as an arm closed around her waist from behind.

'Cold?'

Ron's breath smelled of beer and cigarettes more than chewing gum now. It was warm against her neck.

'A bit.'

'Here, let me take care of that.'

He pulled her into his body, rubbing his hands up and down her back. Heat radiated from his touch and she was glad of it. It seemed to spread from her back down into the cradle of her pelvis. She closed her eyes and submitted to it. She was so tired. Behind her eyelids the world was spinning, so that she suddenly remembered a carousel she'd been on once at the fair on the front at Southend. It had been a school outing, and Miss Birch had bought them candyfloss and allowed them two rides each. Nancy had dragged her onto the swinging chairs first, and then she had chosen the carousel with its painted horses and gleaming barley-sugar twisted poles. She remembered gripping tightly, holding on for dear life as the fairground spun and the faces of the people watching blurred and the music of the organ swelled inside her head. She'd wanted it to stop, to get off, but she was terrified that if she opened her mouth to speak she'd be sick.

Ron's mouth found hers in the dark. His kiss was hard and determined, so different from Charles's. *Charles*. The thought of him jolted her back from the dark vortex in which she'd been spinning. She tried to pull away but Ron's hand was clamped on the back of her head, his tongue jabbing against hers. She couldn't breathe. More desperately now she fought against his kiss, trying to twist her head away and wrench herself out of his grasp, trying to cry out to him to stop. Nausea rose in her throat, like on the carousel; she could see the smudged faces again, spinning around on the inside of her skull. Gathering all her strength she placed her hands against Ron's chest and pushed him away.

He swore viciously as he half-fell backwards, unable to keep his footing on the rubble-strewn ground. As he fell he instinctively made a grab for her and caught hold of her wrist.

She yanked it free and ran, tripping and stumbling down the steps in her haste to get away from him.

Behind her his voice echoed off the ruined walls. 'Hey – *Hey*! Cock-teasing bitch – what's the matter with you?'

She burst out onto the street, retching, pressing her hand to her mouth. A bus was lumbering into the stop at the corner of Aldwych and she forced her trembling legs to run towards it.

I don't know, she thought despairingly, watching the cheerful clippie girl approach. *What is the matter with me?* For a little while he'd made her feel beautiful, desirable, *just like Gene Tierney*. All this time . . . all these lonely months, she thought that was what she wanted.

But now she'd got it she just felt dirty.

9

2011

It was amazing to be clean.

Again and again Jess pressed the button to release another
two minutes of steaming water, long after she'd rinsed the last
of the cheap shampoo out of her hair. She'd paid three
pounds she couldn't afford to use the shower at the leisure
centre and, tipping her face up and letting the water run
down it, she decided it was worth every extravagant penny.

It wasn't just the shower and the shampoo: she'd also
splashed out on soap and deodorant. The fifty pounds was
half gone now and she knew that she had to decide what to
do. Leaving the library the other day she'd picked up a leaflet
from a rack by the counter about 'Housing Advice and
Action Services'. It gave details of emergency shelters and
temporary hostels in the district, as well as how to apply for
more long-term accommodation. One of the shelters was
only a couple of streets away from the library and, feeling
more positive than she had in a long time, she'd walked round

there. As she approached she could see a small group of men huddled in the overhang of the porch outside, smoking. With their angular faces, narrowed, suspicious eyes and hunched shoulders they reminded her of the people Dodge hung out with. She'd kept walking, her heart jumping.

The jet of water dwindled again, and reluctantly she reached for the towel. It was the small, scratchy one from the hook in the bathroom at Greenfields Lane, and it brought the whiff of mildew into the bright cubicle. As she scrubbed herself dry her thoughts slipped into the same worn groove in which they'd circled all weekend. She was like a prisoner endlessly checking the walls of her cell for a means of escape and finding nothing.

To get somewhere decent to stay she needed money. To get money she needed a job, and to get a job she needed somewhere to live. Even if she managed to find a job that didn't require her to submit a CV or application form, she'd need to make herself look half decent.

Towel-drying her hair she caught sight of her face in the little mirror on the cubicle wall. Beneath the halogen lights her skin looked dull and greyish, with red scaly patches on either side of her nose and on her forehead. That's what happened when you washed with soap and didn't use moisturiser. She peered closer. Her eyebrows, which she'd been plucking into fine, sophisticated arches since she was fourteen years old, had lost their shape and crawled across her forehead like black caterpillars. She gave a little groan of disgust and despair. Where did tweezers fit on her list of priorities?

But at least she had some clothes now, thanks to the kind lady in the posh charity shop. Not that leopard print leggings, a pink jumper with KITTEN emblazoned across the chest in sequins and several t-shirts with stuff like 'I want candy', 'WTF' and 'Wild' written on them were exactly what she would have chosen, but she was glad of them. There'd been other, more practical things too. The shoes, for a start, which were a godsend, a little floral shift dress, a denim mini-skirt and a navy cardigan, both of which she was wearing today beneath her leather jacket. In them she felt like someone different from the girl who'd let herself become Dodge's creation, Dodge's punchbag, and from the one who'd hidden beneath a borrowed trench coat. It was a good feeling.

It was Sunday morning, and the foyer of the leisure centre teemed with children. A birthday party was assembling, the kids racing around, fuelled by an excess of excitement. The host's dad was easily identifiable by his air of barely contained desperation as he tried to marshal them. The smell of coffee fought with chlorine, making Jess's mouth prickle. It came from a smart-looking café on the mezzanine overlooking the pool, where parents could pretend to watch their kids' swimming lessons while reading newspapers and drinking the kind of frothy, fancy stuff that Jess couldn't pronounce or afford. Resolutely she squashed down temptation and headed for the door.

Just beside it there was a vending machine. She stopped, looking at it wistfully. Paper cups, powdered milk, bitter instant coffee . . . but it would be hot and she had the beginnings of a sore throat. Guiltily, before she could think herself out of it, she was feeding coins into the slot.

As the last one was swallowed up, the automatic doors to outside swished open, admitting a blast of winter air, and a man. Glancing up as she went to press the button for coffee Jess saw that he was tall, with dark hair and broad shoulders; *rugby type*, she thought absently in the split second before recognition hit her.

Shit. The guy from the house. She looked away sharply – not before she'd seen him notice her, but just in time to realize that the button she'd pressed was for tea not coffee. With the speed and urgency of a pinball ace she pounded the coffee button, which released a second cascade of hot water with no cup to catch it in.

She jumped backwards, out of its scalding stream. When it stopped there was a moment of agonized silence, in which the noise and movement of the leisure centre foyer behind seemed to have been suspended, as if someone had pressed pause. Only the two of them remained. They looked at each other.

Then he spoke, and reality resumed.

'Are you all right? Those machines ought to carry a health warning, and not just for their revolting coffee. Bloody dangerous, boiling water. Did it go all over you? You need to—'

'It's OK. I'm fine. It didn't—'

'Was it coffee? Probably did you a favour.' His smile was gentle, but his eyes held hers, and searched them. 'I – actually,

I think we've met before. The other day — Greenfields Lane, wasn't it? I'm Will Holt. Look —' he dragged a hand through his mop of untidy hair and gave her a sheepish look, 'I'm supposed to be doing an hour in the gym before I head off for a family lunch, but in truth I'd rather boil my own head. You wouldn't let me buy you a coffee to replace this one, would you? The stuff in the café upstairs isn't too bad, if you can put up with the screaming children . . .'

She was shaking her head before he'd finished speaking. 'I don't think — I mean, I can't. I've got to—' She was backing away. 'Sorry.'

And she turned, and the doors slid open to let her escape.

10

1943

Stella awoke with a jolt.

For a second she was disorientated, and gasped with relief when she realized that she was in her own bed. In her fragmented dreams she had been back in the church, stumbling over rubble, forever trying to reach the street she couldn't see. She lay very still. Her body felt clammy and dirty beneath the smooth, clean sheets. Her mouth was dry, her tongue glued to the top of it, making her crave a drink of water. But when she went to sit up it felt like her brain had been scooped out of her skull and replaced with rocks.

No light seeped in around the edges of the blackout, but she could hear the faint song of a lone bird and from that deduced that it must be nearly morning. In the charcoal gloom she peered down at her watch and let out a whimper of horror. Her wrist was bare. The watch given to her by Roger and Lillian with such ceremony at Christmas was missing.

Her hand was shaking so violently she had trouble switching on the light, but when she finally managed, its comforting glow failed to reveal the watch, dashing the hope that she'd taken it off in her drunken state last night. 'Oh God,' she moaned softly, pushing the hair back from her forehead as her mind spooled backwards. There was a clear memory of putting it on as she stood here in the bedroom with Nancy before going out, and then . . . In the dance hall, she'd looked at it in the ladies' cloakroom. She had a sudden flashback to being in the ruined church, when Ron had grabbed her wrist. It must have fallen off then, and she'd been in no fit state to notice.

Desperately her thoughts scuttled backwards and forwards, but could only discover one possible way out: she'd just have to go back and look for it, and be home again in time for church. She pulled on an old tweed skirt and a woollen jumper of Charles's that she'd shrunk in the wash and, treading quietly, went to the bathroom where she gulped down mouthfuls of water and then splashed her face with it. The cold, on top of the arctic temperature and the icy linoleum beneath her feet, made her gasp and set the rocks in her head grinding together. In the small mirror her face was waxy-white and the thought of going out into the frozen dawn was almost enough to make tears of self-pity spring to her eyes. She held them back with the thought that she'd brought all of this on herself.

It was no more than she deserved.

*

The bus was full of munitions workers heading for the early shift. Stella found a seat near the back and alternately dozed and fought back nausea. The sky was the soft mauve grey of a pigeon's breast as she got off on The Strand and the ruined church looked tranquil in the melting pink light, but she was trembling as she went through the door at the end of the broken nave. Memories of last night surfaced like fish from a murky pool.

Inside all was chill and shadowed; the tentative rays of the new day's sun hadn't yet reached in here. There was a bleak kind of beauty to the shattered stone pillars and gaping, glass-less windows. Beneath her feet was a mosaic of broken marble – the pattern of the black-and-white squares still dis-cernible beneath the layers of dirt and sprouting weeds. It must have been the aisle. Brides would have stepped where she did now, satin-shoed, silk train slithering across the pol-ished surface as they walked to the altar.

She looked up, towards the chancel, and froze.

Someone was standing there. A man, head bent, as if in prayer. He was in uniform – unmistakably American – the cut of the tunic making his shoulders appear very broad, his hips narrow. He was standing right beside where she'd sat last night; the place where her watch was most likely to be now. She hesitated, clammy with sudden panic, torn between the temptation to turn around and slip quietly out again before he saw her, and the need to complete the task she'd come all this way to do.

But before she could decide he'd turned round, and she

saw at once that he hadn't been praying at all. In his hands was a black, rectangular box – a camera – down into which he must have been looking to frame a shot. His face registered no surprise as he saw Stella, but a grave smile momentarily touched his mouth as he walked towards her.

'Morning, miss.'

'Morning.'

To her relief he passed her. She stood perfectly still, the throbbing in her head marking the seconds while she waited for him to leave. But instead of heading straight to the door he walked along the wall, trailing his fingers reverently across the stone as if he were reading something there. Then he looked up, past her, towards the spreading pink of the sky above the jagged walls.

Stella looked away quickly, not wanting to be caught staring. Pulling her coat more tightly around herself she hurried down the remainder of the aisle and went up the chancel steps. Since he obviously didn't feel compelled to explain what had brought him here she saw no reason why she should; she would just retrieve her watch and leave. There was the stone slab she'd sat on, the broken bricks heaped against the wall into which Ron had stumbled when she'd pushed him away ... She could even make out the marks in the mud on the tiles where they'd scuffled. It must be here somewhere.

She bent down, peering into the gaps between the bricks, desperately hoping to see a glint of silver. There *was* something – relief flared like a match igniting – a dull, metallic gleam entombed within the rubble. She took off her glove and eased her hand in to see if she could reach it. Pushing back the sleeve of her coat she stretched as far down as she could, fingers scrabbling at the dirt as she tried to block out thoughts of spiders and creepy crawlies. Just as stars were bursting inside her head with the effort her fingertips brushed against something small and metallic. She groped to pick it up and pulled it out.

A silver twist of paper. The wrapper from a stick of chewing gum. Sitting back on her heels she blew out a breath and closed her eyes against the pain in her head and the frustration and misery that were swelling in her parched throat. When she opened them again she saw that the American was looking at her, his camera half raised. Alarmed, she scrambled to her feet.

'I'm sorry, miss. I didn't mean to startle you. I was just wondering if there was something I could help you with?'

In the ethereal light she could see the violet shadows beneath his eyes, as if he hadn't slept much either. He was very good-looking, she thought, bitterly. Very American, somehow, with his strong shoulders and olive-tinged skin and thick, untidy, tawny hair.

She brushed dust from her coat. 'No, thank you.'

'You're looking for something? I mean, something besides whatever it is that people usually come to find in churches.'

'My watch. I was here last — yesterday, and it must have fallen off. You haven't seen it, have you?'

He shook his head. 'Sorry. What's it look like?'

'Small. Silver. Studded with marcasites.'

'Sounds pretty. Was it a gift?'

'Yes,' she said tightly, then turned away and began moving bricks aside, gritting her teeth at the noise they made as they scraped together. She was aware of him laying down his camera and coming up the steps to join her, and she wanted to protest but didn't have the energy. Darkness shimmered at the edge of her vision, like blackout curtains half-pulled across a window. The nausea that had been coiled like a snake in her stomach began to writhe and rise. Oh God. She sat down abruptly in the same place as last night and swallowed a lungful of cold air, hoping it would douse the sickness. It didn't. There was a sort of rushing sound in her ears, like when you were standing on the platform in the underground and the train was approaching. The blackout curtains closed.

'It's OK – I got you.'

She felt his hand on the back of her head, very gently pushing it down. Then the ground rushed up towards her, and everything dissolved into darkness.

'Sugar?'

The woman in the WVS van outside Bush House pressed her lips together as her eyes darted between Stella and the American. It wasn't difficult to work out what she was thinking, why she thought they were out together so early in the morning. Stella turned away, thrusting her hands deeply into the pockets of her coat and trying to disappear down into the collar. She wasn't sure what was more embarrassing – being taken for a tart, or almost fainting and throwing up in front of a complete stranger.

'Two please.'

Stella wanted to say that she didn't take sugar at all, but the words stuck in her dry throat. The WVS woman gave a snort.

'You'll be lucky. It don't grow on trees over here, you know. Rationing – you might not have heard of it.'

'Oh, I've heard of it, ma'am, but the young lady is feeling unwell. I was hoping you might be kind enough to spare a little extra for her. If it helps, I won't have any in mine.'

'Well ... when you put it like that ...' The woman was smirking now, looking up at him from under her lashes as she poured tea into a second cup. 'I expect she's tired out. Needs to get her strength back. Spoon's down there, on the end of that string.'

'Thanks.' Stella took the tea from him without meeting his eye and carried it over to the steps. One of the massive fluted columns that supported Bush House's impressive façade towered above her and she sat down, leaning back against it and taking a tentative sip of steaming tea. It was stewed and made with dried milk, but was so welcome that she didn't care. The American sat down too, a little distance from her. She appreciated that – the distance. His legs seemed too long to fold up comfortably on the shallow steps so he stretched them out in front of him, and put his camera down between them.

'Better?' he said at last, as she drank her tea, cradling the cup with her hands for warmth. She nodded stiffly, grateful for the tea and his kindness but wishing he would go now.

'Perfectly fine now, thank you. If you need to—'

'I'm in no hurry. All the guys I came here with are snoring their heads off back at the hotel and hungover to the back teeth.'

His voice was low and husky, and as he spoke he took a packet of Lucky Strikes from the top pocket of his tunic and held it out to her. She shook her head. 'We're headed back to base today.' Lighting his cigarette he looked up at the soaring columns and arched dome above them. 'Seemed crazy to waste time sleeping when all of this was on the doorstep. I'm with the Air Force, based in East Anglia. You ever been there?' She shook her head again. 'Nothing for miles around but tin huts and mud.' He exhaled a plume of smoke that merged with the steam from his tea. 'Makes quite a change to see proper buildings, I can tell you.'

She could feel the chill of the marble through her coat, but the tea had warmed her from the inside. He was nothing like the Americans from last night. She risked a look at him.

'That church wasn't exactly a proper building.'

'Ah, but it was once,' he said softly. 'St Clement Danes is one of the fifty or so churches built by Christopher Wren after the Great Fire of London.'

'Really?' She hadn't even known its name.

'Sure. In its day I guess it would've represented the best in modern design. It's good to know that it's come back from ruin before. Makes you just about believe that one day it can be rebuilt into something beautiful again.'

They sat in silence for a while as the street in front of them became busier. The dawn's rosy golden magic was fading fast and the city was putting on its working grey to begin another day. Stella's cup was empty. At the WVS van another woman had arrived on a bike to take over the shift and was untying the patterned headscarf she'd worn under her hat.

'Was it one of our guys?' he said in a low voice. 'Last night? I don't want to pry, but if—'

'I must go.' Flustered, she put the cup down and made to stand up. In one smooth movement he was on his feet, holding out his hand to help her. She took it, blushing as his fingers closed around hers. He didn't let go immediately and for a moment they stood, hands clasped, looking at each other. His eyes were the clear blue-green of old glass, tinged darker around the edges.

'Th-thank you. Really. You've been very kind.'

'You're welcome. It's a shame we didn't find your watch. I'm not quite done with taking pictures so I'll take another look around now. You could give me your name and address, and if I find it I'll put it in the post to you.'

'Oh . . .' She was caught off-guard, torn. On the one hand, if there was any chance of getting the watch back it would be sensible to take it, but on the other she instinctively resisted the idea of telling this man that she was Mrs Charles Thorne of The Vicarage, Church Road, King's Oak, though she wasn't sure whether that was for the right reasons or the wrong ones. 'Do you have something to write on?'

He pulled the cigarette packet from his pocket again, along with a pencil. Heart thudding she turned away and leaned against the pillar to write, then gave them both back to him. He looked at what she'd written before putting the cigarettes back into his pocket.

'Nancy. Pretty name. I'm Dan. Daniel Rosinski – 2nd Lieutenant. It's been nice meeting you.'

She kept her hands in the pockets of her coat and looked past him up the street, in the direction she should be going. 'Thank you again, Lieutenant.' She said it in the American way, as he had. 'For the tea and everything. Best of luck when you get back to duty.'

It sounded brisk and flippant and wrong, and she was suddenly struck by a sense of what he was going back to. While for her the war meant queuing at Fairacre's, making up Red Cross parcels, waiting for Charles's letters and putting up with Reverend Stokes, for him it meant – what? Flying into enemy territory? Being shot at? Coping with the knowledge that he might not see another sunrise?

She stood, rooted to the pavement as these thoughts went through her head, wanting to say something but unable to put it into words. He'd already begun to move away, his eyes still fixed to hers.

'I'll be seeing you,' he said quietly with a little mock-salute, and then he turned and walked away.

Liverpool Street Station was one of those flamboyantly grand Victorian buildings the British did so well. Its rows of arched windows and delicate filigree ironwork spoke of Victorian self-assurance; a nation that was wealthy and powerful enough to insist that its public buildings combined function with beauty. It was easy to imagine gentlemen in top hats and tail-coats striding along its wide platforms, although today every inch was covered by a flood tide of American khaki.

It seemed like half the USAAF had been given leave and were now pouring back out of London into the flat fenlands, hungover and subdued, aware that they had had their last taste of freedom and hedonism for a long time, perhaps forever. A Red Cross canteen, distributing much-needed coffee and doughnuts, had done such a roaring trade that it had run out of both and was reduced to handing out cups of water and cheerful smiles, which were almost as gratefully received.

Sitting on his kitbag amid the swarm of men Dan Rosinski felt a little lightheaded from lack of sleep but a hell of a lot better than the three other officers from his crew. Louis Johnson, Jimmy Morgan and Sam Adelman were slumped around him in various stages of recovery. The cloud of alcohol fumes hanging over them was enough to fell an elephant.

'Jeez,' Morgan moaned, without lifting his head from his hands. 'This wasn't supposed to happen. I thought English beer was just about the same as English tea – undrinkable and totally non-alcoholic.'

'It is,' Dan remarked, pointing his camera at Morgan, his co-pilot. 'It was the bottle of whisky that you bought from that guy in Trafalgar Square that did the damage. Tasted like he'd siphoned it out of a fortress's fuel tank.'

Morgan moaned again. 'Next time, stop me.' He looked

up with bloodshot eyes. 'Where did you get to this morning, anyway? Some chick from last night that I don't remember?'

Dan shook his head and held up the camera. 'Wanted to get some photographs of the city before I left.'

'Photographs? What was there to photograph at that time in the morning?'

'You'd be surprised.'

He thought of the shot he'd taken of the girl in the church, kneeling down in the ruins with her eyes closed. He felt bad for taking it without asking, but the moment, the picture, was too perfect to miss.

'Hey, look up there boys,' said Louis Johnson, the crew's navigator, tilting his head back. 'Whaddya see?'

A neat bit of cast iron, Dan thought; delicate and decorative, but strong enough to support the whole damn roof. He guessed that wasn't the answer Johnson was looking for.

'I dunno. Sun's too bright, it's hurting my eyes,' grumbled Adelman.

'Exactly. The cloud cover's lifted. What's the betting *Ruby Shoes* gets her first run tomorrow?'

A groan went up from the small group. Since they'd arrived in East Anglia thick layers of cloud had hung heavily over the flat landscape, making flying impossible and meaning that after two weeks they hadn't clocked up a single mission. The waiting around put a strain on everyone, which was why leave passes were being given out like chewing gum. But Johnson was right. It looked like the endless games of poker and soccer were now at an end and their work as a crew was about to begin.

'I wonder where the other guys are?' Morgan said, looking around as if he'd had the same thought. On the ground a distinction was made between officers and enlisted men, with separate living quarters at the base and different accommodation arrangements for leave in the city, but in the air they would be a unit, close as brothers.

A distant rumbling roar gathered beneath the canopy of the station and there was a surge towards the tracks as the train swung into view. Dan got to his feet and hefted his kitbag onto his shoulder, then hauled Morgan up and shoved him forwards into the crush. Johnson, who had a pregnant wife back home and had already taken on the role of father figure to the whole crew, dodged to the front and claimed a carriage. Adelman and Morgan sank onto the plush seats, moaning.

It wasn't long before they were joined by men from another crew, jostling and squeezing into the carriage, hauling their kitbags onto the overhead luggage racks. By the colour of their faces it was clear they too had taken full advantage of the city's nightlife. The carriage was unheated and it was way too cold to open a window, so by the time the train sighed and slid out of the station the small space was already filled with the smell of stale alcohol, sweat and cheap aftershave.

Dan watched the grimy backs of the city houses slide by, the gaps between them inflicted by the Luftwaffe back in 1940 now overgrown with weeds and wildflowers. By the time the houses had given way to allotments and fields, Morgan's moans had given way to snores and Adelman's head had come to rest on Dan's shoulder. Awkwardly he took the cigarettes from his pocket and lit one, more to burn away the stink of second-hand beer than because he wanted to smoke. Then he turned the pack over.

Nancy. He said the name silently to himself, watching the faint movement of his lips reflected in the glass of the window. It didn't really suit her. Sure, it was pretty, but too brash somehow. Too pert for the bruised, ethereal girl who had knelt in the ruins of Wren's church wearing her unhappiness like a cloak. He'd gone back to the church afterwards to look for the lost watch and, searching amongst the dirt and rubble he'd decided that if he found it, it was a sign that he was meant to see her again.

He hadn't. There were four cigarettes left in the pack, and the rate this train was moving he'd smoke them all before they reached Cambridge. Then he would throw the carton away.

Adelman shifted position on Dan's shoulder, his mouth wide open, emitting guttural snores and the breath of Frankenstein. Clamping his cigarette into the corner of his mouth Dan nudged him over so that his head lolled onto Johnson on his other side, and got to his feet.

'Fresh air,' he muttered to Johnson with a grimace, climbing over legs and kitbags to get to the door.

It was even colder out in the corridor, but at least the air was clean. The train was so crowded that there were guys crouched by the doors, so he walked along the passageway a little and stopped beside an open window, watching the smoke from his cigarette get sucked out into the chilly afternoon. The wintry sun was small and mean and couldn't warm the endless miles of flat grey earth that unfolded on both sides of the train. At intervals the grey was broken up by a field of scrubby green – cabbages perhaps, or maybe the Brussels sprouts that kept appearing on their plates in the mess hall, much to everyone's disgust – and every now and then a great whooping and cheering went up from further down the train as they passed a field with land girls working in it. Dan finished his cigarette and flicked the roach out of the window, then turned away from the uninspiring view.

Behind the glass partition of the compartment opposite more airmen were playing poker. They'd piled their kitbags in the space between the seats to make a flat surface on which to deal and were crouched over it, slapping cards down, jaws working furiously on gum. As he watched one of the men threw his hand down and fell back against the seat, leaving only two of them in. Dan was about to move away, back to his own carriage, when something caught his eye.

The stakes they were playing for had been placed at the end of their makeshift table nearest the glass: a pile of English coins nestling dully in a fold in the canvas, and on top of them something shinier. Something silver.

He backtracked, looked again, but he hadn't imagined it. A delicate ladies' watch lay on top of the coins. Without thinking he slid back the door of the carriage and leaned in. Everyone looked up, except the two poker players who remained intent on their game.

'Excuse me, gentlemen.'

Reaching over, Dan scooped up the watch. One of the

players – the stocky one – gave a yell of indignation and threw down his cards as he leapt to his feet. 'What the hell? Who the fuck do you think you are—?'

Beside him his friend tried to pull him down onto the seat again, muttering, 'An officer, dumbass.'

A tense silence fell while Dan studied the watch and the men in the carriage studied him. Her voice came back to him with its note of misery. *Small, silver. Studded with marcasites.* He turned it over. Something was engraved on the back and he tilted it so that the letters caught the light.

S.T. 1942

Frowning he turned to the guy who'd challenged him.

'Where'd you get this, buddy?'

'Well sir, I think you could call it a souvenir from London.'

'I said, where did you get it?' Dan repeated, his voice soft but insistent.

The airman's eyes slid away from his, looking for escape. Aggressively working his gum, he shrugged. 'Some girl.' He squared his shoulders and looked Dan challengingly in the eye. 'Yeah, this girl I met. She was real nice. It was a gift – to remember her by.'

Dan nodded slowly, one arm braced against the doorway of the swaying train, looking down at the watch in his hand. 'It's a nice gift. Valuable. She must have liked you a helluva lot to give it to you.'

'Well, naturally.' There was a smirk in his tone. 'I gave her a good time.'

'Yeah? You take her to a hotel or something?'

'No sir, nothing like that.' He glanced around at the others, who were all sniggering in collective amusement at some private joke. 'Why pay for a room when the city's full of bombed-out buildings? There was this old church, right there on the main street . . . real quiet, real romantic.'

'A church . . .' His hand tightened around the watch. He had two alternatives – to give in to the urge to punch him and take the watch, or to pay him for it and leave without a fuss. The first was more appealing, but the second was more sensible. With the other one he let go of the doorframe and reached into the inside pocket of his tunic.

'Here.' He tossed a pound note down onto the fan of cards on the kitbag. 'Next time take her to a hotel.'

He didn't give him a chance to respond. Dropping the watch into his pocket he turned to leave the carriage. As he turned to slide the door shut behind him he saw that the slimy bastard had already grabbed the money and was stuffing it into his pocket. Aware of Dan's eyes on him he looked up, bristling defensively.

'What was her name?' Dan asked abruptly.

'Excuse me?'

Both his temper and his patience were hanging by a thread. He cleared his throat and steadied himself before repeating the question. 'The young lady. Her name?'

'Jeez, I—' The airman laughed nervously and hitched up his belt, transferring his gum to the other cheek. 'Renee?'

The Italian-looking guy in the corner of the carriage rolled his eyes. 'Come on, Greenbaum, that was the other ones. Yours was Stella. Nice girl; classy. That was why she blew you out.'

The stocky airman turned on him in a rage. 'Go fuck yourself, Franklin, she was frigid. I swear there was actual ice in—'

He didn't finish the sentence. Dan's fist connected with his jaw knocking him backwards, straight into the lap of his crewman who'd been keeping his head down, shuffling another deck of cards. They flew in all directions, like a scene from *Alice in Wonderland*.

Dan shut the door on the chaos and went back to his carriage feeling a whole lot happier.

11

2011

It had to be said, the All Saints Senior Citizens' Lunch Club was probably not the most glamorous event Jess had ever been invited to. Even so, the prospect of turning up with grey reptilian skin, eyebrows as unkempt as the overgrown garden and no make-up was daunting enough to make her seriously consider giving it a miss.

But it was a lifeline that had been thrown to her from the outside world. If she ignored it, let it drift away from her, how would she ever get back? And there would be a free lunch. Hot food and plenty of it, that's what the vicar in the horrible jumper had said. Her mouth filled with saliva at the thought. Her supplies of cereal, bread and cheese had not yet run out but they were getting pretty monotonous.

And bread and cheese wasn't the only thing she was bored of. She was bored of washing in cold water and creeping around in the dark. She was fed up of silence, of not speaking to another living soul for days at a time, of feeling like a criminal and living like a fugitive because she could see no way out. She was tired of being alone with her problems. It had been a week now since she'd run away from Dodge. At first the house had been a sanctuary, but if she didn't get herself together and move on soon it would become a prison. A tomb, even. Make-up or no make-up, she needed to get out.

Upstairs in the front bedroom she sat on the little stool in front of the dressing table and, taking a deep breath, opened the top drawer. She had avoided doing this, not only from an instinctive sense that it wasn't right to go through someone else's personal things, but also because there was something creepy about it. But she couldn't afford to be squeamish or superstitious any more. Not with eyebrows like hers.

As she'd suspected, the drawer was a museum of ancient cosmetics: a bottle of perfume called 'Flamenco' which had aged to a deep, rancid brown colour, a can of hairspray, a pot of cold cream. (She unscrewed the lid of this and sniffed it, wondering if it would be any good for her red scaly patches.) There was a gross hairpiece, yellowed and matted, like roadkill. Shuddering she moved it aside with a comb, in whose teeth several silvery blonde hairs still clung. The bottom of the drawer was littered with hairpins, but there was no sign of any tweezers.

She shut it and opened the next one down. Dozens of pairs of tights lay coiled like shed snakeskins beside neat piles of gloves, the fingers of the leather ones still slightly curled up, giving them the ghoulish appearance of dead hands. She shut the drawer quickly and pulled open the last one, steeling herself against what she might find.

Nighties. Old-fashioned ones; slithery nylon confections in pastel colours, edged with yellowing lace, a blue quilted bed jacket with fraying pink ribbons at the collar. She went to shut the drawer but was too hasty. It snagged and jammed. Neck prickling with distaste she went to flatten down the bed jacket and felt something hard beneath it. Pushing the garments aside revealed a shoebox, the lid of which had been dislodged and was the cause of the jam.

As she set it straight again she noticed that the box contained not shoes, but papers. Stacked upright, neatly in a row, like in a filing cabinet.

'Blimey,' she said out loud into the mildewed silence. 'Letters.'

6 March '43

Dear Nancy

I hope that you've got as far as opening this letter, and have not just thrown it away when you worked out that it didn't contain your watch. I think I found it, but I didn't want to post it in case it got broken or removed by the censors or something. It's just like you described and has the initials S.T. and a date on the back. If this sounds familiar let me know and we can work out how I can return it to you. I'm hoping to get another couple days' leave next month. Maybe if the post isn't such a good idea I could meet you someplace in London and give it back to you in person.

Since I saw you I've flown my first two missions, which is kind of a relief after all the waiting around for the weather to clear when we first arrived here. It feels like a long road to the twenty-five we have to complete before we're done, but it's a start.

Anyhow, I just wanted to let you know about the watch. I hope it's the one you're looking for, and that you'll be happy to know it's safe. Let me know what you'd like me to do with it.

Take care of yourself
Dan Rosinski.

*

'Well, you're a dark horse.'

Sitting at the table in the Vicarage kitchen Nancy folded her arms and drew her lips tightly together, looking up at Stella with eyes that positively sparked with expectation. Stella turned away from the stove where she'd just set the kettle on the gas and looked back blankly, trying for the life of her to think what she might be talking about. For some reason Alf Broughton's pig club popped into her mind – because she'd been about to take a pail of scraps round to Ada when Nancy had arrived, she supposed – and she wondered if Nancy had found out and was cross that Stella hadn't told her about it. She opened her mouth to make some apology but shut it again as Nancy placed an envelope on the table.

'I think that now would be a very good time to tell me who the blinking heck Lieutenant Dan Rosinski is, and how you come to give him my name and address.'

'Oh.'

Hearing his name caught her off-guard and she pulled out a chair and sat down heavily. She'd tried to put him – all Americans, in fact – out of her mind, and had almost succeeded, so sure was she that there was no chance he'd find the watch. The envelope lay in the middle of the table, directly in the pool of light cast by the bulb overhead, like a piece of incriminating evidence in a police interview room. It was totally flat and obviously contained nothing but paper. Had he written in spite of having found nothing? She was torn between irritation and excitement.

'Go on then – don't you want to know what it says?'

The sounds of the wireless drifted down the passageway from the sitting room, where Reverend Stokes was listening to Tommy Handley, loud enough to fill the Albert Hall. Across the table Nancy was practically self-combusting with curiosity. She had called on her way home from the salon and the sulphurous smell of perming solution infused the kitchen. Maybe the idea of self-combustion wasn't actually so far-fetched. Dumbly Stella picked up the envelope and turned it over. Nancy must have opened it in a hurry and the back was jaggedly torn, revealing a glimpse of the writing on the page underneath. It was nice writing, the same as on the front, sloping and slightly spiky and in black ink. Without warning she remembered his blue, blue eyes, and felt a jolt inside her, like she sometimes got from the lamp in the sitting room.

She didn't want to read the letter there, in front of Nancy, but there was no choice. Her face tingled with the effort of keeping it expressionless, but she was aware of the colour mounting in her cheeks and was powerless to stop it. It was a short note, just a few lines, but reading it made her blood sing.

'Well?'

Nancy, impatient with waiting, prodded her for a response. Very carefully Stella folded the letter again and tucked it back into its shredded envelope.

'Well what? You know what it says. You've read it.'

'Stella! If you don't stop being so bloody mysterious I'm going to come round there and shake you till the truth falls out! I might have read it but that don't mean I've got the foggiest idea what it's all about.'

'My watch. I lost it, when we were in that church – St Clements.'

'You never said.'

'I meant to – it slipped my mind, that's all.' Beneath the table Stella crossed her fingers against the lie. The reason she hadn't mentioned the lost watch was because that would have meant talking about that night, and she'd been afraid that if they did she might not be able to hide her hurt that Nancy hadn't come after her. It was unreasonable, she knew, but she couldn't quite shake off the childish feeling that Nancy had let her down, and a small but significant crack had appeared in the fortress of their friendship. 'I went back the next morning, as soon as I realized, but I couldn't find it. There was this man there – an American, taking pictures with a fancy camera – and he said he'd have a proper look. I had to get back, see? To get Reverend Stokes's breakfast before church. He said if I gave him my address he could let me know if he found it but ... I don't know, it didn't seem right somehow, with Charles being away.'

Nancy's carefully plucked eyebrows shot up and she laughed. 'So you gave him mine? Thanks very much! He could have turned out to be a right nutter!'

Stella shook her head, her shoulders hunched. 'He wasn't.' She smiled faintly. 'But I didn't think for a second that he'd find the watch.'

'But he has, and now he wants to give it back.' Nancy sat back and narrowed her eyes. 'So, what's he like then, this American?'

'What do you mean?'

She shrugged. 'Short or tall? Blond or dark? Nice or a bit creepy?'

On the stove the kettle had begun a muted, sibilant hiss. Stella got up and turned off the gas. 'Why do you want to know?'

'Well, since it's me he's written to, I reckon it's me who'll be replying,' Nancy said archly. 'And it's me who'll be meeting him to get your precious watch back, won't it? So, what's he like? Worth using good lipstick for?'

'No.' The word came out sounding sharper than she'd

149

intended and it bounced off the green gloss-painted walls. Stella felt the heat seep back into her cheeks. 'I mean, it's fine – that won't be necessary. I'll write back myself. And I'll meet him to get it back. It's only fair.'

There was a burst of uproarious studio laughter from the sitting room. Nancy tapped her fingertips on the table. 'What about Charles?'

'Charles isn't here. I'm not doing anything wrong, and it's only polite to go myself when he's gone to all the trouble of looking for it and getting in touch.'

'Well, if you're sure ...'

Nancy was now wearing her long-suffering expression. It was the one she always used when Stella expressed an opinion that didn't quite fit with hers, and it usually made Stella doubt herself enough to reconsider whatever it was they had disagreed on. But as she set the teapot on the table she found that she was able to meet Nancy's eye and say quite calmly, 'I am. I'll write to him tomorrow.'

Spring had arrived, but it was a cheap and shabby version of previous years, as if daffodils and blossom and bright yellow sunshine were on ration along with everything else. Stella gazed out of the dining-room window at the rows of ragged kale and onion leaves, and Reverend Stokes's surplice flapping on the washing line like some ungainly bird. In front of her on the table lay the pad of writing paper that she usually used for her letters to Charles, and her second attempt at a letter to Dan Rosinski.

13 March 1943

Dear Lieutenant Rosinski

    Thank you for your letter. I must admit it was a surprise to receive it, and especially to hear that you'd found the watch. I truly had given up hope of ever getting it back and am most grateful to you.

    I also owe you an apology. Perhaps you guessed that the name and address I gave you that morning were not my own, but belonged to a trusted friend. Forgive me, I acted in haste and didn't mean to deceive.

Things she wanted to say flitted in half-formed sentences through her head, but even without writing them down she knew that they sounded too personal. Too encouraging. She wanted to ask him how he was and to say that she'd been thinking of him, hoping that he was safe – or as safe as anyone could be in the skies above Germany, being shot at by enemy fire. But while she could tell herself that making contact with him wasn't breaching Charles's trust, she knew that the letter had to be business–like. Brisk. Dragging her gaze from the blustery garden she looked down at the paper again and began to write, quickly.

The post service has suffered the effects of the war as much as anything else. It might be best if I was to collect the watch from you in person, if you expect to be in London again in the coming weeks, and if it wouldn't put you to too much trouble. It

would, of course, be perfectly all right for you to write to me at
this address to let me know if this is acceptable to you, and
when and where we might meet.

In the meantime, best wishes and sincere thanks
Stella Thorne (Mrs).

Oh dear, was that too brisk? She stared at the *Mrs*, which now seemed prissy and reproachful. She'd wanted to make things clear before they met again, so there could be no room for misunderstanding, but did she sound like she was showing off, putting him in his place? She should probably write the letter again and leave it out, but her first attempt was already screwed up in the grate, and paper was so scarce . . . Hastily she tore it from the pad and folded it in half, then pushed it into an envelope and sealed it down.

Writing his name on the envelope felt curiously intimate. *2 Lt D. Rosinski.* A shiver went up her spine. But then it was freezing cold in the dining room, where the sun never penetrated and she'd been sitting for a long time. She got up and went in search of a stamp. Probably best to post it straight away before she lost her nerve.

'Lovely day!' Ada called out from her position at the garden fence, where she was talking to Marjorie Walsh. Stella smiled and waved, hoping to make a quick getaway, but the new warmth in the air had put Ada in the mood to hold court. ''Ere – come and see what Marjorie's brought for Blossom!'

Feeling her smile stiffen, Stella crossed the street. Blossom had grown prodigiously in the last few weeks and presided over the Broughtons' backyard like a mini-Empress, accepting the offerings of visitors with regal grace. Peering politely over the door of her sty, Stella saw that this morning she had her snout buried in a heap of dandelions, and when Ada scratched the top of her head she lifted it up to reveal two yellow flowers drooping from the corner of her mouth like Carmen's rose.

'Daft old girl,' Ada clucked. 'Ain't you, eh? Daft old girl.'

'You look very … bright this morning, Mrs Thorne,' Marjorie Walsh said, studying her with a touch of suspicion. 'Have you done something new to your hair?'

'Oh – no, I don't think so.' Self-consciously Stella's hand went to the scarf holding her hair back from her face, while in her mind she cast around for an escape. 'I'd better—'

'Got a bit of lipstick on, that's it,' Ada said approvingly. 'Always makes you feel better, don't it? I knew that night out was a good idea – you've had some colour in your cheeks since. It don't do to sit around pining.' She sniffed thoughtfully. 'Marjorie and I was just talking about the Fete – not long now until Whitsun. Don't it come around quickly? Don't seem like a year since the last one. That was when Reverend Thorne announced you two was engaged, weren't it?'

To Stella it seemed like much longer than a year, more like a lifetime. The Fete was a highpoint of the St Crispin's calendar; a meticulously planned event which was ostensibly all about raising money for good causes and bringing the community together. After one particularly bruising meeting Charles had confessed to Stella that it was just as much about the ladies of the parish vying for control of the tea urn, and that it would be easier to get a place in the War Cabinet than on the St Crispin's Fete committee. The days when he'd confided in her seemed very far off indeed.

'The first committee meeting's on Thursday week,' Ada said. 'Why don't you come along? Do you good to keep occupied.'

The look of stifled alarm Marjorie directed at Ada wasn't lost on Stella, who was a little alarmed herself. As the doctor's wife, Marjorie Walsh liked to think she was at the centre of parish life but also a little above its other inhabitants, and Stella recognized that Marjorie viewed her as a potential rival.

'That's very kind of you,' she said hastily, 'but I'm sure you don't need my help. The fete is always so perfectly organized. A well-oiled machine, Charles calls it. I'm sure the last thing you need is a spare part.'

'Well ...' Marjorie said, with obvious relief.

'Nonsense. A bit of new blood is just what we need. Well-oiled machine it might be, but the war's put a right old spoke in the wheels. No coconuts for the coconut shy, no sweets for Guess the Number of Sweets in the Jar ... We was just saying we need some new ideas, wasn't we, Marjorie?'

'Well ...' Marjorie said again, relief turning to dismay.

'It's very kind of you to ask me. I'll have a think and see if I can come up with any ideas, though I'm sure it'll be nothing that you expert ladies haven't thought of already.' Hoping that was an answer that would cause no offence to either party, Stella began to move away. 'Now, if you'll excuse me I suppose I'd better get this in the post.'

'Ahh,' Ada folded her arms across her floral bosom and beamed. 'Letter for Reverend Thorne, is it?'

'Y-yes. Yes, that's right.'

'Well, we won't keep you then, love, you get on and catch the post. And don't forget to kiss the back before you drop it in the box – that's what I always used to do to the letters I sent Alf in the last one. Convinced it would bring him luck, I was – and look where he is now; dozing in the armchair indoors, so there must be something in it!'

Stella laughed politely as she made her escape, the letter clasped firmly in her hand, address-side carefully averted.

20 April '43

Dear Stella

I have a three-day leave pass for the weekend. I'll be waiting for you in Trafalgar Square on Friday at noon, to return your watch to you. I'm afraid I have no idea where I'll be staying so can't give you a contact address in the event that this time doesn't suit you. I'll wait for a half hour and if you don't come I guess I'll just have to trust the watch to the British postal service.

Hope to see you,
Dan Rosinski

*

The letter folded into itself again, along its old creases. The paper was brittle and yellowed with age, but the ink inside was unfaded. Jess guessed it hadn't been exposed to the light in almost seventy years.

And it was the same handwriting, of course. Stronger and surer, but instantly recognizable from the letter still tucked into the pocket of the trench coat. Dan Rosinski's writing, on another letter to Mrs Thorne.

Stella. That was her name, and she lived at the Vicarage in King's Oak. Where was that? Jess's knowledge of London was sketchy, but she had a feeling it was on the outskirts somewhere, in the suburbs. She slid the letter reverently back into its age-spotted envelope and turned it over in her hands. Her chest felt tight with emotions she couldn't quite identify. Astonishment, perhaps. Excitement. Fragments of fact whirled in her head and she tried to catch hold of them, to pin them down in the right place.

The first envelope was addressed to Miss N. Price – Nancy. She was Stella's friend and she'd been in on the whole thing from the start, providing a front for Stella because she was already married. And if this was Miss Price's house, Stella must have given the letters to her at some point so her husband didn't find them.

Jess ran her thumb along the tops of the envelopes in the box, flicking through them so that she could tell at a glance that they were all addressed in the same hand. There were so many. She put the one she held back into the box, at the front from where she'd taken it out, and checked the date stamped in the circular postmark on the next envelope. May 1943. Whoever had put them there had been careful to make sure they were all in order.

The bed creaked and sagged as she sat back and crossed her legs, staring at the box in the centre of the pink counterpane. She felt lightheaded. In it lay the key to finding out who Stella Thorne was, and where she might be now. In it lay the secret of why Dan Rosinski wanted so much to find her, and the story of a love affair that had happened the best part of a century ago.

The All Saints Senior Citizens' Lunch Club was forgotten. With a shaking hand she slid out the next envelope.

12

1943

The day was blue and full of noise and sunshine. Standing at the edge of Trafalgar Square, Dan felt oddly small, like one of the toy soldiers he used to play with when he was a kid. The guys at the base never stopped saying how tiny England was – you could fit it four times over into Texas, they said – but the buildings around him seemed huge, used as he was to flat fields and squat corrugated iron huts like tin cans cut in half, and looking down on German cities from thirty thousand feet.

This time yesterday they'd been flying over Wilhelmshaven, dropping bombs on the submarine yards there. A week ago it had been Bremen. Only a week? The spaces in his head expanded and contracted, trying to accommodate the horror of the memory: enemy fighters appearing out of the cloud like a swarm of bees, fifteen bombers and their entire crews lost. He rubbed his fingers against his forehead, as if he could erase it.

Wearily he wondered if she'd come, or if she'd send her friend. Either way, it didn't matter. Across the square on the steps of the National Gallery a queue was forming for the lunchtime concert, and he thought wistfully of a still hour with Bach to hush the roar inside him. He checked his watch. Looking up again, he saw her.

She was wearing a dress the same green as the new leaves on the trees at the edge of the square, threading her way through the shifting sea of people. She hadn't spotted him, and so for a moment he watched her, adjusting the reality of her to the girl in his photograph, kneeling in the wrecked church. She looked different now. More buttoned-up. A married woman, not a fragile girl. He was aware of distant disappointment.

He went towards her, unhurriedly, and in the second that she noticed him he saw her falter. She stopped walking, so that people had to step around her.

'Hi.'

'Hello.'

'I wasn't sure you'd come. I mean, I wondered if you might send your friend. Nancy.'

He said it because it was something to say to breach that first awkward moment, but almost instantly regretted it in case it made their meeting seem somehow illicit, or more meaningful than it was. She shook her head and her glossy curls danced, the breeze catching at one and flicking it across her face. Carefully she tucked it back behind her ear.

'I wanted to see you myself, to say thank you for finding the watch.'

It was busy and people, hurrying in their lunch hour, were having to alter their course to move around them. A bespectacled man in a suit narrowly avoided bumping into her as he stepped aside to make room for a couple of ATS girls and a pigeon browsing for sandwich crumbs. Dan took her arm and drew her gently towards him, out of the way. He'd put the watch in an envelope with her address on, so that if he hadn't made it back from a mission there was still a good chance it would find its way to her. He took it from the inside pocket of his tunic now, and gave it to her.

'Here – safely delivered. You might want to open it up and check if it's the right one, although there's not a lot I can do about it if it isn't. *S.T. 1942*, right?'

'Yes. My parents-in-law gave it to me for Christmas.' Relief and perhaps gratitude had melted a little of her stiffness. They began to walk, past the fountains, towards the National Gallery. 'Did you find it in the church?'

He barely missed a beat, dismissing the memory of the leering airman. 'Yep. Right where you were looking. I don't know how you missed it.'

They reached the bottom of the steps, and stopped. At the top, the line of people going into the gallery was inching forwards. There was a frozen little pause, in which he searched his mind for some polite way of saying goodbye and came up with nothing. Life on a bomb group base and extreme fatigue had put him out of practice with social graces. He cleared his throat. 'I thought I might see the lunchtime concert in the gallery there. Myra Hess – I've always wanted to hear her play.'

She startled, like a horse about to bolt. 'I'm sorry, I didn't mean to keep you ... You must go. Thank you again for the watch.'

She was already backing away. In a second she would turn, and in two more she would be swallowed up by the crowd. His heart gave a sudden twist inside his chest, and his mouth opened to say words his brain hadn't had time to process.

'Look – if you're not in a hurry – I mean, if you don't have anything to get back for right away, why don't you join me?'

They walked up the steps together, a little way apart, not speaking as they followed the slow tide of people. Not speaking out loud, anyway. Inside his own head Dan had plenty to say, all of it addressed to himself and heavily featuring the words 'goddamn', 'fool' and 'mistake'.

He hadn't expected her to say yes. He'd expected that little dismissive shake of the head she did, a rushed excuse that would leave him free to walk away with the satisfied feeling he'd done the right thing and to be able to enjoy the concert alone. Instead he had the responsibility for making sure she wasn't bored and for making small talk during the interval, when his brain was so fried that even remembering his own name was an effort.

The gallery's walls had been stripped of their paintings and the frames gaped emptily on the walls, but in Dan's eyes their absence only served to emphasize the fine bones of the building, like a society beauty without her magnificent jewels. Like Stella Thorne, too. As they crossed an echoing hall towards the concert room he stole a glance at her. The girls he'd come across over here, at dances on the base or in the bars in London, seemed to wear the same scarlet lipstick, like it was some kind of unofficial uniform. Her lips were dusky pink and natural. *Naked*, he thought. Jesus. Did she know how much sexier that was? No, of course she didn't.

And that was the other pain-in-the-ass thing. Not only was he too tired to come up with amusing conversation or anything even remotely resembling charm, but he wasn't sure he was up to beating back the onslaught of desire that being this close to a woman like Stella Thorne – young, pretty, shy, married – was inevitably going to bring. He wasn't like some of the guys on the base who rushed down to London on their furloughs with their pants on fire, but he wasn't made of stone either. Despite the best efforts of the Eighth Army, he was still more or less human.

The concert was to be held in the octagonal gallery, and there were rows of chairs set out in three of the rooms leading off from it. It was obvious at a glance that they were mostly already taken, but Dan spotted two seats together at the far end of a row. Taking care not to touch her, he guided her towards them.

They'd just sat down when the musicians began their final tune-up, making conversation unnecessary. Around them the audience – which seemed to be made up of a complete cross-section of the London population, from office workers to soldiers on leave and elderly couples – shifted on chairs as they settled down. Latecomers were still slipping in, and the uncomfortable-looking benches along the walls were filling up too. Above the sound of the orchestra Dan heard a commotion by the door and turned to see a formidable-looking lady in a fur stole with iron-grey coils of hair sitting over her ears. Sighing with ostentatious dismay, she was extending her tortoise-like neck to search for an empty seat while people on all sides pretended not to notice.

Dan's heart sank as the courtesy that had been bred into him fought with more recently acquired exhaustion. But twenty-two years of conditioning were impossible to deny. Lightly he touched Stella's arm and gave her an apologetic look as he got to his feet and raised a hand to catch the woman's eye. Looking mollified she bustled over.

'Thank you, young man. My lumbago, you know . . .'

The bench against the wall was too narrow for comfort, but the old girl had probably done him a favour; at least now he could enjoy the music without being distracted by the nearness of Stella Thorne. But as the orchestra finished tuning up and the famous pianist took to the stage amid a burst of applause, Stella got up from her seat and slipped into the narrow space beside him.

In the second before she sat down their eyes met, and her mouth – her soft, pink mouth – curved into a shy smile.

Silence shimmered over the room, and then Myra Hess began to play the first exquisite, tentative notes of Bach's *Art of Fugue*. Wearily Dan leaned his head back against the wall and looked up at the patch of pale blue sky through the glass dome above.

Goddammit, he thought.

She'd never heard anything like it; had never imagined that such music existed. It bore no relation at all to the wheezy organ in St Crispin's, or the piano Miss Mason used to play in school assemblies, or the thin notes that came out of the wireless and the gramophone. This music seemed to be all around her, inside her, not just something to be listened to, but something to *feel*. It vibrated through her, and when she closed her eyes it was almost as if she could see it too, bright showers of sound in the darkness, drowning out the sour little voice that told her she shouldn't be here.

She wasn't sure why she'd said yes. If she'd had time to think about it she wouldn't have, but the invitation had come from nowhere and she'd accepted before she knew what she was doing. Because the day was bright and spring-like, perhaps, and there was a pulse of excitement beneath the noise of the city that made getting on a bus and going back to King's Oak seem like a screaming shame. Because there was nothing waiting for her there except Reverend Stokes's laundry and a mean piece of reeking haddock to turn into something for supper. Maybe that's why she'd accepted his invitation, and why, steeped in shimmering music, she couldn't be sorry.

Besides, it would give her something to tell Charles about in her next letter, she thought, resolutely averting her gaze from Dan Rosinski's long thigh inches away from hers on the bench. Charles was so cultured and educated, and she was so often aware of how limited he must find her. *I went to one of the lunchtime concerts at the National Gallery,* she imagined herself writing. *Quite by chance and on impulse. It was Myra Hess herself, playing Bach. I adored it . . .*

Shadows moved across the walls and the music swooped and gathered. Gradually she became aware of the tension leaving

Dan Rosinski's body until his leg came to rest lightly against hers. She froze. Sparks shivered along her nerves and her heart began to pound, galloping ahead of the music. Had she got it wrong again? Did he think that by agreeing to come she was—?

But then she glanced at him and the breath left her lungs. With his head tipped back against the wall and the light falling on his face, he was asleep.

There was no final, flourishing chord. The notes died away, echoing and unbearably poignant. There was a moment of pure silence as the enchantment lingered, and then a storm of clapping. Dan Rosinski's hand twitched, his fingers straightening and stiffening, and then she felt him gather himself. He sat upright and moved his leg away from hers as he joined in the applause.

It didn't go on for long. The spell was broken and people were already gathering their belongings and getting to their feet, in a hurry to return to offices and resume the business of the war. Stella knew she should stand too, and in her head she rehearsed a goodbye that would show gratitude without being too . . . emotional. The words eluded her. Neither of them moved, and as the seats emptied he dragged a hand through his hair and sighed.

'I'm sorry.'

'What for?' She picked up her handbag from beneath the bench and pretended to look for something inside it.

'You're very polite. Either that or you're used to people falling asleep in your company.'

She abandoned the pretence and smiled. 'You must have been exhausted.'

'It's been a pretty long week.' A shadow passed across his face, but then he gave his lopsided smile and chased it away. 'I'm also absolutely starving. I think there's someplace to eat here. Do you mind if we go find it?'

That was her chance to make her excuses and leave, but she didn't. Instead she found herself leaning against a balustrade on the stairwell while he queued up for tea and sandwiches at a makeshift counter. She couldn't help but notice that the two starchy, well-bred ladies behind it were vying to serve him, blushing almost girlishly as they arranged teacups and a plate of sandwiches on a tray and took his money. The accent, Stella thought. Or the smile. She braced herself against it as he carried the tray over.

There were no free tables, so they perched on the stairs in the shadow of a mammoth pillar, just like that morning on the steps of Bush House. 'One day I'll take you to a proper restaurant, where you can sit on a chair,' he said with a grin, picking up a sandwich. Then his expression abruptly changed. 'Jeez – I'm sorry, I shouldn't have said that. I guess I'm still half asleep. Your husband – is he away fighting someplace?'

'He's in North Africa, but not fighting. He's an army chaplain.'

She spoke calmly, without apology. It was a relief to bring the spectre of Charles out of the shadows, to be able to feel that she wasn't pretending to be something she wasn't, or playing a game. She sipped her tea.

'He's a minister? I guess I could have worked that out from your address. How long have you been married?'

'Since last August.'

His eyebrows rose a fraction. 'And when did he go away?'

'October.'

She watched him process this; saw the question in his eyes that he opened his mouth to ask. But then he stopped himself and smiled. 'Poor guy. Bad enough to have to leave home, but to have to leave a new wife too . . .'

He didn't have to go. He wanted to.

She sipped her tea and said nothing.

Afterwards, they walked along the Embankment. The sun was bright but the wind whipped cottonwool clouds across it so that shadows washed over them like waves on a beach. Silvery barrage balloons floated high up above the city. The sky looked like such a serene place from down here.

Neither of them had said anything when they'd left the gallery, they'd simply walked slowly together across the square, absorbed in conversation. Something had changed while he'd slept. His guard had been lowered, but she didn't seem to mind. He still felt pretty dazed and out of it, as though the adrenaline had drained from his body and his reflexes – usually on high alert – had been switched off. It was a feeling he only usually got these days halfway down a bottle of bourbon, but which used to be a regular thing back home. A thing called peace.

And so they walked, with no particular destination in mind and no hurry to reach it. He found himself doing most of the talking. She asked questions, and listened with apparently genuine interest as he told her all about home and Pop and Alek. About Mom, who'd died so long ago she'd become little more than a silver-framed black-and-white memory, but who came to life again as he talked.

'Mom's family had settled in Chicago in the '90s, but Pop didn't come over until 1914. He was studying to be an engineer in Warsaw when he saw how things were going to go. He didn't want to fight under the German flag in a war he didn't believe in, and he reckoned America was the land of the future, especially for engineers. There was a big Polish community in Chicago, so that was the obvious place to head to. He met my mom at a dance.'

She glanced sideways at him with eyes full of sunlight. 'Love at first sight?'

'Yeah, though it took her family a while to come around to the idea. They were Catholics and he was Jewish. He had to work pretty hard to convince them he wasn't such a bad match . . .' It always amused Dan to remember how spectacularly Josef Rosinski had proved himself, and he was smiling as he turned to her. 'Sorry. As if falling asleep wasn't bad enough, now I'm boring the life out of you by talking all about myself.'

'It's not about yourself, it's about your family. And it's certainly not boring.'

The sun shone on her hair and made it gleam like well-polished mahogany. He thought of his camera, left with the rest of his things in the dingy officers' club in Piccadilly and wished he'd brought it.

'What about your family?'

By some unspoken consent they'd stopped walking and leaned against the railings overlooking the river. The water was khaki-coloured, as if it too was in uniform and doing its patriotic duty. Next to his her arms looked pale and improbably slender, which made him realize how he'd grown used to being surrounded by men.

'I don't have one. Perhaps that's why I like hearing about other people's. I grew up in the charitable school, with Nancy – she's the closest thing to family I have. And Miss Birch, I suppose. She was the headmistress and not the most maternal person, but I can see now that she was very kind.' The wind picked up that curl again and bounced it across her cheek. 'She gave me away at my wedding.'

'And what about your husband's family? The ones who gave you the watch?'

'They're kind too. Very proper.' She stroked the curl behind her ear and shrugged. 'They had higher hopes for Charles, but they try to make the best of it.'

He frowned. 'How did you meet him?'

'The school finds work for pupils when they're of an age. The housekeeper at the Vicarage left at the start of the war so he needed a replacement.'

'You went to work for him? But you must only have been—'

'Seventeen. I knew nothing at all about keeping house, but in those days there was a lot of other work to do – organizing evacuation rotas and collecting clothing for the refugees that were arriving from Belgium and Holland. I think that was what made him think I'd make a good vicar's wife.'

It sounded like a joyless arrangement. How did a young girl who was as beautiful and gentle and sweet as this one end up thinking that was the best life had to offer her?

'Smart guy,' he said blandly.

'Not really. If I had been, he wouldn't be in Africa now, would he?'

There was something terribly bleak about her matter-of-fact tone. Dan turned to look at her, impulsively putting a hand on her upper arm.

'That's Hitler's fault, not yours.'

She stiffened and turned her head to avoid his gaze. Sensing her resistance, he let her go. Goosebumps had sprung up on her bare skin and she rubbed at them briskly. 'I should have brought a coat. It's colder than it looks.'

He couldn't give her his jacket, it was strictly forbidden. He had no problem with flouting the rules himself but was deterred by the embarrassment it would cause her if they should be caught – the bastard Military Police had a habit of appearing from nowhere.

'Let's keep walking,' he said, sensing again that she might be about to bolt. 'St Paul's is just up there – Wren's finest work. Mind if we go and take a look?'

She was doing nothing wrong. After all, it was a church, and from the moment they stepped through the towering doors they were enveloped in its atmosphere of hushed reverence.

Of holiness. It wasn't like going to a bar or a nightclub, or the Opera House with its pulsing, sensual music and feverish heat.

In fact it was even cooler in here than outside. She felt the shiver of goosebumps on her skin again as she walked slowly across the black-and-white tiled floor, her footsteps echoing in the magnificent quiet. They'd instinctively gone their separate ways when they came in, and Lieutenant Rosinski was somewhere behind her now, gazing upwards with the same grave focus she'd seen on his face in the bombed-out church that morning. She headed towards the altar, pulled by some illogical need to explain herself to God. For all Charles's insistence that He was the universal father who knew and loved everyone, she could never quite stop herself from thinking of Him as a friend of Charles's – a bit like Reverend Stokes or Peter Underwood – who tolerated her for his sake. Like a guest at a party, she felt bound by courtesy to make some sort of formal acknowledgement.

In the gloom of a side chapel, rows of votive candles glowed. She went in and lit one.

Dear Lord, please keep Charles safe wherever he is and let him know that I love him . . .

The words formed themselves in some dutiful part of her head, while in another she imagined God looking down on her with mild contempt. She was very much the third party in this relationship; He would look after Charles on His own say so, without any prompting from her. She was also struck by the irony of needing to ask God to tell Charles that she loved him. As his wife of less than a year she should be able to do that herself. She did do it, in fact, at the end of every letter, but because he never mentioned love in anything more than a general sense in his impersonal replies, she felt like she was standing on a mountaintop and shouting it into the wind.

As she left the chapel she saw Dan Rosinski leaning against a pillar, arms folded, looking perfectly at ease. Too at ease, Charles would think; God was the universal Father, but He was the kind of strict parent you would address as 'sir' and who would frown on such informality. Seeing Dan at a distance she felt an odd lurch beneath her ribs. He was an American soldier; just another one of the thousands that filled the streets of London and towns and cities all across the country, and who appeared on newsreels. And yet he was no longer a stranger. His family was from Poland. His mother was dead. He had a brother called Alek who was with the Ordnance Corps, currently training in Maryland. When he spoke of his father you could hear the affection in his voice. He wasn't just another American soldier, he was her friend.

When he saw her he detached himself from the pillar and came towards her.

'OK?'

She nodded. 'It's a beautiful church.'

'You can imagine when it was built that they were virtually turning them away at the door on Sundays. Imagine leaving your dark home with the low ceilings and tiny windows and coming here . . .'

She could. When he said it like that she understood. It wasn't just a feeling of cowed duty that brought people to church, but genuine wonder. Reverence. The belief that there must be something beyond the small sphere in which they lived their short, dark lives.

'How come you know so much about it? I mean, I'm a Londoner born and bred, and I don't know half of what you do.'

'Back home I studied architecture. I just started my senior year when Pearl Harbor changed everything. I went from sitting in a classroom studying German architecture to sitting in a B-17 and destroying it.' He looked away, out across the majestic sweeping space of the church.

'But if you didn't, the Luftwaffe would have flattened this place by now. Or there'd be red flags hanging down the columns outside and a photograph of Hitler on the altar.'

'Maybe.' He smiled, and the clear, pure light filtering in from above showed up the lines of exhaustion around his mouth and the dark smudges beneath his eyes. 'Come on, I'll show you something.'

He walked back in the direction from which they'd come. Without speaking she followed him up a winding stone staircase, like the ones taken by princesses in fairy tales. They had to step aside to make way for other people coming down, and when they reached the top she was slightly breathless from the climb, and from the astonishing place in which she found herself. They were beneath the dome, on a narrow walkway that ran around its perimeter. Heaven rose above them in an extravagant, painted canopy of gold and blue, pierced by shafts of ethereal light.

'I've never seen anything so beautiful.' All of a sudden her chest tightened and she thought for a painful second that she might cry. First the music, and then this – it was like she'd been walking along a dark corridor lined with closed doors and had suddenly discovered that paradise lay on the other side of them.

'It's called the Whispering Gallery.'

'Why?'

His eyes were warm. 'Sit down right there and I'll show you. When I say, you have to close your eyes and lean your cheek against the wall, OK?'

A stone ledge ran all the way around the walkway. It was smooth and shiny with age. She sat down on it and watched him walk away with his easy, unhurried stride. Laughter bubbled up inside her, and a sort of childish anticipation that she hadn't felt for years. She had to press her lips together to stop it escaping her.

He stopped right opposite her, on the other side of the void, and gestured for her to close her eyes. In the darkness behind her closed lids the laughter was suddenly spiked with something else. Anticipation. A shiver of fear. She leaned closer to the wall and waited. Faint echoes rose from below, footsteps and muted voices, and then a whisper so close and clear it was like a caress in her ear.

'Will you have dinner with me tomorrow night?'

She gasped and opened her eyes, expecting to see him standing in front of her. But he was where he had been before, leaning casually against the wall on the opposite side of the dome. She blinked, and the laughter spilled out, and before doubts and reality and duty could wither this moment of pure happiness she pressed her cheek against the ancient stone and whispered, so softly it was scarcely more than a breath.

'Yes.'

13

27 April '43

Dear Stella

I'm writing this on the train going back to the base, to say thank you. I had the best time last night. OK, so maybe not one of the best dinners, but I've got to say Spam rissoles never tasted so good as they did in your company. (And I think that says a whole lot more for your company than it does for the rissoles.)

I don't know whether I should be writing this letter or not. I don't know if receiving it will make you feel better or worse. I guess I just have to say the things that are on my mind and leave you to tear them up and put them on the fire if they're not what you want to hear. I want you to know how special you are. I want you to see that you are clever and funny and interesting. I want you to realize that you are beautiful, although as I write that and remember the way you looked last night in the candlelight, I know that a part of what makes you

176

such dynamite is that you don't have the faintest idea of how incredible you are.

Believe me, you really are.

Most of all I want you to be happy. You deserve to be. Listening to you last night I got a glimpse of a girl who has lived her short life so far to please others. The fact that you do that is, again, a part of what makes you the amazing girl that you are, but I'd hate for you to be so focused on the needs of everyone else that you forget your own.

Thank you for listening when I talked about flying, and about the crew. The last week was a tough one and I guess the ones ahead won't be a picnic either. It's easier to face them now.

I won't write again. You're married, and I understand the seriousness of that commitment. Of course, I'm selfish enough to wish that you weren't, but I'm also smart enough to have noticed that circumstances aren't exactly on our side anyway. We had dinner, and you took my mind off of the things I wanted to forget, and helped me to remember the good stuff at the time I needed to most. I'll always be grateful for that.

Look after yourself — for me. (I figure that telling you to do it for someone else is the best way of getting you to do anything.)

Dan.

They were just words written on a page, but their immediacy took her breath away. Like a swimmer coming up for air, Jess lifted her gaze from the letter and let it wander around the room, taking in the leaf-sprigged wallpaper, the bright scarlet poppies on the tiles in the fireplace, and saw for the first time not just the neglected home of an old person, but the setting for stories she wanted to hear, of secrets she wanted to know. The wind sighed softly in the chimney, and the outside world felt very far away. Sucking in a lungful of air she took the next envelope out of the box and plunged back under, into the echoing world of the past.

8 May '43

Dear Stella,

It was so good to get your letter. I hadn't dared to hope that you'd write, but I'm sure glad that you did. My crew was flying at dawn this morning – mission #6 completed – and it was here waiting for me when I got back. Reading it was like hearing your voice.

Stella, I don't want you to feel guilty. Since Bremen I've gotten to be quite an expert on guilt and have come to the conclusion that as emotions go it's right up there on the negative scale with malice and jealousy. It poisons happiness and makes us believe that we're not good enough, and that the things we do and the choices we make are wrong. As human beings I guess we're programmed to try to be happy, and guilt tells us that instinct is bad. I don't believe that it is. In fact, sitting in the cockpit of a B-17 with German flak and tracer fire coming at you from all sides, it seems like snatching some happiness is the only thing that matters. Or else, what's life for?

It was just a kiss – a moment on a London street on a warm spring night. You can blame the brandy, or the war, or you can blame me. I'm not sure I could have kept myself from kissing you if I'd tried, and I sure didn't want to try. I could say I'm sorry, but the truth is (and I'm too wiped out to write anything but the truth) I'm not, because I liked kissing you. But you are still Charles's wife. You have not caused him a second's pain or given away anything that belongs to him. It was a moment, that's all. A very precious, special moment.

Look after yourself for me.

Dan

PS. You should definitely go to the Fete Committee meeting – don't let that old girl Marjorie get to you! Hold your head up and remember how strong you are.

17 May '43

Dear Stella

I just finished reading your letter and I'm still smiling. Don't ever apologize for writing about everyday stuff. I feel like I'm right there at the Church Fete meeting, although I have no idea what a coconut shy is so I can't really comment on whether cauliflowers would make suitable replacements for coconuts. But the fortune-teller sounds like a great idea, whatever that Stokes guy says. God might be in charge of our destiny, but I don't know anyone who wouldn't pay good money to find out what He has in store for us all right now.

We haven't flown for a couple days. Every day more crews

are shipping in from the US and they look so green we feel like old hands in comparison. There's a dance on the base tonight, to welcome them all. They're fixing up one of the hangars with streamers and balloons and sending trucks out around the villages to pick up local girls. I guess this all means nobody's going to be flying tomorrow either. I don't know which is worse; the nerves of doing a mission or the boredom of doing nothing.

Remember I told you about Morgan, my co-pilot? Well, this week he finally managed to get himself a bicycle from a kid in the village. Back home Morgan's folks own a farm out in the middle of Arkansas and he claims he was riding a bicycle practically before he could walk, so he was pretty damn pleased with himself for landing one over here, even though he paid well over the odds for it. (The kid who sold it to him might have looked like a scruffed up choirboy, but he drove a deal like a New York hustler.) Morgan set off for the pub in the village on it last night, bragging that he'd have finished his first pint by the time the rest of us arrived, and promptly rode it right into a ditch. Apart from his bruised pride and a few nettle stings he was unhurt, though Adelman, our bombardier, laughed so much he nearly bust a rib.

The village here is beautiful. When we arrived everywhere was brown with mud but now it's all turned green, and the trees are all covered in blossom, like snow. It's hard to imagine a prettier place to fight a war.

Good luck with the rest of the fete preparations – stick to your guns about the fortune-teller, and look after yourself for me.

Dan.

Letters to the Lost

Dear Stella

Thanks for the explanation of the coconut shy, and the drawing too! So the idea is that you aim a wooden ball at a coconut on a stick and if you knock it off you get to take it home? It sounds like my kind of game. And OK, so cauliflowers might not be quite so exotic as coconuts, but you got to work with what you got, right?

For what it's worth, I think you're right about the ginger cake as well as the cauliflowers. Your Marjorie Walsh sounds like she could give the Führer a run for his money when it comes to bossing people around, and I'm proud of you for standing up to her. You'll make a great job of the teas, and I'm prepared to bet that the fete will still be a success even without her scones (but then I'm a Yank and I never had a scone in my life) . . .

Dear Stella

I got a letter from my dad a couple days ago. My brother Alek has finished training and is waiting to hear where he's going to be posted. Pop wrote two places where it was most likely to be but the censors blanked them. I guess if I don't know I can't worry for him . . .

Dear Stella

I co-piloted one of the new crews today. It was supposed to be an easy one, a milk run to help them find their feet. It ended up as a bloodbath. Two of their men didn't make it through their

*first mission and two forts didn't come back. Things are pretty
quiet here tonight . . .*

*Stella, I wanted to say thanks for keeping on writing and let
you know that it makes a difference. I like to hear about the fete
and the kids in the nursery, and I feel like I know Ada and
Marjorie Walsh and the others. I can picture you, sitting under
your beautiful apple tree in the dusk, and it makes things easier.
The way you wrote it was so vivid I can almost smell the scent
of the blossom myself. And in my head I can hear the song
'Apple Blossom Time'.*

Look after yourself, remember? For me.

D.

There were pins and needles in Jess's legs and her neck was
stiff. Her eyes smarted, letting her know that she'd been so
busy reading she'd forgotten to blink. Or eat. As she straightened her shoulders and arched her aching back she realized
that it was long past lunchtime.

Carefully she put the letter she was holding back into its
envelope, and slotted it back in the box with the others, on its
end to show where she'd got up to. Then, sucking in a sharp
breath as the blood flowed back into her cramped feet, she
went downstairs to make a sandwich.

She sliced the last of the cheese mechanically, not noticing
the smattering of mould on the edges of the bread. Dan Rosinski's voice was clear in her head; so clear she could almost hear
it and imagine he was in the room with her. But what about
Stella? Even now she was as elusive, as mysterious as ever.

I don't think I like her very much, Jess thought, mindlessly chewing on the dry sandwich and staring out into the wrecked garden. She seems like a piece of work, starting an affair with an American airman when her husband was away and – what? – just shoving him aside like yesterday's chip paper when her man came back. What kind of woman would do that? She remembered the letter that had arrived here just a week ago; the one marked 'Personal and Urgent'. *I never stopped loving you . . . I tried, for the sake of my own sanity, but I never even got close.*

Jess swallowed the sandwich with difficulty, frowning at the pain in the back of her throat and the loose ends of logic in her head. Stella Thorne had broken his heart, but she had kept his letters. Kept them carefully, like they meant something. Given them to her friend so they'd be safe.

Did that mean that maybe, just maybe, she had loved him too?

14

1943

Local legend had it that the weather was always good for the St Crispin's church fete. Even Jacob Fletcher, King's Oak's oldest resident, couldn't remember a single year when it had rained. Fortunately 1943 didn't look like being any exception to this rule, which was a matter of some relief to the Fete Committee; after such an astonishing run of luck, rain on fete day would seem like failure on the part of the organizers.

'Well, I think that's just about all of it,' Ada said brightly, checking down her list at the final meeting on the eve of the big day. 'The teacups have been given a wash and Mr Crabtree is delivering the milk to the church hall in the morning. Tables and bunting to be put up first thing. Ooh – and I must tell my Alf to get the bits for the coconut shy out from under the stage in the hall. He's managed to collect quite a nice little pile of cauliflowers from down the allotments.'

From around the table in the vestry the response to this last remark was muted and neutral, since the argument over the cauliflower/coconut shy still rankled. The committee had been divided between those who thought Stella's suggestion an amusing improvisation, and those who considered it a shameful waste of good food as the cauliflowers were bound to get smashed up by the hard wooden balls.

'And I trust Mrs Thorne is on top of all the preparations for the teas?' Marjorie Walsh enquired with frosty nonchalance. 'Not that it's any of my concern this year, of course; only nobody knows better than me how much work there is to do beforehand. I'm always up into the small hours making my scones . . .'

Caught in the act of stifling a yawn, Stella could say nothing for a moment. The argument over the teas made the cauliflowers look like small beer, and she still wasn't sure if finding herself in charge was a victory or a punishment. Attending her first committee meeting she'd offered to help out with the teas, and naïvely suggested gingerbread cake instead of scones, to save on margarine. Marjorie had seen this as a hostile takeover bid and dramatically removed herself from both the meeting and her long-standing position behind the tea urn. According to Ada she expected to be wooed back. 'But she can forget that,' Ada said shortly. 'We can manage perfectly well without her.'

Stella wasn't so sure about that. Sunlight filtered down through the high windows, casting criss-cross patterns on the table, around which everyone was now looking at her expectantly – everyone except Reverend Stokes who was peacefully dozing. She cleared her throat and nodded, not daring to admit that in spite of practically offering up her body to Mr Castle at the grocer's she hadn't been able to get her hands on enough golden syrup to make even half the quantity of gingerbread cake needed to feed the hordes. The whole thing had seemed funny when she'd written about it to Dan, but less so now.

'All under control,' she said, trying to sound confident, and like someone who was wide awake and had been paying full attention. 'I thought I'd make some coconut ice, to go with the gingerbread . . .' although Mr Castle had only been able to give her the most meagre amount of desiccated coconut too.

Marjorie gave a strangulated little laugh, but whatever she was about to say was interrupted by a knock on the wooden screen that divided the vestry from the body of the church. Heads turned. An American serviceman stood beneath the carved gothic arch, a piece of paper in his hand. Stella's heart jumped into her throat and she almost let out a scream as she realized that it wasn't just any American serviceman, but the one whose face had haunted her dreams for weeks and whose voice she heard in her head just about every waking moment.

'Excuse me? I'm looking for a . . .' Dan squinted down at the paper. 'A . . . Mrs Thorne?'

In the moment before she leapt from her chair and went to him Stella understood that he was up to something. Ignoring her completely, he was looking at Ada.

'Oh, that's me . . .' Shakily she got to her feet, cheeks crimson, mind racing, her whole body awash with adrenaline. 'Sorry – you are . . . ?'

'Lieutenant Rosinski, ma'am, USAAF. You applied to us under the Special Allocation of Supplies Scheme? For the,' he looked down at the paper again, 'St Crispin's Church Fete? Well ma'am, I'm pleased to tell you your application was successful. Where would you like your tinned peaches?'

A frisson of excitement went around the table, though whether at the words *tinned peaches* or the exotic accent in which they were spoken and the handsomeness of the man who'd said them, it was impossible to say. In the general excitement Dan gave her the ghost of a wink.

'That's wonderful news, Lieutenant – thank you so much.' Walking towards him she could barely keep herself from smiling like a loon. 'Why, I'd almost forgotten that I'd written to you. I suppose they ought to go in the kitchen at the church hall. I'll show you.'

'Tinned peaches?' Reverend Stokes had woken with a start and was clearly afraid that he might have dreamed it, or misheard. 'What the Dickens?'

'From the Yanks – I mean, the Americans,' Ada explained excitedly. 'Under some supplies scheme clever Mrs T. found out about. What was it again?'

'The Special Allocation of Supplies Scheme, ma'am. Or, as we call it for short, "Allies' Supplies". It's our way of thanking you for your hospitality over here, and making sure that items that are hard to get hold of are spread around a little.'

Stella had to bite the inside of her cheeks to stop herself from laughing. God, he was convincing. He could have told them the tinned peaches had been specially delivered by schools of dolphins that had swum across from California and she felt sure they'd all believe him. Even Marjorie couldn't maintain her sour-lemon face at the prospect of tinned peaches.

'Ah – but there is a Judas in our midst,' Reverend Stokes announced darkly, making the laugh die inside Stella's mouth and jerking her heart back into her throat. 'Remember the stolen light bulbs? I'm afraid it would be foolish to put such bounty in the church hall. The kitchen at the Vicarage would be more secure.'

'And more convenient for him to help himself to a tin after his tea,' Ada muttered.

Stella expelled her pent-up breath in a sigh of relief. 'Yes, of course. Good idea. Follow me, Lieutenant and I'll show you where to go.'

After the sunlight outside, the kitchen was cool and dim. Wordlessly she led him into the small, square scullery with the slate shelves that would once have been laden with provisions but were now deplorably empty. The window, set high up in the wall, was covered with a metal mesh to keep out the flies, giving the room a greenish, underwater feel. Dan set the crate of tins down on the floor and straightened up, and they looked at each other properly for the first time.

'Thank you,' she whispered, as they drank each other in with their eyes. They were both smiling, breathless, laughing a little at the craziness of what had just happened; at the audacity of his idea and the completeness of its success. And then somehow the laughter had faded and they were moving together, reaching out. His hands cupped her face, her fists closed around handfuls of his shirt as their mouths met and their bodies slammed together.

The first time he'd kissed her – on the street outside the restaurant on the night he'd taken her out for dinner – it had been tentative and infinitely gentle, as if he'd been afraid of breaking her or frightening her away. This was different. There was no hesitation now, and no fear, just a joyful, hungry urgency. Over the previous weeks their letters had removed any strangeness between them. She had heard his voice so often in her head, encouraging and reassuring her, that it felt like he was almost a part of herself. The clean scent of him made her senses reel. Her lips burned beneath his. Dazed, they pulled apart and laughed again, quietly.

'The Special Allocation of Supplies Scheme?' she whispered. 'Does that actually exist?'

'Nope. Made it up in the jeep on the way in. The Allies' Supplies bit I made up right there on the spot.'

This sparked off another convulsion of laughter. They clung together, shaking with private mirth.

'How did you do it?'

'Natural genius, I guess.'

'Not the name, silly,' she swiped at his arm, 'the whole thing. Coming to my rescue with tinned peaches. How did you know?'

'Your letters.' He took her face in his hands again, stroking his thumbs across her cheeks. In the green gloom his face was suddenly serious, his eyes shadowed. A crease had appeared between them. 'Reading them, hearing about all of this just about keeps me sane.'

'Do you have to go back today?'

'Nope. I'm officially on D.S. – detached service. I'm on stand-down until Sunday and was given the jeep to take some other stuff over to HQ. I'll do that now then head back into town and see if I can get a room in the officers' club. Can you come in later?'

She thought about the gingerbread cakes she still had to make, and the coconut ice – though maybe that wouldn't be necessary now, thanks to the tinned peaches. But she didn't know what plausible excuse she could give for going out the night before the fete, and – more importantly – her hair was badly in need of a wash. Suddenly she was terribly aware of what she must look like, in a greyish aertex shirt she'd had since school and a maroon skirt of singular ugliness.

'I'm not sure . . .'

He kissed her. 'No problem. It's fine.'

'Tomorrow. I'll come tomorrow, after the fete. I'll say I'm going out with Nancy.'

The sound of footsteps on the front path made them spring apart. Over the pounding of blood in her ears Stella heard Ada's voice.

'Hello-o? Just came to see if you need a hand?'

Completely unruffled Dan went out of the scullery. 'That's very kind of you, ma'am,' Stella heard him say, 'but I wouldn't want to put you to any trouble. There's another couple crates in the jeep, but I can manage.'

'Very kind of *you*, more like. Tinned peaches! I can hardly believe it!'

Ada's voice got more distant as she followed Dan to the jeep. Stella could hardly believe it herself; Dan, *here*. Straightening the hideous skirt she left the scullery and went out of the kitchen door. As she went down the side of the house she saw Ada standing by the jeep, looking at it as if it were the golden coach used for the King's coronation. Dan was coming back up the path carrying the two remaining crates, which were obviously very heavy.

'In the same place, Mrs Thorne?'

'Yes please, Lieutenant.'

'Well, I must say, you done us proud,' Ada said admiringly as Stella went to join her. 'Marjorie's face! No one's going to miss 'er scones now, are they?'

Dan came down the side of the house and Stella's heart cartwheeled in her chest. The sleeves of his khaki shirt were rolled back to show tanned forearms and the sun made gold lights glint in his tawny hair.

'Is that an apple tree in the yard back there, Mrs Thorne?' he asked.

'Yes.'

'It's a beauty. Going to be a fine crop this year.'

'You should have seen it a couple of weeks ago,' she said softly. 'A mass of blossom it was, like a cloud.'

'I can imagine.' He was smiling, straight into her eyes.

Then he opened the door of the jeep and picked up a clipboard from the dashboard. He scribbled something quickly before handing it to her.

'If you could sign right there, ma'am. Peaches, three crates.'

His finger tapped the paper where it said: *Trocadero 8 p.m. I'll be waiting.* Swallowing a smile she took the pencil he held out and wrote, *I'll be there.*

15

True to tradition, the day of the fete was the best June had to offer; warm and golden and with a brisk breeze that tugged at the tablecloths of the trestles outside the hall and made the faded bunting flap and dance.

Word had got out about the peaches. Ada had told Alf at teatime, just before he went for his Friday pint of half-and-half at The Albion, which was as good as standing on the scrubby ground beside the church hall and announcing it through a megaphone. Consequently the St Crispin's fete enjoyed a record turnout, with the queue for the tea table stretching right out of the door of the hall, 'Like the first day of the sale at Debenham and Freebody,' huffed Ada.

Of the three crates of peaches, two and a half had been portioned out carefully into saucers (the most elegant method of presentation the church hall kitchen could supply in such quantities) for sale alongside the teas, while half a crate's-worth of tins had gone to provide prizes for the raffle, garden-on-a-plate, and fancy dress competition, and to add some much-needed pizzazz to the tired-looking array on the tombola table.

At least one had also been lost to Reverend Stokes. Stella, coming into the ginger-scented kitchen the previous night, had discovered him lurking in the scullery with a tin-opener and spoon. She'd retreated quickly, not wanting a confrontation, but had felt quite justified in going up to run a bath and fill it with twice as much hot water than the regulation five inches and luxuriate in it until it cooled, feeling no guilt about keeping him waiting beyond his regular and strictly-adhered-to half past ten bedtime.

Lying up to her chin in steaming water, her blissfully clean hair floating around her like pondweed, she'd gone over every detail of what had happened earlier, from the moment she'd looked up and seen Dan standing in the church, to the outwardly formal handshake beside the jeep before he'd driven off. Slipping beneath the surface and listening to the boom and echo of the underwater world, she'd relived the kiss . . . Relived it until red flowers blossomed in the darkness and the desire that had swirled quite languidly through her veins grew more urgent. She surfaced again, gasping in air, and swept the water from her face as she counted the hours until tomorrow night.

There wasn't time to think about anything as she poured cups of tea and handed out peaches. She was so busy she didn't see Nancy until she was standing at the table in front of her, even though she was dressed to be noticed in film-star sunglasses and scarlet lipstick. Smiling across at her Stella felt like wilted lettuce. 'I didn't expect to see you here.'

'Yes well, heard you had peaches, didn't I? I suppose it's only one dish each?'

'Yes, sorry – there's plenty of gingerbread cake though.'

Nancy slid her glasses down her nose and peered at it. 'Hmm. Think I'll just take the peaches, thanks.'

Stella was too preoccupied to take offence. Glancing quickly around she said quietly, 'Listen Nancy, I need to ask you a favour. I've got to judge the fancy dress in a bit – meet me outside?'

Half an hour later the peaches were all gone and Stella took off her apron and gratefully handed it over to Dot Wilkins. Outside, the playing field was gratifyingly crowded, and the wind cooled the sweat on the back of her neck. The White Elephant stall was doing brisk business, and the tombola table contained only meagre pickings now. Shouts of 'behind you!' from the children watching the Punch and Judy competed with the baying onlookers around the tug-of-war, almost drowning out the Co-op band playing *You Are My Sunshine*. Stella was relieved to see that quite a large group of women were clustered around the coconut shy, rising to the challenge of winning a cauliflower for supper. She spotted Nancy, sitting on the grass with her face tipped up to the sun, a cigarette creating a hazy halo of smoke around her head, and sat down beside her.

'You got a dilemma with this fancy dress, I can tell you. Been having a look while I've been waiting and they're none of them much cop, apart from him.' Nancy took a suck on the cigarette then waved it in the direction of a small boy standing solemnly by himself beside the makeshift platform where the fancy dress line-up was scheduled to take place next. He was dressed in what was clearly an older brother's Scout uniform, with the addition of a black tie and a red armband featuring a swastika. His hair had been Brylcreemed down from a side parting and on his top lip was painted a black toothbrush moustache.

'Blimey. That's scary.'

'He's totally in character too – you should see him goosestep. So – what's this favour you want to ask me? Bear in mind I'd do pretty much anything for a tin of peaches ...' Nancy gave a saucy wink and Stella had a flashback to the dark church and Nancy's legs entwined around the waist of the GI. She quickly banished it.

'You don't have to do anything, really, just back me up in a bit of a lie. I was hoping ...' She plucked at the grass, torn between shame and excitement. 'I was hoping it would be all right if I said I was going out with you this evening.'

With slow deliberation Nancy moved her glasses down her nose again and fixed Stella with a searching stare. 'That sounds interesting. Do you mean to tell me, Mrs Thorne, that you are intending to escape the Vicarage this evening with the purpose of enjoying a bit of entertainment of an illicit nature? With a person or persons such as the vicar might disapprove of?'

'Shhh ...' Stella was laughing now, blushing, as the excitement she'd managed to squash down all morning came bubbling up. She looked around. Luckily no one was watching them, and the noise of the band and the tug-of-war crowd made it impossible for them to be overheard, but she felt nervous even so. 'It's the man who found my watch, Lieutenant Rosinski. He was the one who supplied the peaches. He's in town tonight and he asked me if I could meet him.'

Not long ago such explanations would have been unnecessary; they'd shared every detail of their lives and the secrets of their hearts. But now there were gaps. Big gaps, that Stella couldn't really attempt to fill.

'And being human, female, alive and not *entirely* barmy, you said yes . . . ?' Nancy looked impressed.

'Being married I should have said no.'

'Pfft.' It was somewhere between an exclamation of disgust and an exhalation of smoke. 'Forget that. Got to grab hold of a bit of fun wherever you can in these uncertain times. If you shut yourself away in that tomb of a vicarage, the Rev will come home and find you fossilized at the kitchen sink. You did the right thing. Course I'll cover for you. I tell you what, I fancy a go with this Madame Anoushka.' The matter of Stella's marriage vows dismissed, Nancy's butterfly mind settled on a new topic of interest and she nodded in the direction of the fortune-teller's faded tent. 'I wouldn't mind knowing what fate has in store for me, so long as it's not a direct hit in an air raid.'

'If you knew that you could get yourself a Morrison shelter and sleep in it every night. I don't think she's very reliable though. Ada booked her; apparently her real name is Annie and she mostly works in a pub in Potters Bar.'

'Spoilsport. 'Ere, she's got no one in there now. Why don't you nip in first, while I finish my ciggy? Punch and Judy's not finished yet – you've got time before you have to judge the fancy dress.'

It was the last thing she felt like doing, but Stella didn't have the heart to argue, not when Nancy had just agreed to help her out. Together they went over and while Nancy stood outside the shabby little tent with its faded sign she drew back the canvas flap and went in.

It smelled of fermenting grass and mildew, undercut with the sharper tang of sweat. The light was murky and the air damp. Madame Anoushka was nowhere to be seen, but just as Stella was about to go out again she appeared from behind a flimsy curtain made from a moth-eaten shawl.

'Sit down, my child.'

Her voice was husky, a mixture of Russian and Cockney. She was wreathed in scarves and cigarette smoke – the old girl must have been having a sneaky fag out the back of the tent. Behind their layers of kohl and mascara, her eyes gleamed when they came to rest on Stella, as if she had just remembered some private joke.

She slid a small enamelled dish across the table into which, Stella realized, she was supposed to put money. She fumbled in the pocket of her dress and reluctantly put in half a crown because she had nothing smaller. It didn't seem appropriate to ask for change.

With impressive sleight of hand Madame Anoushka

whisked the money out of sight beneath the purple chenille tablecloth and busied herself pouring tea from a tarnished silver spirit kettle. Stella's mood lifted a little – having been on her feet all afternoon serving tea to other people, the prospect of a cup for herself was very welcome. The brew was black and smelled strongly of bonfires. The woman peered at her through the steam with the beady relish of a blackbird watching a worm.

'We start, I think, with the 'and. I sense you will have honest 'ands. Show me.'

Blimey, thought Stella, placing them uneasily on the purple chenille. She hoped they weren't too honest.

Madame Anoushka seized her wrist and turned her hand palm upward, bending over it so that Stella could see the seam of white at the roots of her orange hair. She looked for a long time, twisting her hand this way and that, as if reading actual print. Stella stared over her head at the potted aspidistra behind her and let her thoughts drift deliciously ahead, as the noises of the fete floated in from the other side of the canvas. The fancy dress judging was next, and then there would be prize-giving to endure, and clearing up . . . It would be six o'clock at least before she could hope to be finished. Salad for supper; Reverend Stokes could complain all he liked. Her dress was hanging up on the wardrobe door – only the navy and white spotted one she usually wore for church, but aside from the green she'd worn last time it was the best she had. She wondered if she could get away with another bath before she went out—

'You are married.'

Stella started in alarm, almost jerking her hand from the fortune-teller's grip. It took her a second to realize that it was a statement of fact, not a reproachful reminder.

'Oh . . . yes! Yes, I am.'

It was hardly proof of her psychic power, since Stella was wearing her wedding ring and Ada had undoubtedly pointed her out as the vicar's wife. 'There is break in marriage line . . . This shows separation – living apart.'

There must be an awful lot of people with breaks in their marriage lines at the moment, Stella thought. Restlessness was building inside her. Madame Anoushka was tracing a line across her palm with a long, slightly dirty fingernail; the sensation made her shiver involuntarily.

'I sense passion. Great passion. But caution too. You are fearful. You do not trust easily.' She ran her nicotine-stained claw along the curving line beneath Stella's thumb. 'But you have much to give – this passion again, and love. Very much love you have to give. Now – drink your tea.'

Stella took a mouthful of the dark brew – it tasted like it had been made with the contents of the ashpan rather than tealeaves. She was beginning to feel uncomfortable and longed to reclaim her hand. And wash it. Madame Anoushka was pressing her thumb over her palm now, as if testing the freshness of a piece of steak at the butcher's.

'You have needs to meet. The needs of a woman.' There was something lascivious in her tone, as if she was taking some kind of vicarious pleasure in saying such things. Really, it was too much, but just as Stella was about to snatch her hand away she let it go. 'Now, let us see what is written in the leaves.'

At least she wasn't required to finish the tea. With relief she watched Madame Anoushka swill the remaining liquid around then tip it out into the saucer. She studied the flotsam of leaves washed up around the inside of the cup and gave a crow of triumph.

'Ha — there it is!' The claw hovered over a nondescript clump of tealeaves by the rim of the cup. 'The oyster! And there too, the harp! Each are symbols of love, romance . . . *Desire*. And right at the top of the cup — that is indication of the present.' She looked up from beneath her orange floss of hair with a coquettish smirk. 'This passion will have outlet *tonight* . . .'

How did she know? Stella got to her feet, suddenly dizzy. Her breath seemed to be stuck painfully behind her breastbone. 'Thanks,' she said in a strangled voice. 'It's been fascinating, but I—'

She stumbled towards the tent door, fumbling for the opening in the canvas and desperate to be out of the fetid atmosphere. Nancy pulled back the flap and watched her emerge with mild surprise.

'Steady on. You all right? You look like you've seen a ghost.'

Stella was about to demur; to reassure her that she was fine and it was just the heat inside the tent and the voyeuristic suggestiveness in the creepy old woman's tone. But something caught the periphery of her vision and made her turn to look across the field, to the figure standing beside the platform, surrounded by a little crowd of people. The blood left her head.

'Oh my God . . .' she croaked.

Nancy turned to follow her gaze.

'Bleeding hell,' she muttered. 'That's no ghost. It's bloody Charles.'

He looked different: older, thinner, more weathered. His skin was too fair to turn brown, and it had a reddened, flayed appearance. There were new lines around his eyes, from squinting into the African sun.

'I should have sent a telegram, but it was all so last minute, there really wasn't the opportunity. Is it a terrible shock, darling?'

'Well, yes, but . . . a good one, of course.'

Her voice seemed to come from a hundred miles away. She sipped the tea Ada had brought her and looked out of the hall window onto the field where the children were assembling for the fancy dress parade. There was no sign of Nancy; she must have gone in to see the fortune-teller. She should have saved her money, Stella thought with a flash of anger. The shameless old fraud – she must have seen Charles get out of the taxi while she was having her cigarette at the back of the tent, and come up with all that claptrap about passion and romance being imminent. If she'd had any genuine psychic ability—

'I'm afraid there's another surprise in store, but I hope this one won't have quite the same effect. Who should I just happen to bump into at Victoria, but Peter? Got a few days' leave too, and no specific plans for it, so I told him to come back here with me. He's gone to the Vicarage, to wash off the travel grime. I hope you don't mind?'

'Peter? Peter Underwood? No, no of course not.'

In truth the news was curiously unsurprising, and came as a relief. Having Peter in the house meant that she wouldn't be alone with Charles.

'That's very good of you, darling.' Charles put down his cup and saucer and looked around. He was jiggling his knee in an excess of nervous energy, making the table vibrate and rattling the china, though he didn't seem to notice. 'I must say it's quite a scene to come home to. Tranquil old England. The "green and pleasant land" of fetes and cake and afternoon tea.'

He said it almost like a criticism. There was a square of gingerbread cake on the plate in front of him from which he'd taken one mouthful and crumbled the remainder into dust. She wanted to remind him that it wasn't always like this, and that the teeth of rationing seemed to bite deeper every week, but she reminded herself of where he'd come from and kept silent. Marjorie Walsh came over to take away their empty cups.

'It's marvellous to see you, Vicar, and looking so well! I'll tell Gerald you're home. Bearing up all right out there, are you?'

'God is taking care of me, thank you Marjorie, but it's good to be back and to see how well you ladies are keeping things going in my absence. The fete looks splendid – though I confess I'm disappointed there are none of your famous scones this year. They're the only reason I came home!'

'Thank you, Vicar. I wanted to make them, but there were those who decided otherwise. Have you finished with that? I'll take it away, shall I?'

She picked up the plate of gingery crumbs and shot Stella a superior look as she bore it back to the kitchen.

Ada appeared in the hall doorway.

'Sorry to drag you lovebirds away from your reunion, but they're ready for you to judge the fancy dress now, Mrs T.'

On the platform a parade of ragged flower fairies, storybook characters and a League of Nations display of Dutch girls, Spanish dancers and Chinese ladies fluttered and shuffled, while the mini-Führer scowled and stared straight ahead, one arm raised. 'My goodness,' Charles exclaimed uneasily.

'Standard's not what it has been,' Ada remarked. 'Every spare scrap goes into making proper clothes these days, there's nothing left over for fancy dress. Still, the Chinese girl's very clever, with the dressing gown and the knitting needles in her hair . . .'

'Really, Hitler is the best,' Stella said. 'Such a simple outfit, but brilliantly done.'

'Poor taste,' Charles said briskly. 'No, Ada's right. The Chinese girl.' He clapped his hands and said loudly and heartily, 'Well done everyone – splendid effort all round, but this year's prize goes to our lovely Oriental lady!'

There was a ripple of desultory applause. The Chinese girl simpered and the Führer's military bearing dissolved, his despotic scowl melting into a little boy's expression of naked disappointment. Stella turned away, anger quickening her blood. Across the grass Nancy was just emerging from the fortune-teller's tent.

'Here, Mrs T. – you can present the prize,' Ada said, holding out the inevitable tin of peaches.

She shook her head, already moving away. 'Charles decided. He ought to do it.'

'Foreign travel!' Nancy called as she came towards her. 'I says to 'er – I hope that means I marry a Yank and go back to the States, not join the bleeding Wrens. She says, could be. There was an oyster in my tealeaves which means passion, apparently. So –' she dropped her voice as she came level with Stella, 'how's that for a shock? What you going to do about your American?'

'I don't know.' Dan's face came sharply into focus in Stella's mind and she was suddenly afraid she might cry. 'Obviously I can't go now, but I don't even know where he's staying to get a message to him. He'll be waiting for me, and he won't know why I haven't come.'

'Where were you supposed to meet him?'

Stella repeated the message she'd read on the clipboard.

'Hmm – the Trocadero, very nice, I must say.' Nancy snapped open her handbag and took out a little square mirror. 'Well, don't worry; just leave it to your Auntie Nancy,' she said, checking her make-up. 'Does he know you're married?'

'Yes, of course. Oh Nancy, would you really do that? Thank you, thank you. Tell him I'm sorry and that I'll write as soon as I can . . .'

'Shh – that's enough now. Here comes the vicar.' Looking past Stella she smiled her pussycat smile. 'Hello Reverend Thorne – fancy seeing you here.'

'Nancy.' Charles's voice was as stiff as his smile. 'Nice to see you.'

'Likewise, looking tanned and handsome with all that African sun.' She dropped the mirror back into her bag. 'I'd love to stay and talk but I'm afraid I'll have to love you and leave you. Important date to get ready for this evening.' She winked at Stella.

'Come for tea tomorrow,' Stella suggested slightly wildly. 'You can tell me all about it!'

'I wouldn't want to be in the way—'

'You wouldn't at all. Charles's friend Peter is staying, and Reverend Stokes will be there, so the more the merrier. Isn't that right, Charles?'

'Quite,' he said, but without bothering to make it sound like he meant it.

He was her husband, and yet he was still a stranger. She knew that it must be difficult for him, adjusting to being home again after the things he had seen and experienced in the desert, but with Peter staying there was no opportunity for her to talk to him and find out what those things were, and she had the feeling that he despised her slightly for not knowing. Not understanding. Absence had not made his heart grow fonder. Rather, it had hardened the spaces between them into something impenetrable.

I am a bad person, she told herself, coming back from church alone while he stayed to talk to his parishioners. *My husband has come home and I am not glad to see him. In fact, I resent him for being here.* She closed the door behind her and leaned against the wall in the chill of the scullery, where Dan had kissed her. *I am irritated by the way he treats me like a child and assumes I can't do anything properly, and most of all I resent him for keeping me from the man I want to be with.*

It was a relief to put it into those stark words. Laid out like that in her head she could see how selfish she was being, how unreasonable. Faithless and weak-willed, like the worst kind of stereotype of a wife left behind while her husband did his bit for King and Country. Ashamed and sobered, she collected the cauliflower (slightly battered) from the scullery shelf and took it into the kitchen.

Through the window she saw Peter Underwood, sitting on the old bench beneath the apple tree. He was reading a book, his dark head bent, legs crossed in that very precise, particular way he had, as if somehow trying to make as little of himself as possible come into contact with the mossy, peeling paintwork. It was like that when Charles touched her, she'd noticed. Although he was good at saying the right things and going through the motions of courtesy she could feel him shrinking away, as if she was contaminated.

Peter hadn't come with them to church. When she'd

expressed surprise to Charles he'd been tight-lipped, as if it were a grown-up matter that she wouldn't understand. Peter had been asking some questions about his faith, he said tersely; that was why they'd stayed up so late talking last night. Charles was hoping to help him through the crisis, but until then Peter didn't feel able to pray in church and needed peace and space to think. His tone made it clear that the subject was closed.

Except of course, it was still very much *there*. At lunchtime, as the cauliflower cheese cooled and congealed Charles said an extra-long Grace, thanking God not only for the food, but also for friendship, loved ones, the gift of days spent together. Throughout Peter stared out of the French windows, where leaden clouds had taken up residence in yesterday's delphinium skies. Glancing at him surreptitiously Stella saw the expression of elaborate resignation on his thin, sardonic face, and when Charles had finished he said, 'Nice try, old chap.'

Reverend Stokes broke the tension by picking up his fork and prodding the cauliflower cheese.

'Sunday lunch isn't what it used to be.'

'No,' Charles agreed testily, 'it isn't.'

Conversation over lunch was stilted and sporadic, the atmosphere curiously tense. Peter Underwood pushed his cauliflower cheese around his plate with barely contained distaste and laid his fork down with half of it still uneaten. Reverend Stokes brightened visibly when Stella brought out the rice pudding, but Peter looked at it, then laid his napkin on the table and quietly asked if they would excuse him.

Charles watched him leave the dining room then, after a few seconds, stood up and followed him, redness blossoming on his cheeks as if he'd been slapped. Reverend Stokes looked up from his pudding in mild surprise.

'Underwood chap not feeling well? Pity for him, but all the more for us.'

After lunch Reverend Stokes retired to the sitting room with the newspaper and the wireless. Stella was washing up in the kitchen when Charles came in and announced he and Peter were going for a walk. It had begun to rain now, a steady summer downpour. He looked so fraught that she felt sorry for him.

'You poor thing. It hasn't been a very restful homecoming for you,' she said, drying her lobster-pink hands. 'You're supposed to be on leave from other people's spiritual problems.'

'Being a minister is hardly a job with conventional hours,' he replied, as if spelling out something very obvious to a simpleton. The little flame of sympathy was snuffed out. She only just managed to stop herself sticking her tongue out at his departing back.

Mercifully, Nancy arrived early. Stella was rolling out pastry to make jam tarts with the last of Marjorie Walsh's rhubarb and carrot jam when she heard the front doorbell over the din of the Home Service coming from the sitting room. She ran to let Nancy in with floury hands, and ushered her down the gloomy passage to the kitchen, where she shut the door and gave her a swift, fierce hug.

'Well?'

'Nice to see you too, I'm sure.'

'Sorry – it's always wonderful to see you, you know that, but I've been on pins all day. I'm dying to know how it went last night – did you see him? Was he cross that I didn't come?'

'One question at a time would be good. And put the kettle on – I couldn't half do with a cuppa.'

She should have known better than to try and rush her; Nancy's stubborn streak meant she only ever did things in her own time and on her own terms. As her nerves screamed with impatience Stella filled the kettle and waited while Nancy went over to the stove, flapped her wet skirt and proceeded to narrate the story of how she'd been planning to walk, until the rain began to come down in stair-rods, so she'd caught the bus. Eventually, when she'd got that off her chest, she perilously lit a cigarette from the gas ring and settled herself down at the table. 'So – quite the charmer, isn't he, your Yank?'

'You found him all right?' Stella's knuckles were white on the rolling pin. She was caught between dread and excitement.

'Oh yes. Recognized him straight away, didn't I? He was the handsome one sitting at the bar with his eyes fixed on the door and a sort of hungry look on his face, like a dog outside the butcher's.' She giggled. 'Poor love. Mind you, he didn't have to look so disappointed when I told him you wasn't coming and he'd have to put up with me instead. I almost cut my losses at that point; left him to drink on his own.'

'You didn't though, did you?'

'Nah, course not. Wasn't going to pass up the chance for a free drink. Or several, as it turned out. Not mean with his money, is he?' Nancy flicked ash into a saucer. 'I like that in a man.'

'So what did he say? I mean, what did you talk about?'

'This and that. You mostly.'

Happiness rose inside her, like a fat, pink sun and she laughed. 'Not the most exciting evening out you've ever had, then.'

Nancy picked up the spoon Stella had just put down and ran her finger over it, sucking off the precious jam. 'Course, he wanted to know all about the vicar, too.' She dropped her voice and cast a furtive glance towards the door. 'He'd had a bit to drink by then. Kept asking if he loves you.'

Quite suddenly the laughter had evaporated, like the sun going behind a dark cloud. 'It's all right, he's out. If Charles loves me, you mean? What did you say?'

'Well, I didn't know what to say, did I? So I decided to tell it like it is.' Nancy's gaze held an edge of defiance as she slid her finger into the bowl of the spoon so that jam oozed over it like blood. 'I said I wasn't sure. I mean, it should be obvious, shouldn't it? He should be going round with a grin a mile wide on his face to have landed a wife like you.' She shrugged. 'I might be speaking out of turn here, but I'm not sure he even notices you, never mind loves you, and that's the God's honest truth.'

Stella turned away, stricken, opening the oven door and slipping the tray of jam tarts into it. Hearing someone else, even if it was only Nancy, say out loud the secret that had been haunting her for months was shocking. Instantly a dozen responses bobbed to the surface of her mind: *He's just not the kind of person who shows his emotions . . . His faith makes it hard for him . . . The war has made it impossible to have a normal marriage . . .* but she didn't want to say them aloud and expose them to Nancy's inevitable scorn.

From along the passageway they heard the front door slam, and the sound of voices in the hall. It cut through Stella's thoughts, galvanized her into action. Flustered she looked around the messy kitchen.

'They're back – and I haven't made the sandwiches yet, or laid the table.'

Nancy's expression was difficult to read as she got to her feet. 'Where's the bread? I'll make a start on the sandwiches. What are you putting in them?'

'There's not much. I was going to grate a carrot, and there are lettuces in the garden . . . I'll open a tin of Spam.' She grabbed the dishcloth from the draining board and was scrubbing at the sticky residue of pastry on the table when the kitchen door opened.

Charles's cheeks were pinker than ever and crystal droplets of rain sparkled in his sandy hair. Coming into the kitchen he looked uneasily around, and although he took in the floury surfaces, the open jam jar on the table and the spoon resting stickily beside it, he seemed not to notice Nancy.

'Tea will be ready soon, I hope? Peter needs to catch a train.'

'Yes. I was just about to lay the table.' Stella gestured to the tray on the worktop, on which she'd put the cups and saucers and plates ready. Charles frowned.

'Those cups?' He made a little irritated sound that wasn't quite a laugh. 'Could we not use the ones Aunt Edith gave us as a wedding present? The rose-patterned ones?'

'Of course ... Sorry, how silly of me. It's been so long since I used them I'd forgotten all about them. I'll get them out now.'

She went past him into the dining room and opened the door of the oak sideboard. The tea set was stacked carefully on its shelves and she took out the cups, wiping the dust off them with her apron. She'd been so thrilled to receive them – how odd that she should forget about them. Placing the cups on the top of the sideboard she looked at the wedding photograph that stood there and noticed that it too was dusty. She'd just picked it up and was rubbing the corner of her apron over the glass when Charles appeared in the doorway.

'You found them?'

'Yes.' She held up the photograph and smiled, feeling suddenly shy. 'Almost a year. It hasn't been the best start for a marriage has it?'

It was intended, perhaps not to bridge the chasm that lay between them, but at least to acknowledge it. To re-establish some connection, however tentative.

'I'm sorry it hasn't lived up to your expectations,' he said coldly. 'I suggest you stop reading those appalling novelettes

213

and filling your head with romantic nonsense. Now, if we could manage to give Peter some tea before he leaves?'

He went out, and she stood there, still holding the photograph, feeling utterly foolish. *Nancy's right*, she thought with a little gasp, setting it down again. *He doesn't love me. He never has. I've always known but I didn't want to admit it. He really doesn't love me at all.*

She waited for the hurt to kick in, but instead the realization was like a weight falling from her – the burden of her guilt, she supposed. In her head the clouds rolled away and the sun came out.

16

Dear Stella

It was good to get your letter. I didn't want to cause
trouble for you by writing when Charles was home, but I got
worried when I didn't hear from you for so long. I don't know
what I was worried about, exactly. Maybe I just missed
hearing your voice.

I guess it's not surprising that Charles isn't being sent back
to Tunisia – things look like they might be a whole lot
quieter in North Africa for a little while, thanks to your guy
Montgomery. How long will he be at the training camp before
this new regiment gets shipped out? I got Johnson to look up
Barnard Castle on those navigator's maps of his. In English
terms he reckons it's a pretty long way away, which is great. I
probably shouldn't say that, but – what the hell. I hate it
that the guy doesn't appreciate you, which I guess is
reasonable. I also hate it that he stopped me from seeing you

215

that night, which I know is not. It was great to meet Nancy and put a face to the name (she actually looks like a Nancy) but it would've been so much better to see you.

This Peter Underwood guy sounds like quite an oddball . . . From what you say he sure seems to have a strange kind of a hold over Charles. Let's hope he doesn't happen to bump into him again the next time he gets leave.

I'm glad the peaches went down well. You don't have to thank me — at least, as I remember, you already did (and I do remember it . . . over and over. I really liked your Ada, but she has lousy timing). Three crates of tinned peaches was a small price to pay for a kiss like that.

Look after yourself for me, beautiful girl.

Dan

27 June '43

Dear Stella

Edge of Darkness hasn't reached the movie theater in Bury St Edmunds yet, but I'll sure look out for it. Last week it was showing I Married a Witch — again. I didn't like it much the first time around, but Morgan is nuts about Veronica Lake so I somehow found myself sitting through it a second time. Guess what — I fell asleep. Sleeping through Veronica Lake in the company of a guy I spend far too much time with anyway is nothing compared to sleeping through Myra Hess with you. (You know, I actually can't believe I did that, or that you were so sweet about it.)

It sounds like the machines you saw on the newsreel were the same ones I fly — B-17s. They're big, but not as big as the B-24s that are coming over from home now. They all have names and pictures painted on the nose, though don't ask me how that started. Ours is called Ruby Shoes, and she has a painting of a beautiful redhead wearing a pair of glittering red shoes and not a whole lot more. We picked the name for our ball turret gunner, a kid called Joey Harper. He's the youngest member of the crew and was so homesick the first three weeks of training that he barely spoke, except to say how much he wanted to go home. Since he comes from Kansas we figured that what he needed was a pair of ruby slippers like Dorothy's in The Wizard of Oz (did you ever see that movie?). The attractive lady wearing them is just a bonus.

Things have been busy around here. We've almost reached the fifteen mission mark, which is when they give you a medal (I guess they figure they ought to give us something now because they don't think we'll make it to twenty-five). They don't count the extra rides I've taken with other crews. I thought it would get easier, the more missions you flew, but if anything it's harder because you can't help thinking about the odds getting shorter. It's best not to think about it at all.

Take care of yourself.

D x

2 July '43

Dear Stella

Forget what I said about flying and medals and odds – it was a stupid remark that I never would have made if I'd thought about it for even a half-second. You're not allowed to be worried, OK? Right now there's nothing at all to worry about, except that I'm going to bankrupt myself at poker. Every morning we get woken up before first light and go through briefings and breakfast, only to make it down to the flight line and have the mission cancelled because of cloud cover over the targets. After that there's nothing to do all day but play cards and soccer, which can get pretty competitive sometimes but hasn't resulted in any casualties so far.

I've put in for a leave pass. I don't want to tempt fate and assume I'll get it, but I think there's a good chance – they don't want us all hanging around here and going slowly crazy with nothing to do. If I did, what would you say to going away someplace? If that sounds presumptuous, ignore it and I'll never mention it again, I swear . . .

Take care of yourself for me.

Dan x

Letters to the Lost

Dear Stella

That's a yes? You're sure? I mean, you didn't quite write it big enough . . .

So – where should we go? I guess New York and Paris are both out, and London isn't exactly an escape for you. Should we head for the coast? Is there any coast left that hasn't been barricaded up with barbed wire and gun placements? Will it be difficult for you to get away?

Take care, for me.

D x

Dear Stella

Ah – so Nancy has a long-lost mom? And a long-lost mom who's chosen right now to get back in touch? I think I love this woman (or the woman who made her up). Of course it's natural that you'd want to be with your friend when she went to visit. And, if she lives somewhere nice, with a great hotel, well – that would be just perfect.

I've never been to Brighton, but from reading your description I'm pretty sure I don't want to. I couldn't give a damn about being by the sea – I see enough of the stuff flying over it – and you're right about the trains. How about Cambridge? It's a beautiful city, and a great place to get lost in, and we won't waste a precious day to get there. Do you think that maybe Nancy's mom might just live in Cambridge?

Another two missions down. No word on the pass yet. With any luck it won't be long, but when these things come through they tend to be pretty immediate. Will that be a problem?

Take care of yourself for me.

Dan x

The light was nearly gone and it was almost impossible to make out the words. But excitement rose like wreaths of smoke from the page as the plans for those stolen days seventy years ago were made.

Jess sensed a change, and wondered what had happened to bring it about. Their initial tentative friendship had entered a different phase, and there was a sort of exuberance in Dan Rosinski's tone. She remembered what he'd said about a kiss – a kiss that had been worth three crates of tinned peaches. A kiss that had meant so much it had made him able to forget that he was regularly flying deep into enemy territory and not knowing if he'd come back. A kiss like nothing Jess had ever experienced.

The book in the library had outlined the facts, and the odds that were stacked against the young American airmen who poured into East Anglia during the war. She'd skimmed over a lot of it, her attention diverted by the photographs; crowded dance halls decked with streamers and balloons, airmen queuing for coffee and doughnuts at Red Cross vans, crews lined up beneath their planes – pin-up girl paintings just like the one Dan described visible in the background. But one statistic stuck in her mind. A tour of duty consisted of twenty-five missions in 1943, she'd read. The average life expectancy was seventeen.

Dan Rosinski must have known that, but apart from that one bit about the medal for fifteen missions, he didn't mention it. He talked about his friends and the films they'd seen, and he focused his mind on planning a trip he couldn't guarantee he'd be alive to take with the woman he hadn't meant to fall in love with.

She lay back on the pink counterpane in the evening gloom, and thought about Dodge. Even at the beginning, when she'd actually believed that he loved her, she couldn't imagine him doing anything like that for her. But then she couldn't imagine him setting aside his own needs, his own comforts, his own plans for anything that didn't directly line his own pocket. His swaggering selfishness had almost, ironically, been part of his attraction – it was as if his belief in his own importance had made her believe it too. Dodge prided himself on being a seasoned veteran of many a violent warzone but they were all ones that didn't require him to move from the horrible black PVC sofa in the flat, or shift his eyes from the huge flatscreen TV as he gunned down enemies with a beer in one hand and a spliff in the other.

When she met him she'd been working in a bar in Manchester, taking to the stage in the cave-like club downstairs to sing on Saturday nights. Living with her dad, she'd been desperate to save up some money to rent a place of her own. Lisa, her dad's new partner, made no secret of the fact she didn't want her there, and Jess couldn't blame her; Lisa had two small kids of her own who'd each had their own bedroom before Jess came on the scene.

Singing was the only thing that made the long hours behind the bar and the awkward atmosphere in the cramped house bearable. For those few hours on a Saturday night she could believe that her life was going somewhere, and that there was still a chance she might achieve her ambition and be the star Gran had always said she was. Even though for the rest of the week it seemed about as likely as moving to Mars.

And then Dodge had appeared. One night, watching her from the side of the stage with measuring, speculative eyes.

He knew people, he said, in London, and she didn't doubt it for a second. He came and went, city to city, dropping the names of clubs and DJs in his wake like stardust. That first night he'd pressed her up against the wall in the corridor and told her he'd look after her, make things happen. He said she had a voice like dynamite, and a body to match. She thought he'd release the neon-bright dreams that lit up the inside of her head and let the colours come shining out of her.

He hadn't. It all turned out to be lies – all those hints about friends in high places and industry connections – and gradually she'd realized that she was part of the pretence; another fake accessory to enhance his image and bring in a bit of above-board cash from small-time gigs in pubs while he got on with whatever it was that paid for the TV and the BMW and the moving around from town to town. It had been pretty obvious from the moment she'd left Manchester with him that he hadn't loved her – anyone with half a brain could work out that dragging someone off the bed by the hair wasn't a sign of affection – and yet she'd believed him when he said he was sorry, and felt almost flattered when he told her she made him crazy. She'd known at the time that wasn't love, but she hadn't understood until now, reading Dan Rosinski's letters, what real love was.

With a sigh she sat up. Did men like that still exist, or was Dan Rosinski the last of a dying breed?

The phrase sent a shiver up her spine. She thought of the letter downstairs and felt a hot pulse of alarm. *I don't have much time left . . . Forever is finally running out . . .*

The sky beyond the filthy window was dark, but there was still a thin strip of pink behind the chimneypots of the houses opposite. The shops wouldn't be closed yet. She still had time to buy writing paper and envelopes, and candles.

She had read so many of Dan Rosinski's letters, but now it was time to write one to him in return.

17

1943

The train was dirty and crowded, like all trains were these days. Stella had walked along virtually its entire length, gritting her teeth and feigning indifference to the whistles and catcalls of the soldiers crammed into the corridors, as she looked for a carriage that wasn't full of khaki. Eventually she'd spotted an empty seat in a compartment with two sleeping sailors, and a harassed-looking mother with two children. It was only after she'd stowed her small case on the overhead luggage rack and sat down that she noticed the greenish pallor of the smallest child.

'Travel sick,' sighed the mother, meeting Stella's eye. 'Threw up three times on the train from Maidstone this morning. Wish I never gave 'im 'is breakfast – waste of bread and marge.'

Stella smiled faintly, wondering how she'd failed to pick up the smell that hung around the child, and whether it was too late to grab her suitcase and leave. Maybe she should just get off at the next station and go back to London – it was a mistake to have ever agreed to this. She turned to look out of the window in the hope of deterring the woman from making further conversation.

The signs had been removed from the stations at which they stopped, making her feel more disorientated than ever. Her face was a ghostly smudge reflected in the glass – as white as the little boy's. The train plunged into a tunnel, bringing it into sharper relief and revealing two black whirlpools for eyes, incongruously topped off by the jaunty little straw hat that was Ada's latest trophy from the donations haul.

She tugged it off. It looked ridiculous. *She* looked ridiculous, trying to be sophisticated in her remodelled jumble sale dress. Oh God, what was she doing? Risking everything she'd got, everything she'd ever wanted – a home, security, a family of her own – for what? A dirty weekend? That was obviously what he had in mind, what all the letters and the planning and scheming had been about. But he hardly knew her. Two kisses – not enough to put him off yet. She thought of the slinky silk slip beneath her dress and panic surged up inside her like milk coming to the boil. He'd probably take one look at her in it and change his mind, like Charles had on their wedding night. Oh God . . .

'You all right, love? You look a bit peaky yourself.'

'Just going to the loo,' Stella muttered, getting to her feet.

The lavatory at the end of the carriage was taken, so she walked down the swaying train, past clusters of servicemen smoking out of the windows and passing round pictures of girls in bathing suits, to one that was empty. Inside it was cramped and reeking, the smell almost worse than that in the compartment she'd just left. She faced herself in the mirror. *Too late to turn back now. You've started this and now you have to see it through.* From her handbag she took the lipstick Nancy had pressed on her before they left – together, so it looked like they were going to her fictional mother's – and twisted it up. What did the magazines call it? The red badge of courage. Tentatively she dabbed it on. It looked gruesome against her corpse-like pallor; garish and wrong – a little girl's clumsy attempt to be a lady. She tried to rub it off again, though it was hard to get rid of the stain.

Someone knocked sharply on the door, startling her. Muttering apologies she stumbled out. She couldn't face going back to her seat so stood by an open window, letting the wind buffet her face. It wasn't a long journey – that had been the point – and far too soon the train was sliding between the backs of houses, past scrubby gardens where washing flapped across rows of vegetables.

In a few minutes they'd be there. She went back to her seat to collect her case. The smell of vomit hit her as soon as she opened the door to the compartment, where the woman was scrubbing furiously at the seat with a handkerchief. Stella collected her case and retreated hastily.

The blur of faces on the platform came into focus as the train slowed, then came to a halt with a great shuddering sigh. Out in the corridor Stella hung back, pressing herself against the window to let the people who were spilling from compartments out onto the platform ahead of her. For a long, lightheaded moment she stood in the empty corridor, staring at the open door until a guard appeared.

'Cambridge, love. You getting off here?'

The station was a sea of khaki, retreating now, like the tide. She was shaking, curiously cold even though she could feel the sweat soaking under her arms, terrified that he wouldn't be there, dreading that he would be.

He was.

Leaning against the wall by a machine dispensing Fry's chocolate, his hands in his pockets. He straightened up when he saw her, unhurriedly, and came towards her. His face was grave, his smile gentle, as if he sensed her uncertainty. And shared it?

'I'm glad you're here,' he said ruefully, picking up her case. 'I was half expecting to see Nancy striding down the station. And don't get me wrong, I like Nancy, I just don't want to spend a couple days with her.'

It wasn't like the reunions she watched with Nancy at the pictures. But then, she wasn't like those women, those Hollywood actresses with their shining hair and well-cut clothes and photogenic vulnerability. He didn't try to kiss her, or even take her hand as they walked out of the vast whale's belly of the station and into the unfamiliar city.

Maybe he was having second thoughts too.

Maybe he'd changed his mind already.

*

He felt like a kid who'd captured the most beautiful, delicate butterfly and was sickened at the sight of it, trapped and helpless inside his net. He'd been so focused on grabbing this time with her that he hadn't actually thought what he'd do when it came. Actually, that was a big lie. He'd thought about it plenty – in fact, thinking about it had been just about the only thing that had stopped him losing his mind these past two weeks. It was just that all of the things he'd imagined seemed completely inappropriate now.

With heroic effort of will he held back, resisting the urge to gather her up into his arms and bear her back to the hotel like a caveman. She was as brittle as glass, and he was afraid that if he touched her she'd shatter. Guilt, he guessed, trying hard not to mind, and to direct his frustration and anger – unfairly perhaps, but what the hell? – at her cold-hearted bastard of a husband. He wasn't just making the cold-hearted bastard bit up because it suited him, Nancy had been pretty forthcoming on the subject of Reverend Charles Thorne. 'Bastard' had actually been her word, along with 'arrogant', 'humourless', 'disapproving' and 'stuffy'. The thought of Stella throwing herself away on a man like that, a man who didn't even love her, made him feel incandescent with fury.

'How about we drop your case back at the hotel, then go for tea someplace?' he asked as they stood at the bus stop outside the station. In the bright summer afternoon her face was white as paper, her lips unusually red by contrast. They twitched into an unconvincing smile as she nodded, but she didn't meet his eye.

228

On the short bus ride she sat beside him, but might as well have been a hundred miles away as she gazed out of the windows and folded her ticket into tiny pleats with trembling fingers. Dan felt the happiness that had sustained him through the past week — the sense of anticipation and excitement at seeing her again — cool and set into something entirely different. Something that felt like despair.

The hotel was the best Cambridge had to offer; an imposing gothic edifice overlooking a pretty stretch of grass that for once wasn't disfigured by rows of Brussels sprouts and potatoes. He'd deliberately arrived early and checked in, anticipating that she would find the whole business of pretending to be married awkward and painful, so he led her straight past the uniformed doorman with the poker up his ass and through the echoing lobby to the stairs, to spare her the inquisitive eyes of the elevator bellboy. His heart was beating too fast again, adrenaline sluicing through his veins and making him feel a little shaky. It was happening more and more lately, not just on the flight line in the morning when they were warming up the engines for take-off, but at other times, stupid times, like at 3 a.m. when he should be asleep.

He was painfully aware of her, trembling like a convicted woman on the way to the gallows, as he unlocked the door to the room he'd been given earlier, and stood back to let her go in first.

The bed, with its plump, blue satin eiderdown, seemed huge and threatening. She walked around it and went to stand at the window, her back to him and her arms crossed over her chest. Dan put the suitcase down, at a loss. Everything was wrong and he didn't know why, or how to put it right. The wrongness was also a shock. For weeks her letters had been the only thing that felt right, the thing he had come to rely on in a world full of uncertainty and fear. He felt like a guy who'd just pulled the rip-cord on a parachute only to discover that the canopy hadn't opened.

'Stella . . .'

'I'm sorry.'

Her voice was low, vibrating with nerves. Her head was bent, her hair partly obscuring her face. He wanted nothing more than to take her in his arms, to hold her gently until she'd stopped shaking and the tension had ebbed out of her shoulders, but everything about her resisted approach. He thrust his hands into the pockets of his trousers, and sighed.

'It's OK . . . You don't have to apologize. You don't have to stay either. Forget going out for tea. I can take you straight back to the station, if that's what you want.'

She said nothing, but nodded her head jerkily.

Disappointment solidified in his throat, and he didn't trust himself to speak. He couldn't blame her for not wanting to stay – he should never have put her in this position by asking her here in the first place. He'd turned into one of those men on the base: crass, graceless, clumsy. He rubbed a hand over his eyes, and when he dropped it again and looked at her he saw a single crystal tear fall and shatter on the floorboards. Self-disgust washed through him.

'Stella . . . I'm sorry. I shouldn't have suggested this. I was wrong to push you.'

'You didn't push me.'

'It was my idea. I wasn't thinking straight, I guess.' He dragged a hand through his hair and gave a hoarse, rasping laugh. 'I guess I wanted it so much I didn't stop to think about you. About what you want.'

'I do want it.'

Her voice was so small that he thought he'd misheard. Her head was still bent, her face hidden.

'What did you say?'

Slowly she lifted her head and her hair fell back. 'I *do* want it . . . more than anything . . . but I don't know . . .' Her eyes were haunted. 'I don't know if I can—'

'I don't understand. Is it him? Charles? Because I—'

'No. It's not him, it's me.' She was whispering, twisting her wedding ring around and around on her finger. 'I'm . . . I'm no good . . .'

Confusion buzzed in Dan's head. Turning away from her he paced across the room, needing to put some distance between them so he couldn't see the shimmer of tears on her eyelashes or the trembling of her mouth. 'That's not true. Stella, you are good through and through, and if that bastard, or the church, or *anyone else* has made you feel that you're worth less as a person because we—'

She made a hiccupping sound, half-laugh, half-sob. 'I don't mean it like that. I mean I'm no good . . . at *that* . . .' Her eyes moved meaningfully towards the bed and the tears that had been brimming in them overflowed and spilled down her cheeks. 'I shouldn't have agreed to come. I shouldn't have let you think—'

Jesus. His self-restraint dissolved and, covering the distance between them in two long strides, he took her in his arms. She was absolutely rigid and he could feel the frantic beating of her heart against his chest as he rocked her gently, shushing and soothing.

'I'm so sorry. I've ... tried ... with Charles, and ... and he ...'

'Shhh.' Very gently he kissed her mouth, silencing her. After a moment of stillness her lips parted and she was kissing him back; hesitantly, tremulously. Triumph, relief, hope pulsed through him. And desire, but he fought that down again. Sliding his fingers into her hair he moved his mouth from hers to kiss along her jawline. Pausing by her ear he took the lobe gently between his lips and breathed, 'With all due respect, Charles is an idiot.'

That was only a half of his theory, but he didn't want to go into the rest of it now, not with her delicious body arching against him, her fingers digging into his biceps as his mouth moved across her collarbone. Through the thin fabric of her dress he could see the outline of her nipples and had to brace himself as lust hit him like a sledgehammer in the gut.

'Christ, Stella. You're ... incredible ... You have nothing to prove, and you don't have to do anything that you don't want to.' With mammoth effort he lifted his head and held her close again, burying his face in her hair. 'We're going out for tea now, right? And then afterwards you can decide if you want to stay, or if you want to go back to the station. It's up to—'

She cut him off with a shake of her head. 'I don't want to go back to the station,' she said, pulling out of his embrace. 'And I don't want tea. I want you ... *this* ... But I'm scared.'

'Sweetheart, I won't hurt you.'

'I'm not scared of that.' Her eyes were like spilled ink; the dark centres blotting out most of the blue. 'I'm scared how much I want it. And ... that I won't be good enough for you.'

He shook his head, incredulous. 'I can promise you this ... You are the most magical ... the most astonishingly beautiful woman I have ever seen. Just holding you like this is setting me on fire ... The thought of undressing you ...'

He groaned and dropped his mouth to cover hers again, gathering her body into his as if he could absorb her into himself. She arched up to meet him, her hips bumping against him and the pressure on his erection was almost too much. Oh God, he mustn't rush her, but she was fumbling at the buttons of his tunic, her fingers trembling. His heart swelled with protectiveness and – less nobly – annihilating want. Without letting his lips leave hers he helped her; shrugging off his tunic, then tugging at the knot of his tie.

Slowly, for pity's sake ... Don't scare her ...

She unbuttoned his shirt and pushed it back over his shoulders, stepping back to look at him. Her hands moved slowly over the planes of his bare chest; wonderingly, reverently. She touched his silver dog-tag and let the chain slide through her

233

fingers, then moved lower, her splayed fingers spanning his ribs, her palms brushing the line of hair just beneath his navel. He stood very still, letting her touch, gritting his teeth against the longing that swamped him. When he could hold out no longer he reached for the buttons of her dress and unfastened them, forcing himself to go slow. It was like opening a parcel on Christmas day, fighting the temptation to tear off the wrappings quickly and greedily. Only when all the buttons were undone did he gently push the dress back from her shoulders so it slipped to the floor.

Christ alive. He took in the delicate, decadent peach silk underwear that had lain beneath the rather sensible dress and a moan escaped him. She hung her head, trying to cover her body with her arms. 'It's silly, I know . . . I shouldn't have . . .'

He couldn't wait any longer and couldn't begin to form an argument in words. In answer he swept her up into his arms and lowered her gently onto the bed.

They watched the squares of sky between the blast tape on the window change from forget-me-not to lavender, and the shadows across the bed stretch and slant. For a long time they didn't speak. Stella's head was on his chest, his arm around her shoulders, their legs tangled together. His fingers traced lazy arcs across her back as they drifted on their own thoughts in this new landscape.

She felt perfectly at peace. The doubts of earlier had dissolved like sinister shadows when the light is switched on. The clean, warm scent of his skin – so difficult to recapture when she wasn't with him – filled her head, and when she closed her eyes the shapes of the windowpanes turned orange and lit up the darkness. It felt like that inside her body too. A delicious languor, like nothing she had ever experienced before, spread through her, radiating outwards from somewhere deep in the centre of her. It was as if her blood had been replaced with warm honey.

Dan raised his head and kissed the curve of her shoulder. 'You OK?'

'Yes. Just wondering if I've died and gone to heaven.'

'Me too.' He smiled sleepily. 'If this is what it's like I can't see what I was so scared of all these weeks.' Altering his position, he propped himself up on his elbow so that he could look down into her face. 'You don't have to talk about it if you don't want to, but what's the story with Charles?'

Stella sighed. She hadn't had to tell him that it was her first time; it must have been obvious from her uncertainty and the way she'd tensed against the anticipated pain. She'd expected it to hurt, but it hadn't – not really. Or at least, pain was so entwined in the rush of entirely unfamiliar sensations that she hadn't registered it as being something separate. It was a bass note in the wild, crashing symphony he unleashed inside her.

'I honestly don't know.' His hair was untidy, sticking up in all directions and she smoothed it back, loving the silken feel of it between her fingers. 'I tried, I really did. Miss Birch told us all about the birds and the bees and made it sound very matter of fact so that I assumed it was something that just *happened*. When it didn't I thought it must be me; that there was

235

something I was getting wrong, or that I was trying too hard and making a fool of myself. Or that I was ... I don't know ... dirty.'

'You're exquisite.' His voice was husky as he bent his head and dropped a kiss on her breast. 'Impossibly ... distractingly ... perfect. I can prove it to you if you need a little extra reassurance ...'

She laughed, wriggling in delight as the hand that had cupped her breast moved downwards and she felt his erection against her thigh.

'Can I ask you something?' she said, suddenly remembering. 'That rubber thing – what was it?'

'French letter.' He was laying a path of kisses down her ribs. 'To stop you having a baby.' His mouth moved down to the sweep of her midriff. 'I figure that's one explanation you'd rather not have to make to Charles. Christ, you are so beautiful. I want to get to know every inch of your body ...'

He slid further down the bed, almost disappearing beneath the sheets. She stiffened as his stubbled jaw grazed her thigh. 'Dan! No! Not that bit—'

'Oh yes ... that bit's one of my favourites ... And I think you'll find it could be one of your favourites too ...'

'Dan!'

What started out as a shriek of protest somehow became a cry of pleasure. And was quickly followed by another, and another, echoing off the hotel's high and tastefully papered walls.

*

Later she hurried down to the bathroom at the end of the corridor and began to run water into the enormous old claw-foot bath. After five minutes, as the tiled walls were starting to blur and dissolve in a haze of steam she heard Dan's discreet knock and let him in.

The meagre water allowance (strenuously enforced by signs printed in capital letters, placed above the taps, on the windowsill and pinned to the back of the door) seemed more plentiful with two people. It lapped at her breasts as she lay beached on Dan's chest, and made bronzed islands of his raised knees. No sun penetrated the bathroom's tall, opaque window, and blue dusk closed around them like a tent. From through the open window voices drifted up from the kitchens; good-natured shouting and someone whistling *The White Cliffs of Dover*. The smell of cooking reminded them that they were starving and they got out of the cooling water.

As they stole back along the corridor, wrapped in thread-bare hotel towels and holding hands, an upright couple were coming towards them on their way down to dinner. He had a monocle and military bearing, she had silver hair set in Marcel waves and a green crêpe de chine evening dress. A squashed-looking fox bared its teeth and stared beadily from her shelf-like bosom. All three wore identical expressions of icy disapproval.

'Evening sir, ma'am,' Dan said, with impeccable American courtesy as they passed. They only just made it back to the room before collapsing with laughter.

'We'll probably wind up sitting at the table next to them in the dining room,' Dan said when they'd recovered enough to speak. 'Maybe we'd better find somewhere else to eat.'

'I'm afraid I don't have anything smart to wear.' Stella went over to where Dan had left her suitcase, re-securing her towel.

Dan watched her from the bed. 'You could have the smartest dress in England and you wouldn't look any more beautiful than you do now.'

She gave a snort of laughter. 'I wonder if that couple would agree?' Opening the case on the dressing-table stool she looked at its contents. The familiar, slightly mildewed smell of the Vicarage rose from their folds; the smell of home, and sadness. She took out a flower-sprigged dress and held it up.

'That's pretty,' Dan said.

'But not nearly smart enough for the dining room. It's from Ada, like most of my clothes. She thought it would be perfect for visiting Nancy's mother. I didn't think I could ask if she could lay her hands on an evening dress and some satin gloves too.'

'Hey, it doesn't matter.' Dan levered himself off the bed and pushed back his damp hair, so that it stuck up even more crazily. 'I don't want to go out to some god-awful stuffy restaurant anyway, and have to spend hours keeping my hands off you for the sake of some watery old English stew that tastes like boiled socks.' He went over to the telephone on the little writing desk and picked it up. As he waited for someone to answer he half-turned away, giving her the chance to stare at him properly without feeling self-conscious.

It was a pleasure, looking at him: a real, sensual, visceral pleasure, like eating a chocolate from one of those posh assortments, or holding your hands out to a fire on a freezing day. His body was hard-planed and golden and entirely beautiful. She'd always sensed in Charles a sort of shame in his own lividly pale, etiolated limbs, which he was at pains to keep hidden from her – unlike his distaste for her body, which he didn't bother to hide. In King's Oak Vicarage, nakedness was embarrassing, disgusting. Here it was glorious. Goosebumps spread over her skin and her empty stomach squeezed and knotted as her eyes travelled across his shoulders and down the elegant length of his back. The towel had slipped down onto his narrow hips, so she could just see a strip of paler skin beneath the gold.

'Hi, this is Lieutenant Rosinski, room 43. I was wondering if we might have some dinner sent up to the room please? Sandwiches?' He turned to Stella and gave a helpless shrug. 'Well, I guess if sandwiches are all there is, then sandwiches will do just fine.' From across the room his eyes held her. 'And if you could possibly find a bottle of champagne, that would be even better.'

He put the phone down and came towards her, a slow smile spreading across his face as he gently pulled the towel off.

'There. You're dressed perfectly for dinner.' He pulled her towards the bed. 'May I show you to your table?'

18

Three days. Not even that; two and a half. Not much, out of a whole lifetime, but Stella knew that every moment would stay with her. It was a turning point, the end of one era and the start of a new one. It was the time at which she stopped being a passive being, controlled by others, and became herself.

They talked. His gentle questioning unearthed fragments of her past that she'd all but forgotten, which, when pieced together gave her a clearer picture of herself. Nancy was the person who knew her best in the world, but for the first time Stella began to see herself without the filter of Nancy's gaze and started to feel that she existed outside the slot into which Nancy had placed her; the compartment labelled 'safe, cautious, conventional'. With Dan she was fearless, adventurous. *Sexy.*

They played cards. He taught her poker, and let her win the first few games. And then he introduced her to the idea of strip poker, and mysteriously her luck seemed to run out.

They made love. She found it almost incomprehensible how something as astonishing as sex could have existed all this time without her knowing about it. Discovering it was like being given the key to paradise. She felt lit up inside, golden and glowing. But maybe that wasn't sex, she thought. Maybe that was love.

They explored the city. In the syrupy July warmth they walked along narrow streets between ancient, honey-coloured buildings and ducked through ornate gateways to peer into college courtyards. It was a glimpse into another world, one which would have made her feel excluded and inferior if she hadn't been with Dan. He was a foreigner, and yet he seemed perfectly at home. With an arm draped around her shoulders and a cigarette hanging from his bottom lip he pointed out details on beautiful buildings and told her their names. *Cupola. Oriel. Pilaster.* He photographed them, and her, making her giggle and blossom under his warm, appreciative gaze.

He bought a postcard showing different views of Cambridge and scrawled a message to his father on the back. *In one of the most beautiful cities in Europe with the most beautiful girl in the world. Who said war was all bad?* In a cobbled street in the shadow of one of the city's many churches they queued for sausage rolls in a butcher's shop and bought strawberries from a stall in the market square. Carrying these treasures they made their way towards the river. In a hotel beside the greenish water Dan persuaded the landlord to sell him a bottle of wine, and they picnicked beneath the drooping branches of a willow, feeding each other strawberries, sucking the sweetness from their fingers and kissing the juice from their lips.

Afterwards they lay together, hidden by the acid–green curtains of leaves and dozed. Punts slid past, mostly piloted by American servicemen whose voices floated across the water. On the opposite bank was a little row of whitewashed cottages, their windows open against the hot afternoon. A woman in a red headscarf was working in the garden of one of them. Drowsily Stella watched her picking beans and dropping them into a bowl. A few moments later she carried it inside and in her mind Stella followed her, picturing a simple kitchen with a stone-flagged floor and a range, a pine table with its surface scrubbed white. She'd just added a jug of flowers – delphiniums and stocks – on a dresser, when Dan said, 'Penny for them?'

'Those houses over there. I was just imagining what they must be like inside.' It was the kind of banal thought she would have felt stupid sharing with Charles. Not that he would have ever asked anyway.

'Nancy told me that you always wanted a house.' He was stroking her hair, picking it up and running it through his fingers. 'She said that whenever you got the chance to have a wish – like blowing the candles out on your birthday cake or something – that was what you always wished for. A house of your own.'

'We didn't have birthday cakes with candles, but we used to find all kinds of excuses to make a wish. If you saw a black cat you made a wish, and when there was a new moon. Another one was if you ever said something at exactly the same time as someone else, and whenever you crossed a bridge . . .' She smiled, remembering. 'Nancy always wanted something different – a box of rose and violet creams, or a particular boy to like her – but I always wished for the same thing.'

The sun glittered between the leaves. In this tent of shimmering green, London and her old life seemed very far away; far enough to give her a detached kind of overview on it. She thought back to Charles's stiff, business-like proposal and her own grateful acceptance.

'I think that's why I agreed to marry Charles, so I'd have a house of my own to keep. I wanted to make jam and sew pretty cushion covers and put little jugs of flowers on every surface. I wanted a baby in a little swinging crib with a patchwork quilt I'd made myself. Not much of an ambition, was it?'

'I don't know,' he said softly. 'Having a family and creating a home, giving them the kind of love and security you never had yourself . . . I think that's a pretty good ambition to have.'

'It's just a shame I didn't realize how impossible it would be to fulfil in St Crispin's Vicarage with Charles.'

Across the river the woman in the red headscarf had come outside again. She was carrying a cup of tea and what looked like a newspaper or magazine and she sat on a bench beneath the kitchen window and began to read.

'So, where would it be, your perfect house?' Dan asked, his fingers still sifting her hair. She was glad he'd steered the conversation away from the Vicarage. The day was too perfect to be soured. She closed her eyes and luxuriated in his touch, like a cat being stroked.

'I don't know – I never really thought about that. An ordinary house in an ordinary street, I suppose. Nothing grand.'

'I always wanted to build my own house right by the ocean,' he said sleepily. 'A house like you've never seen before, with big open rooms and glass walls so that you could see all of the horizon.'

She tried to picture it in the dappled, gold-splashed darkness behind her closed eyes. 'Go on.'

'The floors would be all wood, but pale wood – beech probably, or birch – and the walls would be white, to reflect the colours of the sky and the sea. The rooms would flow into each other and everything would be spacious and open, so you could really breathe.'

'Wouldn't it be cold?'

'No. The sun would stream in and warm it up. And in winter there'd be a fire. Right in the centre of the living room. Raised up a little.'

'Oh, that's good . . .' She was smiling as she added this detail to the image in her head. 'With a soft rug in front of it?'

'If you put one there.'

'I would. A big one. It might be fur. Yes . . . white fur.'

They were quiet for a moment. His breathing was soft, his body warm and solid against hers.

'White fur. Mmm . . . I like the sound of that. And I'd make love to you on it, right there in the firelight.'

She tipped her head back to kiss him, and murmured, 'I like the sound of that too.'

On their last day the mood changed. Like a cloud stealing across the sun the brightness left them. Their voices were more subdued, the silences longer, and there was a new intensity to their lovemaking. They woke in the early morning and Dan drew back the curtains and raised the blackout so that they could see the sun rise over the city's spires and domes and let its rosy light wash over the bed. He showed her how to sit astride him, so she could look down into his face as she moved her hips. Their gazes fused. He kept one hand on her waist, guiding her, and with the other, worked his gentle, expert magic. Her orgasm gripped her like a lightning strike, and she collapsed onto his chest. He gathered her up into his arms and cradled her as, inexplicably, she cried.

In the aftermath she felt fragile, shaken. The atmosphere between them was achingly tender as they went out into the sunlit morning and, by some unspoken, instinctive agreement, headed away from the city's heart, wanting to leave behind the streets filled with people and noise and uniforms. Reaching the river, they followed its course south-west.

In King's Oak the summer meant snapdragons and sweet peas in Alf Broughton's garden, the smell of hot tarmac and the shrill voices of children playing in the street long into the blue dusk. Here the season was marked by rippling fields of greenish gold, and trees as big and cool as cathedrals. There was a stillness that seemed timeless, and reassuring. They found a pretty pub, with a slightly wild garden that sloped down to the riverbank, and had a lunch of cheese and home-made bread at a wooden table with ducks dozing beneath it. The only other customers were two elderly farm-hands silently supping cider on a bench by the door.

Stella watched Dan walk through the long grass, ducking beneath the low branches of an apple tree choked with hon-eysuckle, carrying the drinks he'd just bought at the bar. He set them carefully down on the table, which lurched at a dis-tinctly drunken angle: a pint of beer for him, a half for her.

'Thank you.' She dipped her finger in the creamy froth at the top of the glass. 'I've cost you a fortune, with all this wining and dining.'

He looked around the unkempt garden, with its uncut grass and buttercups and tangled streamers of honeysuckle, and held up his hands in mock despair. 'Yeah, you're a real expensive date. I'm bankrupting myself here trying to keep up with your excessive demands.'

'I'm being serious!'

'Well, don't be.' He picked up his beer and took a long mouthful, then looked at her. 'You don't have to worry about it. Money isn't a problem. But even if it was . . .' He smiled that crooked, rueful, beautiful smile. 'Even if it was, I'd have sold everything I had for these few days. They say you can't buy happiness, but . . .' He looked away, out across the river to the humming shadows beneath the trees on the bank, and shook his head, struggling for words. 'Jeez, Stella . . .'

The tenuous laughter of a moment ago was smashed,

swamped, swept away by a tidal wave of emotion. Across the table their hands touched, clasped tightly, as if across a void.

'What are we going to do?'

He sighed. 'Carry on as before, I guess. I have nine missions left to fly before my tour ends. Depending on the weather and the mood of the guys in charge it might be two weeks or two months.'

Or never. He didn't say it, but it was there. A fact. An obscenity, too appalling to acknowledge. From the deep, black waters at the back of her mind questions surfaced about odds and statistics and current expectations. She drowned them all.

'And then what will happen?'

'In the normal run of things I'd get sent home, given a few weeks to rest up, and then get sent around the good old US of A selling war bonds or something.' He let go of her hand, picked up his pint and drank. 'I'm going to apply to stay here. To transfer to a different squadron or fly with rookie crews or something. Anything. I'm not much of a cook, but hell, I could have a go at that too, if it meant they'd let me stick around.'

'The war brought us together, but it's going to keep us apart too. The unfairness of that makes me—' Her breath caught awkwardly in her throat, in a sort of silent sob.

'I know.'

Long moments passed. She took a mouthful of beer and, putting the glass down again, traced patterns in the condensation clouding its sides. She didn't want to look at him because she knew that she would cry. The future had unfurled itself before them. In the distance there was happiness – the house he was going to build on the beach, the fur rug in front of the fire – but it was on the other side of a vast chasm. Crossing it safely seemed impossible.

'What about me? What shall I do? I don't want to be married to Charles any more. Life is too short and love too precious to waste in pretending.'

'Will he agree to a divorce?'

Stella considered this for a moment before answering. 'I think he has to. I mean, I know the whole sanctity of marriage thing is important to him, but it's obvious he doesn't even like me very much, never mind love me. I noticed it last time he came home, when he brought Peter to stay, and it struck me that he's never looked at me or spoken to me with anything like the warmth he shows to him. And he can't go on pretending that ours is a normal, happy marriage when it's obvious he finds touching me as appealing as stroking a slug. I think even he would have to agree that the whole thing has been a rather terrible mistake.'

'This Peter guy . . . You told me about him in your letter. He and Charles seem pretty close.'

'Oh yes, they knew each other from theological college, long before I met Charles. They used to go on fishing holidays together.'

She said it in a way that was supposed to make him laugh, but his face stayed thoughtful. Serious.

'It was quite a coincidence, them being on leave at the same time, and then meeting up at the station like that.'

'Yes . . .' Stella felt her smile falter. She'd said the same thing to Charles at the time, but he had snapped that she was being ridiculous; thousands of military personnel passed through Victoria every day. She had shut up then, and not bothered to explain that that was what she'd meant; that the chance of them bumping into each other in the flood of people seemed so small.

Across the table Dan drained his beer and put the glass down carefully. 'It's just a hunch, but something about what you said in your letter got me thinking . . .' He looked up at her with a wry smile. 'And finding out that Charles isn't driven wild with desire for you has got me thinking a whole lot more. I might be wrong . . . but I'd say the marriage may not have been a mistake, exactly. More of a . . . smokescreen.'

'What do you mean?'

He took a packet of Lucky Strikes out of his pocket and slid one out. He knew her well enough not to offer her one now. 'There are some men – women too, come to that – who aren't attracted to the opposite sex, but to their own. It's more common than you might think.'

'But . . . but isn't that against the law?'

'Yep.' He paused to light the cigarette, cupping his hand around the lighter flame, then continuing as he snuffed it out again. 'But there isn't a legal system in the world that can control people's feelings. And if I'm right about Charles, I guess that's why he felt the need to marry, so he could carry on feeling how the hell he likes in private. Hey, I might be completely on the wrong page, but—'

'No . . .' Stella was distracted, fascinated. It felt like she'd been stumbling around in a landscape where everything was blurred and indistinct and he'd just given her a pair of spectacles that brought it all into focus. 'It all fits, including why he asked me to marry him in the first place. He obviously knew I was stupid and naïve enough not to suspect anything. And since then, he's used that to make me believe that I was to blame for everything that was wrong in our marriage.'

Dan took a long, deep lungful of smoke and exhaled slowly. 'It doesn't change much, though. You're still married.'

'At least I understand now. Actually, I feel rather sorry for him – I've always sensed how unhappy he is, deep down. I thought it was all tied up in his calling, and his belief that he somehow wasn't good enough to please God, or his parents. But now I can see . . . How horrible it must be, loving someone and wanting to be with them forever, and knowing that it's hopeless.'

He looked at her through the haze of blue. 'Like us, you mean?'

'No.' She stood up and went around to his side of the table. Moving his empty glass to one side she hitched herself up so that she was sitting in front of him on the rough wood, then leaned forward and took his face between her hands. 'It's not hopeless for us. Charles tricked me into a charade of a marriage under false pretences. There's nothing he can do to make me stay now. All you have to do is come through this safely. *Alive*.'

It sounded so simple. In the damp green garden, with the

scent of honeysuckle and rank earth and the river, and her face only inches from his, it was obvious. Stay alive. He'd almost believed it was possible.

But the 3 a.m. demons had woken him again, trailing their icy fingers down his back and whispering their sour-breathed truths in his ear. *Two out of three airmen don't live to see the end of their tour. Losses in the Group currently standing at seventy-two per cent after seventeen missions.* The faces of crewmen he no longer saw in the mess hall emerged from the darkness at the edges of the room and crowded around the bed. There was the ball-turret gunner who'd taken the hit on the milk run to Fruges, the side of his head a bloody pulp as it had been when Dan had watched him get carried off the plane; the pilot and co-pilot of *Sweet Georgia Brown* whom he'd last seen through the glass of the cockpit before their ship spiralled downwards, engulfed in flame.

Sweat drenched his body and his heart punched his ribs. Beneath the sheets his legs twitched from the flood of adrenaline. He turned his head on the pillow, inhaling the scent of Stella's hair like oxygen, listening to the sound of her breathing and trying to hold on to its slow rhythm. He wanted to pull her into his arms and bury his face in her neck, knowing that she'd turn to him and wrap herself around him and allow him to lose himself in her again. Instead he sat up and, taking care not to wake her, slipped out of bed.

In the afterglow of a bone-melting orgasm sleep had come easily, but he knew that it wouldn't be back tonight and it wasn't fair to keep her awake too. In the darkness of the blackout he groped for his cigarettes and went over to the window. Raising the blind a couple of inches he saw that the sky was the smudged grey blue of the hour before dawn, the city still folded in its shadows. He lit a cigarette, noticing the tremor of his hand in the lighter's flame.

As she'd said herself, none of it was fair. The war. People in Europe being herded into camps because of the family they were born into and the building in which they worshipped. Flak that whistled past one boy's shoulder and hit another right in the head. Him bringing her here, sleeping with her, talking about a future he knew damned well wasn't his to promise.

Things were happening; the whole USAAF was alive with rumour and speculation. Meetings had been held, new strategies decided. Fresh crews had been arriving to take up the empty beds at Palingthorpe and all the other bases. An announcement had been made about the Combined Bomber Offensive, which was to see American and Brit flyboys harness their efforts and rain bombs down on Germany day and night, to destroy the Nazis' military, industrial and economic strength. It sounded great, until you remembered that the Nazis were pretty shit hot at trying to stop that kind of thing, and the only reason new crews were being trained up and spat out onto the ground so fast was because the guys in those meetings knew they'd be needed. Because they knew what the losses were going to be like.

In the bed Stella sighed and stirred. Light was seeping into the sky; cool and pearly but enough to bring her face into focus, like a photograph developing in a darkroom. His heart squeezed. It was nothing new for him to be awake in the small hours and thinking of her. Over the months since he'd met her, since he'd started flying and watching ships fall out of the sky and men get shot to pieces or consumed by fire, she'd been his safe place. It had been her letters, her voice, her smile he'd focused on when the demons whispered and the adrenaline wouldn't stop pumping. She'd been his escape from the fear of dying.

Now she was the biggest reason for it.

He looked over to where she lay in the wreckage of the hotel's immaculate bed, the sheets twisted around her naked body, her hair spread across the pillow. And in that moment he almost wished he'd never found that watch.

'Our bed. I can't bear the thought of other people sleeping in it. Making love in it, when we're miles apart from each other.'

The covers were pulled straight and tight, the blue satin eiderdown retrieved from the floor and placed neatly on top. The room was respectable again. Neutral. It was impossible to tell that for three days it had been their whole world, and the setting for such joy.

He had saved the treats he had brought to give to her now, to lighten this moment of parting, and took out nylons and chocolate from the bottom of his kitbag, and tins of pineapple. There was two of everything – 'For you and for Nancy,' he explained. 'To thank her for being on our side.'

Stella's throat felt sore with the effort of not crying. She didn't want their last moments alone together to be tainted by sadness, and made a convincing attempt at a smile.

'I'm sure Nancy will be keen for us to visit her mother as often as possible for all those treasures. Will we be able to do this again soon?'

'I hope so.'

She nodded, glimpsing the continent of uncertainty that lay beneath his words, and understanding. 'If this is all there is . . . If these three days are all we ever have . . . I want you to know, they were enough. Enough happiness to feed off for a lifetime.'

He kissed her, fiercely, as if he was trying to imprint himself on her. When they finally fell away from each other her cheeks were wet with tears.

'This isn't all there is,' he said, gently wiping them away with his fingertips. 'Letters. We still have letters. Whatever happens, just keep writing, OK?'

19

Sweetheart

I got back to the base an hour ago. It's 6 p.m. and I have the hut to myself since everyone else is either in the bar or the ablutions block taking a shower before heading out to the pub in the village. Lying here I can just about catch the scent of your skin on mine. It's just as well I'm alone because the others would think I'm crazy.

Johnson tells me I haven't missed much. There's been cloud over Europe and not much flying. Too bad. I was hoping they'd have nailed the Nazi bastards while I was away.

I love you. Look after yourself for me.

D x

26 July '43

Darling Stella

A couple of days ago the sun came out, as the weather guys predicted it would. We're back in the air. They seem to be ready to pull out all the stops, which hopefully means things will start to move in the right direction now. It should also mean that I rack up these last few missions quickly. We've done two in as many days and we're on the list again tomorrow. I guess they won't keep scheduling us to go up like that as we're all pretty tired, but I'd fly all day and all night if it meant getting to the end of my tour quicker.

There's no time to think of anything on the way out or when we're over the target, but it's when we're headed home it always feels like I'm flying right back to you.

Take care sweetheart, for me.

D x.

Darling girl,

Your letter was waiting here when we got back today. I didn't even wait until after the debriefing to open it.

I guess he had to get Embarkation Leave sometime. Fourteen days sure seems like a long time, but it's nothing, not really, I promise you. It'll pass, and when it has and he's gone I might be finished my twenty-five. We're nearly there. Now is not the right time to tell him about us, not when he's going away – it wouldn't be fair. Also, with any luck he'll give you up without a fight, but right now there's not a damn thing I could do about it if he didn't. Just two weeks. Hang on in there, beautiful girl. Send him off with a smile and we'll sort everything out properly when he gets back.

The war has to be over soon. These missions we're doing are big ones, and from twenty thousand feet up they look pretty damned successful. After what happened in North Africa it sure feels like the tide is turning in our favor.

I know it's going to be hard for you to write me when Charles is home so don't worry about it. It sure is good of Nancy to offer her services as delivery girl – I still had her address from that first time. I'll write whenever I can, I promise, and I know that you're thinking of me.

Johnson's wife had her baby – the flight chief was standing on the control tower waving a blue towel when we landed today. A boy. Mother and baby both doing well back home in Ohio. I don't think I ever saw anyone so happy. So you see, that's another reason why we have to stay safe and finish up real soon.

I love you, and I'm counting down the days until we can be together. Look after yourself for me.

D x

28 July '43

Sweetheart,

Sorry this is going to be a short one. It's late and I'm on standby again for tomorrow, though it seems we only just got back from today's mission. It was the longest and the toughest I've ever done. Our target was ▮▮▮▮▮ *and when we got there we could see that the RAF boys had been there before us. The city was pretty much on fire. Even from 10,000 feet up we could feel the heat.* ▮▮▮▮▮▮▮▮▮▮▮▮▮▮▮

▮▮▮▮▮ *We watched the crews to either side of us bail out.*

▮▮▮▮▮▮▮▮▮▮▮▮▮▮▮▮▮▮

▮▮▮▮▮▮▮▮▮▮▮▮▮▮▮▮▮▮

▮▮▮▮▮▮▮ *I guess I'm lucky to be here.*

I think about you all the time, though it doesn't bring me the same kind of peace as usual, knowing that he's with you. I hope he's treating you well. He doesn't know how lucky he is.

I love you. Take care of yourself for me.

Dan x

Jess's head pounded and her hand was shaking too much to put the letter back in its envelope. It had crept up on her while she'd been reading, this feeling, stealthy and sinister as sea fog, and now it engulfed her, swallowing up familiar landmarks so there was nothing else but her aching body. The black, blanked-out lines of the letter spread across her vision. Still holding it, she lay back on the bed and closed her eyes.

They were almost there. Neither Dan nor Stella knew for sure that he would survive his twenty-five missions, but Jess did. She knew that he would live to the grand old age of ninety, in a house on the beach in Maine. Without her. So what had happened?

Beside her on the bed the box of letters offered up its secrets. The afternoon light was still bright enough to read, but it was too bright for her eyes, which burned behind her closed lids. Her throat felt like she'd swallowed rusty razor blades. She longed for hot coffee to soothe the pain, or even water, but couldn't face the thought of going downstairs. She was cold. So very, very cold. Moving from the warm hollow she'd made on the bed was out of the question.

Whimpering slightly she pushed down the pink bedcover. The blankets beneath felt impossibly heavy and tight and gave off the chill breath of the tomb, but she slid beneath them, still fully clothed. Every muscle screamed a protest at the movement, and so she tucked up her knees and lay very still, waiting for the pain in her head to subside and the shivering to stop.

'I brought you a coffee. Thought you might need it.' Bex set a cardboard carton from the coffee chain across the road on Will's desk and looked down at him with eyes full of compassion. 'You all right?'

Will dredged up a crooked smile. Having discovered that one whole branch of the Grimwood family tree had been signed up by a rival company, Ansell had been on particularly bruising form this morning and, as usual, Will had taken the flak. It hadn't been pretty.

'I'm marvellous, thank you. Never better. After all, I had Sunday lunch with my parents. My ace-barrister brother was there, with his ace-barrister fiancée and my father's sarcasm is always particularly biting after half a bottle of Chateauneuf, so I'm at the top of my game when it comes to dealing with ritual humiliation. A day in the office with Ansell is like a picnic in the park in comparison.'

Bex gave a sympathetic cluck. 'Don't you get on with your brother, then?'

Will considered this for a moment as he took a sip of his coffee. It was a latte, full fat; a calorific habit he had vowed to give up, but he didn't have the heart to tell Bex that. 'You don't so much "get on" with Simon as bow down before him and pay homage to his brilliance. I'm not sure he has friends, exactly. There are probably other barristers and maybe the odd brain surgeon that he plays squash with or − providing their girlfriends have a brand of handbag Marina approves of − goes out to dinner with in very, very expensive restaurants, but I'm not sure they're what you or I would call friends.' He took another mouthful of coffee and added gloomily, 'I suppose I shall find out at the wedding.'

It was lunchtime and the office was quiet. Ansell, in punchy and belligerent form had, with typical insensitivity, borne Barry off to the pub.

'Is Marina his fiancée? When are they getting married then?'

'April.'

'Oooh, nice,' Bex said admiringly, hitching one black-stockinged thigh onto his desk. 'A spring wedding. Where are they having it?'

'My parents' house. In some kind of incredibly elaborate marquee affair. Marina's father owns half of Scotland and they would have had it at one of his castles, but they decided that it was too far for their busy and important friends to travel.'

'Wicked.' Bex didn't really get irony. Her false lashes quivered in awe, like the wings of some exotic butterfly. 'So, are you best man then? Him being your brother and all?'

Will almost snorted coffee out of his nose at the ridiculousness of the suggestion. 'God, no! The whole wedding is pitched to impress — as the big day approaches I'm half expecting him to issue me with a gagging order to stop me opening my mouth in front of his top-notch colleagues. I gather there was a handful of possible candidates for best man, and the eventual winner was selected on the grounds that he was president of the Oxford debating society so will give a clever speech, and will also look good in the photographs.'

'Not too good, I 'ope.' Bex giggled, finally catching on. 'Your brother wouldn't like it if he was better looking than 'im.'

'It probably hasn't entered Simon's head that there could possibly be anyone better looking than him.'

Bex stood up, but as she did so she nudged the computer mouse on Will's desk and woke up the screen. Glancing at it, she frowned. 'Oh Will, what are you like? That's not the

Grimwood file, that's the one we shelved – Nancy Price. You won't find any of Stanley Grimwood's relatives in the records of –' she leaned closer to read the name at the top of the screen – 'Woodhill Charitable School, you daft so-and-so.'

She leaned right over him, practically suffocating him in her magnificent cleavage (reminding him, bizarrely, of bobbing for apples when he was a boy). Clicking Nancy Price's file shut she typed 'Grimwood' in the search box, her rhinestone-trimmed nails clipping on the keys like Wellington the Labrador's claws did on the flagstoned floor at home. A new file appeared on screen.

'There. Grimwood. Remember, the Ipswich lot have already been signed, so we're not bothered about them. It's the cousins on the paternal side you're working on now, basing the search around Canvey Island.' Straightening up she looked down at him with an air of benevolent frustration. 'Honestly, you are a case.'

'Aren't I ?' Will said, not meeting her eye.

The afternoon delivered, like a great big gift from the gods of serendipity, a trip to the registry office in Cheshunt. It was four o'clock by the time Will had collected the relevant birth certificate and phoned the information through to Barry. Too late to battle through traffic right across London to get back to the office.

He passed a petrol station on the way out of town and turned in to feed the ever-hungry Spitfire. He was pretty hungry himself, but standing in the queue to pay in the kiosk he deliberately averted his eyes from the display of sweets and chocolate. There had, of course, been the obligatory ribbing about his weight on Sunday. His father, leaning back to show off his trim stomach – the result of a pre-TV series diet and twice weekly sessions with a personal trainer – had commented that he knew of an extremely good upholsterer if Will needed a new suit for the wedding. Everybody had found it immoderately amusing. Will's efforts in the leisure centre gym that morning had suddenly seemed pitifully inadequate. And not only in the actual gym. His attempt at a chat-up line had been pretty pitiful too.

That failure stung more than the jibes from his family. He'd driven to Oxfordshire with his fists clenched around the steering wheel and the black dog of despair panting down his neck, fighting the urge to turn the Spitfire round and roar back to London to seek her out. And then what? Apologize for getting wrong what he'd wanted so badly to get right and ask her to give him a second chance, he supposed. Find out what it was she was afraid of. In fact, finding out her name would be a good start, given the amount of time he seemed to spend thinking about her.

And thinking about her brought him right back to the place he'd first seen her, outside Nancy Price's house, which reminded him of the promise he'd made to Albert Greaves. He did a quick mental calculation: Church End wasn't far off his route, he could call in on the old man on his way home and use the key he held to have a look inside Nancy Price's house. His furtive trawl through the records earlier had confirmed that there really was no solid information to go on, and (much as he hated to admit it) Ansell had probably been right to drop the case. No money, no heirs – it was a complete non-starter. All that Will could do was contact the council and see that the estate was dealt with officially, though he had a feeling such an impersonal dispersal of his friend's effects wouldn't go down well with Albert.

The queue shuffled forwards, and he found himself standing next to a display of cakes and biscuits. On impulse he picked up a couple of packets – perhaps Mr Kipling's exceedingly cheap cakes might sweeten the disappointment. Of course, there was always the possibility that he might find something significant inside the house; something that would change everything, like a mattress stuffed with money and an address book bulging with relatives ...

Or not, he thought wryly. Miracles might happen, but only to other people.

20

1943

Stella was waiting by the sitting-room window, looking out for Nancy. In the street a pack of boys were playing some complicated game involving milk bottles half-filled with soil and piles of stones. With the school holidays well underway they had a grimy, feral appearance. As Nancy rounded the corner by the church they shrank into the shadows beneath a blowsy buddleia in Alf Broughton's garden, pressing themselves against the fence as she passed.

Stella grabbed her handbag and ran to the front door, disturbing the stillness of the empty house. When the dates for Charles's Embarkation Leave had come through, Reverend Stokes had tactfully announced he would go to visit an old friend from his teaching days, and her protests that this was unnecessary fell (very literally) on deaf ears. Without the wireless playing all day at high volume the Vicarage seemed eerily quiet.

Nancy jolted to an alarmed standstill on the path as Stella appeared.

'Blimey, you look like a prisoner on the run. I thought you said he was away?'

'He is. I was looking out for you, that's all. Didn't want to miss the bus.'

'Wanted to find out if I've got a letter for you, more like,' Nancy said, throwing Stella an arch look as they started walking. 'Sorry to disappoint. Nothing today, but you know what the bleeding post is like. Probably three'll arrive together tomorrow.'

Stella nodded mutely, blinking back tears. Without being conscious of it she had been keeping herself going for the last two days on a combination of hope and excitement, and having both removed so abruptly left her feeling like a puppet whose strings had been cut. As they passed the lurking boys Nancy took her arm and gave it an encouraging squeeze.

'Now, no moping allowed. You got to stay positive; look on the bright side. Smile, smile, smile, as the old song goes.'

Of course, she was right, Stella thought bleakly. The whole world was missing someone, mourning someone. It was horribly self-indulgent to brood, not to mention boring for everyone else. She forced her mouth into a smile.

'Too right. It's not often we get a whole afternoon together these days. And you look gorgeous – is that a new coat?'

'D'you like it?' Nancy looked smug and secretive, dropping Stella's arm to pull the belt of the gabardine trench coat a little tighter and putting her hands in the pockets like a mannequin. 'Len got it for me. God knows where it came from, but ask no questions, get told no lies. Got friends all over the place, Len has. I'm dying for you to meet him. You'll get on like a house on fire. A right charmer, he is.'

Stella didn't doubt that, but she was less sure about the house on fire bit. From what she could make out, Nancy's new man was a bit of a shady character. He'd been wounded at Dunkirk – a collapsed lung, according to Nancy – which prevented him from going back into uniform. Now he was working in something that was 'very hush hush'. Stella suspected it was the black market.

'It's a gorgeous coat. Really elegant. Makes you look like Katharine Hepburn.'

Nancy patted her hair. 'That's what Len said too. So where's the Rev gone then? To see his lah-di-dah parents?'

'No, Devon. To visit Peter Underwood.'

Charles had announced his intention to spend 'a few days' of his fortnight's Embarkation Leave in Devon quite casually: in fact, the naïve, gullible, pre-Cambridge Stella wouldn't even have noticed the slight note of defiance in his tone or the defensive set to his jaw, never mind understanding what they signified.

'Oh well, it's given you a bit of breathing space. How's it been, you know, since he's been back?'

They were the only people at the bus stop, which meant Stella didn't have to lie. 'Awkward,' she sighed. 'I know he's got a lot on his mind, but he won't share any of it with me.

Sometimes I wonder if he's forgotten he married me and thinks I'm still his housekeeper.'

'Blimey.' Nancy's pencilled brows shot upwards. 'No bedroom action?'

Stella shook her head. She wished she'd been honest from the start about the fact that there'd never been any 'bedroom action' in their marriage, but felt it was too late to confess that now.

'He's either shut away in his study or in the church. I went across there yesterday when he didn't appear for supper and found him crouched on the altar steps. He was sort of . . . collapsed. I thought for a minute he was having a heart attack, but it turned out he was just praying.'

The episode – his fervour and his despair – had reminded her of their wedding night, only this time she understood. With the benefit of her new insight she felt huge sympathy for him, almost tenderness. She would have liked to reach out to him, offer him comfort and a human ear to listen, but his coldness made it impossible.

'Praying? What for?'

'God knows.'

The joke was lost on Nancy, who was looking past her to the end of the road.

'Ooh, good – here's the bus. So what do you want to do first, shops or cinema?'

The house was as quiet and still as ever when she got back. Shutting the front door she stood for a second in the hall, watching the dust motes swirl in a shaft of light from the sitting room and breathing in the mildewed smell that she'd never succeeded in changing. Then she put down her bag on the hallstand and went into the kitchen to make a cup of tea.

She moved automatically, without being aware of what she was doing, so that when she went to spoon tea into the pot she couldn't remember if she'd done it already. Despite the silence of the house her head was full of noise; the noise of engines roaring, planes thundering forwards and taking off.

Dan's kind of planes. They'd been on the newsreel again, before the film started, and she'd watched in an agony of hunger and hope and horror for a glimpse of the redhead in the sparkly shoes on the side of one. '*Every morning at airfields all across the east of England our American allies are taking up the baton from the RAF,*' the voice-over had announced in clipped tones, over incongruously cheery music. '*As our Lancaster Bombers return from night raids on the centre of Germany's war industry, the American B-17s are setting out to keep up the pressure. There is no let-up. Aerial photographs show the results; seven square miles of Hamburg's war centre virtually wiped off the map. As the squadrons return, the gaping holes in many a bomber are testament to the intensity of German fighter resistance.*'

Stella's eyes had burned. She wanted to stand up, to scream at the people whispering and passing bags of sweets along the row to shut up as the camera hovered over jagged holes torn in the side of planes, shattered glass, painted ladies riddled with bullet holes. It had closed in on a crew lowering an injured man from the hatch. '*Morale amongst these brave men remains high as the effectiveness of this combined offensive becomes clear. They won't stop until the job is done.*'

The rest of the film had passed in a blur. The actors could have been speaking in Chinese for all she took in of the plot, though she was glad of the darkness of the cinema and the respite from having to talk to Nancy of normal things and smile. She'd squeezed her eyes shut and called out to him inside her head, hoping she could somehow make him hear her, let him know that she was thinking of him. Loving him. She remembered with absolute clarity how it had felt to lie on his chest in the bed in Cambridge. He had seemed so strong. But he was made of skin and bone and muscle, like everyone else, and those things could be so easily shattered and torn apart. He was fragile. Fragile and so precious . . .

Oh God, where was he? He'd promised to write – why had no letters reached her?

Outside, inky clouds were massing above the rooftops and the summer afternoon had taken on a bilious yellow tint. She'd washed the sheets from Reverend Stokes's bed and they hung on the line, glowing eerily in the acid light. Listlessly she went outside to unpeg them. The air was still and sulphurous. She carried the sheets inside and, taking them upstairs, draped them over the banisters to dry completely in the way that Charles hated. He considered it vulgar to have laundry on display.

As she came down again the light in the hall had turned purple and yellow, like a bruise. A shaft fell across the picture of the Virgin Mary on the wall, making her face look sickly and liverish. In the moment that she turned to look at it again something caught her attention. A sound, nothing she could name; a breath perhaps, or the creak of movement. She froze, the hairs rising on the back of her neck.

A few feet away the door to Charles's study was ajar. Had it been earlier, when she'd left to go out with Nancy? With a hammering heart she went towards it and pushed it open, thinking as she did so that she should have armed herself with something – a candlestick from the dining room was the thing that came to mind – in case an intruder was hiding in there. So vivid was the image of a sinister stranger pressed against the wall behind the door that it took her a stunned second to process what she was really seeing.

'Charles!' Her hand flew to her mouth. 'You ... You're back! I didn't know – I mean, I didn't expect you until tomorrow at least!'

He was sitting at his desk, and swung the chair round towards her. There was something skull-like about his face; the skin was stretched tight across his cheekbones and his eyes were sunk into black hollows. It shocked her.

'I came back early. As you can see.'

'Is – is everything all right?'

'Perfectly.' His peculiar, bland smile didn't falter. It was as if it had been nailed on. 'You were out when I got back.'

'Oh, yes. Yes, I went out with Nancy. Just uptown – we had tea at the Kardomah in Piccadilly and then saw a film. Gary Cooper and Ingrid Bergman – not terribly gripping.'

271

She was babbling guiltily, as if she had done something wrong in going out, but as she spoke she noticed a glass on the desk, amongst the scattered papers. A glass containing amber-coloured liquid that she would have been certain was whisky or brandy if it wasn't for the fact that Charles never drank. 'I was just making a cup of tea – would you like one?'

She fled to the kitchen and got another cup down with shaking hands. Something must have happened – something terrible – but what? Had he somehow found out about Dan? Her mind swept the possibilities like a searchlight: had she left a letter lying around before she'd gone out? She dismissed the idea – the last letter had been four days ago, and was now tucked safely into a nightdress case and hidden at the back of a drawer; her underwear drawer, the contents of which were so distasteful to Charles that he would never open it. Which brought her face to face with the other possible reason for Charles turning to drink.

Peter.

She poured the tea and carried a cup through to him. He was sitting where she'd left him, but the glass was now empty. She wondered whether to take it away when she put down the tea, but thought better of it, not wanting him to feel that she was reproaching him.

'I thought perhaps an early supper . . . ? There isn't much, but you must be hungry after travelling all the way from Devon . . .'

'Thank you.'

It was a dismissal. She went back to the kitchen and began

to tidy it, since there seemed little point in laying the table in the dining room for powdered scrambled eggs. Outside the rain had begun to fall, washing away the other-worldly light and replacing it with an underwater gloom. When the eggs were cooked (though it was always difficult to tell and seemed to make little difference to the taste) she called down the passageway to him. She spread oily margarine onto the toast and was spooning egg on top of it when he appeared.

In spite of everything her heart went out to him. His eyelids were swollen and his sandy hair was sticking up where he'd pushed his fingers into it. His dog collar was askew, as if he'd wrestled to loosen it. 'Sit down,' she said, setting a plate in front of him. 'I'll just get a jug of water. Unless – well, unless you'd like something else? Something stronger?'

'Of course not.'

He picked up his fork and began, mechanically, to eat. No Grace. No comment on the dismal food. Surreptitiously Stella watched him, longing to know what had happened but unsure how to ask. As the silence stretched, broken only by the clatter and scrape of cutlery and the rain on the window, she said cautiously, 'How was Peter?'

'Well. Peter was . . . very well.'

'Has he heard if he's to be sent overseas again?'

Charles laid down his knife and fork, his mouth twisting in a bitter parody of a smile. 'No, he's not going to be sent overseas just yet. He's going off to a training camp, somewhere unpronounceable in Wales.'

'Training? What for?'

'The army, of course,' he drawled. 'He doesn't feel able to deliver the message of a gospel in which he no longer believes, so he's renounced his position as Chaplain and is joining the ranks.' He was drunker than she'd realized and his words ran into each other, as if there were no spaces between them. 'He's fired up with passion at the idea of fighting side by side with the youth of England. He wants to kill and be killed in the name of freedom and justice.'

Stella didn't know what to say. She couldn't imagine fastidious Peter Underwood doing anything as messy as fighting, although with the new insight Dan had given her she could see the attraction of the youth of England.

'I'm sorry,' she said softly. 'I know how difficult—'

He stood up abruptly – too abruptly, so that he staggered a little and his chair tipped backwards and fell with a crack onto the tiles.

'You don't,' he spat. 'How on earth could *you* possibly know? You haven't been out there. You haven't seen how things are. Men die, like dogs. Every day. Blown to bits. Shot through the head, the neck, the stomach, the heart. They die of disease – malaria and typhoid. They get bombed and trapped in burning tanks, or cars or planes. There are so many ways to die in this fucking war . . .'

Hearing him swear shocked her more than the outburst itself. His face was contorted with pain and fury, and flecks of white spittle had collected at the corners of his mouth. He had become a different person from the mild, academic man she knew. And yet she understood that she didn't really know him at all. He had kept the most fundamental part of his character hidden from her. Hidden from everyone, except Peter Underwood.

She stood up, thinking only of going to him and trying to offer him comfort but he backed away, raising his hand to shield his face, almost colliding with the door as he left the kitchen. A moment later she heard another door slam – not his study this time, but the sitting room. In the sudden silence of the kitchen she let out a shaky breath and began dazedly to clear away the remains of supper.

It was frightening, seeing him like that, but as she washed the dishes she was surprised to discover that there was something liberating about it too. The rigid mould of their relationship – which cast her in the role of powerless child and him as wise, capable adult – had cracked open, providing an unexpected opportunity for change.

Unhurriedly she tidied the kitchen, deep in thought. Then she made coffee and laid a tray and, full of calm purpose, carried it along the hall to the sitting room.

'Sorry. I'm behaving like a boor.'

He was standing beside the radiogram. In the dull light of the rainy evening his face was desolate. Records, pulled out of their paper sleeves, lay scattered about him like coins in a busker's cap and another glass of whisky was balanced precariously beside the turntable, on which a record was spinning. Stella put the tray down on the table beside the sofa and straightened up to look at him.

'Bach,' she said softly, recognizing it from the concert at the National Gallery.

His face registered surprise and he picked up his glass and held it up to her. 'Very good. Bach indeed. I didn't think you knew about music.'

'I didn't, but I do now. I know about a lot of things now that I didn't before.'

He drained half of the glass in one mouthful and laughed. 'Fancy that. The war has turned my little wife into a woman of the world. Worldly wise. Tell me what you know about, worldly wife.'

'Perhaps you should have some coffee now.'

'Disappointing. I was expecting something more profound than that.'

She could feel the heat climbing to her cheeks, but knew that she had to hold her nerve. If she didn't take this chance to speak she might not get another one. 'All right,' she said carefully, perching on the arm of the sofa and folding her hands together to stop them trembling. 'I know more about people, and relationships. I know about love. And I under-stand about you and Peter.'

His head jerked backwards as if she'd struck him. His face was oddly rigid, flooded with colour, and veins stood out at his temples. He made an awkward attempt at a laugh, which emerged as a kind of hoarse gasp.

'Don't be ridiculous. You're talking nonsense.'

'Oh Charles . . .' She could see the muscles of his throat working as he struggled not to cry, and she went forwards, her arms instinctively opening. 'It's all right, you know, you don't have to hide it from me any more. I know that you want to be with him and—'

The blow came from nowhere; she didn't even see him raise his hand. She reeled backwards, covering the side of her face where he'd hit her, her mind a kind of startled blank.

'There is nothing between me and Peter.' His voice was an animal snarl, vibrating with fury. '*Nothing*. Do you hear? How dare you make such a disgusting suggestion.'

'I'm sorry,' she gasped. 'I'm sorry. I just wanted to let you know that—'

'What?' He made a lunge for her. Grabbing her chin he forced her head up and back so that she was looking into his face, blasted by his sour whisky breath. 'That you think I'm one of *those* men? That you think I'd go against God's law and commit . . . sodomy?'

'There's nothing wrong with loving someone, whoever that person is!' she said desperately, and with difficulty. 'Love can never be wrong!'

'Of course it can – do you not read the scriptures? *"Thou shalt not lie with mankind as with womankind: it is abomination. If a man also lie with mankind as he lieth with a woman, both of them have committed abomination, they shall surely be put to death."'* He was speaking from between tightly clenched teeth, still gripping her chin. 'The Bible makes it quite clear. *"The unrighteous shall not inherit the kingdom of God. Neither fornicators, nor idolaters, nor adulterers, nor effeminate, nor abusers of themselves with mankind."* Sodomy is a sin. A perversion. A degrading passion.' He pushed her backwards, so they were standing on the rug in front of the fireplace. His face was dark red, his eyes bulging. ' *"The men abandoned the natural function of the woman and burned in their desire toward one another,"'* he quoted, ' *"men with men committing indecent acts"*. Indecent acts.'

With a sick jolt she noticed that his other hand, the one that wasn't gripping her jaw, was fumbling with the buckle of his belt. Her first thought was that he was going to pull it off and beat her with it, as a punishment. What happened next was so unexpected that it felt unreal. Somehow she was on the floor, face down, her cheek squashed up against the tiled edge of the hearth. The rug smelled old and musty and there was grit — ash perhaps? — in her mouth, and a metallic taste which she recognized as blood.

These sensations came to her in fragments, one at a time. Her shoulder hurt where she'd fallen on it, and the ache radiated downwards into her ribs. There was more pain too, in her lower back and her hips as he gripped them hard and held them high, bending her spine the wrong way. He was pulling at her underwear, but even that didn't prepare her for the searing stab of pain that felt like she was being torn apart.

Her cry was muffled by the rug, but Charles wouldn't have heard it anyway. She couldn't see his face, but he was still talking. Grunting. Spitting out the same words with every savage thrust.

'*Men with men. Committing indecent acts.*'

She tried to separate herself off from the body on the floor, but the image her mind produced was one of Mr Fairacre the

278

butcher, hacking into a carcase on his scarred and blood-stained block, the red flesh splitting beneath the blade of his cleaver. Her cheekbone bumped against the edge of the fireplace and her lips stretched in an endless silent scream. She thought longingly, helplessly of Dan and then tried to banish him to some safe, sacrosanct part of her brain so that he wouldn't be tainted by this ... abomination. This indecent act.

She didn't try to fight him off. But just as she thought she could bear it no longer she felt Charles give a convulsive shudder and fall forward. He let go of her hips and the weight of him pushed her down so that her head twisted against the tiles and she thought her neck might snap. The immediate relief that it was over was dimmed by the clammy blanket of nausea that wrapped itself around her.

They lay like that for several long, dazed minutes, the silence broken only by the ticking of the clock on the mantelpiece and Charles's ragged breathing. She wanted to tell him that she thought she might be sick, but the words were stuck in her dry throat. And then, from a long way away in the ordinary world outside she heard the click of the front gate, and footsteps coming up the path.

For a second neither of them moved and then they both tried to spring up at once. Charles, lying on top of her, was quicker. She felt the rush of release as her body was relieved of his weight but had only managed to raise herself unsteadily to her knees by the time he had reached the sitting-room door. He paused to fasten his trousers and buckle his belt. He had done all of that – committed the entire indecent act – without undressing at all, she realized with a sort of dull surprise. The doorbell rang.

Charles threw her a warning look as he left the room. A moment later she heard him open the door. 'Oh – Charles! I thought you weren't back until tomorrow.'

'Nancy—' Stella croaked, struggling to her feet and instantly doubling over as her battered insides screamed in protest. Blackness swirled across her vision like smoke. From outside in the hallway she heard Charles's voice.

'I came back early. Missed my wife – nothing wrong with that, I hope?'

In the mirror above the fireplace Stella's face appeared strangely obscene against the familiar backdrop of the sitting room. There was a white indentation in the puffy red skin on her cheekbone and her bottom lip was swollen, so it looked like she was pulling a comical pouty face.

'Is she in?'

Please . . . Stella willed silently, staring into her own desperate eyes. *Oh please, Nancy, come and help me out of this nightmare . . .*

'Yes, but you've called at a rather inconvenient time.' Charles's voice was chilly and defensive and she heard Nancy laugh.

'Charles, you sly old thing!' She'd evidently taken in his state of uncharacteristic disarray and was amused and delighted by the idea of catching them in the throes of marital passion – oh, why hadn't Stella been honest with her from the start? 'All right, I'll leave you to it. Tell her I called though, won't you? And tell her I've got something for her – she'll know what I mean.'

A letter. Oh God – *Dan*. Her mouth stretched into a silent howl as she heard the front door shut and, a moment later, the door to Charles's study. Knowing that he wasn't coming back in, she ran to the window, pressing her palms to the blast-taped glass, willing Nancy to look round and see her. She half-turned to close the gate and Stella saw her face, still wearing its amused smile. And then she flicked her hair over her collar and began to walk away, taking the letter with her, and whatever news it contained.

Then she was gone and the street was empty. Stella stood, a warm rush of stickiness oozing out of her, and felt completely alone.

21

2011

In Jess's dream there was a fire.

She couldn't see it because everything was so black, but she knew it was there because she could hear its roar in her ears and feel its heat on her face. Convulsed with shivers and frozen to the bone, she longed to get closer. The darkness glowed red as the heat started to lick through her, and then it was orange and yellow and then the fierce bright white of midday sun and she was burning from the inside. She tried to escape but tree roots and undergrowth twisted around her – not just around her legs and feet, but her whole body – holding her fast. She writhed and struggled and then, above the rage of the furnace inside her she heard a voice telling her that it was OK, she was going to be all right. That she was safe.

Dan Rosinski. It was him, she knew it. He came out of the fire and his face hung in front of her – old at first, but changing before her eyes until he was young again. Handsome, with dark hair and gentle eyes. His hands were cool. At his touch the roots and brambles fell away. She tried to sit up and tell him that she'd read the letters and knew about Stella. It was very important to tell him she was going to find her, but he was easing her down again, saying it didn't matter.

And when he said that she knew it wasn't him. And through the heat and the roar and the ache in every nerve and muscle and bone in her body she recognized the man from the leisure centre.

'It's all right,' he said again, as his face began to shrink and swim out of focus. 'I'm going to get help. Just hold on, I'll be back soon.'

Will had never phoned for an ambulance before. As he dialled 999 he wondered if he was being ridiculously melodramatic and was about to end the call when the operator came on the line to ask which emergency service he required.

'Sorry – ambulance please.'

'What's the nature of the emergency?'

'A young lady – I've just discovered her, in an empty house. I think she's sleeping rough in there, or squatting per-haps—

'Do you need police assistance?'

'No! No, it's not that – she's not well. I'm not sure what the problem is, but she seems to have a fever. She's very hot, and she's—'

He faltered. He was going to say that she'd been hal-lucinating; about letters, and someone called Stella and how she was going to find her, but he baulked at the word.

Hallucinating made it sound like she was high on something. The possibility hadn't occurred to him until that moment. Was he being terribly naïve in thinking that she was actually ill?

'Is the patient conscious and breathing?'

'Breathing, yes.' Rasping breaths that made her chest squeeze like bellows. 'Conscious – I don't quite know. She's talking, but not rationally, if you see what I mean. Nonsense, really.'

'Could you give me details of where the patient is, please?'

He gave the address and was told, quite briskly, that an ambulance would be there soon, and then the line went dead.

He'd left his mobile in Mr Greaves's kitchen and had to go back there to make the call. When he'd done it he went through to the lounge. Mr Greaves was sitting upright in his chair. His eyes, behind his bottle-bottom glasses, were the size of satellite dishes.

'So, what did they say then?'

'They're sending an ambulance. It shouldn't be long.'

'Ambulance? What are they bothering with one of them for? Police, that's what they ought to be sending to someone what's broke and entered. That's a crime, that is. How did she get in then, the little beggar? Through the back door most likely – broke the glass I'll bet, and that's criminal damage, for starters. I knew that would happen when I wasn't there to keep an eye on things. Kids these days – no respect, that's the trouble. And drugs—'

Behind his outrage Mr Greaves was thoroughly enjoying the drama that had arisen from Will's visit to Nancy Price's house. 'You see what you can find – there must be something there that can help you get things sorted,' he'd said as he handed over the key. Neither of them had suspected that the first thing that Will would find would be a girl, shivering and delirious in the bed upstairs. And yet, in some detached part of his mind Will wasn't surprised to discover that it was her. He'd almost known it all along, but not quite trusted his instincts.

'And a girl too,' Mr Greaves was saying now, gesticulating forcefully with his one good hand as he warmed to his subject. 'That really puts the tin lid on it! I mean, I know you see them on the news, staggering around as inebriated as sailors on shore leave, but breaking and entering?' He shook his head. 'I don't know – in my day, ladies was ladies. Except for the odd one, of course—'

Will moved towards the door and cleared his throat anxiously, cutting Mr Greaves off before he could begin to air his experience of ladies of questionable morals. 'I ought to get back to her, Mr G. She's really not well at all—'

'Well – serves her right, don't it?'

'Oh, I don't know ... She's quite young, you see and, I think, possibly rather frightened.' He remembered the way she'd jumped and backed away from him when he spoke to her. He remembered the tension in her movements and the panic in her wide eyes, and he wondered what had happened to her to put it there. 'It's my guess – and I know this doesn't make breaking into a house any less serious – but I imagine that she must only have done it because she had no other choice. I'm sure she's there because she has nowhere else to go.'

Sitting in his chair Mr Greaves was quiet; so quiet that for a heart-stopping moment Will thought he'd had another stroke and was fleetingly, massively glad that an ambulance was already on its way. Then he gave a little grunt of acquiescence.

'It's that government's fault. Kids today, what is there for 'em? No trades, no housing. No wonder they end up on the streets.'

'Exactly.' Will opened the door, to make good his escape. 'I'll wait with her until the ambulance comes and then I'll be back.'

The old man gave another grunt. He was staring out of the window, his face softened. 'You've just reminded me of something Nancy said to me once, years ago. She said she came to that house when she had nowhere else to go. So maybe it ain't so bad after all, what this one done.' He chuckled quietly. 'It's just history repeating itself.'

As soon as Will opened the front door the cold wrapped itself around him and the damp settled like a smothering hand over his nose and mouth. No wonder she was ill, living like this for God knows how long. The afternoon was turning into evening and he flicked the light-switch at the bottom of the stairs with more hope than expectation. The gloom remained undisturbed, and he wondered how she'd managed without heating *and* light; without the means to cook or boil a kettle. He remembered when he'd seen her at the leisure centre, feeding coins into the machine to buy cheap coffee and he almost groaned out loud into the silence. If only she'd let him help her then. He just hoped it wasn't too late to make up for it now.

'It's only me,' he said as he went upstairs. 'I'm back.'

She was still there. Improbable though it was, he'd half expected to find that she'd bolted, like she had the last two times he'd seen her. She was quiet now, and still. His heart squeezed with fear as he went over to the bed and gently smoothed back her damp hair to lay a hand on her forehead. It was radiator-hot. She was asleep, that was all.

He looked around the room. At this hour of a winter February day it was at its most dismal. The only colour came from the pink bedcover, but the place was tidy enough. His gaze flickered to the dressing table, then the nightstand. His own experience of drugs was limited to a few lumpy cigarettes at college balls during his first year at Oxford so he was a little hazy about the practicalities of drug taking, but there didn't seem to be any evidence of it here. No hypodermics or charred teaspoons, not so much as a cigarette lighter. He felt a rush of relief, though he wasn't quite sure why.

Sirens were part of the everyday soundscape of city life, so it wasn't until the ambulance had turned into Greenfields Lane and the wail was echoing off the buildings on either side that he noticed it. The flat, colourless half-light that filled the room was suddenly broken up by flashes of blue sliding across the walls. He went back to stand over the bed.

'The ambulance is here now. You'll be in safe hands.'

In a moment the professionals would come in and take over, and he'd be surplus to requirement. The thought should have been comforting but it made him feel oddly bereft. He gazed down at her ashen face against the pillow, wanting to imprint her features on his memory before he had to say goodbye. To his surprise her blue-tinged eyelids flickered open. Her eyes were dark and glittering with fever.

'Don't go,' she whispered, so softly that he might have thought he'd been mistaken if she hadn't stretched out her hand. He took it. Her fingers were hot and dry and small.

'I won't. I'm right here.'

There were voices downstairs. A woman's voice called, 'Hello? Anyone there?' The girl's grip tightened on his hand.

'Up here.'

And then they were there, a man and a woman in green all-in-one suits, filling the room with efficiency and crackling radio static and kindness and the scent of outside air and anti-septic. The space was too small. Will retreated. His fingers tingled where she'd held them.

He waited downstairs. While the male paramedic stayed upstairs, asking the girl questions in a cheerful, encouraging voice, his colleague came down to talk to Will. Once she'd taken down his details she looked around with a visible shudder. 'There's something wrong with the world when kids end up living in places like this. No wonder the poor girl's ill.'

'Where will you take her?'

'Most likely the Royal Free. It looks like she'll need to be on IV antibiotics for a while.'

'What do you think's wrong with her?'

The paramedic shrugged, tucking her pen back into the pocket of her overalls. 'Probably started off as good old winter 'flu and thanks to this place she's got a nasty dose of pneumonia on top of that. Just as well you found her when you did.'

They brought her down in a stretcher chair. Swaddled in blankets, her face covered with an oxygen mask she looked impossibly fragile. Will wrestled the damp-swollen front door open as wide as possible to allow them to get through. As they passed, her eyes found his. They stayed there, unblinking, as if she was holding on to him to stop herself falling. He walked alongside her, keeping that contact until they reached the ambulance.

The male paramedic opened the doors. 'Here you are Jess, love – your carriage awaits. Or should I call you Cinderella?' he joked. Her eyes were still fixed on Will's.

'This is as far as I go for now,' he said. 'Take good care of yourself for me.'

After her incoherence earlier, he wasn't sure how aware she was of what was going on. But when he said this she gave a little nod, and her eyes suddenly filled with inexplicable tears.

The doors shut and the ambulance moved away, lights circling crazily, its siren beginning its long, crescendoing wail like the saxophone note at the start of *Rhapsody in Blue*. Will watched it go. And for once in his life he felt like he'd done something useful. Something good.

22

1943

Stella's bruise spread and blossomed like an exotic flower.

The flesh across her cheekbone puffed up until it was tight and shiny, and the swelling pushed her eye half-closed. She tried to cover it up with face powder and pin on the hat Ada had given her at an angle to hide it, but ended up looking more alarming than ever. And so, unable to face the curious stares of strangers and questions from people she knew, she stayed in the house.

Nancy didn't call round again. The question of whether she had letters to give her from Dan beat around in Stella's brain like a bird trapped in a sealed room, sometimes quite frenziedly, at other times with an exhausted hopelessness. Confined to the gloomy rooms of the Vicarage in those still, hot late-summer days it felt like she'd shrunk into some small space inside herself. Like in the worst days of the Blitz, when they'd got used to retreating to the shelter in the cellar while destruction rained down from the sky, emerging when the All Clear sounded to assess the damage. Now she wondered if it would ever feel like the danger had passed. If she'd ever feel safe again.

Charles never once referred to what she privately thought of as 'the indecent act', but his attitude towards her underwent something of a transformation. Over the few remaining days before his departure he showed her great solicitude — tenderness, even — though the effort this cost him was obvious. It was as if he was determined to rewrite their marriage; as if he believed that by putting on a convincing display of normality he might persuade her she'd imagined everything that had gone before. Also, she couldn't quite escape the feeling that he was almost pleased with himself. As if he'd claimed her at last. As if he'd proved something.

He prayed more than ever. A kind of earnestness had replaced the despair she'd sensed in him before he'd gone away. He wanted her to pray with him, and asked her to kneel beside him on the floor before getting into bed at night. Clasping her hand painfully tight he begged God to deliver them from base, human desires and temptations of the flesh, as if she had been the one to defile him.

Much of his time was taken up with preparing a sermon for his final Sunday service. Its theme, he told her gravely over breakfast on Sunday morning, was love and forgiveness. It was more important than ever in a time of war, he said. He was using St Paul's epistle to the Corinthians as the reading.

'The one we had at our wedding,' Stella remarked dully. Peter Underwood had read it.

'Oh yes,' Charles said vaguely. 'I'd forgotten that.'

On Sunday both of them seemed to accept without saying anything that she wouldn't be going to church; her face was still too much of a mess. Clearing away the breakfast things she wondered what he'd say to the people who asked where she was. When she heard him leave she sank down into a chair at the table and dropped her head into her hands.

It was only ten o'clock in the morning but she felt inexpressibly tired, and the prospect of getting up and carrying on – with the washing up, making the bed, breathing, living without Dan – was utterly overwhelming. After a while her cheek began to throb where it was pressed against her folded arms, so she twisted her head round to the other side.

And that was when she saw him.

Maybe she'd fallen asleep and was dreaming. Or hallucinating. Or maybe her mind had simply lost its reason and conjured up the thing that she most desired, like a mirage of an oasis appearing before weary desert wanderers. His hands were cupped against the kitchen window as he peered in. She sat up and blinked stupidly, and was trying to decide which of the three possibilities was the real one when he saw her. His hands flattened against the glass.

'Stella!'

In an instant she was out of her seat, throwing herself across the kitchen towards the back door. She hadn't got round to unlocking it from last night and her hands were shaking so much she could barely slide the bolt back. But then the door was open and he was there, in front of her, pulling her roughly into his arms, kissing her mouth, her eyes, her bruised and swollen cheek.

'Christ Stella, what happened? Did he do this to you?'

She didn't want to talk about it; not at that moment when there were so many other, more important questions to ask. Not when she could spend those precious moments kissing him. Her fists closed around the collar of his tunic and she pulled him downwards so that his mouth covered hers again, kissing him as if her life depended on it. Like she was breathing his oxygen into her own starved lungs.

'What are you doing here?' It was gasped between kisses.

'I wrote . . . Didn't you get the letter from Nancy?'

She shook her head as kisses rained on her face.

'Flak farm. A week.'

'What's . . . a flak farm?'

'Where they send you to stop you cracking up . . . when things get too much. Some god-awful country manor house . . . with a butler and Red Cross girls all over the place. I left.'

Gently she pulled away and looked at him properly for the first time. There were lines etched around his mouth that hadn't been there before and hollows in his cheeks. 'My God, Dan — are you all right?'

He exhaled shakily. 'I'm good now I've seen you. That's all I needed, to know that you're here and you're OK. Except that you're not. Tell me what happened.'

They'd been standing in the sunless lobby between the back door and the scullery — almost the same place in which he'd kissed her last time — but now she turned and went back to the kitchen. 'Let me make you a cup of tea. We're safe for half an hour.'

'Forget the tea.' He was right behind her, taking hold of her shoulders and twisting her round to face him. 'He did it, didn't he? Jesus Christ Almighty ... Come with me, Stella. Come with me now. I can't leave you here.'

She cut him off. 'That would make things much worse in the long run. He's leaving the day after tomorrow, and it'll be months – years perhaps – before he's back. I can stick it out for two more days. It won't happen again.'

'How do you know?'

'I tried to tell him that I knew he – that I knew about him and Peter. He was drunk, and angry. He denied it. He wanted to prove – I don't know – that he was a proper man, or something.'

'Goddammit Stella ...' He let her go and took a few steps back, rubbing a hand over his face as the implications of her words sank in. 'Jesus. *Jesus.*'

'It's all right. It's over now. And you're here ...' She still couldn't be certain she wasn't dreaming. 'How long have you got?'

'I'm back on duty Thursday.'

Thursday. She thought quickly. Charles was leaving on Tuesday, but not until the afternoon. He had to be at Waterloo at five o'clock.

'That gives us Tuesday night and all of Wednesday.' Not enough, never enough, but a gift nonetheless. Their eyes met across the table. 'Where?'

'Don't worry. I'll find somewhere.'

*

Leaving her was like cutting off his own arm. The shadows were back in her eyes as she stood at the back door of that great bleak tomb of a house and watched him walk down the path to the gate.

The sound of singing drifted over from the ugly Victorian brick church across the road. He recognized the hymn: *Love Divine, All Loves Excelling.* Hatred blackened his heart. What did that bastard know about love? He imagined slipping in through the arched doors and striding right down the aisle to land a punch right in his face in front of his blind, adoring congregation. It took just about every ounce of willpower to keep walking.

He had no sense of where he was going, his head too full to take in any detail of the streets he passed along. His thoughts were not distinct from one another but a dark mass, a swarm of bees. He could hear Louis Johnson's voice calmly telling him to keep going forward, just like he did in dense cloud cover at twenty thousand feet, though Johnson had been hit in the chest by a twenty-millimetre shell on the Hanover mission and had died somewhere over the English Channel on the return to base.

The small of his back was wet with sweat. He felt slightly dizzy, like he hadn't slept for days, though they'd given them tablets at the flak farm that knocked them out for ten hours straight. Fitcham Park it was called. It was some big fancy pants Neo-Palladian pile in the country that was supposed to supply the battle-weary officer with every comfort he might desire.

It had given Dan the creeps. The library-like silence that weighted the air in the huge rooms felt unnatural, and meant that the noises inside his head – the constant roar of engines, Louis Johnson's voice – were all the louder. The smiles of the Red Cross girls had been painted on a little too brightly, and the empty days which they were supposed to fill playing croquet or shooting skeets gave him too much time to think. About Hamburg's burning schools and burning houses. About Louis Johnson with his flying suit all dark and glistening with blood, his baby boy without a father. About Stella. He knew that seeing her for five minutes would do him more good than five weeks at Fitcham Park.

Leaving had just been a matter of signing out; the Red Cross girl on the desk had expressed regret but hadn't tried to stop him. Adelman and Morgan had been more difficult to get past, but since neither of them had been sober since they'd arrived their objections were half-hearted. He'd caught the train to London and spent last night in the only hotel he could find with a room available; a tall, narrow building on Greek Street, that got progressively dingier and more down at heel on each successive floor.

He stopped at a crossroads now, totally disorientated. He had no idea where he was, nor how to get back into the city, though it occurred to him that he didn't particularly want to go back there, either to the crowded streets or the depressing hotel room. The day stretched ahead of him and he felt the familiar panic begin to rise, filling his legs with sand.

A bus was swaying up the road. On impulse he stuck out

his hand and swung onto the platform at the back, then climbed the narrow stairs to the top deck.

'Where to, sweetheart?'

The woman with the ticket machine was blonde and stout and matronly. She smiled at Dan with great kindness, which told him how rough he must look.

'I don't care. Anywhere.'

It was warm. The sun on his cheek and the rocking and swaying of the vehicle were soporific and soothed him into a welcome half-doze. The branches of trees brushed against the windows and the streets were Sunday quiet. They passed people spilling out of a church into the sunshine and it made him think of Charles goddamn Thorne, which jolted him awake again.

He sighed and felt in his pockets for cigarettes before remembering he'd smoked the last one instead of having breakfast. Dammit. He turned to look out of the window, the brief spell of tranquillity broken. They were passing between rows of pretty Edwardian villas but a little further along the street, beyond a grassy gap where a house must once have stood, he could see a row of shops. He got to his feet and staggered down the steps.

As the bus lumbered away he found himself standing on a neat high street. There was a butcher's shop, its blinds pulled down and a sign saying 'Closed' hanging on the door. Next to it was a dress shop called Uptown Fashions with a headless, handless mannequin in the window, wearing a grey dress of notable ugliness. Beyond that was a greengrocer, a tiny drug-store and — right at the end — a newsagent and tobacconist's.

It was closed.

Of course. Sunday. A great surge of frustrated fury rose up inside him and he grasped the brass handle on the door and shook it roughly before falling forward against the glass, rest-ing his hands and his forehead on its cool surface. A mosaic of hand-written cards was stuck behind the glass, making it dif-ficult to see anything inside. *LOST: BLACK AND WHITE CAT*, he read on one of the cards. The paper was yellowed, the ink faded — along with any hope of recovering the cat, Dan imagined. He glanced at the other cards, all of which seemed to be of a similar vintage: *Daily Help Wanted by Gentle-man, Weston Park, Lunch Provided. SEWING BEE, Tuesdays 10 am — 12 noon, All Saints Church Hall, all welcome. HOUSE FOR SALE: 4 Greenfields Lane, Church End. Contact J. B. Furnivall Solicitors, Highgate 8369.*

His pointless anger spent, he was about to turn away but something made him look back and read the last card again. Then he felt in his pockets and dug out the bus ticket he'd just bought. On the back, very small, he wrote the name and tele-phone number of the solicitor, as out of the chaos of his raging thoughts, a plan began to emerge.

J. B. Furnivall's office was on the ground floor of his home, a handsome Georgian townhouse on a leafy square. At five min-utes to two on Monday afternoon, Dan was shown into the waiting room by his secretary. She had the solid proportions and stately profile of a ship's figurehead and Dan assumed she was the person he'd spoken to that morning, who'd made out that it was both hugely inconvenient and nigh-on impossible to grant Dan an appointment at such short notice. Mr Furnivall was engaged with other business, she informed him now, gesturing to a row of hard chairs lined up against the wall. Dan waited, trying to ignore the smell of mutton that hung greasily in the air and mentally recreating the room as it must have been before partition walls had cut through cornices and mouldings to divide the space. Eventually Mr Furnivall appeared. It was quite obvious that the only business he'd been engaged with was lunch.

As briefly as possible, Dan outlined the reason for his visit and opened his cheque book. The solicitor steepled his plump fingers and gave a patronizing smile.

'I'm afraid, Lieutenant Rosinski, it's not that simple. I don't know about Chicago, but over here these things take time.'

'And I'm afraid, Mr Furnivall, I don't *have* time.'

He kept his voice even, pleasant, but his patience – frayed by another impatient, sleepless night in the Greek Street hotel – was down to its last thin threads.

Mr Furnivall sighed and began rearranging the papers on his desk. 'As I hope my secretary made clear, I too am very busy. However, I will endeavour to get a letter sent off to Mrs Nichols by the end of the day. She's the current owner of the house, now residing at Blackstone Hall in Dorset.' Dan wondered if this detail was intended to intimidate him. 'Then, when I have had her reply I will contact you and arrange—'

'How about you telephone her?' Dan interrupted. 'Now. Save yourself the job of writing the letter.' He managed to stop himself from prefixing the word 'letter' with 'fucking', but only just.

'Telephone her?'

'Sure. You said she was living in some big house – Black-something Hall – so she must be on the telephone there, right? Tell her I'm sitting right here with the money and I'd like to buy her house. I guess she wants to sell it, so it really is quite simple.'

'If I may just point out that you don't exactly have the money, Lieutenant Rosinski. You have a cheque, from the –' he leaned forward, sliding his spectacles down his nose to peer at the cheque with elaborate disdain, 'Illinois National Bank; a cheque which I have no proof will be worth any more than the paper on which it is written – which, although a valuable commodity in these troubled times, doesn't quite cover the price of a house.'

That was J. B. Furnivall's attempt at a joke, Dan realized. He could tell from the way his lips stretched into his attempt at a smile.

'Does the name JMR mean anything to you, sir?'

'The motor manufacturing company?'

'Got it in one – the motor manufacturing company that produced most of the tanks that ground Rommel into the dirt in Africa earlier this year. Perhaps you don't know that those initials stand for Josef Marek Rosinski; my father, who founded the company. I have no worries that the Illinois

National Bank will honour this cheque, or that my lawyers in Chicago will be able to handle the paperwork arising from the purchase of one small, vacant London property. Now please, if you would put a call through to Mrs Nichols I can buy her house before I go back to my base to get shot up over Germany again.'

Furnivall glared at him coldly but reached for the telephone. In a tone of quivering superiority he asked the operator for Blackstone Hall, Upper Compton, switching to oily ingratiation as Mrs Nichols answered.

For a man who claimed to be busy he sure didn't seem to be in a hurry as he enquired after first her health, and then that of Mr Nichols. When he finally got round to raising the subject of the house, he made it sound almost like an irrelevant detail. An *American* gentleman, he said regretfully, looking past Dan towards the portrait of a pinched-looking man in a wig and gown above the fireplace. 'Lieutenant Rosinski, an airman in the US Air Force. He's keen to conclude matters as quickly as possible, though of course I have pointed out to him that that's not necessarily in your best interests, Mrs Nichols.'

He said this like he expected it to conclude the matter. Dan felt the last glow of hope begin to fade and clenched his fists in impotent rage. In that moment it struck him how much hope he'd invested in this plan: the only hope he had left.

He'd asked about the house yesterday, in the pub where he'd bought cigarettes. The landlady had given him directions that led eventually to a little row of four cottages tucked away like overlooked children between the shops along the main street and the backs of tall Victorian houses. Workers' cottages of absolute architectural simplicity; unadorned London brick, small square windows beneath a low slate roof. There was something honest about them. Something clean and straightforward that appealed to him.

An ordinary house in an ordinary street.

When he'd said he'd find somewhere for them to be together he'd meant a room in one of the better hotels — better than Greek Street anyway. But then he'd thought of the bruise on her cheek and he knew that he had to offer her something more solid than that. More permanent. Somewhere that would be hers, and would keep her safe and give her the chance to get out of her god-awful travesty of a marriage if he didn't survive.

And now some bastard of a solicitor was about to close off that escape route. Slumped in the chair he felt a blast of utter desolation. Sure, there must be other houses, but he didn't have the time to go looking for them. He didn't have the time to hang around waiting while Furnivall shuffled paper and sent laborious letters and took two hours for lunch. With nineteen missions behind him, the odds shortening, luck running out and the targets getting more ambitious he had a feeling he didn't have the time for anything much any more.

He was just about to get to his feet and stop wasting whatever time was left to him when he saw Furnivall's expression change. The smugness was abruptly wiped away and replaced with alarm.

'Now? Yes, I have him here, but—' A pause. 'Of course.' Alarm hardened into flinty dislike as he held out the receiver to Dan. 'Mrs Nichols would like to speak to you.'

'Close your eyes.'

'Dan! I'll fall over!'

'You won't. I've got you. I'm holding you. I'm not going to let you fall.'

In the darkness all her senses were sharpened. She was aware of the rank green smell of shrubbery in late-summer gardens, the dusty street, Dan's clean, warm scent. His arm was around her waist, guiding her forwards and holding her firm. An involuntary smile tugged at the corners of her mouth, like a kite catching the breeze. All this secrecy reminded her of the Whispering Gallery in St Paul's and the moment she first knew she was falling in love with him. She wondered what special surprising thing he was going to show her now.

They stopped. She felt him bend to put her suitcase down; he'd taken it from her the moment she stepped out of the cab. In it were the mysterious items – two sheets and a blanket – he'd asked her to bring when he'd telephoned the Vicarage after Charles had left. She'd joked that he was taking her to spend the night in some musty army bell tent, but he'd simply said she'd have to wait and see.

There was grass beneath her feet, long grass that tickled her bare ankles, making the tent idea seem more plausible than ever. But where could you put up a tent in London? Curiosity almost got the better of her but he stood behind her and covered her eyes with his hands – gently, so as not to hurt her bruised cheek, even though the swelling was mostly gone.

'Dan! Where are we?'

He kissed her neck and dropped his hands. 'Home.'

23

2011

Somehow it was Thursday again.

This week the Bona Vacantia list was full of the kind of names that were a probate researcher's nightmare – Evans, Thompson, Collins, Jones, Taylor. The sky in the gaps between the blind's vertical slats was still dark when Ansell had his first epic meltdown of the day, and after that it just got worse. By nine o'clock Will had been given his first sacking threat and by eleven the list of insults that had been thrown his way included not only several instances of the standard 'posh boy' and 'twerp', but one 'fucking fairy' and one 'inbred ponce', which only came out on special occasions. And all before he'd finished his second cup of coffee.

The afternoon brought respite in the form of a trip to Harrow on the Hill to collect a birth certificate, but the release of pressure was brief. The certificate proved that the information upon which they'd spent all morning construct-ing a family tree was wrong and the case collapsed like a house of cards.

Finally, after the painful start, things began to come together towards the end of the afternoon. At five o'clock Will parked outside the address of the only definite potential heir they had, and rang the doorbell. Long minutes passed, during which he could hear the blood-curdling screams of small children and a woman's voice shouting. He rang again. This time the door was answered almost immediately, by a blonde woman wearing a floral apron and a murderous expression.

'Hi – Mrs Maynard? I'm Will Holt from a firm called Ansell Blake. We're probate researchers, and it's about an inheritance—'

He wasn't quick – or maybe convincing – enough. Her face darkened, and in the bright light of the modern chande-lier above her head her eyes had the sinister glitter of a woman on the edge. He took a step back.

'An "*inheritance*" you say? Hurrah! That's marvellous, but unless I'm going to inherit two slightly less dysfunctional chil-dren, a husband who – just for once before they reach the age of eighteen – might get home from the office in time to put them to bed, oh – and a very large bottle of gin, I have to say at this point that I really couldn't give a toss. Nice to have met you, Will.'

The door shut.

There was an off-licence on the corner, although the term

didn't quite do justice to the array of products Will discovered inside. Weaving his way around displays of artisan olives, high-end patisserie and a mini designer florist counter he found his way to the booze aisle, where at least fifteen exclusive brands of gin jostled for shelf space beside the champagne. He almost had a panic attack as he handed over his credit card, but he calmed his private hysteria with the knowledge that thirty-eight pounds spent on posh gin today might just save him from losing his job tomorrow, and convince Bryony Maynard he wasn't a cheap conman.

He rang the doorbell again. The screaming had died down now, and given way to a tired and miserable sobbing which increased in volume as the door opened. Before it could be shut in his face again he thrust the bottle into the gap.

'I can't make any firm promises about the children or the husband, but I can at least offer you the gin.'

An hour and a half later he had read two *Thomas the Tank Engine* stories, played one game of Connect Four and explained the family link between Louisa Evans and Bryony Maynard, which meant the latter was in line to inherit the bulk of the former's estate. The house was quiet now, the children in bed, and Bryony was a good three-quarters of the way down her second large gin and tonic.

'Great Aunt Louisa – gosh, I haven't thought about her for years. She was a bit of a joke in our family. She wore a lot of tweed and couldn't pronounce her Rs properly. Bwyony, she used to call me, which I thought was too hilarious. She

had a friend who lived with her called Millicent. Oh gosh—'
Her eyes widened and she almost choked on her gin. 'It
never occurred to me until now that they were more than
friends, but of course they must have been! Good old Aunt
Louisa. She was always asking me what I wanted to do with
my life and saying I must get out and see the world. I just
wanted to paint my nails and listen to Spandau Ballet in my
bedroom.'

Discreetly Will's eyes slid back to the clock above the Aga.
He'd followed the journey of the minute-hand pretty much
every step of the way for the last hour, hiding his impatience
with heroic effort. 'Well, you'll be able to get out and see the
world now, with the money she's left you. We're not sure how
much it'll be yet, but now you've signed the paperwork we
can get the claim moving.' He began collecting his things
together. 'Talking of which, I should—'

He stood up. Bryony Maynard stayed where she was. Taking another swig of gin she stared at the wall, but in a dreamy
way that suggested she wasn't seeing the daubed finger paintings or messy collages. 'A friend of mine went on a yoga retreat.
To Ibiza. I'd like to do something like that ... but maybe
without the yoga.'

He let himself out, promising to be in touch. It was half
past seven. Visiting hours at the Royal Free were six until
eight. If he hurried he might just make it.

There was nowhere to park. At ten to eight he abandoned
the Spitfire on a kerb by some kind of loading bay and ran. In
his hands he cradled the bunch of flowers he'd bought at the

last minute from the posh shop at the end of Bryony Maynard's road.

They were snowdrops. He'd noticed them when he paid for the gin, and all the time he'd been reading *Thomas the Tank Engine* and playing Connect Four and explaining to Bryony about her potential inheritance he'd thought of them. They were small and delicate. Fragile. And with their little white faces and their bowed heads they'd reminded him of her. Jess.

That was the only name he had for her; no surname, so it had taken him a full ten minutes of frustration, diplomacy and a little bit of creativity with the truth to find out which ward she was on. He'd rung the hospital from his mobile in his snatched lunch break, which had at least distracted him from the urge to buy chips, which was his default coping strategy on crap days in the office. At the end of the call he'd secured the information he needed. Ladies' Medical.

He had to fight against the tide. Visiting time was almost over and people were beginning to flow out of the hospital. He found himself wasting valuable time holding a door open for streams of people who didn't even acknowledge him. It went against the grain to push through himself, but eventually he did it. A large clock, of the kind you saw in stations and Bryony Maynard's kitchen, hung over the corridor and as he passed beneath it he saw the minute-hand flicker to the vertical position. He started to run.

He was breathless and sweating when he arrived at the ward. There was no need to ring the buzzer; the door was open for people to leave. He slipped through them and went straight to the nurses' station.

'I've come to see Jess—'

'Visiting time's just finished, I'm afraid.'

She must have seen his face fall. She must have taken in his heaving chest and red face and his handful of snowdrops and felt sorry for him because her expression softened and she put a hand on his arm. 'Not to worry, she's asleep – has been on and off all day since she came up from ICU. You wouldn't have got much out of her this evening anyway.'

'ICU.?'

'Intensive care. She's much better now, responding nicely to the antibiotics. Come back tomorrow and I'm sure she'll be much brighter. What pretty flowers – I'll find something to put them in and take them for her, shall I? She'll be sorry she missed you. She's been asking for you, even though she's not even properly awake. You are Dan, aren't you?'

'Oh . . .' Will stepped back, caught between acute embarrassment and utter, wretched foolishness. 'No, actually, I'm . . .' He shook his head, suddenly defeated. 'It doesn't matter. Thanks anyway.'

He walked away, leaving the nurse holding the snowdrops. Their stems were crushed where he'd held them too tightly and their silken petals were starting to wilt.

The invitation arrived on Saturday morning, while Will was having breakfast.

Mr and Mrs Hugo Ogilvie
Request the pleasure of your company
at the marriage of their daughter
Marina Rosamunde
To
Simon Richard Alexander Holt
On Saturday 17th April 2011 at 11.30 a.m.
At St Mary's Church, Deeping Marsh,
and afterwards at Deeping Hall
RSVP

It was plain white card, stiff and smooth, edged in gold. No embossed doves or gilded horseshoes for Marina and Simon; everything was impeccably correct and aggressively tasteful. Opening it, Will's fried egg sandwich had turned to ashes in his mouth.

April 17th. Shit. The Save the Date card had arrived months ago – long enough for the wedding itself to seem remote and unreal. He'd binned it immediately, preferring to remain in a state of happy denial about the entire event, but there was no avoiding it now. Still in the t-shirt and boxer shorts he'd slept in, he abandoned the half-eaten fried egg sandwich and stood in front of the mirrored door of the wardrobe.

Throughout school and university he'd rowed and played cricket and rugby, which had kept him effortlessly in shape. Now, without the daily training, the twice weekly matches, once-rigid muscle had softened and his lean silhouette had filled out. In some rational part of his brain he knew that he was still a normal, healthy weight, but the trouble was in his family, normal wasn't the benchmark. Simon was. Simon, who played squash and ran marathons and spent his holidays skiing and scuba diving; who ordered in sushi instead of Indian takeaways and would never scoff a whole packet of M&Ms without even noticing. Will sighed. If he gave up carbs and refused Bex's well-intentioned lattes would that stop people choking on their canapés when they discovered he was Simon's brother?

But the physical comparisons were only part of the problem. He rehearsed a conversation with his reflection in the mirror. *Me? Oh no, I'm not a barrister. Or a historian. No, I'm a sort of failed-historian turned third-rate probate researcher. Well, it's like a door-to-door insurance salesman. No, I'm not married myself, and unlikely to be since the last girlfriend I had was in the second year at university and she dumped me while I was in the psychiatric unit. I know, I can't think why either! I'm such a catch!*

The pasted-on smile slipped and he turned away from the mirror.

In the therapy he'd had in the hospital they used to say that every challenge was an opportunity. Back in the kitchen he threw the sandwich into the bin and put the invitation on the front of the fridge, secured with a magnet bearing the telephone number of the local pizza takeaway. He would look on it, not as total freaking nightmare, but an opportunity. To turn his entire life around. In six weeks.

*

It was warm in the hospital. The bed was firm and crisply clean. The world outside felt like a different planet.

Jess floated through the hours in a daze. Her mind felt as white and blank and clean as the sheets. She didn't want to think; about what had gone before or what would come after, about what would happen when she was well enough to leave or where she would go. She slept a lot. And in the space halfway between sleeping and waking she thought about Dan and Stella, reliving their story.

And when she was awake she looked at the snowdrops in the glass on her bedside locker and she thought of Will Holt. His strong hand holding hers, his dark eyes and his sad, sweet smile.

And she wished for him to come back.

After lunch (a joyless quinoa salad with reduced-calorie dressing bought from the local posh supermarket) Will set off to visit Mr Greaves. The unexpected turn of events of last time had meant he hadn't had a chance to have a proper look around Nancy's house, and because the electricity was turned off it made sense to go during the day rather than in the evening after work. This time, determined not to be shaken in his new resolve, he took with him not cake, but fruit: a small pineapple, a pomegranate, grapes and blueberries.

The old man was dozing when Will arrived. He could see him through the net curtains, tipped over to one side in his big armchair, as though the dead weight of his arm was pulling him downwards. Will was just retreating to wait in the car for half an hour when Mr Greaves's eyes shot open and he sat up, gesticulating for Will to go around to the back door.

A narrow alleyway ran up the side of the first cottage, the one with the window box of herbs, and along the back of the row of gardens. At the far end it was swallowed up by towering weeds and overgrown shrubbery spilling over the hedge of number four. By contrast Mr Greaves's garden was neat and sparse, its few plants confined to pots standing at the edges of the crazy paving like sullen teenagers at a disco.

The back door was unlocked. Will let himself in and went through to the front room. Mr Greaves was sitting upright in his chair with an air of eager anticipation.

'You thought I was asleep but I spotted you! It's being on them bleeding convoys, I tell you – learned to sleep with one eye open, we did.' He looked at the supermarket carrier bag in Will's hand. 'What you got there then?'

'Fruit. Pineapple and blueberries, and a pomegranate—'

Mr Greaves's face fell. 'Oh well. Not to worry, there's some of them cakes left from last time. Cherry Bakewells – my favourite. Why don't you put the kettle on and we'll have one with a cup of tea before you go and carry on at Nancy's.'

After the cosy clutter of Mr Greaves's house, number four seemed cold and bleak. Will wasn't quite sure where to start looking for clues to Nancy Price's past. He wandered through the small rooms, trying to imagine what the house must have once been like, before the damp seeped in, stippling the walls with florid patterns of mould.

He opened drawers in the sideboard and half-heartedly sifted through their contents; instruction manuals for long-defunct appliances, tattered paper poppies, a scattering of old Spanish coins. In a drawer in the kitchen he discovered a hoard of money-off coupons and a Post Office savings book. Turning the pages to find the last entry he discovered that it was made in 1968, and that the balance of the account was seven pounds, four shillings and sixpence.

He left the kitchen and went back to the stairs. They were in darkness; both doors at the top closed. Going up he tried to open the one on the left, but it remained firmly shut – even when he leaned his shoulder against it and shoved. He briefly considered ramming it harder, splintering the wood, but dismissed the idea almost in the same second it came to him. It was the kind of thing people did in police dramas on TV, not in real life, and aside from Albert Greaves's say-so he had no authority to be there. Besides, the chances of finding a stack of gold bullion and a couple of Van Goghs hanging on the wall seemed pretty remote.

Instead he turned and pushed open the other door, into the room where he'd discovered Jess. Hesitating on the threshold, he looked at the bed, then went across and sat down heavily. The pink counterpane was pulled back, the sheets creased from where they'd twisted around her hot body. The pillow still bore the imprint of her head, and he smoothed his hand over it, remembering how her dark hair had clung to her face in damp strands. With a shuddering sigh he thrust his fingers into his hair.

He liked her. He couldn't even say why, because God alone knew she hadn't given him any grounds to. But something about her touched him. Maybe because he sensed she needed looking after and it awoke in him some primitive masculine instinct. Maybe because she'd held his hand and looked right into his eyes like she felt the same connection he did.

'Because she was ill, you idiot,' he groaned into the silence. 'She was delirious. I could have been anyone. She looked at me and probably saw David Beckham, or the Pope.'

Or *Dan*, whoever he was. Her boyfriend, presumably. The love of her life.

He hauled himself to his feet and straightened the pink cover. As he did so his foot struck something, half pushed under the bed. He pulled it out.

It was a box. A shoebox, filled with letters. From way back, by the looks of them, all stacked neatly, and possibly holding exactly the kind of clues to Nancy Price's family and past he'd been hoping for. His pulse stepped up a pace. One of the letters was out of its envelope and had fallen down between the bed and the nightstand, as if someone had dropped it while they were reading it. He picked it up.

Sweetheart, sorry this is going to be a short one. It's late and I'm on standby again for tomorrow, though it seems we only just got back from today's mission . . .

Will's jaw dropped. He checked the date at the top. He might not have finished his history degree but he knew that in July 1943 the Allies had been stepping up their bombing campaign over Germany. He'd chosen Twentieth Century

Conflict as one of his subjects in the second year, and would have gone on to do his dissertation on the Second World War if he hadn't cracked up first.

Our target was ▮▮▮▮▮▮ *and when we got there we could see that the RAF boys had been there before us. The city was pretty much on fire. Even from 10,000 feet up we could feel the heat.*

Hamburg. Their target must have been Hamburg, where firestorms had rampaged through the city and devoured it. Will read on avidly, his heart thudding properly now. And then, as he reached the signature at the bottom, it stopped.

Dan.

Dan?

The same Dan as—? Did that mean—?

He looked at his watch. Afternoon visiting hours started at three. Picking up the box he left the room and clattered down the narrow stairs, two at a time.

24

1943

It was like a dream; surely it must be. As he opened the front door and turned to scoop her up into his arms to carry her over the threshold Stella half expected Winston Churchill or the King to appear, in the illogical way of dreams. But they didn't. It was just her and Dan, his strong arms holding her as he carefully manoeuvred her through the narrow doorway.

'Aren't you supposed to do this when you get married?' she murmured.

'I'll do it again then.'

He led her through the rooms. Dazed with disbelief she loved it all, from the worn green-and-cream chequered linoleum in the kitchen stuck onto the back of the house, to the poppies that bloomed on the fireplace tiles in the bedroom at the front. They crossed over the little square landing at the top of the stairs and Dan ducked through the doorway into the back bedroom. Sunlight sloped across its bare floorboards and gilded the faded violets on the wallpaper. A big, old-fashioned brass bed with a bare ticking mattress stood against the wall and the scent of roses drifted in through the open window.

Stella reached for him and buried her face in his shirt, too overwhelmed to speak. After a while she looked up at him through her tears.

'I can't believe it. Is it really ours?'

'Yours. All yours, forever – or for as long as you want it. It's a safe place, if you need it, and someplace we can be together whenever we get a chance. And if Charles is home, I can write you here, so we don't have to rely on Nancy to act as go-between.'

'It's perfect.'

He grinned lopsidedly. 'With a few minor exceptions. We can fix it up, make it nice, though it's not easy with everything in short supply. The landlady at the pub lent me a whole lot of things to get it cleaned up yesterday.'

She left the circle of his arms and went over to the bed, running her fingers wonderingly along its tarnished rail. 'Where did you get the furniture?'

'All part of the sale. The lady who lived here left in the Blitz to go work as a housekeeper in Dorset. She got a furnished house with the job so she left it all here. No sheets though. That's why I asked you to bring some.'

'I didn't forget. They're in my suitcase.'

He came to stand behind her, wrapping his arms around her and kissing her neck, below her ear.

'How about we put them on now?'

*

Later they dressed again and, their appetites awoken, Dan went out to queue up for fish and chips from the shop on the high street. Left alone, with the evening sunlight sloping through the open back door Stella felt like a little girl playing house. She wiped down the gateleg table beneath the window of the back room and folded out one of its leaves, then went out into the tangled jungle of garden in the hope of finding some flowers to put into the milk bottle that had been left on the kitchen windowsill.

It was immediately obvious why the rose perfume upstairs was so strong: a rambling plant massed with yellow blooms smothered the back of the house, the weight of the flowers pulling it away from the wall. Bees browsed in the wildflowers that had sprung up in the tiny patch of meadow that must once have been a lawned garden. Thistledown drifted on the still, evening air, like sunlit summer snow.

She snapped off stems of dandelions and buttercups and some delicate, papery poppies that she found beside the hedge. Returning to the kitchen she looked wistfully at the roses, but their stems were too thorny and tough to pick with her bare hands. Instead she leaned against the windowsill and breathed in their perfume. She held her breath, as if by doing so she could preserve the perfect, pure happiness of the moment inside herself, forever.

The sound of his key in the front door took her back into the kitchen, blinking in the sudden gloom. He was bearing greasy newspaper-wrapped parcels which they ate, in the end, sitting cross-legged at either end of the deep horsehair sofa in the front room, with the milk bottle vase of flowers in front of them on the mantelpiece.

Shadows gathered in the corners of the room and it grew cooler. There were no curtains at the windows so they couldn't switch on the light. Lying against his chest, Stella was glad.

'How did you find this place?'

'Same way I found you. By chance, or fate, or because it was all part of some great plan that was written in the stars. Buying it was a little more of a problem though. Luckily the lady who owned it was real nice. She moved in here as a young bride in the summer of 1914 and lived here with her husband until he went away to war. And then he got killed and she lived here by herself until the Luftwaffe came along and scared the daylights out of her. She answered an advertisement for a housekeeper at some big old house in the country and ended up marrying the guy she was working for. She's no spring chicken but she's one serious romantic. She was happy to think of the house being filled with love again.'

A shiver had run down Stella's spine at the thought of the young bride who'd so quickly become a young widow. To banish her unease she stretched up and kissed him, slowly and deeply. 'In that case, we mustn't let her down,' she murmured against his lips.

Then she took his hand and led him up the darkling stairs to the bedroom.

They woke the next morning to the sound of birdsong and the sun streaming across the rumpled sheet. Being used to the blackout it felt astonishingly bright and precious, like liquid gold. They lay together, drifting gently into wakefulness.

'I guess today we have to go shopping.'

She turned her head to kiss his bare chest. 'There's bread, and a tin of Spam. And since you cleverly managed to get tea and milk I think we have everything we need . . .'

He laughed throatily. 'Except cups to drink it from. And plates, and knives and forks, and a pan to make fried eggs for breakfast.'

'We don't have any eggs.'

She said it happily, as if that settled the matter. He laughed again. 'I thought women were supposed to love picking out new stuff?'

'I love being with you more.'

'You will be with me.'

'But not like this.' She sat up and stretched her spine luxuriously, then went to the door, naked, aware of his eyes following her.

'Point taken.'

The stone-floored bathroom at the end of the kitchen was as cool as a cave. There was no mirror so she couldn't see her face, but she pressed her fingers over her cheekbone experimentally and found that it felt better. She felt better inside too. She'd been worried that Charles had damaged her, that what he'd done to her would sour the sweetness of how it was with Dan, but it hadn't. A tingle of warmth spread across her skin as she remembered last night. It really hadn't.

She was brushing her teeth at the tiny basin in the corner

when there was a banging on the front door. Her heart gave an uneven thud; thinking about Charles had made her jumpy. She heard Dan's feet on the stairs and peered cautiously around the door to see him hastily fastening his trousers before he went to open the door.

'Morning sir.' The voice reached her faintly; cheery, impersonal, unfamiliar. 'Delivery for you.'

Emerging from the bathroom once she'd heard the front door close again, Stella saw that he was carrying an enormous wooden crate, almost the size of a tea chest. 'For us? Who on earth is it from?'

'The guy who delivered it had *F. Carter, Dorset* painted on the side of his wagon.'

'Mrs Nichols? The lady who lived here? What would she be sending to us?'

'Let's take it upstairs to find out.'

Stella climbed back onto the bed and hugged her knees as she watched Dan lever off the lid. There, lying on the packing straw, was a note. He handed it to her and she read it out with increasing wonder.

My dear Lieutenant Rosinski,

I do hope you won't be offended, but after we spoke on the telephone earlier it occurred to me that you might be in need of all sorts of household items as you set up your new home with your wife . . .

Stella paused and raised an eyebrow. 'Your wife?'

He looked sheepish. 'I couldn't exactly tell her you were someone else's wife, could I?'

Apart from the saucepans and blankets I donated to the local WVS and some items of sentimental value, many of the things I brought with me when I moved from Greenfields Lane were still packed away in the cases they came in, as I have no need of them here. I thought they might be of use to you in a time when such things are hard to come by.

'The little beauty . . .' From beneath the layers of straw Dan lifted a green lustreware teapot and four cups and saucers. These were followed by four plates patterned with ivy and a bundle of bone-handled cutlery, tied up with string. A small milk jug bearing the legend 'A Present from Margate' emerged next, then a little mirror with an oak frame that crossed at the corners, and a pressed glass cake stand. At the bottom of the crate was a chipped enamel milk pan and a frying pan, cheap and barnacled with use, but worth a price beyond rubies. Dan held it aloft like a trophy, grinning.

Stella read on, incredulous at such generosity.

I hope you will accept them as a house-warming gift and indulge a foolish woman who is getting sentimental with the advancing years. It pleases me to think of these things being used once more in that dear house, and I wish you all the happiness that I enjoyed there.

Kindest Regards
Violet Nichols.

P.S. I have included a little present from my 'girls' – who are yet another unexpected joy of my new life in the country. I hope it has survived the journey!

They looked at each other, mystified and a little over-whelmed.

'Her girls?'

'There's nothing else in here ...' Dan was looking in the crate, sifting through the packing straw and lifting it out to make sure he hadn't missed anything. It had spilled out onto the bedroom floor and drifts of it lay across the bed, giving the room a rustic feel. Dan had straw in his hair, and there was straw sticking out of the spout of the teapot. Idly reaching to remove it Stella gave a gasp of surprise.

'Dan, look!'

Tucked inside the teapot in their own little nest of straw were two speckled brown eggs.

'Well I'll be ... If she didn't think I was already married I'd be heading down to Dorset to tell Mrs Violet Nichols that I love her.'

Stella settled herself back on her bed of straw and laughed delightedly.

'Instead you can head downstairs to make me breakfast.'

In the early afternoon she took the bus back to King's Oak. Praying not to bump into anyone she knew she hurried along the street from the bus stop and let herself into the Vicarage. The boiled vegetable smell enveloped her as soon as she closed the door.

In the kitchen she collected her ration book from the drawer and went outside to grub up a few potatoes and a lettuce for dinner, then picked some raspberries. They were almost too ripe, and oozed dark crimson juice into the bowl, which helped to assuage the nagging guilt she felt about taking them. Although she'd be coming back tomorrow and staying until everything was resolved, it felt like in some fundamental way the Vicarage had already ceased to be her home.

Perhaps it never was, she thought, leaving the kitchen and going back along the silent passageway to the hall. *I've only ever been the housekeeper.* She stood for a moment looking around as the Virgin Mary gazed at her with hooded, blaming eyes from the wall. What had Violet Nichols said to Dan? *A house filled with love.* The Vicarage had never been that, no matter how much she'd tried.

The air was warmer outside. She walked the familiar route to the row of shops on Oak Street with a new vitality in her step. In the butcher's shop Mr Fairacre commented that she was looking very chipper. *Oh dear*, Stella thought, *Charles has just left and I'm supposed to be miserable.* She tried to look appropriately grave as she asked for two lamb chops.

Mr Fairacre gave a low whistle as he weighed them out. 'Special dinner, is it?'

Nosy old bugger. She wished she could use her coupons

somewhere else. 'Just Nancy coming over to keep me company. The house seems very empty on my own.'

As she left the shop she bit the corners of her mouth to stop herself from smiling. How easy it had become to lie.

In her absence Dan had knocked on the door of the next house but one and introduced himself to the neighbour – an elderly man called Mr Chapman with a bristling white moustache and a pronounced limp 'from fighting the Boers' – in the hope of borrowing something to cut the lawn. In the end, seeing the unkempt state of his lawn too, Dan had offered to cut that one as well, in repayment for the loan of the mower.

It was a tiny push-along thing, like a tin toy, and essentially unequal to the lush meadow of a lawn. When Stella got home he was still battling with it. Stripped to the waist, a cigarette hanging from his lower lip, his golden skin glistened and his damp hair was untidy where he'd pushed it back from his forehead. When she kissed him he smelt of fresh sweat and fresh grass.

While he returned the lawnmower she ran him a bath and he lay in it with the door open, talking to her as she moved about the kitchen, assembling their supper. The simple domesticity of it gave her a sense of profound, serene joy.

There was no towel. He came into the kitchen wearing only his shorts, with droplets of water beading his chest and back. In his hands he carried, miraculously, two bottles of beer.

Stella's jaw dropped. 'Where did you get those?'

He looked very pleased with himself. 'I was passing the pub this afternoon. I left them in water in the sink, so they should be good and cold. I never can get used to the way you drink it warm over here.'

He had an alchemist's gift for conjuring up treats from thin air, making magic from the mundane. They took them outside and sat on the damp, freshly cut grass in the evening sunlight while the swallows performed their aerial acrobatics in the warm blue air above. Then, while Stella cooked the lamb chops Dan carried the gateleg table out into the centre of the lawn and laid it with the plates and cutlery Violet Nichols had sent.

'All that's missing is a silver candelabra,' he said when they'd finished eating and the sky had turned to deep blue velvet above them.

Stella tipped her head back and looked up into the indigo infinity. 'We couldn't risk it. Apparently the Luftwaffe can see you strike a match on the ground.'

'Load of baloney.'

'Is it? I often wondered. It seemed unlikely somehow. What can you see?'

His sigh melted into the soft evening. 'I don't know much about night missions, but I guess they're kinda the same as daytime ones, which means you can see pretty much nothing at all. Cloud. Smoke. Flak. Tracer fire. No one's going to notice some guy standing on a street corner lighting a cigarette with all that going on. The night flyers get to see the pretty lights when the bombs hit, but I don't suppose they have any more

329

idea than we do whether it's the target that's on fire or a bunch of houses.'

He turned away, but even in the dissolving light Stella could see the set of his jaw and the muscle flickering above it. A little silence fell, but it was tainted with the bitterness of his words, which lingered between them. Leaning across the table she took his hand.

'Dan, I'm sorry.'

'Me too.' His voice cracked, letting the despair seep out. 'Me too.'

'Tell me about it.'

'About what?'

'About whatever happened that made them send you to that place. The flak farm.'

For a moment she thought he was going to brush her off. He sighed again, a sigh of bone-weary resignation and hopelessness, but then he began to speak. 'They send most of us there at some point – or those of us that live long enough to need it. We had a run of bad missions, long range into Germany. Those are the most dangerous ones; all those miles on our own over enemy territory once the fighter escorts have waved goodbye and turned back for home. They're the most tiring too. I love our fort, but she's heavy to hold for eight, nine hours at a time. There were big losses; forts falling from the sky with whole crews gone. We ... we lost one of our men. Just one, which is probably pretty damn lucky.'

'Who was it?'

'Our navigator. Johnson.'

Instantly, automatically, she felt her eyes fill with tears. 'Oh Dan, I'm so sorry ... His wife had just had a little boy. He was your friend.'

'Yeah. He was a good guy. Good navigator, good friend, and he would have been a damn good father too, if he'd had the chance.' He closed his eyes and his face, veiled in twilight, wore an expression of profound pain. 'The thing is,' he said softly, 'I can't imagine going up there without him.'

Stella's fingers tightened around his. 'How many more?'

'Six.'

'You're nearly there.' She said it almost pleadingly. 'Nearly through.'

'Maybe. It doesn't feel like that. I've been lucky so far – Christ knows why – but luck changes in an instant. Think about it. Six missions; that's maybe thirty-six hours in a rattling tin can loaded with enough fuel and ammunition to go up like a firework on the fourth of July, and the Luftwaffe's finest spraying you with incendiary fire, and all it takes is a second – one second – to end it all.'

He pulled his fingers from between hers and dropped his head into his hands.

'I'm sorry. At the base I never think about this stuff. Nobody does. It's kind of easier to accept it there, somehow – I guess because it's so normal. It's only when you get away that you realize what a screwed-up world we live in. But you don't need to know all of that stuff. I shouldn't be saying—'

'You *should*.' Her voice was low, certain. 'I'm not a soldier and I'm not fighting in this bloody awful war, but I'm not a child either. I don't want to be protected, Dan. I want to know what you have to go through, and if there was anything – *anything* – I could do or give up or suffer to make it even the tiniest bit more bearable I'd do it in a heartbeat. But there's nothing I can do, except listen. And love you. And tell you that it's all right to be scared and it's good to talk about it.'

His shoulders heaved, and he looked at her with eyes that were wide and darker than the evening sky. 'I am scared, Stella. Scared of dying. Scared of leaving you. Scared ... *so* scared that this is all we're ever going to have. And I want more. *Years* more with you ...'

She got up and went to him, cradling his head against her as she soothed. 'Shhh ... we'll have that, we have to believe it. What we have is too big to be destroyed in a second. Whatever happens, this is it – for life. Every day, every hour, I'll go on loving you whether you're with me or not.'

'No.' He shook his head, detaching himself so he could look at her. 'I wouldn't want that. If I don't come through it I'd want you to move on. Not with Charles, but with someone else. Someone who'll take care of you and love you like you deserve to be loved. Promise me?'

She didn't want to argue, so she tilted his chin upwards and bent to kiss him, deeply and with infinite, aching tenderness. The future lay beyond the inky garden, unformed and impossible to know. The only certainty was now, and this precious, magical summer's night. The warmth of his mouth against hers.

'I don't want to think about it,' she said quietly. 'And I don't want anyone but you – not now, not *ever*.'

He got slowly to his feet, and she felt his hands circle her waist; his long, strong fingers spanning across her back as he pulled her against him.

'I love you. Jeez, Stella – *I love you*.'

The jagged edge of panic was still there in his voice, and so she captured his mouth again and kissed him, on and on, stroking her fingers through his hair, massaging the rigid, corded muscles of his neck and shoulders until she felt it warm into urgency of a different kind. His breath was uneven as he pulled away and rested his forehead against hers, drawing her into the moonlit pool of his gaze. The moment of crisis had passed and she had pulled him back from the edge of the abyss.

'Dan . . .' It was a sigh. A surrender.

'You ever made love outside?' he murmured.

Her lips blossomed into a smile. 'You know I haven't.'

'Want to try it?'

'We can't! The neighbours . . .'

'The blackout. The whole city has closed its eyes. Nobody's watching.'

It was true. All around the houses were dark and shuttered, their occupants oblivious inside. They could do anything. Standing in the middle of the lawn he unbuttoned her dress and slipped it off her shoulders.

25

2011

Of course, he was late.

By the time Will had gone home, ransacked his wardrobe for a decent, ironed shirt and tried to tame his hair it was quarter to three. It took him another ten minutes to choose something to take for her in the mini-supermarket at the end of the road, and he had just got into the car and driven to the end of the street when he remembered what a nightmare it was to find a parking space. He reversed all the way back to his house (the Spitfire's engine screeching in protest) and abandoned the car, then sprinted to the bus stop and had to wait fifteen minutes for a bus.

It was almost half past three when he walked up the corridor to the ward, carrying the shoebox of letters and a giant bar of chocolate. He was already regretting his choice of gift. In the shop he had picked up boxes of chocolates, but put them back again on the grounds that they were too clichéd, too hopefully romantic. He'd briefly considered more flowers, but what use were they, really? Remembering her pale, pinched face he'd settled on chocolate in bulk, but now it seemed ridiculously cheap and crass. He dropped it onto an empty trolley as he passed, and hurried on. After the cold outside it felt blastingly hot in the hospital, and his shirt was sticking to his back by the time the nurse at the desk directed him to Jess's bed. He almost turned round and went home.

But then he saw her. She was in the bed at the end, sitting back against the bank of pillows with her knees tucked up and her arms wrapped around them, and was easy to spot because she was the only patient not surrounded by chattering visitors. There was a drip stand beside her, to which she was tethered by a plastic tube taped to the back of her hand. Her head was turned to look out of the window, but as Will approached she looked round. When she saw him, a faint tint of pink washed her pale cheeks.

'Hi ... Jess? I hope you don't mind me barging in on you like this. I'm Will. We've met before but you probably don't remember.'

'Oh ... Yeah. Yeah, I do.' She was blushing properly now, her eyes downcast as she made nervous pleats in the hospital sheet. Her voice was hoarse and a little raspy, as if it hurt to talk. 'Sorry about being in the house. I know it was out of order but it was just until I sorted something else out, and I really tried not to do any harm or touch anything that wasn't mine.'

'Oh God – I'm not here about that! Honestly, it couldn't

matter less to me – except, of course, that you're OK.' Since she obviously almost wasn't, he rushed on. 'I've been back to the house. I'm trying to sort it out for her neighbour, and hopefully find out if Nancy Price has any living relatives who'd be heirs to her estate. While I was looking for information I came across these.'

He put the shoebox on the bed. She stared at it, and a fresh wave of pink infused her cheeks. When she looked up at him her eyes were troubled.

'They were hidden at the back of a drawer. I found them by accident. I shouldn't have been looking, but I—'

'Thank goodness you did. You saved me a whole lot of time and bother.' Her eyes were grey, he noticed. They reflected her mood like the weather. 'Somewhere in all this lot might be exactly the information I need. I don't suppose you've read them by any chance?'

It was like approaching a nervous horse. One wrong move and he sensed he wouldn't see her for dust. Not that she could actually go anywhere this time, but even so. He wanted to win her trust.

'Some,' she said cautiously. 'I know I shouldn't have, but . . .' Nervously she moistened her lips and rubbed at the cannula in the back of her hand. 'But they're not really Nancy's letters. After the first one, they're addressed to someone called Stella Thorne, see?'

She moved aside the envelope at the front of the box and showed him. *Mrs S. Thorne, The Vicarage, Church Road, King's Oak, London.*

'So they are . . .' Will said, surprised. 'I didn't even notice. So who is she, this Stella Thorne?'

She hesitated, like she was wrestling with some private dilemma, and then took a rapid little breath. 'I don't know yet. But I really need to find out.'

It was a relief, finally, to tell someone.

She tried to keep it brief, but was aware as the words came out of her in stop-start bursts that there were bits that sounded weird and made no sense. He didn't stop her though. He'd sat down on the chair beside her bed and listened as it came spilling out. All of it: about Dodge and that last gig at the pub in Church End. About how he'd left the wad of money in the van and she'd seen it. Seen her chance. About how she'd run, and kept running until she found herself in a back road, looking at a house that had obviously been empty for years. About the letter from Dan Rosinski, marked 'Personal and Urgent'.

'It felt like fate. I know that sounds insane.'

He smiled. It was a kind of lopsided smile, bittersweet somehow, and it gave her a fluttering feeling in her chest. 'Not to me it doesn't, and I know all about insane.' He flicked through the letters in the box, releasing a faint scent of age and damp that took her right back to the house. 'So have you found out anything that'll help you find her?'

'Nothing yet. She was married right from the start, when they met. Her husband was a vicar – a chaplain in the army. He was away in North Africa when she met Dan. He was an American pilot.'

Will picked a letter from the box and scrutinized the address on the front. Its series of scribbled numbers and initials had meant nothing to her, but he seemed to be able to decipher them. 'Palingthorpe, in Suffolk. He would have been with the US Eighth Army, flying B-17s on daylight bombing raids into occupied territory. Dangerous work. Not a great survival rate.'

'But I know he did survive. He's still alive now, in America – Maine, to be precise. What I don't know is where she is, or what happened to them. They were in love. They wanted to be together when the war was over—'

Her chest heaved and cracked beneath the strain of talking and she was gripped by a fit of coughing. There was a jug of water and a glass on the locker beside the bed, but to get it she'd have to reach right over, and as the stupid hospital gown was fastened by ties at the back there was no way she was going to risk it. She coughed on, burying her face against her knees until she felt him beside her, gently touching her arm. He must have understood the issue and had come round the bed to get the glass for her. She took it and gulped gratefully.

'Better?'

She nodded, fighting for breath. In the aftermath of a coughing fit she always felt like a rag doll that had been picked up and shaken by a dog, then dropped again. She was getting better, feeling stronger every day, but the coughing still ripped through her body like a tornado.

'So, where had you got up to?' he asked, gently. 'With the letters?'

'I'd read about three quarters of them, I think. Once I started I couldn't stop. They didn't mean to fall in love, but you can see it happening. At first I thought she was stringing him along, wanting a bit of excitement while her husband was away, but I know it wasn't like that now. She seems to have been the only thing that kept him going. That's why I don't understand what could have happened.'

She slumped back on her bank of pillows and waited for him to say something dismissive or flippant about it just being a wartime fling. She was worn out, with coughing and talking, and felt suddenly exposed – not just by the stupid hospital gown, but by having shared the story of the letters. Dan and Stella were hers; she'd come to care about them and – in that strange time when fever had blurred the boundaries between day and night, waking and dreaming, reality and imagination – she'd felt she inhabited their world. She was afraid that now she'd opened it up to the brisk breeze of normality, and the fragile layers of the past would be scattered forever.

Will Holt got to his feet. 'I expect you've been dying to find out. Why don't I go and get us a cup of tea while you read on?'

31 July '43

Darling girl,

Today was insane. Crazy, like some kind of nineteen-hour nightmare. I'm still not sure I'm awake, because I can hear the engines in my head and my hands feel like they're still clamped around the throttle and the control column. I need to sleep, but I need more to talk to you, even if it can only be on paper. Stella, I'd give just about anything for a night with you now. Just to hold you and breathe in the scent of your hair would be enough.

Two more missions down. Four more to go. If I get through them you will marry me, won't you? Somehow? I don't care if it's just the two of us standing in the ruins of St Clement Danes at dawn, just so long as you'll promise to spend your life with me.

I love you Stella. Take good care of yourself for me.

D x

8 August '43

Darling Stella

Sorry for the long silence, and for my last letter, which I have a feeling might have sounded kind of crazy. I didn't know it at the time but when I wrote it I was right in the middle of coming down with the 'flu. It was the real deal — fever, hallucinations and aching so bad all over that I was sure I'd been shot up and couldn't remember it happening. When I came round in the hospital I thought the blonde nurse was German.

The worst thing is that the boys have finished their tour without me, but since they've also finished without Johnson and Harper I guess I'm the lucky one. Morgan and Adelman came to see me after their last mission. They smuggled in a bottle of bourbon and we managed to get disgustingly drunk before the nurse rumbled us and threw them out. If there's one thing worse than having the 'flu, it's having the 'flu with a crushing hangover, I can tell you that.

I've been stood down for ten days, and lying here hour after hour I can't help thinking that if I hadn't got sick I could be done by now. I could be in London, in the house in Greenfields Lane, with you. I think about you all the time, and it's a bittersweet kind of pleasure. Bitter because it makes me miss you more, and sweet because — well, for obvious reasons.

I'm hoping to be passed fit for flying again in the next couple days, and will be assigned a new crew. That'll be tough, but only four more missions and I'm done, and we can make a start on the rest of our lives. I don't know what will happen, but we'll always have a place to be together now, however and whenever.

Take care of yourself for me, darling girl.

Dan x

Jess was smiling as she finished reading; smiling because there it was — the first reference she'd found to the house in Greenfields Lane — and also in sympathy with Dan Rosinski and his 'flu. She knew how he'd felt, especially with the confusion. The weird thing was that while she'd been in the same situation it was him she'd been dreaming about. Him and Will, anyway; the two had become kind of interchangeable. She felt her cheeks heat up again remembering how he'd appeared through the fever's fire and chaos and touched her face with his cool, gentle hands. The rest of the world had long since slipped out of focus and she wasn't sure what was real and what was delirium, but she'd felt his strength and his kindness. And she'd known she could finally stop struggling because he was there, and she was safe.

She must remember to say thank you. God, she wished she had a mirror – she probably looked all kinds of hideous. Gingerly she altered her position in the bed, taking care not to knock the tube in her hand as she tried to tug the ugly gown into some kind of arrangement where it didn't look like a paper sack. She turned towards the window again. The outside world was nothing but a pewter grey background in which the brightly lit ward was reflected, and she was just pulling her fingers through her lank, greasy, sawn-off hair when she caught sight of him coming back. She turned round quickly, her heart giving an odd little skip.

He was carrying a tray on which were two cardboard cups and a piece of fruit cake wrapped in cellophane. He had nice hands, she noticed as he put one cup down on her locker, then pushed back the hair that had fallen over his forehead. Nice hair too. And an incredible smile.

'The cake looks fairly sad, but there wasn't much else and I thought you might be hungry.'

'Thank you,' she said, and the tightness in her chest was nothing to do with pneumonia.

26

1943

'Are you going to eat that?' Nancy eyed the dried piece of Genoa cake that Stella was absent-mindedly turning to crumbs. 'Only, if you're not, I will. I'm starving.'

Stella pushed the plate across the table. She'd only ordered the cake because she'd sensed the disapproval of the Nippy when she'd only asked for tea; Nancy had been late and, it being a Saturday, there were lots of other people waiting for tables. She had no appetite lately – the worry, she supposed. Dan was out of hospital now and back on duty and every day she woke up with a sick feeling in her stomach, knowing that he could be in the sky and heading for the heart of Germany, all the guns of the enemy ranged against him.

Across the table Nancy polished off the cake and took a packet of expensive-looking cigarettes from her handbag. Lighting one, she settled herself back in her seat. 'My feet are killing me,' she said, crossing her legs and drawing attention to her high-heeled cream leather shoes. She'd given up the salon and, funded by Len, devoted her days to the pursuit of beauty, though it didn't seem to bring her much satisfaction. 'I've already been all round Debenham and Freebody looking for a dress but honestly, I wouldn't scrub the floors in the flimsy old rags they're selling in there. I want something stunning. Something sophisticated.'

'Have you got coupons?'

'Oh yes, loads.' Nancy waved her cigarette dismissively. 'Len can always lay his hands on them. It's finding something worth spending them on that's the problem. I need nylons as well,' she sighed, extending her leg and picking at a run with scarlet-tipped fingers. 'Don't suppose there'll be any of those to be had in the shops for love, money nor coupons.' She looked up at Stella with sudden interest. 'Here, don't suppose you've got any lying around, from your Yank . . . ?'

'I've got the packet he gave me in Cambridge, but they've been worn a good few times. They're not bad though – you can borrow them if you like.'

Nancy's face fell again. Being with Len had spoiled her for second-hand. 'Thanks all the same.' She exhaled a plume of smoke with an edge of irritation. 'You'd think he'd keep you well supplied with little treats like that, wouldn't you? I mean, it's not like they're short, is it? Bit tight if you ask me.' She shot Stella a sly glance. 'Not giving them away to someone else, is he? One of them village girls he's met at a dance on the base?'

Nancy always became sharp when thwarted, but since she'd been seeing Len it was as if any softness she'd once had had been stamped out, or hidden beneath the black-market silk blouses and the mysteriously acquired trench coat. Anger flared through Stella's veins like a flash fire, and she set her cup down in the saucer very carefully. 'He gives me lots of things,' she said quietly. 'More than I ever dreamed I'd have.'

'Yes, well, there's a war on. Fancy promises of undying love don't keep you warm and looking presentable, do they? Give me a few pairs of nylons and a decent lipstick any day.'

'He's given me more than promises.'

'Oh yes? Got a ring, have you?' Nancy looked at her with withering pity. 'Stella, angel, you're too nice for this world. I don't want to sound cruel, but I don't want to stand by and see you get hurt neither, because you can bet as soon as he's flown his last mission he'll be off into the wide blue yonder and he won't look back. I'm not saying it hasn't meant something, but let's face it, it ain't going to last. A wartime romance, that's what it is. God knows, we need a bit of romance. It's about the only thing that's in plentiful supply these days.'

Coming to the end of this speech, Nancy took another drag on her cigarette and stared moodily out of the window. It was a bright September afternoon, but cold enough for people to have unearthed threadbare coats from the backs of wardrobes. The year was turning.

'A house,' Stella said softly, almost to herself. 'He bought me a house.'

It was as if the words stopped time for a second. Nancy froze, and when she moved again her face and voice were curiously blank.

'A house?' She tapped her cigarette over the cheap tin ashtray on the table and gave an abrupt little laugh. 'Where?'

'Church End. It's tiny and old and hidden away on a little back lane. I love it.'

She said the last bit almost defensively. Nancy ignored it. 'Blimey. So you're leaving the Rev then?'

Stella nodded and swallowed the last of her tea. It was cold and almost made her gag. 'You were right. I should never have married him. I . . . I had no idea. About anything.'

'So when are you going to tell him?'

'I don't know.' A wave of inexpressible weariness crashed over Stella, as it did so often these days. 'It's hard to find a good moment when he's hundreds of miles away in Italy. It's not the kind of thing I can put in a letter, sandwiched between news of the runner bean glut and Reverend Stokes's latest sermon. Maybe I'll even have to wait until the war's over: I've been listening to the wireless — it seems we're making proper progress so it surely can't be too long. In many ways I think he'll be relieved. I know appearances are important to him, but he knows as well as I do that the marriage was a mistake.'

Nancy's pencilled eyebrows shot up, though whether her scepticism was directed at the idea of the war, or Stella's marriage ending wasn't clear. 'What about the God thing? Marriage vows made in church being unbreakable and all that?'

'I know it'll be difficult for him, but I hope he'll see that we have a right to try to be happy, especially after all these

346

years of struggling and hardship. Surely that's what God would want?'

Viciously Nancy squashed the end of her cigarette into the ashtray and ground it down. 'I don't think it's that simple with God. After all, he's a man, ain't he?'

Double summertime had ended and the days seemed to shorten rapidly. In the garden everything was ready at once, making the challenge of feeding Reverend Stokes slightly easier but providing endless amounts of tedious work; picking, peeling, slicing, sterilizing jars and eking out sugar for jam. Another season of apples swelled and sweetened, and Stella made apple sauce in preparation for Blossom's impending demise.

She wrote to Dan and told him how she could no longer bear to go round with scraps from the kitchen and watch her snuffling through them, rooting out the choicest bits with surprising delicacy, oblivious to the fate that was soon to befall her. It seemed like a betrayal. It also gave Stella a sense of superstitious unease: what if God was looking down and watching her going about her daily chores, similarly oblivious that disaster was about to strike?

No matter how hard she tried to shake it off, a sense of doom stalked her through those late September days. Even receiving a letter from Dan – while wonderful – offered small comfort because she knew that it would have been written three or four days earlier, and was well aware how much could change in that time. The censor ensured she only read half of what he wrote to her about operations, but combined with what she picked up from the nine o'clock news on the wireless it was enough to know that a major air offensive was underway.

Leave passes were like hen's teeth. Since those enchanted first days in the house they had never had another night there, although twice they managed to snatch a handful of hours together when he'd been on stand down and had hitched a ride on a supply truck. He'd been able to give her no notice, and she had no idea if or when such a meeting might be possible again, which only added to her unsettled feeling. Each day was a round of hope and dread, waiting and disappointment.

To make matters worse, the last time they had met at the house they'd come close to arguing. She had already been there when he arrived and he had walked straight into her arms as she opened the door. Wordlessly they had gone upstairs and made love with silent intensity, until tears slid from her eyes and into her hair.

Afterwards they lit a fire in the grate downstairs and sat in front of it, drinking the whisky he'd brought with him as the sweet autumn afternoon cooled into evening outside. The raw feeling she'd had for weeks was back, as if she'd lost a layer of skin which had left her emotions too close to the surface. She'd reached for him again, wanting to wrap herself around him and feel the strength of him inside her. Reluctantly he'd pulled away, murmuring into her hair, 'I haven't got another rubber.'

'I don't care.'

'I do.' Sighing, he sat up and raked a hand through his hair. Muscles moved beneath the skin of his bare back – he'd lost weight since he'd been in hospital, and the realization made her want to hold on to him even more. 'I care about you too much to land you with a baby.'

'I *want* a baby.'

'So do I. But not now, not like this. I want to raise our kids in a safe world. One where we can be together all the time, not just in furtive moments that feel like they're stolen from someone else.'

'But what if you don't survive to see that perfect world?' The words sprang like malevolent toads from the dark swamp of despair inside her. Tears were streaming down her cheeks, dripping onto her raised knees as she hugged herself on the floor. 'Dan, what if you don't come back? Couldn't you at least let me have a part of you to live for?'

'Sweetheart, you would have.' He knelt in front of her, his expression terribly sad. '*You're* a part of me, and if that happens, if I don't come back, I'd want you to live for yourself. I'd want you to have choices and the freedom to make them; to leave Charles, if that was what you wanted, and come here and be safe. It would be hard, but a whole lot harder if you had a baby.'

She knew he was right, but that only made it worse. Later, before he left, she had apologized for her childish, unreasonable behaviour and he had kissed her gently, sweetly; utterly forgiving. But she couldn't quite forgive herself for spoiling their precious time together. It played on her mind and added to the sense of dread. What if that was the last time she saw him?

All of this was going round in her mind as she stood at the sink washing Reverend Stokes's breakfast dishes one morning. She had run out of soap and the water was greyish and greasy, with bits of powdered egg floating like primitive life forms in it. A sulphurous whiff rose from it, like bad drains. Her throat constricted with nausea.

There was a knock on the back door. The effort of going to open it seemed too great, so she shouted, 'Come in!'

Ada appeared, her old tweed coat thrown over her kitchen pinny, her head swathed in a scarf. She bustled over to the table, carrying a wicker basket and the clean, cold smell of autumn.

'Morning love. Thought I'd bring you the first pickings.' She lifted a bloody newspaper bundle from the basket and dropped it proudly on the table. Stella looked at it in horror.

'What is it?'

Laughing, Ada folded back the red-edged pages to reveal a glistening mound of crimson flesh and nest of greyish snakes. 'A good bit of liver, some loin, some chitterlings, bacon of course—'

Blossom.

The iron tang of blood filled Stella's nostrils. She clamped a hand over her mouth and nose to block it out, and, cannoning off the table and the wall just about made it to the lavatory beside the scullery before she was violently sick.

*

'Better?'

Ada watched her with a mixture of sympathy and concern as she sipped her tea. Blossom's mortal remains had been wrapped up again and removed from sight, though Stella could still smell the metallic reek of flesh. Since when had her nose been so sensitive?

'A bit, thanks.' She took another dutiful sip. In all honesty she would have preferred water, but it would have been ungrateful to say that when Ada had been kind enough to make a pot of tea. Wearily she acknowledged that it would also be ungrateful, and ungracious, to say that she was still feeling wretched and would rather be left alone. Ada had taken off her coat and hung it on the hook on the back door, and seemed to be prepared to stay until she was sure Stella was all right. Pinned by her sharp gaze, Stella dredged up a smile. 'It's the change of seasons. Always a bad time for illness.'

'Felt like this for a while, have you?'

'A week or so, although I haven't been sick before. I thought I was fighting it off, but obviously not. I've been so tired . . .'

Ada gave a soft little chuckle. 'Poor lamb. You're in the club, ain't you?'

For a moment Stella was nonplussed. She thought of the bloodstained newspaper parcel and its gruesome contents. The pig club. She was in the pig club, that's why Ada had come round.

'What I mean is . . .' Ada's voice gentled. 'Could you have started a baby?'

Stella's jaw dropped. Thoughts chased each other like leaves in a gale across her mind. A baby? But Dan had been so careful ... so determined. Could fate have intervened, just like it had when it had brought them both to the church, and taken him to the house? *Some great plan that was written in the stars* ...

'A baby?'

Tentative joy glowed inside her, like the first traces of pink dawn on the night horizon. He couldn't mind now it had happened, could he? A baby. Dan's child. She could almost hear its laughter echoing through the little house on Greenfields Lane.

Ada chuckled affectionately. 'Don't sound so shocked, love. It happens. And my guess is that you must be about two and a bit months on, which is exactly how long it is since Reverend Thorne was home on 'is Embarkation Leave.'

Oh God ...

Charles.

Her cheek grinding against the fireplace and grit in her mouth. Slime between her thighs. *Indecent acts.*

The pink glow died and there was nothing but darkness.

The bell sounded for the end of visiting time, jolting Will back into the present. Looking up, he was surprised to find that while he'd been reading the letters it had gone completely dark. The windows were squares of black; shiny like tar, sealing off the world outside.

He stretched and rubbed a hand through his hair and looked down at the letter in his hand. Reading quickly – a

352

skill he'd perfected at university – he'd almost caught up with Jess. He could understand how she'd become so involved in the lives of Dan Rosinski and Stella Thorne. Even without being able to read Stella's side of the correspondence their story had leapt from the brittle pages and dragged him in.

He replaced the letter in its envelope. Up and down the ward people were standing up, stacking plastic chairs they'd brought in from the day room, rustling plastic bags as items to leave and items to take home were exchanged. Only Jess was still, curled up on the bed with her back to him, her knees tucked up. He wondered if she was asleep. Through the narrow gap between the ties of the hospital gown he could see the pale ridge of her spine, as delicate as an ammonite. He averted his eyes, and was just wondering whether to slip quietly away when she stirred and turned towards him.

Her eyes were swimming with tears, shimmering like pebbles in a clear stream. Uncurling herself she held out the letter she'd been reading.

'Look.'

He took it from her. *Dear Stella,* he read, *This is one of those letters I hope you don't ever read, the one I'm going to leave on my bunk to be posted by the CQ if I don't come back . . .*

'He must have got shot down,' Jess said softly. 'I guess she thought he was dead. She gave up on him.'

27

1943–44

The high-up windowsills of St Crispin's were decked with swags of ivy and fronds culled from an overgrown conifer hedge at the back of the village hall field. There were a few sprigs of holly too. Candlelight made its glossy leaves shine, and showed up the few berries, gleaming in jewelled clusters against all the green.

You couldn't beat candles at Christmas. Ada glanced up at the windows where, at four o'clock, the light was already beginning to fade from the day. If old Stokes didn't get a move on they'd have that fusspot Jim Potter slapping a fine on him for breach of blackout regulations. She glanced across to where Jim was sitting with his wife. The fact that it was Christmas Eve and he was in his best suit rather than his ARP uniform wouldn't hold him back from doing his official duty.

At last Reverend Stokes announced the final hymn and they all roused themselves to sing *O Come All Ye Faithful*. It was one of Ada's favourites, though it was hard to imagine all the nations arising joyfully together at the end of yet another year spent bashing each other to pieces. Really, it seemed never-ending, and harder to bear or comprehend at Christmas. All the suffering. All the loss. She sent up another swift and silent prayer of thanks that her Harry was safe at home, sleeping off the effects of a thirty-six-hour journey to get there. There were many as weren't so lucky. Reverend Stokes had read out a list of names of those from the parish who wouldn't be spending the festive season at home. It was no wonder the service had gone on so blooming long.

Ada's gaze came to rest on the solitary figure in the front pew and her hearty singing faltered a little. The poor mite. From the back you couldn't tell at all that she was expecting; she was thinner than ever. Too thin, in Ada's view. The mound of the baby seemed stuck on, like it was nothing to do with the rest of her body. She'd been sick as a dog at first, of course, but she should have got over that by now and be blooming, as much as anyone could bloom in this endless winter of an endless war. But she wasn't. Her hair had lost the lustre it had had in the summer, and her eyes had lost their shine. You'd think instead of looking forward to a birth she was mourning a death.

The organ swelled as Marjorie Walsh thundered triumphantly through the last verse. *Born that man no more may die,* Ada sang wistfully. Babies always brought hope. Maybe Stella would pick up once the little one was actually in her arms. In the meantime, Ada resolved to keep a close eye on her, make sure she was eating properly and not letting that old goat Stokes take all her rations.

As the congregation filtered out of their pews, moving slowly towards the door and the frosty twilight beyond, she abandoned Alf and caught up with Marjorie and her husband. Dr Walsh had taken the half hunter from his waistcoat pocket and was looking at it, saying, 'If we hurry we might just catch the end of the Festival of Nine Lessons and Carols on the wireless.'

'We've just had carols,' Marjorie hissed.

'Hardly the same standard.'

Marjorie was about to reply when she noticed Ada and was forced to present a polite smile. 'Lovely service, I thought. Very festive with the candles, though we ought to blow them out quickly now as it's getting so dark. And such a nice letter from Reverend Thorne, though even he sounds like he's struggling to hold on to hope and stay cheerful.'

'Aren't we all?' Ada looked past Marjorie to where Stella was collecting hymn books. Smiling was obviously an effort and made the tendons stand out in her neck. 'Mrs Thorne's shockingly thin – there's not an ounce of flesh on her bones. It's not right in her condition. Is there anything you can give her, Doctor?'

Dr Walsh tucked the watch back into his pocket and rocked back on his heels. 'Some women just don't take well to childbearing. It's a question of temperament, and I'm afraid there's little we in the medical profession can do about that.'

Pompous old so-and-so. Ada almost wished she hadn't asked. 'Oh well, I daresay she'll pick up when she's got a little one to nurse.'

'Perhaps.' Dr Walsh smiled with patronizing gravity. 'Though I'm afraid I'd have to say that, in my experience, that's when the problems can really start.'

Usually in nightmares you woke up just before the really terrifying thing actually happened – when you were falling and about to hit the ground, or when the shadowy figure who was chasing you was almost within grabbing range. But there was no such relief from this nightmare. It just went on and on and on.

Dan was gone, and yet she had to stand here in the church hall, pouring tea and handing out Marjorie Walsh's mince pies ('Yes, isn't she clever – you can hardly tell there's no currants in the mincemeat') and smiling. Smiling until her face hurt almost as much as her heart.

It all felt ridiculously surreal, but then she supposed that all nightmares were. She continued to act out the role of Vicarage wife and say the simple, meaningless things that people expected to hear from her, while behind the rigid mask of her face the real her was screaming. Sometimes she imagined dropping the act and letting the mask crack and fall away. She imagined setting down the teapot now and sinking to the floor behind the table and just sobbing and sobbing, like she did in bed at night, but loudly and without restraint. The idea was mesmerizingly seductive.

'Careful,' Dot Wilkins squeaked, snatching her cup away as tea overflowed into the saucer. 'You'll have a caution for waste if you carry on like that.'

'Sorry. I was miles away.'

'I could see that. Missing him, are you?'

Stella nodded, clenching her teeth hard against the need to cry out. *Missing him like you wouldn't believe. Missing him so much that I think I might die. Wishing I could die.*

'It's always worse at Christmas. I remember when Arthur was away in the last one, and just thinking of him out there in the freezing cold, having bully beef and biscuits and the Queen's plum pudding for his Christmas dinner made me so miserable for him I couldn't eat a mouthful of mine. My mother was furious, she always said it was a sin to waste good food.' She picked up the brimming saucer and tipped the tea back into the cup. 'There'll be happier times ahead though, you wait and see. When the war's over and you've got your little family . . .'

Right on cue the baby inside her stirred, butting irritably against her drum-tight skin. Now it was bigger its movements always felt cross, like it too resented having to share her body. *There won't*, the real Stella behind the mask replied coldly to Mrs Wilkins. *You're quite wrong. I'll never be happy again because the man I wanted to have a family with is gone. Missing presumed dead.*

The fake Stella smiled her painful, plastic smile. 'Of course.'

'It must be such a comfort to Reverend Thorne, knowing there's a baby on the way. "A blessing, and evidence that God has not deserted us in these dark days" – that was what he said in his letter, wasn't it? I thought that was lovely.'

At this, Stella's ability to deliver the appropriate lines deserted her. She excused herself, muttering something about getting more milk. In the kitchen she closed the door and stuffed her fist into her mouth to stifle the sob that tore up through her.

Missing does not mean dead.

That night she sat on the edge of the bed in the darkness, Josef Rosinski's letter clutched in her hand. She hadn't drawn the blackout and the thin moonlight made shapes on the floor and across the bed. It wasn't bright enough to enable her to read the old-fashioned handwriting, but she didn't need to. She knew the letter by heart and whispered the words into the silence, to make them seem more real.

There's still hope, and we must not lose sight of that.

It had taken her a month after she had got Dan's letter of farewell to muster the strength to go back to the little house in Greenfields Lane. Grief and morning sickness felled her, though at least she was able to hide the former behind the latter as an excuse for keeping to her bed and abdicating responsibility for the house, the church, the Red Cross Parcels and crèche.

The idea of returning to the place where she'd known such brief and perfect happiness was almost unbearable, but in the end some kind of masochistic need took her back. The little house was cold and there were shadows where before there had been sunlight. The remains of the fire they'd lit on that September afternoon was still in the grate, but the sheets had long since lost the scent of his skin. They felt damp against her cheek when she lay on them to read the letter she had found waiting for her amid the scattered skeletons of leaves on the doormat, addressed to Miss S Thorne.

Dan's father had reached out to her across the miles of icy, treacherous ocean. She had been inexpressibly touched by his generosity and gentleness, which reminded her so poignantly of Dan. But she was also choked by guilt.

Reading his letters I was in no doubt about how much my son loved you. Loves you. I believe that he's still alive somewhere and, spurred on by the thought of you, he will find some way to make it back so you can have the life together that he had planned.

She hadn't written back. She wanted to, but knew that doing so would mean choosing to deceive this kindly, grieving old man or to compound his hurt by telling him that she was carrying the child of another man.

Outside it had begun to snow; tiny, feathery flakes that dissolved almost before they'd touched the wet ground. Like wishes. Like plans.

January came. A new year, but one with little new hope. At least once the scrappy attempts at festive decorations were taken down and the old routine resumed, there was no longer the same pressure to be cheerful. Everyone was snappy and fed up. Stella was in good company.

As the baby grew inside her she felt as if she herself was shrinking, and her world too. The journey to the shops seemed longer and became almost overwhelmingly arduous over icy pavements that she could barely see for the mound of her stomach. Church End seemed as far away as the moon. She ached to find out if another letter had come from America, but the opportunity seemed constantly to elude her. Mornings were taken up with shopping, as supplies grew shorter and queues longer, meaning that by the time Reverend Stokes's lunch was cooked and cleared away she was on her knees with weariness. In the afternoons when she wasn't due at the church hall for crèche or parcels, Ada had taken to calling round 'to check if you're all right, love', and help her make a start on the supper.

It was Ada she assumed she'd see when she opened the door one afternoon towards the end of January. The sight of the telegram delivery boy sent the air rushing from her lungs.

'Telegram for Mrs Thorne. Here, do you need to sit down?'

'No. No, I'm perfectly fine. Thank you.'

She shut the door on him abruptly and fell back against it, tearing open the telegram, struggling to hold it steady enough to read as hope and terror sluiced through her.

REGRET TO INFORM YOU THAT YOUR HUSBAND,
REV. CHARLES THORNE, HAS BEEN INJURED IN AN
INCIDENT 22nd JANUARY 1944, NORTH ITALY.
FURTHER INFORMATION TO FOLLOW BY LETTER.

28

2011

Stella Thorne.

Will typed the words into the box on the screen and pressed enter, then waited for his cheap and unreliable laptop to digest them. It wasn't, as Ansell would have pointed out, the best name to work with; not unusual enough, and with a chance of spelling variations in the surname. But it was a start. The information necessary to find the girl with whom 2nd Lieutenant Daniel Rosinski had fallen in love in 1943 was out there, all that was needed was the knowledge of where to look, the patience to work through the possibilities and a little bit of inspired guesswork and lateral thinking. Oh – and an incentive for all of the above, which in his case came in the form of Jess Moran.

He could tell how much it meant to her. Shut away in that forgotten house, hiding from her bastard boyfriend, he could understand why she'd become so swept up in Dan and Stella's story, and so desperate to help bring about its happy ending:

other people's problems – especially ones that were over half a century old – always seemed easier to tackle than your own. And she certainly seemed to have had her share. Will was no stranger to loneliness and isolation, but just imagining what she'd been through made his heart turn over inside his chest.

It also put his own issues into perspective and gave him a new determination to get himself together. It was Sunday, which usually meant a lie-in until lunchtime, a large fry-up, and an afternoon slumped on the sofa watching whatever sport was in season with a beer in his hand. Today however, he'd got up early and done an hour at the gym, shopped for proper wholesome food and given the flat the cleaning of its life. With fresh sheets on the bed, the week's laundry picked up from the floor and put into the washing machine and actual fruit in the bowl beside the toaster he'd been able to stick two fingers up to the invitation stuck to the fridge as he got the milk out for his coffee.

He grimaced as he took a mouthful. It had gone cold. On his screen the circle of doom continued to rotate, so he turned his attention instead to the pad of A4 paper beside him.

At Ansell Blake the starting point was a death certificate. It was from there that they gleaned all their information; a date of birth, the place of death, the name of the informant (who was likely to be known to the deceased and therefore a good source of additional information), a married woman's maiden name. It provided a few bare facts; dry seeds from which shoots and roots might, with the right nurturing, sprout. But this search was different.

Hesitantly at first, and then with gathering confidence he listed the facts he had.

Stella Thorne, maiden name —? Married Charles Thorne — Minister (C of E?) King's Oak, North London, Army Chaplain — sometime before 1943. Born —

He paused, calculating. She'd been young enough during the war years to be swept off her feet by an American airman — the typical age of whom was late teens to late twenties — putting her in roughly the same age bracket?

Born — 1913 — 1925??

The screen of his laptop brightened, showing the results of his search. All one thousand, eight hundred and seventy-four of them. Applying the dates he'd estimated narrowed it down, but still there were one hundred and thirty-seven Stella Thornes with husbands called Charles. The online archives were always frustratingly general, encompassing all name combinations and variations. Without knowing her maiden name or the exact date and place of their wedding it was impossible to know which one was likely to be the love of Dan Rosinski's life.

He puffed out his cheeks and exhaled slowly as he stared at the computer, his mind spinning fruitlessly like the circle on the screen. At a guess Stella Thorne might have got married in King's Oak, at the church where Charles was minister, but to find out for sure he'd have to make an appointment with the current vicar to look through the parish register, and when would that be possible? Not on a Sunday, he was pretty sure of that.

He'd made a deal with himself that he wouldn't go back to the hospital to visit Jess until he had something concrete to tell her, some information that would move her search forward. Impatience and frustration made his nerves fizz like badly wired electrics and he got up from the sofa and paced over to the window (a journey that would have been extremely hazardous before his tidying blitz). The information was out there, he just had to work out how to find it.

He headed to the kitchen to put the kettle on again for more coffee. The wedding invitation on the fridge door mocked him with its smug, gilt-edged traditionalism. *Mr and Mrs Hugo Ogilvie*. He parroted it aloud in a childish comedy voice, and was just reflecting that he'd spent too much time around Ansell the Arse when a thought struck him.

Leaving the kettle to boil noisily to itself he shot back into the sitting room.

Like many women of her time, Stella's life might have gone pretty much unrecorded, but he was prepared to bet that her husband's hadn't. He typed *Barnard Castle WW2* into the search engine. That was the place Dan Rosinski had mentioned in his letter; the faraway place where Reverend Charles Thorne had been posted, and finding out what happened to him was a good place to start finding out what happened to his wife.

With infuriating languor the screen produced a list of results. Clicking on the first one, Will discovered that 54th

Training Regiment of the Royal Armoured Corps had had a camp at Barnard Castle. A little more searching down the labyrinthine alleyways of amateur enthusiast forums led him to the regimental diary of Charles Thorne's Tank Regiment, digitalized and uploaded by some extremely helpful tank geek.

And there he was. Reverend Charles Thorne, Chaplain to the Forces, 4th Class. Joined the Regiment June 1943, embarked for Italy from Glasgow 29th July, arrived Naples 8th August. Injured 22nd January 1944, sent home on board hospital ship No.12, arriving Southampton 3rd February. There was another link, to a document this time. Will clicked on it and found himself looking at a miniature facsimile of a medical card. The handwriting was typically illegible, but when he enlarged the picture to its maximum size he could just about make out what it said.

'Vehicle accident. Severe trauma to upper left arm. Transhumeral amputation.'

*

Nancy offered to go with her to visit Charles. Stella accepted gratefully, relieved that she wouldn't have to face the ordeal of the journey or the daunting prospect of seeing Charles on her own, and glad that the strain of her last few meetings with Nancy had been swept aside by this new turn of events. Nancy had always been good in a crisis.

Predictably, the train was loaded to the gunwales with sailors returning from leave. Nancy was in her element, simpering and batting her eyelashes so that they were ushered onto the train like royalty. Waddling along in her wake Stella felt invisible, which was ironic given her size. But she was profoundly glad of it.

At Southampton station Nancy sought out a porter for directions to the hospital. Outside seagulls screamed and swooped overhead as they queued for a bus with several other white-faced women also accompanied by mothers, sisters, friends. Without the distraction of the sailors Nancy's attention turned to Stella. She took her limp hand and squeezed it.

'You all right? Not going to throw up are you?'

Stella shook her head and smiled weakly. She felt more faint than sick. The whole trip had an air of unreality, like it was part of the nightmare. She hadn't thought ahead to what she might find at the hospital, but as the bus juddered its way along bomb-scarred streets she forced herself to confront it. Charles; wounded, changed. His injury had been the result of a car accident, the medical officer had said in his letter. A mountain road, an icy night; no one's fault. The jeep had been open-sided, which accounted for the injury to Charles's arm. 'He was lucky,' the letter had said. 'It could very easily have been his neck that was broken.'

She wondered if they'd told him she was coming and couldn't imagine that the prospect of seeing her would bring him any comfort whatsoever. The two of them were nothing more than apathetic actors on a flimsy film set, like the ones in Charlie Chaplin pictures where the house folded inwards at the slightest touch. She was his wife, but she already knew to her cost that she was the last person he would open up to in a time of difficulty or distress.

The hospital was vast and palatial, a Victorian extravaganza in red brick and creamy white stone. Dan would have loved it, Stella thought with a thud of misery as she struggled down from the bus. Nancy straightened her skirt as they approached. 'Blimey. Makes you feel like you're going to tea with the King.'

Inside the corridors were as wide as Mile End Road, with tall windows facing out onto the landscaped grounds and the sea beyond. Patients in hospital blues moved slowly along them, some of them with a sleeve or a trouser-leg pinned up. Stella's skin felt clammy with sweat. A harassed-looking orderly directed them towards the Surgical division. Nancy walked with her, trying not to show impatience at her slow pace, until they were outside the double doors to Charles's ward.

'This is as far as I go, angel,' Nancy said. 'Pecker up – you'll be fine on your own from here. I'll make myself comfortable on that bench there and have a ciggy, so you take as long as you like.' She suddenly looked worried. 'You are allowed to smoke in here, aren't you?'

Stella was ten years old again, being sent to Miss Birch's special Latin lessons, while Nancy was heading to Domestic Science. The walk down to the nurses' desk seemed endless, the stern-faced sister in the starched apron and nun-like veil seated behind it impossibly intimidating without Nancy's bolstering presence. In the short time she'd known him Dan had

369

given her independence, confidence, but they seemed to have vanished along with him. *Oh Dan – help me . . .*

The nurse's expression softened when Stella told her who she was, and her pale, protruding eyes flicked down to her abdomen. She got up and came round the desk.

'Mrs Thorne. The medical officer has told you about his injury? Try not to be shocked when you see him – or at least don't let him see it, please. His arm is healing well, but we're keeping him under sedation for the time being. He's been rather . . . agitated – upset, if you like – when the medication has worn off. It's understandable, given this kind of injury.'

'His arm is healing? But I thought—?'

'It's been removed, yes, above the elbow, but there's a bit of the upper arm remaining, which is good news for the future. Here we are, dear. Fourth bed down on the right.'

It was Charles, but not Charles. He was asleep, and against the fat white pillow his face was yellowish, his lips scabbed and crusted. Stella sat in the hard chair at his bedside and looked at him, because there was nothing else to look at without intruding on the privacy of neighbouring patients and their visitors. His hair had thinned, and the bones of his skull gleamed beneath the stretched skin on his temples. His truncated arm lay outside the blankets, swathed in bandages. It reminded her of the swaddled baby Jesus in the picture that hung on the wall in the room they used for Sunday School at St Crispin's.

In sleep his face twitched irritably. The mummified stump

of his arm rose and dropped back onto the blankets. And then his features convulsed and his mouth stretched into a silent howl of anguish. He made a peculiar choking sound as tears oozed from beneath his closed eyelids.

'Charles—' She heaved herself from the chair and went to him, reaching across to take the hand that plucked at the sheets on his other side. 'Charles, it's me – Stella. It's all right, you're safe in hospital, in England.'

He opened his eyes and stared at her glassily. His pupils were tiny pinpricks in the cold blue. He blinked and struggled to raise himself, as though embarrassed to have been caught in a moment of weakness and determined to gloss over it.

'I didn't know you were coming,' he muttered.

'It's fine – don't try to sit up, just lie still. I came as soon as I found out where you were. I'm so sorry, Charles. You've been through such a horrible ordeal, but at least you're on home ground now. And the nurse says you're doing very well and getting better . . .'

She trailed off as the banal stream of words ran out. Her mouth was dry. She swallowed with difficulty. 'Are you in pain?'

'No. I feel . . . numb.'

'That's good.' Was it?

'Some water, please.'

His eyes went to the jug on the cabinet. She moved around the bed to pour it and, turning to give it to him, caught the look on his face as he glanced at her swollen stomach. He's more shocked at my altered body than I am at his, she thought sadly. She went to hold the glass to his lips but he twisted his head away angrily.

'I can do it.' With difficulty he raised himself up and took the glass from her with his good hand.

'Would you like some tea? Perhaps if I ask—'

'They're nurses, not Nippies in a Lyons Teahouse. They have better things to do than run up and down with trays of tea.'

Stella subsided onto the chair again, at a loss. The suggestion of tea had been as much for her benefit as his and would have at least provided a diversion. Charles was lying back on the pillows now, staring resolutely ahead, his jaw set. She sifted through the contents of her head to find something suitable to say, and was just about to resort to making some remark about the frustrations of the journey when she noticed that his chin was quivering and tears had begun to seep from his eyes again.

'Oh Charles . . .' Her heart contracted with pity. She pulled a handkerchief from her pocket – reasonably clean – and very gently blotted them away. He flinched but said nothing. Encouraged, she pulled her chair a little closer, and said softly, 'Does Peter know that you've been injured? Would you like me to write to him and tell him where you are?'

His eyes closed and lines of profound suffering etched themselves onto his face.

'You can't.' He spoke from between gritted teeth. 'Peter is dead. Monte Cassino, in January.'

And then she understood, and suddenly the senseless

accident didn't seem so senseless or accidental any more. For a moment he lay rigid and motionless, struggling with the invisible demons of grief that Stella knew so well herself. Then he opened his eyes and gave her a frozen smile. 'Thank you for coming, it was good of you. But please don't feel you have to make the journey again.'

He came home on a bitterly cold day in March.

From the moment a date for his discharge from hospital had been tentatively settled, the St Crispin's ladies swung into action, preparing a welcome for their wounded warrior. Reverend Stokes had never been very popular in King's Oak and his leaving passed with barely a murmur, such was the focus on Charles's return. Another banner was made, using the same striped flannelette sheet as for Charles and Stella's wedding. On the reverse side of it Alf Broughton painted, at Ada's instruction, *WELCOME HOME*, and beneath it in smaller letters, *King's Oak is Proud of You*. Rations were pooled for a small buffet tea in the church hall and a rolling menu of nourishing soups, stews and milk puddings (or their wartime equivalent, made from recipes in Marjorie's magazine) was planned to boost his recovery in the coming weeks. Distantly, through the deadening layers of scabbed grief, Stella was grateful, but anxious. This was a different Charles from the bookish, boyish vicar they'd all enjoyed spoiling in his bachelor days. She hoped their feelings wouldn't be hurt if he failed to respond to their kindness with appropriate gratitude.

But in the end she worried for nothing. Three weeks in a convalescent home just outside Newbury had not only restored some of the colour to his cheeks, but a little of his old charm. She watched him as he sat in the hall, surrounded by a little crowd of ladies vying for the honour of bringing him sandwiches and the inevitable scones. He played his part well, accepting their attention with good humour, even joking that the empty sleeve of his jacket was merely a ruse to secure such royal treatment. It broke the ice and made it all right for them to stop pretending they hadn't noticed it.

He's much more at ease with them, Stella thought bleakly. *It's just me he can't bear to look at or talk to.* On the banner hanging above the stage she could make out the mirror image of the words 'The Happy Couple' through the thin fabric, behind the message of welcome. *Dear God.* It seemed almost laughable now, if it wasn't so bloody hopeless. She pressed her fingers into the small of her back and rubbed at the ache there as, without warning, she thought of the sunlit bedroom with the violet-strewn walls. Grief reared up and kicked her hard beneath the ribs so she had to bend and lean on the table for support.

'You all right, love?' Was there nothing Ada didn't notice? 'Got a pain? Baby's getting ready, that means. Won't be long now, you mark my words. Reverend—' Before Stella could stop her Ada was bustling over to him, nudging Marjorie and Dot and Ethel out of the way, puffed up with the importance of her mission. 'I'm quite sure you've had enough listening to us old birds. You've got a girl that needs to put her feet up here, bless her, and I reckon you two have got some catching up to do. You take her home now.'

Stella looked at Charles, hoping to transmit a silent apology and disassociate herself from the hatching of this plan, but he was too busy thanking everyone and saying goodbye to notice. Dutifully he slid his good arm through hers as they went to the door. She could feel the stiffness in his body, and understood the effort it was costing him to put on this front.

We have more in common than he realizes, she thought as they crossed the road to the Vicarage, the wind slicing through the gap between them. Two lost souls with their hearts broken and their other halves torn away.

The Vicarage was as cold and damp as a tomb. Muttering awkwardly, Charles retreated to his study and Stella went into the kitchen to prepare supper. It wasn't strictly necessary as there was a corned beef hash in the larder made by Ethel Collins, but she didn't know what else to do to fill the hour until suppertime, or the days and weeks and years that stretched ahead of her. Leaning against the scullery wall where Dan had kissed her she buried her face in a tea towel to stop herself screaming. The only way it will be bearable is if we can be honest with each other, she thought desperately. If we can share our pain, maybe we can find some way of going forward with it and making some kind of life together. Not the life we thought we'd have when we married, not the life either of us wanted in our hearts, but *something*. For the baby.

In her head she began to piece together what she would say to him over supper, putting out of her mind what had happened last time she'd tried to talk to him honestly. Because what could he do to her now? The worst had already happened. He could kill her, she supposed, and the idea was curious but not frightening.

In the end, what happened was completely unexpected. Just as she was taking the corned beef hash from the oven he appeared in the kitchen carrying a bottle of champagne.

'Part of the case my father bought for our wedding,' he said sheepishly. 'It's rather a disgrace that we've left it unopened for so long. Do you think you could do the honours? I'm afraid it's one of the many things I'm discovering for which two hands are a minimum requirement.'

Taking it from him she smelled the sweet-sharp tang of alcohol on his breath. He'd obviously worked out how to open the whisky bottle. She tore off the foil, trying to beat back the memory of watching Dan do the same thing in the hotel room in Cambridge. It was impossible. She could see the muscled ridges of his bare stomach as clearly as if she was looking at a photograph.

Wrestling the cork out was much more difficult than Dan had made it look and a flume of froth cascaded over her hand. Charles brought in a pair of champagne coupes, dusty with lack of use, rattling together as he clutched them awkwardly in his unsteady hand.

'I thought we should drink to the future. To the baby,' he said with forced heartiness, raising his glass and looking at her with a sort of determined fondness. 'I know things have been far from easy for you. I know that not many men are as lucky as I am in having a wife who's as understanding as you've been and I want to put the past behind us and make a new start.' His eyes crinkled as he attempted a smile. 'Don't worry, I'm not going to inflict myself on you like this,' he lifted his arm so that the empty sleeve of his jacket twitched. 'I thought it would be best if I moved into the small room at the end of the landing.'

Stella nodded, speechless with surprise and numb with misery. He drained his glass in one mouthful, and poured another, and she understood that the toast to the baby was incidental. His main purpose was simply to drink.

Later, after they'd eaten in stilted silence and she'd washed the dishes she went up to make up the bed. It was the room Peter Underwood had used when he'd stayed at the Vicarage. She didn't blame Charles for wanting to have it now.

Her body was so cumbersome it was a major undertaking to manhandle the sheets and blankets into place and tuck them neatly under the mattress. Charles came in just as she finished and was sitting on the edge of the bed, red-faced and damp-haired. He was carrying his pyjamas.

'Forgive me, darling, I'm rather tired. Would you mind if I turned in early?'

She scrambled to her feet. The 'darlings' made her profoundly uncomfortable. 'Of course not. I'll go and make some cocoa, shall I?'

'Mmn, super.'

When she brought it up to him he was wearing the

pyjamas, though the jacket was hanging open and he was fumbling helplessly with the buttons. Putting the mug down, she went over to him. 'Here, let me do that.'

He didn't resist. The set expression was back on his face, the rigidness in his jaw, but he made a visible effort to smile. 'Thank you, darling.'

His chest and stomach seemed weirdly pale and soft-fleshed after Dan's. She finished doing the buttons as quickly as possible and went over to the bed to turn down the sheet. 'Is there anything else I can do?'

He didn't reply straight away, and when she turned she saw why. His face had contorted into a childlike mask of anguish, and tears were flowing down his cheeks.

'Oh Charles . . .'

There was nothing else to do but go to him and take him in her arms, as well as she could with the mound of their ill-begotten child between them. He leaned on her heavily, sobbing without restraint, his inhibitions removed by all the whisky and the champagne he'd put away during the evening. She shushed and soothed automatically, until eventually he pulled away and groped blindly for the handkerchief he'd left on the bedside table.

'Sorry . . . how revoltingly indulgent of me. Do forgive me, darling.'

'There's nothing to forgive,' she said woodenly. 'You've suffered a great loss. It's going to take time to adjust.'

'Yes.' He looked away, his throat working again. 'There have been times when, God forgive me, I've wanted to die –

and wished I had died, on that dark road. It didn't seem right that I should be spared when other men ... b-better men than I ... had not been.' For a moment his shoulders shook with sobs, but then he gathered himself and turned back to her with a broken smile. 'But God did spare me. I don't know why, but I must be thankful to Him for giving me another chance. For giving me the opportunity to feel the love of a father for his child.' He reached out then, and placed his hand on the mountain of her stomach as tears fell in a silent stream down his cheeks. It took every ounce of strength she had not to recoil from his touch. 'Oh Stella ... If it wasn't for the baby I don't know how I'd find a way through this. He truly is a gift from God – my reason for carrying on.'

29

2011

Will woke up on Monday morning with a curious feeling of optimism. Listening equably to Keely's loathsome electro-alarm music from upstairs he tentatively examined the contents of his brain to find out why this should be, and remembered yesterday's burst of productivity. The flat was tidy and he was lying beneath crisp bedlinen that smelled of washing powder. He'd had all five recommended portions of fresh fruit and vegetables, and though he hadn't made much headway on finding Stella Thorne, as he'd brushed his teeth last night he'd remembered something obvious; something that would give him a cast iron reason to go back to the hospital without seeming like some weird stalker or sad act.

Clothes.

Jess must have some. He'd seen her twice, and she'd been wearing different things each time, so there must be some of her things back at the house that he hadn't noticed. He'd been meaning to pay Albert Greaves a visit anyway. He'd go tonight and have a look.

It was a quiet day in the offices of Ansell Blake. Grimwood was all but wound up, and no other relatives had been traced for Bryony Maynard's long-lost great aunt. With no new cases, and none expected until Thursday's Bona Vacantia list, Ansell was at his most trying. Pressure made him volatile while lack of it made him bored and belligerent, and prone to casual bullying. Thankfully he left the office at 2 p.m. 'for a client meeting', giving them all a chance to relax and regroup. Barry, who'd watched Ansell drive out of the car park, remarked that he didn't know what kind of client meeting required golf clubs, and Bex confided that she'd overheard a phone conversation and knew for a fact that he was trying to join the Freemasonry.

'He thinks it'll be a good way of finding out about cases before the competition,' she giggled.

Will snorted. 'I thought the basic entry requirement for the Freemasons was being of good moral character?'

Following Ansell's departure, the afternoon passed peacefully and Will switched off his computer at 5 p.m. exactly. He arrived at Albert Greaves's just as the carer was leaving. It was a different one from the lady who'd answered the door to him the first time. This one was young and blonde and pretty, with a neat figure that was showcased by her tailored blue tunic. Mr Greaves was eating the supper she'd just served him from a table designed to fit over his armchair. His eyes sparkled as she let herself out of the front door.

'She's a little smasher, that one. Do nicely for you, she would. Mind you, she can't cook for toffee. None of them can.' He prodded the pale slop on his plate disgustedly with his fork. 'Supposed to be fish pie, but I wouldn't mind betting there's nothing in here that's ever been within a mile of the sea.'

'Correct me if I'm wrong, but I think she's a nurse, not a cook,' Will said with a smile. 'And that's a microwave ready-meal. It's not her fault if it's not good.'

'My Dorothy was a marvellous cook. What she couldn't do with a scrap of meat and a bit of pastry wasn't worth doing. I'm not bad in the kitchen myself, neither. Well, until I had this stroke. No use now. No use for nothing now.' Albert sniffed morosely. 'Come to have another look around Nancy's, have you?'

Perhaps after his own extreme tidy-up Will was seeing the room through the eyes of the newly converted, but it seemed smaller tonight, the clutter more oppressive. He thought of the long hours of the day when he'd been at the office, driving across the city, talking, having a laugh with Barry and Bex, and Albert Greaves had been here. Alone. Hemmed in by photographs and china ornaments and horse brasses and memories, listening to the clock ticking.

'Not today. I thought I ought to pick up the things that Jess – the girl who was sleeping there – left. But mostly I came to see you.'

Mr Greaves looked pleased. 'Ought to be out with a young lady, that's what you ought to be doing of an evening. Getting spruced up and taking her to the pictures or up town. Got a girl, have you?'

In his mind Will saw a pair of grey eyes; dark-lashed and troubled. He smiled crookedly. 'I wish.'

The old man dropped his fork and pushed his plate away with an air of recklessness. 'Here, if you go and get us a plate of fish and chips for tea I'll put a word in for you with that young nurse.'

Will grinned. 'What's the point? I'm no competition for a man like you. But I'll go and pick up these things from Nancy's and then go on to the chip shop.'

The first thing he noticed when he opened the door of number four was the letter lying on the floor right in front of him. The envelope was pale, creamy and expensive and for a crazy second he wondered if Nancy Price had been invited to Simon and Marina's wedding. He stooped to pick it up, and saw the name on the front.

Miss Jess Moran.

Of course. She'd written to Dan Rosinski, and this was his reply. There was something rather exciting about a letter; an envelope with a handwritten address and an overseas post-mark, and who knew what secrets and answers inside it. A feeling that he'd probably last experienced on Christmas morning when he was about five years old fluttered in the pit of his stomach and for a second he regretted the whole fish and chips plan, which had blown out of the water any chance he had of making visiting time tonight. He sternly squashed the thought. Albert Greaves had precious little enjoyment in life; the least Will could do was treat him to a fish-and-chip supper.

And tomorrow he would visit Jess.

She wasn't going to look at the door. She wasn't going to spend the next hour as she'd spent the last one, looking up every time another visitor came in, her heart giving a little skip in case it was him. She wasn't going to allow herself to feel that dip of disappointment every time it wasn't, because that meant that she'd expected him; that she'd actually thought he wouldn't have anything better to do than visit a girl he barely knew in hospital. A drop-out, who he'd found sleeping rough and been kind enough to help because he was that sort of nice person. So nice that he must have loads of friends – people like him, with posh accents and cool cars and great clothes. She imagined him now, in some fancy wine bar, surrounded by girls with swishy blonde hair and skiing tans. And neat eyebrows.

Crossly she turned over so that her back was towards the door. At least she could move more easily now that the drip had been taken out. A woman called Claire Trent had come to see her this afternoon, from Housing Services. She'd sat on the chair beside Jess's bed, asking questions, filling in forms and smelling of perfume. Jess had stared at her arty, interesting silver earrings and her well-cut blonde hair and felt childish and resentful, which was completely stupid since Claire Trent was trying to help her.

Grudgingly, imparting the minimum of information, Jess

told her about Dodge, and about the men she'd seen smoking outside the hostel in Church End. 'I'm not being funny, but I can't go somewhere like that. He knows people everywhere. He'd find out. He'd find me.'

Claire Trent had listened earnestly. She was pretty old, Jess decided, definitely over forty, but she had really good skin. She pictured a row of expensive bottles and jars in a bathroom that looked like something from a magazine, all white tiles and gleaming glass, and the resentment melted into envy. Would she ever have a home that was all her own?

'Don't worry, we'll make sure you're completely safe. There are women's hostels, where security is taken very seriously.'

Jess's heart had sunk at the word. Hostel. It sounded pretty dire; too much like hostage and nothing like home. But of course it was a start. An address. The bottom rung of a ladder. She felt like she'd fallen into a deep, dark hole and now she had to climb out of it, slowly, one step at a time. On her own.

She picked up a magazine that had been circulating the ward and began flicking through it, hurrying over the features on 'Cosy colour schemes for winter decorating' and 'Vintage style for bedrooms'. A late visitor came in. Without thinking she looked up, unable to stop the hope that flared. Or the disappointment that followed a moment later when it was extinguished.

One of the few things that Will actually liked about his job was that no two days were the same. This was one of the factors that had prevented him from handing in his notice long ago.

Just when it looked like Tuesday was going to continue in the same ad hoc way as Monday afternoon (although with the unpleasant addition of Ansell, whose mood suggested that he hadn't stepped right onto the welcome mat at the Masonic lodge and been greeted with a secret handshake) the post arrived, bringing a letter from a client with a case to research. Jobs like these were usually initiated by someone with inside information who knew there was a worthwhile sum of money to be gained, and without the race-against-time-and-competitors element of Bona Vacantia cases they were heir hunting gold.

After two hours of research a family tree had taken root and grown, its branches extending across several pages. Walter Cooke was one of eight children; born in Crewe, he'd worked all his life on the railways. At the time of his death he was living in a modest property in Watford which, it emerged, was stuffed to the gills with rare railway memorabilia and a valuable collection of vintage model train sets. These were expected to make the estate a substantial one.

'You ever been to Crewe, Posh?' Ansell drawled in his comedy Bertie Wooster voice. 'Frightful imposition I know, but can you bear the thought of venturing beyond the Home Counties? Are your refined lungs capable of breathing the air beyond Birmingham, because I'd really rather like you to get up the motorway smartish and start signing up Walter Cooke's nearest and dearest. Best go home and get your butler to pack a case – this might be an overnight job.'

Will could have wept with frustration as his plans for the evening dissolved before his eyes. Back at the flat he put a clean shirt, boxers and a toothbrush in an overnight bag and collected his laptop. The carrier bag he'd discovered in the bedroom of the house in Greenfields Lane was standing beside the door, with the letter from Dan Rosinski on top. He picked it up. Sod Ansell: it might not be the most direct route, but he was going to Crewe via the Royal Free Hospital.

It wasn't strictly visiting time, so he got a parking space relatively quickly. He found he was walking ridiculously fast up the corridor to the ward, and knew that it had nothing to do with being in a hurry to get to the M1 and everything to do with the fact that in a minute he would see Jess. He'd spent so much time thinking about her since Saturday, reliving the things they'd said, remembering the sweet way she pronounced her vowels. He pictured the delicate bumps of her spine beneath the hospital gown and was almost winded by a great surge of protectiveness. He hadn't wanted to look through the carrier bag of clothes, but he hoped there were some pyjamas in there.

The door to the ward was shut. His hand was shaking as he pressed the buzzer. A crackly voice came over an intercom.

'Yes?'

'I've – er – I'm dropping off some things for Jess Moran. Clothes and—'

The door swished open before he could finish. His pulse

suddenly rocketed as if he was doing a hundred-metre sprint instead of walking perfectly normally towards the nurses' station. One of the women sitting behind it got up as he approached and came round to take the bag from him.

'Thanks very much. I'll make sure she gets it.'

'Oh – great, thank you. Er – look, I know it's not visiting time, but I don't suppose I could see her? Just for a moment?'

He was blushing like a schoolgirl. The nurse smiled at him kindly, obviously feeling sorry for him and his great big tragic crush.

'Sorry love, you've just missed her. She's gone down for a chest X-ray. Want me to give her a message when she gets back?'

'Oh. No.' He backed away, trying hard to appear casual and indifferent, almost tripping over a floor cleaning machine. 'No, don't worry, it's fine. Thanks anyway.'

From then on things got worse. As he drove North the weather got colder, and by Northampton it had begun to snow, in slushy great splodges that the Spitfire's windscreen wipers smeared into a sheet of ice. Walter Cooke's family proved to be large, complicated and very chatty, and at each house he called at, memories of the late Walter were taken out and dusted off along with the best china; aired in great detail before papers were signed. It was after ten o'clock when he had finished his final call. Getting into the car, he'd planned to give the cheap motel Bex had booked for him a miss and drive back to London while the roads were quiet, only to find that the Spitfire refused to start.

It had eventually been towed off Walter Cooke's sister's drive by a tattooed mechanic called Warren, who had given Will a lift to his hotel in the cab of his truck and promised, with frustrating nonchalance, to get the car mended 'as soon as possible, mate'.

And so he was stuck, in Crewe, on a sleety Wednesday morning, with nothing to do but wait. He found a coffee shop advertising free wifi facing onto the empty square and went in. The woman who took his coffee order asked for his name to write on the cup, though there was no one else waiting at the counter and only a handful of other customers scattered around. Will took his drink over to a table by the window and got out his laptop.

While it connected to the network he sat back on the faux-leather sofa and looked out into the grey morning. He felt disorientated and uprooted, like he'd woken up in the wrong life. Opening up his email, the name Evelyn Holt instantly jumped out at him.

It had taken a while for his mother to trust modern methods of communication, and even now she used email rather like the telegram service of yesteryear; while her messages didn't quite contain the word 'stop' at the end of every sentence, they might as well have done. 'Don't forget wedding present for S and M,' she wrote. Will sniggered. 'Best items going from list fast. Also, they want to know whether you're bringing a +1 for seating plan. Said I very much doubted.'

His smile stiffened and splintered.

His mother had never quite forgiven him for letting Camilla slip through his fingers at university. Milla, like Marina, had had all the qualities Evelyn Holt considered desirable in a daughter-in-law: namely, the right accent, the right parents, and a thorough grounding in the rules of polo, bridge and what cutlery to use at a formal dinner. Although she'd never said as much, Will knew his mother blamed him for not doing enough to keep Milla interested. Not *being* enough. For selfishly having a mental breakdown. For not being like Simon.

He'd always suspected that the benevolent fairies who'd blessed the infant Simon with brains and looks and sporting prowess had all had a previous engagement on the day of his own christening. The achievements that came so effortlessly to his brother eluded Will, no matter how hard he strived for them. He might have made the teams at rugby and rowing, but he'd never been captain, like Simon had; he'd got good grades in his exams, but never gone up on Speech Day to collect the prize for Outstanding Achievement. The greater his efforts, the more significant his failure, in his parents' eyes. Realizing that was what had tipped him over the edge five years ago.

He closed the email and took a steadying sip of coffee. Sometimes he wondered what it would be like to have no family, like Nancy Price: no parents to assign you a role as constricting and uncomfortable as someone else's too-small, cast-off clothes, no siblings to keep you in their shadow ...

Pretty good, he thought, staring out of the window onto the deserted square. And then an image of Jess Moran superimposed itself on the misted glass, hugging her knees on her hospital bed, completely alone.

He sighed shakily, running a hand through his hair. No, not good. No one should be alone, not like that. A wave of longing crashed over him, winding him for a moment and making him feel more disorientated than ever in its wake. Blindly, he turned back to the screen in front of him, sweeping his fingers over the mousepad. Nancy Price's file jumped out at him and he clicked on it, desperate for the distraction it offered.

The Woodhill School roll of pupils was the first document that appeared. It was a screenshot of the archive record he'd been going through that day when Bex had interrupted him; the names and dates of birth of all the children who'd been registered at the school in 1932, listed in exquisite copperplate handwriting.

And suddenly it struck him – maybe Nancy Price did have brothers and sisters? Albert had said she was a Poor School girl and had grown up without a family, but that didn't necessarily mean her parents hadn't had other children. Sitting more upright on the leather sofa Will began to scroll through, looking for other Prices. And then something caught his eye and made him stop. He scrolled back.

Stella Holland.

Stella. It wasn't the most unusual of names, but still ... The hairs on the back of his neck prickled. Stella Thorne was

391

Nancy Price's friend – that much was obvious from the fact that she'd entrusted her precious love letters into her keeping. It was likely that their friendship would have started at school . . . Hastily he looked through the list to see if there'd been another Stella at Woodhill Community School in 1932.

There hadn't.

It took less than five minutes to log onto the genealogy website, enter this new information into its search facility and get the results. Stella Elizabeth Holland married Reverend Maurice Charles Thorne, August 1942, Middlesex. The two women behind the counter broke off their conversation and looked at him in alarm as he gave a muted *Yessss* of triumph.

'Sorry,' he said with an apologetic grin, barely tearing his eyes away from the screen. His fingers were tingling, clumsy: it took two attempts to type Stella's details into a new search. He submitted the information, and sat back, waiting for the next part of her story to be revealed.

And there it was.

In April 1944 Stella Thorne had had a baby. And the father was registered not as Dan Rosinski, but as Charles Thorne.

30

1944

At first the pain was good. She'd been labouring in the oppressive air for so long that she could barely breathe, and at last the storm had broken. She was scared, but she was ready, braced to meet its fury and open her throat to give voice to the grief and frustration and rage that she had carried inside her like a second, invisible child.

But it went on and on, like the nightmare, only this time there was no escaping it, no pretending. It swallowed everything, even time. Days and nights were chewed up in its vicious jaws until they became indistinguishable: a blurred, bloody scream.

Faces appeared and disappeared: Charles, Ada, Nancy, Dr Walsh. Not Dan. Never Dan, even though she willed him there with all her remaining strength. Jesus looked down on her from his cross, His carved wooden compassion morphing into impassive boredom. *Pain?* He seemed to say. *Tell me about it.*

And then at some point Jesus disappeared, along with the green walls and ugly curtains of the bedroom, and different faces hung above her as she was rushed along draughty tunnels. In addition to the unseen hands that had seized her insides and were wringing them like sheets on washday, other hands held on to her arms, her legs, pinning them down and pulling them wide apart.

Indecent acts. An abomination. The unrighteous shall not inherit the kingdom of God. Someone was thrusting something up inside her. She couldn't see who it was because he was wearing a paper mask across the lower part of his face, but she didn't think it was Charles this time. And then there was a syringe, with a long needle. They were going to use it to burst the tight balloon of her stomach, she was sure of it. She tried to put her hands over her ears to protect them against the bang, but they were a long way away and too heavy to lift, and it was going dark.

When she opened her eyes it was still dark, but the storm of pain had passed. She was lying on her back, but there was no weight pressing up against her diaphragm and her body felt slack and empty. In the distance she could hear a baby's reedy, warbling cry. As she sat up her insides seemed to slosh and surge, like liquid in a barrel. Standing, she felt a downwards rush, a warm gush that weighted the wet wadding between her legs.

She stumbled past rows of white-humped beds and out into the cavernous corridor. A light burned dimly some distance along its length and she went blindly towards it, arms outstretched as if asking for something she couldn't name. The crying continued, gathering fury. The chair behind the desk was pushed back, vacant. Beyond the desk a slab of soft light from a window slanted across the linoleum. Behind the glass she could see rows of canvas-sided cribs, each one containing a sleeping baby. At the sight of them something strange happened inside her body; a prickling, like tiny needles in her breasts, resonant of the sensations Dan had woken in her but sharper, harsher, making her suck in a breath.

The click of footsteps behind her heralded the arrival of the nurse. 'Mrs Thorne! What are you doing out of bed?' She clicked her tongue disapprovingly. 'You shouldn't be up. You've lost rather a lot a blood – and still are, by the look of that gown. Come on, let's get you cleaned up.'

She spoke in a well-bred accent, but there was nothing genteel about her iron grip on Stella's arm.

'My baby – he's crying, I can hear him. I must see him!' Stella tried to shake off the nurse's hand. 'I want to see my son!'

'Now, now, Mrs Thorne, what a lot of nonsense. Your baby isn't crying, nor is it a boy. See – there she is, sleeping peacefully. Now, let's get you back to bed.'

With a strength she didn't know she had Stella wrenched her arm from the nurse's grasp and pressed her palms against the glass, peering in. Through the mist of her breath she gazed at the sleeping bundle that was her child. Her daughter. She was bigger than the babies on either side of her and the pale moon of her face was distorted and disfigured by a purple swelling on her left cheek.

'Is she all right?'

'Perfectly fine, considering what she's been through. It was a very difficult birth. Dr Ingram did marvellously well,' the nurse said warmly, and Stella felt like she herself had had nothing whatsoever to do with the whole affair. 'He was all scrubbed up and ready to operate but in the end he managed to get Baby out with forceps. That's what caused the mark on her face. It'll disappear in no time. Now come along, back to bed with you.'

Reluctantly Stella allowed herself to be led away. Back beneath the papery starched sheets she looked up into the darkness and touched her own cheek. Indecent acts. She wondered whether Charles minded that she had failed to deliver his expected son. Would he love a girl?

I don't care, she thought fiercely and her heart swelled and bloomed. She's mine, all mine. I'll love her enough for both of us. Enough for the whole world.

The maternity ward was its own enclosed world, quite cut off from the one outside. It was a world from which men were absent, except for an hour each evening when those who weren't away on active service trooped in looking uncomfortable. The war, which had so dominated everyone's lives for what felt, in the spring of 1944, like forever, seemed distant and irrelevant here. In their beds the women knitted cosily, not with scratchy khaki, but tiny garments in pastel lengths of whisper-soft lambswool unravelled from pre-war sweaters and cardigans. With babies nestled at blue-veined breasts they chatted, and veterans like Hilda Goodall in the bed opposite Stella's dispensed advice to the first-timers.

'I don't care what that nurse says, you'd be mad to wake a sleeping baby. It'll feed when it's 'ungry, and it'll soon let you know when that is, take it from me. Get some shut eye while you can.'

Hilda, a quivering mountain of a woman, milky like a blancmange, had just given birth to her seventh. The only break she ever got was when she was in the hospital having another, she said. It wasn't hard to see why; after an hour watching her grimy, whining brood squabble and sprawl at visiting time, the whole ward was desperate to see the back of them. The newest addition to her clutch of children was as noisy and demanding as the rest. Raymond Goodall had been the bawling infant Stella had heard on her first night.

By contrast her own baby was angelic. When brought from the nursery every four hours to be fed she was invariably fast asleep, so that when the other mothers were discussing eye colouring Stella realized that she had no idea whether her daughter's were the dark blue that appeared to be the norm amongst the others. She lay in Stella's arms, limp and passive, inscrutable behind resolutely closed eyes. She showed none of the instinct for feeding that the other babies displayed, rooting hungrily for their mother's nipple with quivering lips and frantic flailing fists, and when she fed it was apathetically, taking a few desultory draws before seeming to forget what she was doing and lapse back into a doze. Initially Hilda assured Stella it would be better once her milk came in, but the opposite proved to be the case. A stinging cascade of milk would be unleashed just as the baby lost interest, and she would splutter and choke and cry, a mewling cat-like sound quite distinct from the sound that came from the others.

The nurses frowned when they picked her up. 'Funny-looking little fing, ain't she?' Hilda remarked. 'Big 'ead. No wonder you had trouble getting that out.' Stella was too polite to say anything. Compared to baby Raymond, who was perpetually regurgitating all the milk he gorged and had jug ears, her daughter was perfect. Even with the bruise yellowing on her pristine new skin, she was the most beautiful thing Stella could imagine.

And Charles was smitten too. As a vicar his parish duties had included visiting the sick so he was more at ease on the ward than the other fathers, and his clerical collar and his empty sleeve meant he was treated with deference by the nurses. They made a great fuss of helping him to hold the baby securely, though he wasn't able to pick her up. He came most days, usually with Ada or Marjorie or even, on one occasion, Miss Birch.

'What are you going to call her?' she asked, holding the baby with surprising assurance, her stocky body swaying instinctively to some timeless rhythm.

'Yes darling, we really must decide,' Charles said. 'I must confess I hadn't got as far as thinking about girls' names. Perhaps Lillian, for my—'

'Daisy,' Stella said dreamily from her snowy mountain of pillows. 'I'd like to call her Daisy.'

Charles looked uncertain, but Miss Birch beamed approval. 'How beautiful. Daisy. A fresh start.'

One by one the faces in the beds around Stella's changed, until eventually it was her turn to leave the ward and go home. She had stayed longer than was usual because of the baby's continued failure to feed properly, but as the days passed she sensed the nurses' concern give way to exasperation, as if Daisy was being deliberately stubborn and Stella wilfully inept.

In the mildewed gloom of the Vicarage the iridescent bubble in which she'd been floating burst. The scent of milk, white soap and femininity was replaced by the inescapable cabbagey reek. It was as if Daisy sensed the change in atmosphere too. She became more wakeful, less placid, crying her high-pitched, off-key cry sometimes for hours on end. 'She's half starved, poor mite,' Ada clucked, 'why don't you try her with a bit of flour and water?' Desperate, Stella took her advice, and was almost relieved when Daisy wouldn't take that either, since it made the problem seem less like a personal failure on her part. Surely when she was hungry she'd eat? The bruising had gone down on her face, leaving only a crescent-shaped mark, and when she was wrapped in one of the blankets that had been knitted for her by the parish ladies she looked perfectly normal. But when she undressed her for her bath Stella noticed how tiny her body appeared in relation to the size of her head and felt panicky and helpless.

People were kind. They called at the Vicarage in a constant stream, their concerned gazes taking in the dirty dishes in the kitchen sink, the pail of evil-smelling nappies in the scullery, the state of Stella's lank, unwashed hair and milk-stained clothing. In the mornings Ada called in on her way to the shops to collect Stella's ration book and ask what she wanted. Dazed and reeling from yet another broken night, Stella mostly left it to Ada to decide. Soups and milk puddings continued to appear, made by Dot and Marjorie and Ethel. Charles tucked into these with great enthusiasm, marvelling at the generosity of the parish, but Stella felt her well of gratitude running dry. Their kindness felt like a criticism, an accusation that she had failed as a mother as well as a wife.

It was true, of course, which was why it hurt. Looking after Daisy, coaxing her to feed, coping with her crying, processing the mountains of washing she generated while also keeping up with the housework, washing her own hair, cooking and looking after Charles seemed overwhelmingly impossible, like the tasks presented to fairy-tale heroines to make them prove their worth. It wasn't that she didn't love her baby, but loving her only made the anguish of failing her all the more profound.

Dr Walsh came, not to look at Daisy, but to talk to Stella. Charles was worried, he said. In a tone of bluff heartiness, he asked her about her appetite and how she was sleeping, while his watery eyes bored into her over the top of his glasses. She answered him truthfully, because she couldn't imagine how anyone could meet Daisy's round the clock demands and still eat and sleep normally. He left her with the promise that he'd 'keep an eye on things'. Though perhaps it wasn't a promise so much as a threat.

The only silver lining in this sky full of black clouds was that exhaustion and the demands of a new baby blunted the edge of the pain of losing Dan. She carried the ache with her constantly and never forgot it, but it was deeper; the kind of pain you lived with rather than one that killed you. She adjusted. The brief spell of happiness they'd enjoyed last summer took on the aspect of a dream. Sometimes, in one of the restless, shallow slumbers that were about all she managed around Daisy's waking, she would see him, and it would bring her a bittersweet comfort, like a candleglow in the dark, and sustain her through another bleak morning.

She tried not to think about the house on Greenfields Lane. It was a painful reminder of the past she had lost and the future she would never have. As the months passed her hope quietly died. Dan had taken off from Palingthorpe in a cold, crisp October dawn and as the seasons turned once more and the apple blossom on the tree flowered and fell again in showers of confetti she mourned him, silently and secretly.

31

2011

The Spitfire was mended.

Will had got the call on his mobile just before 4 p.m., by which time he'd eaten a rubbery cheese toasted sandwich and a chocolate brownie and drunk enough coffee to give him a cardiac arrest. When he'd arrived at the garage he'd found his car parked outside, paintwork gleaming. Warren had managed to get a spare part from a mate of his, he'd told Will as he handed him the bill. It was about a third of what Will would have expected to pay in London.

On the motorway a spectacular pink sunset spread across the sky and he fought the urge to press his twitching foot to the floor. 'Don't thrash her for a while,' Warren had warned. 'Break it in gently, like,' but the temptation to ignore this was strong. Will was at Milton Keynes at six o'clock, when visiting time would be starting at the Royal Free. To distract himself from the thought (and from the need to pee – why had he drunk all that coffee?) he went over everything he'd discovered about Stella Thorne; everything he had to tell Jess.

There had been no more children. Daisy Lillian Thorne, born 27th April 1944 was an only child. There had been no divorce either, from what he could tell. Stella Thorne had stayed married to Charles (or Maurice, as he now knew him to be legally named) until his death in 1967, and had not married again since. The absence of a second marriage certificate and also a death certificate suggested that there was a chance she was still alive. Her daughter, however, wasn't. Daisy had died in 1980, in Berkshire.

The sunset finished its extravagant display. The seven o'clock news came on. Sod breaking the new part in gently. Will covered the rest of the distance to London in the fast lane, his shoulders tense as he hunched forward over the steering wheel. At ten to eight he turned into the hospital car park. God, he absolutely had to pee before he went in to see her. He found the toilet, and looked at his reflection despairingly in the mirror. His shirt was crumpled, his hair sticking up wildly where he'd pushed his hands through it as he'd driven. He tried to dampen it down but it looked even worse, like it hadn't been washed for a week or something.

The buzzer went for the end of visiting time as he raced through the doors of the ward. A nurse he hadn't come across before was sitting behind the desk. She looked up in surprise and faint distaste when Will approached, panting.

'Can I help? Visiting time has just finished.'

'I know ... Been stuck in traffic on the ... motorway.' Christ, he was unfit. 'I need to see ... Jess. Jess Moran.'

'Sorry—'

'*Please*. Two minutes, that's all. I know it's the end of visiting time and I know it's a pain in the backside for you when shambolic idiots like me come running in at the very last second, but please. *Please*. I really need to see her.'

Instead of being won over by this impassioned speech the nurse looked simply impatient. 'Well, you can't. She was discharged this morning. She's not here.'

'Discharged?'

'That's right. Now if you'll excuse me—'

'But where to? Where's she gone? She didn't have anywhere—'

The nurse's expression became positively frosty. 'We're under strict instructions not to disclose that information to anyone. Now, perhaps you'd be good enough to leave my ward before I call security?'

It wasn't a bad place.

If you ignored the screeching kids and the blare of other people's music and the television turned up to full volume in the common room and the raucous laughing and arguing that went on in a variety of languages and accents pretty much around the clock, it was OK. The communal kitchen was without a doubt the most untidy place Jess had ever seen in her life. Venturing in there for breakfast on her second morning

404

she had found the cold remains of a takeaway curry spread all over the table (and much of the floor) and a dirty nappy by the toaster.

But Jess was glad to be there. She was glad to have a room of her own, with a bed and a radiator that belted out heat and a tiny en-suite shower room with hot water (most of the time). She was glad to have lights that worked and a duvet that didn't smell of old mushrooms. It was stupid to wish, even for a second, that she was back at Greenfields Lane where Will Holt might find her. Especially since it didn't actually look like he wanted to. After all, he'd known where she was and when he could come in and see her, and he'd chosen to drop off the bag of clothes and the letter when it wasn't even visiting time. When he wouldn't have to stay.

At least he had delivered the letter – that was another thing to be glad about. Now she had somewhere to live her top priority was to find work, but helping Dan Rosinski with his quest to find Stella came a close second. She'd hoped to have Will Holt's help, and that day in the hospital when they'd sat together and read the letters in companionable silence she'd actually been daft enough to think they might continue the search together. Now she wished she hadn't told him about it. He'd made a good job of looking interested at the time, but that was just because he was posh and polite. Anyway, she was determined to find Stella Thorne on her own. Somehow.

She wasn't entirely on her own. Dan Rosinski's letter had included a mobile phone number and an email address. On her second day in the hostel she temporarily suspended her search for work and went to the library where, armed with her new address, she filled in the forms to get a library card. She took it straight upstairs to the computer room.

It took approximately ten minutes to set up an email account, and at least three times that to compose her message. Blood drummed in her ears as the cursor hovered over 'send' and she read back over what she'd written. Was it too personal? Would he think she was some unreliable drop-out who was going to con him? Would he inform the police and ask them to arrest her for breaking and entering or squatting or something? She was just about to start deleting bits and rewriting them when her hand slipped. With a muted whooshing sound the email sent.

She let out a little gasp of horror, attracting the attention of the man to her left, who glared at her as if she had broken some cardinal library rule. Bugger, but it was too late now. She resisted the urge to drag the message up from the 'sent' box to read through again and hovered her fingers over the keyboard, wondering what else she could look up to take her mind off it. She'd just typed in 'Job Vacancies Church End' and looked up the first few results when the little message icon flashed up in the corner of her screen. With her heart leaping into her mouth she clicked on it.

Wow – you have email! I really appreciate you taking the trouble to set up an account. It sounds like you've been going through a pretty tough time lately.

I can't tell you how much I appreciate you trying to help me out like this – a stranger; some old, sick guy on the other side of the world, but I guess I'm kind of resigned to the fact that mine is a lost cause. I've spent weeks searching for Stella online, following all the leads I can think of to find a mention of her. Writing one more letter to the house I bought her was my last hope. I don't have too much time left to waste, but I'm pretty darned sure that there's a whole bunch of other stuff you should be doing instead of chasing ghosts that are probably best left undisturbed.

I sure am glad you're over the pneumonia but you take it easy now. England can feel like the coldest, wettest corner of the planet in wintertime. You need to rest up and eat well. Take care of yourself.

Dan.

No! Without pausing to think she clicked 'reply' and began to type, hurriedly and clumsily, with two fingers.

Please don't give up – not before we've really tried every possibility! I want to help. I want to find her.

The thing is, you don't feel like a stranger to me. That might sound weird, and I hope you won't be angry, but while I was at the house in Greenfields Lane I found the letters you wrote to Stella. All of them, I think, from the one you wrote when you found her watch to the one that was sent to her when you didn't return to your airbase. I know I shouldn't have read them and I'm really sorry. Well, sort of. I can't be completely sorry because they were amazing. I never realized until then what love really was.

If she's alive, I believe that we can find her. Please, let me keep trying.

Jess.

She was sitting rigidly upright as she finished typing, and sagged a little as she pressed 'send'. This time his reply wasn't immediate. Scrolling mindlessly through pages of irrelevant results for 'Job Vacancies Church End' she had just about convinced herself that he was so angry at the idea of her reading his letters that she'd never hear from him again when a message dropped into her inbox.

Oh Jess, you sure are persuasive. Here am I, trying to be as rational as I can and convince myself that it's a no-hoper, and that I should spend the next couple of months writing letters to congressmen, pushing for change, campaigning for justice and all kinds of things that'll make a difference to the world when I'm gone. And there's you – the voice of my heart, not my head, telling me not to bother trying to change a place I'll have no part in and to spend the time I have left finishing my own story.

So you found the letters. I don't know whether I'm happy that she kept them or sad that, wherever she is now, she left them behind. The house was hers, you know. I bought it for her when I was on sick leave in August 1943 and her husband had beaten up on her. It was supposed to be a safe place for her to go if I couldn't be there to protect her and a place where we could be together. Wishful thinking. It didn't quite turn out like that.

I sent more letters, afterwards, when I got home. For years I wrote regularly, in case she changed her mind. Did you find those letters too? There must be hundreds of them somewhere. She never replied and I always wondered whether she ever read them. If not, what happened to them?

You see, there I go – doing what I've tried to avoid these past 68 years; asking questions I'm never going to be able to answer. Leastways, not unless I find her.

So, where do you think we should start looking?

Jess's heart was thudding as she finished reading. She thought of Will. He would know. He'd know which records to look up, and how to go about it. But the ridiculous thing was she didn't even know where to find him now.

I don't know, and I don't know what happened to the other letters. The ones I found were in a shoebox, carefully filed in date order. The last one was the one you wrote to be sent if you didn't come back. But if you bought the house in Greenfields Lane that must mean you still own it, right? And if you own it and you give me permission, surely I can go back and have a proper look? I didn't really want to touch anything last time I was there. It didn't feel right, if that doesn't sound weird after what I did, breaking in in the first place.

The thing is, I don't really understand what happened. I mean, I got as far as guessing that you got shot down or something and that she must have thought that you were dead. But surely you went to see her when you got back? I can't imagine how that must have been for her – finding out that you were alive. Actually, I can. It must have been AMAZING. Like the answer to all her prayers. So why didn't the two of you live happily ever after?

Do you mind me asking all this?

She watched the screen, barely blinking. Ten minutes stretched to fifteen. To twenty. Her shoulders ached, and as she flexed her neck she became aware that the man at the next computer was looking at her strangely. She realized then that she'd been leaning forward, staring fixedly at a blank screen with her hands balled into fists in front of her face. Hastily she tried to look like a normal person and pulled up the job search results again.

Head chef. Motorbike delivery driver. Shiatsu therapist. Bench joiner. She assumed not knowing what a job title meant was a pretty good indication that you weren't qualified for it. There was a vacancy for an assistant in a bookmaker's shop and she was about to look up the details when she thought of Dodge and his gambling habit and changed her mind. All the rest of the jobs posted were Nanny positions. She was just weighing up whether having no previous experience, an address in a women's hostel and a recent spell as a nightclub-singer-cum-squatter might make some parents wary of employing her to look after their kids when the message icon flashed.

She leaped on the mouse like a hungry cat.

I don't mind you asking.

For years I didn't talk about it, mostly because there was nobody I could talk about it to. My brother Alek died in the liberation of Normandy in '44, and when my Pop – who was the only other person who knew about Stella – got Alzheimer's disease he got pretty mixed up about everything. He forgot people who he'd known for years, so there was no chance he was going to remember a girl I'd talked about in my letters home. A girl he'd never met.

You're right. I got shot down. It was a mission to Zwickau in Germany. We made the target but ran into a bunch of BF 109s on the way home. Our plane was badly hit, there were two engines gone and a fire in the tail section. Two of the crew were wounded and the tail gunner was killed. There was no option but to bail. The men who weren't wounded helped the others out, but I stayed at the controls too long to use my parachute so I got separated from them and had to attempt to land.

It could have been a hell of a lot worse. I came down in a field – got out with just a cut on my head where it hit the rudder. We'd been briefed about what to do in the event of a crash landing and I knew I had to set fire to the fort so it

411

didn't fall into enemy hands. That was a low moment; Ruby Shoes had looked after me through a whole lot of scrapes and she felt like a friend.

After that I walked and kept on walking. The whole place was crawling with Gestapo so I avoided the roads and kept to the fields. I walked all of the first night, and through the next day, heading north. I figured that every step was taking me closer to Stella. I found a farm – a run-down sort of a place – and waited for it to get dark before I slipped into a haybarn to sleep. But later, when the old guy came out his dog must have picked up my scent. It started going crazy, barking its head off. I thought I was done for.

But I was lucky. As soon as this guy found out I was an American airman he took me inside and gave me soup and cider, and a place to sleep in his attic. Man, that cider was knockout stuff – I must have slept for twelve hours straight. When I woke up there was a woman there. She turned out to be a teacher at the local school, and an active member of the Resistance.

I don't know how much you know about the Resistance movement in occupied France? I hope if you've heard or read or been taught anything it's that they were incredible people. Ordinary, but braver than most of us can imagine. A lot of people helped me in the weeks and months after that, and every one of them risked torture and death for me, even though they didn't know me from Adam. I was moved every week or so, from Rheims to Amiens to Paris and a hell of a lot of other places with names I couldn't pronounce at the

412

time and can't remember now. I wanted to get word to Stella, to tell her I was alive, but to do so would have been to put all of those people in danger. I just had to wait, and trust that one day I would get back to her.

I guess it never crossed my mind it would be too late.

32

1944

After a promising spell of sunshine at the end of May, for the first time in living memory the day of St Crispin's church fete was marred by bad weather. While across the Channel, British and American troops bravely battled rough seas and squally, soaking rain to land on the beaches of Normandy, in King's Oak the ladies of St Crispin's fought against sharp gusts of wind that tore down the bunting and whipped the cloth off the tombola table, carrying it high in the air and throwing it down in a pile of manure left by the milkman's horse on Church Road.

Buckling under the weight of her other responsibilities, Stella had had no input in the fete this year, though as the date approached and Charles's afternoons were taken up with committee meetings it was impossible not to let her mind be pulled back twelve months. The time seemed distorted, like a fairground mirror, in some ways hugely stretched so that it felt like a century ago that she had battled with Marjorie over ginger cake and scones, in other ways truncated. She closed her eyes and remembered Dan kissing her in the green gloom of the scullery. She could recall every detail, from the prickle of stubble on his jaw to the taste of mint and cigarettes and the silk of his hair through her fingers, as if it had happened yesterday.

How could it be that the man who lived so vividly in her mind was no longer alive?

The fete was already well underway by the time she managed to get herself and Daisy ready to go out. She'd hoped to have a bath and wash her lank hair, but Daisy had cried whenever she was put down in her cot, and the sound grated on Stella's raw nerves too much to endure it. The few clothes she had that fitted her newly expanded bust were all dirty. Taking out the least obviously stained blouse from the wardrobe she deliberately averted her eyes from the apple green dress hanging beside it; the dress she'd worn to meet Dan the day he'd taken her to the concert, and to St Paul's. She was about to shut the wardrobe door when she was seized by another impulse. Reaching inside she pulled it from its hanger and bundled it up to give to Ada for the WVS collection. This was her life now; Daisy and Charles and their attempt to be a family. There was no point in hanging on to relics of past happiness.

Outside it was cold – more like February than June – but at least that meant she could cover up the dirty blouse with a coat. Daisy was quieter in the pram (a stately Silver Cross obtained by Lillian from one of her bridge friends), soothed by the rocking motion and the flicker of acid-green leaves above her as they moved in the sharp wind. Her eyes had started to cross slightly, Stella noticed with a stab of anguish. On his last visit Dr Walsh had muttered darkly about 'abnormalities' and Charles had laughed heartily and called him an old woman, worrying about nothing. Secretly, Stella wondered if Dr Walsh might be right.

On the field the scout tent had been hastily erected and the stalls were huddled beneath its snapping canvas. Without the draw of tinned peaches on the tombola table or as prizes for the hoopla there was precious little to attract customers this year. Only children, impervious to the cold and oblivious to the purple clouds that were massing above the roofs of the surrounding houses, were crowded around the coconut shy (cabbages this year, Stella noticed dully) and the stocks, where Mr Potter, the grumpy ARP warden, was getting a soaking. She went into the hall, which was noisy and crowded. The tea urn had created a steamy fug which had turned Ada's cheeks pink and made the curl drop from her hair. Marjorie, handing out her scones, looked very full of herself.

Stella spotted Charles sitting at a table in front of the stage. It was hopeless trying to take the pram in, and since Daisy looked like she was about to fall asleep she left it in the vestibule and went over.

'There you are, darling!' Charles said in his hearty, vicar's voice, getting up to kiss her cheek. 'I was hoping you'd come soon. Where's Daisy? I thought she could have her first portrait taken – what do you say?'

In a controversial break with tradition the fancy dress parade had been abandoned this year and the stage had been set up like a photographer's studio, using a roll of painted scenery from a long-ago production of *Anything Goes*. Sitters posed in front of a backdrop of sea and ship's railings, while Fred Collins snapped their portraits with his Box Brownie for sixpence.

'Lovely,' Stella said dully, 'but she's almost asleep.'

'Go and get her now, darling, before she drops off.'

Gritting her teeth Stella made her way back through the crush and gathered up her daughter. Charles was already on the stage when she went back in, standing expectantly beside Fred Collins.

'You sit there, Mrs T.' Fred Collins gestured to the single chair. 'And if you can bring the baby down onto your arm so we can see 'er little face . . .'

Stella allowed herself to be arranged and manipulated into a pleasing little family group. She wondered if she could remember how to smile.

'Perhaps I should stand on the other side . . .' Charles said. 'My arm, you see.'

'That's perfect, that is,' Fred Collins boomed, bending to scowl into the viewfinder. 'No, just as you were Mrs T., looking up at the Reverend like that . . .'

Obediently she turned her head again, and that was when she saw the figure standing in the doorway of the hall. Tall. Uniformed. Broad shoulders almost filling the doorframe. Narrow hips and long legs, a bit like . . .

No.

She got to her feet.

'*No . . .*'

'*Darling . . . I say, darling, you were fine just as you were . . .*'

His skin was tanned deep brown, but his cheeks were hollow, his cheekbones too sharp. There were black shadows around his eyes. He was looking at her, gazing with a mixture of despair and longing and anguish that banished all doubt. Even as her head was whispering *it can't be,* every cell in her body sang with recognition.

'Dan.'

Beneath her, on the floor of the hall, people had started to notice. Heads were turning, following the direction of her gaze to the man in the badly fitting American uniform standing in the doorway, but she was oblivious to everyone else but him. The blood swelled in her head. She couldn't take her eyes from him; was afraid that if she blinked he'd disappear.

'Darling . . . ?' Charles's voice had turned icy. He moved to stand in front of her, blocking her view of Dan. Suddenly she was aware that the clamour of conversation in the hall had died away to uneasy murmurs. Charles's face was crimson, his lips white. 'Do you know that man?'

'Yes,' she whispered, stepping backwards. 'Yes, I do.' And with that she clattered down the stairs, cradling Daisy against her shoulder. The people on the floor below fell back to let her pass, their astonished stares following her all the way to the door.

Beside the tea urn, Ada's jaw dropped. 'Tinned peaches,' she muttered incredulously to Marjorie. 'That's that American what brought them last year. I knew I'd seen 'im somewhere before.' Her face hardened and she shook her head. 'Well, who'd have blooming thought it? The poor Reverend. I thought Mrs T. was better than that. Selling herself to a Yank for a bit of tinned fruit.'

A baby.

Jesus Christ Almighty. A *baby*. He felt like he'd swallowed the sun; that it was so big in his throat it was choking him. He was shaking. Adrenaline sluiced through his veins, making him unable to speak.

It had been days since he'd slept for more than a few snatched moments, and reality had broken up into jagged fragments that didn't quite fit together. He'd got back to England yesterday and the last twenty-four hours had been spent debriefing with British and American intelligence. He'd had a shower and accepted a new uniform, but turned down the offer of a bed. The thought of sleep was enticing, but the need to see Stella swamped everything else.

As she came towards him he was distantly aware of the other people in the hall behind her and the hush that had fallen, but he didn't care. This was the moment he'd longed for. Lived for. His fingers itched with the need to pull her into his arms and kiss the living daylights out of her, but instead he took her hand and held it tightly as their gazes locked and the rest of the world dissolved.

'Let's go.'

They moved quickly, their hands clasped so tightly that it

hurt. A good pain. As they left the hall the heavens opened and he felt a jolt of primitive alarm and an overwhelming urge to protect the tiny creature cradled against Stella's shoulder, its feet, in pink knitted boots, drawn up. Pink – that meant it was a girl, right? His heart crashed. He didn't care if it was a girl or a boy or a baby goddamned elephant—

Impatiently he dashed the rain from his face and ripped open his tunic, shrugging it off so that he could hold it over Stella and the baby. Her closeness made his head reel. Half-running they crossed the road to the Vicarage, and she went ahead of him up the path, pushing open the unlocked front door.

Inside it was murky and cold. They faced each other in the gloom, staring helplessly for a long moment before she gave a muted cry and stepped into his arms. He held them both, her and the baby, as his heart smashed against his ribs and their mouths found each other. She smelled different; milky, womanly, but she tasted the same. Christ, how he'd missed her. How he'd craved her. His hand slid through her damp hair, cupped her cheek, his thumb pressing against her mouth as he kissed her jaw, her eyelids. He felt incandescent with love. And want. He pulled away before it burned him up, brushing the top of the baby's silky head with his lips.

'It's really you, isn't it?' she murmured. 'I didn't think – I thought – I thought you were dead.'

In the dirty light her face was as pale and luminous as a candleflame. Her eyes were huge. Haunted. Like she was looking at a ghost.

'I nearly was. The other guys – my crew—'

He wanted to make light of it and take the terrible anguish from her eyes, but he found he couldn't. Clearing his throat he tried again. 'Sorry. It's really me. I wanted to get word to you but it was impossible; it would have put too many lives at risk – the lives of people who were helping me. The only thing I could do was try to get back to you as soon as I could. If I'd known – about—'

Emotion shattered the words in his throat, and he reached out and stroked a finger down the baby's velvet cheek. She was sleeping, the picture of rosy serenity, undisturbed by the cataclysmic events going on around her. She was clean and new and whole and miraculous; a promise of hope after the things that he'd seen.

'What's her name?'

'Daisy.'

Stella's voice was a whisper. A breath. As she spoke the tears that had been brimming and shimmering in her eyes spilled over, down her cheeks.

'It's beautiful. *Daisy* ...' he repeated reverently, trying it out. Daisy ... His daughter ... 'It's the most beautiful name in the world, and she's the most beautiful girl.' He bent to kiss her head again, inhaling her creamy scent and feeling an obliterating rush of adoration. 'Sweetheart, let's get out of here. I have a car. I told the driver to wait at the pub. Get your things and we'll go.'

He saw panic flare in her eyes as she glanced towards the front door. 'Where to?'

'Greenfields Lane, for now. They've given me a few days' leave before I have to report to HQ. We can work out what to do with the rest of our lives.'

She hesitated, opening her mouth as if she was about to argue, but then she shut it again and darted towards the stairs. He followed her, thrusting his arms into his jacket again. The house was like a crypt, all dark wood and dead air. Stella didn't belong here: she never had. In the bedroom she laid Daisy in the sagging centre of the bed while she hefted a suitcase out from beneath it. From the wall, a sinuous, pain-racked Christ stared down at the sleeping baby. Dan shuddered, fighting the urge to snatch her up and cradle her. Soon. Soon there would be time—

'I'll get her things, if you tell me where they are . . .'

Stella was bundling clothes into the suitcase. There was a kind of desperation about her movements now, as if she was trying to outrun a hurricane that had appeared on the horizon. 'Next door,' she said breathlessly. 'Her clothes are in the chest of drawers, and the nappies are folded in a pile on the shelf. She'll need nightdresses, and nappy pins – and I mustn't forget the ration books—'

'Hey.' He crossed the room swiftly and took her face in his hands, kissing her into silence. 'It's OK. It's OK. She'll have us – you and me – that's all she needs. Anything else we can get hold of, from someplace.' Holding her steady he captured her gaze. 'It'll be fine. Stella, I promise. I'm here now. There's nothing to be afraid of.'

She was trembling, he could feel it against his palms. He

was suddenly reminded of Cambridge, and how she'd stood at the window in the hotel and looked out, rigid and quivering with nerves. He'd thought then that all was lost and she was about to walk right out of his life forever. He'd been wrong. So maybe the sense of impending doom that was squeezing the air out of his chest right now was misplaced too.

Her eyes were fixed on his, huge and imploring. 'Dan . . . You have to understand . . . She's not . . . yours.'

Her voice was little more than a shivering breath, but the words hit him with a physical pain, like the lash of a whip. His lungs heaved in air and he floundered for a straw to clutch.

'But . . . But y-you didn't sleep together . . . ?'

She closed her eyes, and tears ran across the backs of his fingers. 'Just once, remember? It seems like that was enough.'

He pulled her against him, wrapping his arms tightly around her and burying his face in her hair as he fought back bitter disappointment and impotent rage. At Charles Thorne and what he had done to Stella. At himself. A memory of that afternoon in the little house on Greenfields Lane suddenly came back to him with astonishing clarity: the taste of whisky on their lips and the smell of autumn and woodsmoke. She'd begged him to leave her with the hope of a child, and he'd refused. The one thing she'd ever asked of him. He'd wanted too much and he'd aimed too high. He'd been so careful. He'd tried to protect her, but in doing so he'd extinguished all doubt. All hope.

Fiercely, gritting his teeth against his own stupidity and arrogance he whispered into her hair, 'It doesn't matter. I

423

don't give a damn if she's his or mine. I love her already because she's a part of you. She's yours, and she'd be *ours*. Our daughter—'

She broke free of his embrace and tipped her face up to his, parting her lips as she sought his mouth. 'I love you,' she sobbed, between kisses. 'I love you so much. I didn't dare hope—'

He smoothed the hair back from her wet face. 'You shouldn't have doubted. Don't ever doubt how much I love you, Stella. Now please, let's get your things together and get out of here.'

On the bed the baby slept on as they packed hurriedly, then Stella gathered her into her arms while Dan took the suitcase and they left the oppressive bedroom. In just a few more seconds they'd be free of this house and he would be able to breathe again, and surrender to the flood of emotions that had risen in him. All those months in France – every footsore step of his journey North, all the waiting and lying low in safehouses, the claustrophobic hours spent hidden in lumbering carts and stinking lorries – it had all been to bring him to this point. He felt lightheaded with exhaustion and exhilaration. Reaching the top of the stairs their hands brushed and he captured her fingers, squeezing them tight and raising them to his lips. He kissed them, and below, in the hallway, the front door opened.

'What the devil do you think you're doing?'

In Dan's mind, Charles Thorne had taken on the aspect of an ogre, but the man who stood at the foot of the stairs was laughably ordinary; tall and thin and typically English with his colourless hair and pink complexion and ridiculously misplaced indignation. It would have been easier, somehow, if he had been the monster Dan had imagined, and if he hadn't had one empty sleeve pinned into the pocket of his jacket. Instead of hatred, Dan felt only pity, and distracted irritation.

'Charles—'

Stella was in front of him on the stairs. Dan couldn't see her face, but he heard the fear in her voice and felt the sudden tension radiating from her body like a forcefield. Irritation hardened into dislike.

'Reverend Thorne. Stella and Daisy are coming with me.' Dan kept his tone reasonable. He willed Stella to keep moving down the stairs – if her husband tried to stop them Dan would have no trouble getting past him – but she stood rooted to the spot on the top step. A few feet below, Charles Thorne's face set into a mask of rage.

'I don't think they are.'

'Charles, please . . .' Stella said. '*Please* . . . I'm sorry it's happening like this, but you know as well as I do that our marriage was a mistake. We tried – *I* tried to make you happy, but it's no good. We don't love each other – not how we're meant to. You know that.'

Her courage and bravado, and the slight tremor in her voice made Dan's heart turn over. Her husband remained unmoved. He gave a brief, mirthless laugh.

'I'm afraid it's not that simple. We're married. Those vows

were made in church, before God. You can't just decide it was a mistake because you've had your head turned by some . . .' His pale eyes flickered dismissively in Dan's direction, 'flashy Yank.'

Dan's pulse was loud in his ears as it pumped anger through his veins. Every reflex in his body was directing him down the stairs to grab Charles Thorne and throw him across the hall and out of their way. It took the last of his strength to hold back, for Stella's sake. Stella and the baby.

'It's more than that, Charles. I *love* him. I didn't know what love was until I met him, but I do now. Please Charles – I'm begging you – let me go.'

'We have a child,' he said coldly. 'What about her? Do you just expect me to relinquish my daughter; all my rights as a father to your fancy man?'

'Don't talk about *rights*.' Dan's words escaped though tightly clenched teeth. Both his hands were balled into fists, held rigidly at his sides, and even to his own ears his voice sounded like the snarl of an animal. 'If you'd behaved like a decent human being you wouldn't have a daughter. You have no *rights*.'

'Dan—' Shaken by the blast of his anger, Stella turned. Standing on the step below him she had to tip her face up to look at him and the light from the mean little stained glass window at the top of the stairs cast a yellowish tint across her cheek. It reminded him of the bruise she'd got from her husband's hand. In her arms the baby slept on, folded in on herself like a flower.

'I think you'll find that I have,' Thorne said. His tone was stronger now; more certain, more arrogant. 'I am her husband. It is my name on the child's birth certificate. You're in England now, airman, not the Wild West. We have the oldest and best legal system in the world, and I can assure you that the rights of a husband over an adulterous wife are robustly upheld.'

It was too much. The final thread of Dan's self-control snapped and he made to launch himself down the stairs to the man at the bottom, ready to beat his self-satisfied face into a bloody pulp. But in the same second Stella moved towards him; stepping up, putting herself and the sleeping baby between him and the object of his fury.

'*Don't* Dan, please . . .' It came out as a sob. 'It's no good.'

He staggered backwards until he hit the wall behind him, thrusting his fingers into his hair in impotent despair as she pressed against him, holding him with her free arm, trying to contain his rage and anguish.

'He *raped* you, Stella! He beat you and he . . . raped you.'

'How dare you say those things in front of my wife?' Thorne's voice rang with icy outrage from the hallway below. His face was white but his cheeks were mottled crimson. Turning, he stepped to the side, as if making way for Dan to come down the stairs. 'I think it's time you left now.'

'You fucking hypocrite. You *did* those things.'

Charles Thorne didn't flinch. He remained where he was, standing like a sentinel at the foot of the staircase, staring at a picture of the Virgin Mary on the wall in front of him. 'Don't be absurd,' he said stiffly, as if he were addressing the Madonna, instead of Dan. 'The things that take place between a married couple are private, and entirely legal.' He gave a blustering little laugh. 'A man can't *rape* his own wife.'

'The hell he can't,' Dan said in a low voice. Stella's cheek was against his shoulder, Daisy's head resting over his thudding heart. His arms were around them both and he wanted to keep them safe like that forever. 'And he can't keep his wife against her will either.'

'No, he can't.'

For a moment Thorne sounded almost reasonable. A jolt passed through Stella's body, and when she lifted her head there was hope written across her tearstained face.

'Let me make myself clear,' Thorne continued. 'Stella is perfectly at liberty to leave. I won't try to stop her.' He looked up with a thin-lipped smile and gestured vaguely to his empty sleeve. 'I think we all know that I couldn't, even if I was the kind of man who would resort to force.' The smile hardened as his pale eyes rested on Stella. 'You can go with him, but be assured of this: there will be no divorce. And the child stays here. If you leave, to live against the word of God with another man, you will not see her again.'

Stella gave a gasping cry, breaking out of the circle of Dan's arms. 'But I'm her *mother* . . . She *belongs* with me.'

'Then you have to choose. To go with him. Or to stay with your daughter.'

And that was when Dan knew it was hopeless; when the strength that had driven him from the moment the first blast had almost knocked his fort out of the sky and kept him going on his perilous, painful, frustrating journey through France finally deserted him. Blindly he groped for the stair post and held on to it for support as his vision darkened and a vortex of panic swirled around him. He wanted to say something to make it all right. To make it how he'd imagined it would be as he walked those endless miles, when he'd thought that all he had to do was stay alive and get back to her.

No words came. None that would put back together what Charles Thorne had destroyed with his brutal logic. The odds had been stacked against them from the start, he thought dully. It should come as no surprise that the law was too.

He shook his head, to clear the fog from in front of his eyes. Stella's face swam into focus, as pale as the moon, her eyes huge with horror. He opened his mouth to cast out his last lifeline, his one remaining hope. *We could have another one. Our own child . . .* But then she lifted Daisy to hold her against her shoulder and, disturbed by the movement, the baby gave a sudden cat-like mewling cry. It split the air between them like forked lightning, and struck him dumb. In silent agony he watched as Stella rested her cheek against the tiny head, folding Daisy more tightly into her body as the distance between them seemed to widen.

'I can't leave her, Dan. I can't . . .' Her voice was barely audible.

'I would never ask you to.'

He was all out of ammunition and the battle was lost. He knew that at some point during its course he had sustained wounds that he couldn't yet feel, but that soon, once the numbness had worn off the pain was going to be bad.

He closed the gap between them, sliding his hand into the warmth of her neck, beneath her hair, bringing his mouth to her ear.

'This isn't goodbye, Stella, I promise you that. I won't let it be.' His lips were stiff, his voice hoarse. 'It's not over – not for me. I'll wait for you, however long it takes – forever, if I have to. And I'll write. And I'll never stop loving you, or hoping. As long as we're both alive I'm not going to give up hope.'

He let her go. Without trusting himself to glance at the man who had destroyed his chance of happiness he went down the stairs and out of the front door, into the drenching summer downpour and the wreckage of the rest of his life.

33

2011

In accordance with the proverb, March came in like a lion, if that meant it was fiercely cold. A couple of sudden and heavy snowfalls at the end of the first week turned London's parks into enchanted playgrounds and its pavements into death runs. With only three weeks to go until the wedding, Will's mother was in despair about the garden being anything like ready. She'd been banking on the magnolia being in bloom for the photographs, as well as the hundreds of bulbs she'd had put in last autumn especially for the event.

Will was in despair too, only he was less vocal about it. Thanks to Warren, the Spitfire was no trouble to start on icy mornings, but going to work early on the first snowy day he had lost control on an ungritted road and skidded, slowly and gracefully, into a new, top of the range Mercedes. His car had skimmed along the side, denting the rear wheel arch of the Mercedes before scraping the gleaming paintwork over both doors. As a twenty-five-year-old male, the cost of insuring an

ungaraged classic sports car in London was already astro-
nomical and he couldn't afford the premium hike if he made
a claim. He could barely afford the Mercedes owner's six-
hundred-pound repair bill either, especially not on top of
Simon and Marina's wedding present. He'd been shocked to
discover that the cheapest thing on the list they held with an
exclusive Chelsea design store was a corkscrew at seventy-
nine pounds.

Any faint and foolish hope he might have cherished of
striking gold with Nancy Price's estate had also officially
been dashed. He'd gone, as promised, to Albert Greaves's
early on the Saturday morning after he'd got back from
Crewe, only to find that, when he went to open the front
door of number four, the key wouldn't fit. It was only then
that he'd noticed the brightness of the metal keyhole and the
scratched paintwork around it, and realized that the locks had
been changed.

'Who the 'eck's done that?' Albert asked, indignantly.

'The council,' Will guessed. 'They must have been notified
about the house by the police and the paramedics. They'll
have got a court order to deal with the contents and, if no
heirs come to light, process a sale.'

'If I'd have seen the cheeky blighters doing it they'd have
had a piece of my mind,' Albert spluttered. 'They've got no
right.'

There was no point explaining that they had, and, with no
paperwork relating to the property's ownership, were following
correct procedure. Will knew that Albert was as disappointed

as he was. To both of them number four Greenfields Lane was more than a decaying old house filled with the flotsam and jetsam of a lifetime. It had held dreams; for Albert, of the past, for Will the future. Their abrupt removal was a bitter blow.

Will could remember quite clearly how he had felt five years ago when it had all gone wrong. The details of what happened and what he'd done – the uncontrolled drinking, the long walks through silent streets in the small hours, the scrambled essays and missed mealtimes – were a blur, remembered largely because of his housemates' reports afterwards. But the feelings . . . the *thoughts* were still there, like a shadow on his brain. As events eluded his control he was aware of that shadow spreading and darkening.

He couldn't stop thinking about Jess; wondering where she was and whether she was all right, torn between the certainty that she had simply moved on with her life and the nagging belief that maybe, wherever she was, she might just be thinking of him too and not know how to reach him. That was the thing that tormented him most. Not knowing.

Small things. Small things mattered. One of his therapists had described a set of scales inside his mind on which everything came to rest, and explained that even the tiniest events made a difference to the balance. The image had stayed with him, and as March slipped by and spring didn't come; as the wedding got closer, Ansell's jibes got crueller and he relinquished all hope of seeing Jess Moran again, he knew that if he couldn't take control, he had to take care. To do small, positive things to counterbalance the negative.

And so, in the absence of anything else to focus on, he applied himself to the task of finding out what had happened to Stella Thorne.

*

The pills lay in the palm of her hand like tiny bombs.

Two of them. She squeezed her eyes shut for a second and then looked again. Definitely two – that was right, and she hadn't taken them already this morning. Had she? Tuesday. She said the day out loud to fix it in her head, then put the pills into her mouth and gulped down water. It would be an hour until they began to work their magic fully, but she felt calmer already, just knowing that soon the sharp edges of the day would begin to blur again and questions that chased themselves round and round in her head would lose their urgency.

She didn't know what she would do without the pills. After the day of the fete (the ill-feted day, as she sometimes thought of it, when the pills gave her thoughts that warm fluidity) things had been very bad, but Dr Walsh had turned out to be an unexpected ally. 'Difficult times, my dear, difficult times. These will help,' he'd said smoothly, the nib of his fountain pen scratching on the paper. After the coldness meted out to her by Ada and Marjorie and the rest of the parish ladies, she was astonished and relieved and grateful.

If it wasn't for Daisy she would have simply given up. Often, during the hot sleepless nights she would find herself wondering which would be the quickest, the least painful, the cleanest way to end it. Those were some of the questions that circulated ceaselessly around the passageways in her brain, like a clockwork train. But then she would remember that she had given up her future with Dan to stay with Daisy and a new series of questions would begin: how was she to get through each day of the rest of her life without him?

Before, she had had the comfort of fantasy to keep her going. Even while fearing he was dead, she had been able to sustain herself with hope and wishes and what-ifs. *If only he would come back safely, everything would be all right.* But he had come back; fate or God or his own courage and determination had brought him home, and it had been she who had sounded the death-knell on their future together. Each time she remembered that, panic pulsed through her, making her blood fizz. Was it too late to change her mind?

She knocked on the door of Charles's study. He didn't look round when she went in, but even the back of his head seemed to radiate cold disapproval.

'I'm taking Daisy to the shops.' Her voice sounded odd – muffled and echoey, as if she were underwater. 'Is there anything you need?'

'No thank you.' He turned round and regarded her coolly over his spectacles. 'Do you have to take Daisy? Isn't it time for her nap? Dr Walsh has said numerous times how important it is for her to have a routine. She'll never settle properly if you constantly fuss with her like some . . . doll.'

'She'll fall asleep in the pram. She's almost dropping off already. Dr Walsh also said it was important for her to get fresh air, and it's such a lovely day . . .'

She trailed off, exhausted by the effort of putting the sentence together. Charles made a little grunt of impatience, or possibly disgust. 'Very well then. It's very hot; make sure she's shaded by the pram hood.'

It was obvious he wanted her out of his room. She went, closing the door carefully behind her. Since the fete Charles had lost enthusiasm for playing the part of loving husband. He had stopped asking her to help with the little things he couldn't manage and relied instead on Ada and Dr Walsh. A new curate had arrived; an earnest young man called Owen or Ewan, and he had quickly become, almost literally, Charles's right-hand man.

The August sun was hard and white, and its heat pressed down on Stella's head as she walked along the baked pavement. Beneath the fringed hood of the pram Daisy wailed fitfully. Stella watched her little mouth stretch in her screwed-up face, but the pills had started to work and the sound that came from it was disconnected. Reaching the row of shops at the bottom of the hill she parked the pram outside Fairacre's and joined the queue inside. Ada was there, talking to Ethel Collins. She glanced at Stella as she came in and pointedly turned her back.

Since she'd been revealed as an adulteress it had been the same story, of conversations ended abruptly, pursed lips and hostile stares. Stella leaned against the doorframe. It was just as well, she thought vaguely; she'd rather be spared the effort of dredging up words from the soup in her head and arranging them into a conversation. Flies circled drunkenly in the thick air and one of them blundered into her face. The hot, meaty smell of blood coming from the counter very suddenly reminded her of Blossom and an inexplicable rush of tears stung her eyes.

She stumbled out of the shop, dizzy and stricken. The fly seemed to follow her. Its buzzing filled her head, so that she thought it was caught in her hair and shook it wildly to get rid of it. The noise got louder, deeper, until the sky boomed with it. She put her hands over her ears and started to walk quickly, keeping her eyes pinned to the pavement and the flicker of her own feet. Running now. Running. Running, running, running—

The explosion made her stop. The ground jerked and the hot air seemed to suck itself in before expanding again in a hot rush. Everything shimmered and became liquid and insubstantial for a moment, as if the world itself was dissolving.

But it didn't. The boom died away and the vacuum of silence in its wake was filled again, by the distant sounds of ringing bells and shouted voices. Smoke billowed like a black parachute unfurling above the rooftops, but the houses around her resumed their solid outlines. Stella looked around, blinking as she tried to get her bearings. She didn't recognize the street in which she stood, but the smoke rose like a shadowy skyscraper in the direction from which she'd just come. From the shops.

Where she'd left Daisy.

34

2011

Morning Dan. Just checking in quickly to fill you in on how it went yesterday in King's Oak. Not exactly brilliant, I'm sorry to say. Got the bus over there and found the church, no problem. It's exactly how you described it – a great big ugly dark red building, so nothing's changed there. It was all locked up and so I went to the Vicarage across the road. It felt pretty weird – good weird – to walk up the path of Stella's old home, but when I knocked the woman who answered looked at me like I was a plague carrier or something and said that it wasn't anything to do with the church any more and she pointed to a sign by the front door that said THE OLD VICARAGE. The new one is a bit further down, next to the community hall. It looks like a shoebox with windows.

The vicar wasn't much help, to be honest. I don't think he liked me and he didn't make much effort to hide it, which I thought was pretty bad since he's supposed to be a

Christian. Anyway, he did go away and dig out this massive book of parish records and showed me the bit about Charles Thorne. It just said that he was there from June 1937, and the next guy took over in September 1945. If old grumpy trousers had any idea where Charles went after that, or how I could find out, he wasn't going to tell me, that was for certain.

One thing was interesting, though. The list of all the vicars was pretty formal, with middle names and everything. Our guy was listed as Maurice Charles Thorne. I can see why he preferred to be called Charles, but I guess if Maurice was his proper first name that might be why you haven't been able to find him in documents and stuff?

Have you made any progress on the house? And how are you feeling? I hope the new drug they gave you is working well, and with no nasty side effects.

I'm off to the lunch club today. I'm massively nervous because last time one of the ladies – Vera, who I told you about, the one who knew Nancy Price pretty well and called her a 'fast piece' or whatever it was – managed to get out of me that I wanted to be a singer. Or used to, before I realized what a hopeless ambition it was. Well, she made a big fuss about it and announced it to everyone, and it seems like they've got a piano in the room where they have their tea and coffee after lunch, and one of the old girls plays it, so you can guess what's coming, can't you? I'll try to get out of it, but those ladies are a pretty determined bunch, I can tell you.

And then after that I have an interview! It's for a job my case worker at the hostel found out about, in a dry cleaner's of all places. I can't say the prospect thrills me much but I haven't heard anything about all the other jobs I've applied for, so I guess I can't be too fussy.

Wish me luck!

Jess x

The library had become a sort of home from home. She had got into a routine of going there every morning, partly to get out of the hostel, but also to exchange emails with Dan and continue their quest to find Stella. In the long computer room she had a favourite machine; the one at the end, which was beside a radiator and had a view over the little park and the bench where she'd eaten her sausage roll all those weeks ago.

It was weird to reflect how far she'd come since then. It had got worse before it got better, but finally she felt cautiously optimistic that her life was heading in the right direction. She had somewhere to live; choices, independence, purpose. All good. But without Will Holt she would have had none of those things, and she would have liked the chance to say thank you. And for him to see her when her hair wasn't plastered to her head with grease and she wasn't wearing a paper sack.

She gazed out over the stretch of grass. Beneath a tree there were daffodils, and an image of the cards they made at school for Mother's Day flashed into her head; three-dimensional ones, with bits cut from egg boxes for the daffodil's trumpet.

Of course, she used to make hers for Gran, without thinking twice about it, but she suddenly recalled with startling clarity a girl called Jacey Reed asking her why she didn't have a mum. Jess remembered the yellow paint, thick as egg yolk, the satisfaction of stroking it onto the cardboard trumpet. 'She buggered off, didn't she?' she'd replied, and subsequently spent her playtime sitting outside the head's office for swearing. Fifteen years later her indignation at the injustice was as vivid as on that long ago March day. She'd only been repeating what she'd heard Gran say.

Feelings, she thought, gazing out into the sharp-edged morning. They're all stored up inside us, like in some kind of freezer that keeps them fresh for years. Like Dan, at ninety, still loving Stella.

Hey Jess – great to get your message. Today's a big day! I'll be thinking of you.

That's great that you went to King's Oak – I really appreciate you taking the time and the trouble. Your discovery about Charles Thorne's name is pretty significant, I'd say. That explains why I've had no luck finding him online.

My lawyers are still working on the house. It seems like the place where the paperwork was stored was damaged by fire from an incendiary bomb in 1945, which is why no one over your side of the Atlantic knew who owned it. Right now it seems that the council have taken charge. My lawyer has sent over copies of the paperwork from the initial sale – not much by today's standards, but hopefully enough to prove ownership. I transferred the property into Stella's name in September '44. I was back home then, and still writing to her pretty much every week. I never got a reply, but I remember telling her in one of the letters that while she kept the house I'd keep hoping. If she sold it, I'd know it was the end of the line. My lawyer thinks that if she can't be found it's pretty straightforward to get the property deeds reverted to me. But like everything, it takes time. And of course, we ARE going to find her, right?!

The new drug is great. I mean, not a miracle cure or anything, but I feel like my grip on life has grown stronger. That could just as easily be talking to you though. Hope is better than any drug.

Good luck with the singing and the interview – knock 'em dead kid!

Dan x

Jess typed a quick reply.

I'll do my best – will tell you later how everything went! I'm coming back this evening to look through the marriage records again. It was pretty hopeless before without Stella's maiden name, but how many Maurice Charles Thornes can there be?

J x

She logged out and picked up her bag. Over the past weeks she'd grown close to Dan Rosinski; amazingly close, considering they'd never even met. The man she talked to by email was the same gentle, unassuming, courageous person whose voice had haunted her in the letters. His story had given her something to focus on while her own life was in a mess. She felt privileged that he had shared it with her.

She also, from time to time, felt very anxious.

Supposing she let him down? Supposing she just couldn't find Stella Thorne, or discover what had happened to her before Dan's illness got the better of him? It was leukaemia, he'd told her. He could fight it for a little while longer, but it would beat him in the end. The thought of saying goodbye to him was bad enough, but saying goodbye without having helped him close the circle was unbearable.

She was frowning as she made her way through the library's reading room, so wrapped up in her thoughts that she didn't notice the chair that had been left sticking out slightly from beneath a table, just enough for her to stub her toe on its leg as she passed. She gasped and dropped her bag, gritting her teeth against the pain. And the embarrassment; around her, people at other tables raised their heads and stared. Feeling foolish she sank down onto the chair to gather up her scattered belongings.

There was a newspaper on the table and she glanced at it, trying to look nonchalant as she waited for her blush to evaporate. But it didn't. It intensified as she read the front page, until it felt like her whole head was alight.

DAWN RAID BUSTS DRUGS GANG. Five appear in court.

443

Below the headline there were a series of photographs of the accused.

RINGLEADER: *Darren Michael Hodgson, 26, of Elephant and Castle is charged with fifteen counts of supplying Class A drugs and four counts of possession with intent to supply.*

Dodge's face glared straight at her, wearing an expression that suggested his arrest was her fault and he'd make sure she paid for it.

Except he couldn't, she thought dazedly, stumbling to her feet. Not now he was in police custody with no bail and looking at a very long prison sentence. If he was found guilty, of course, but he would be, she had no doubt about that. Dodge had screwed too many people over to inspire much loyalty. There would be people queuing up to get into the witness box and see him sent down.

It was almost too much to take in, but as she left the library she smiled with disproportionate warmth at the man who held the door open for her, and walked to work without once looking over her shoulder.

The phone was ringing.

On and on and on and on, the bell seeming to get shriller and louder and more insistent with every ring. Will buried his head under the pillows and wrapped them tightly over his ears to block out the sound.

It would be Ansell again, no doubt. He'd rung yesterday too, approximately a minute and a half after Will had put down the phone from explaining to Bex that the doctor had signed him off work for two weeks. 'Stress?' Ansell had bellowed down the phone. 'Fucking tell me about it! Paying members of staff to arse about in bed all day while the rest of us have to do their share of the work – *that's* fucking *stressful.*' Will had hung up without listening to any more, but it had taken him two hours to stop shaking.

The doctor had prescribed antidepressants. 'Just a mild one, to get you feeling more like yourself again.' If there had been pills to make him feel like someone else – Simon for example – he'd have downed them like sweeties, but since he wasn't sure that feeling like himself was a good thing he hadn't taken one yet. It seemed like a final admission of defeat.

The phone stopped ringing. Cautiously he sat up, pushing the heels of his hands into his eyes as the brightness of the day made them sting and smart. The red digits of his clock radio showed that it was 10.26 a.m. Last night he'd lain awake in the small hours, staring through the gloom at the stain on the ceiling while the contents of his brain churned frantically, like a washing machine stuck on the spin cycle. Eventually he'd got up and sat in the dark sitting room with his laptop, staring at the screen with unblinking eyes and filling the vortex in his head with the search for Stella.

It was pathetic really. He'd scoured every record he could access and scribbled down dates and snippets of information, filling sheets of paper with illegible scrawl and scattering Post-it notes around him like showers of confetti. He'd made a list of Charles Thorne's incumbencies, and trawled the internet for his name in the appropriate local newspaper archives. He had discovered that he'd awarded the prizes in the Stoke Green dog show in 1949 and held a special Coronation service of thanksgiving in St John's church, Bristol in 1953. He'd even turned up a picture of him – a lean man with hollow cheeks and pale hair – shaking hands with the Bishop of Bath and Wells in 1956. But of Stella and Daisy there was nothing. Like ghosts, they remained just out of sight, beyond his reach.

It had been getting light by the time he'd finally given up and stumbled back to bed, exhausted and numb with failure. But waking up now to the glare of another day he saw clearly that it didn't matter. It wasn't important. It wasn't really Stella Thorne he wanted to find. It was Jess.

35

1944

Sunlight lay in watery diamonds across the green linoleum floor.

It was warm, sitting beside the window, though the nurse who had brought her pills came in rubbing her hands and saying how nippy it was outside.

The trees weren't green any more, but orange. Red. Yellow.

They made her think of the scent of woodsmoke, so vividly that it overlaid the smell of carbolic and urine that pervaded the hospital. She recalled lying in front of the fire in the little house in Greenfields Lane, as Dan's fingers trailed lazily over the ridges of her ribs.

She turned her face towards the window and closed her eyes so the sun glowed through the lids, shutting out the nurse. Shutting out now. Shutting out everything but the memory of him.

*

Nancy came. Her face loomed through the fog in Stella's brain, and her mouth moved but the sound was all distorted, like a gramophone that needed winding.

'Can you hear me, Stell? Christ Almighty, what have they done to you?'

Stella wanted to ask the same thing. Nancy's face was all wrong. Her mouth was too big, and one eye had almost disappeared in a pad of spongy flesh. *Indecent acts.* She opened her mouth to try to explain but the words were glued to her tongue. Nancy leaned in closer through the fog, so that Stella could see through the layers of powder to the purple bruise beneath.

'Listen to me, Stell. I need your help. I don't know who else to turn to. Do you understand?'

Stella nodded. Nancy was holding her hands, but they felt like they were a long way away, like her arms were six feet long. The pills always did that. Made things feel distant. Detached. It was good.

'I need somewhere to stay. I can't go back to the flat. I need somewhere that Len won't find me.'

The hospital ward was like the dormitory at school: beds in rows, lockers beside them, noises all through the night. There wasn't a bed free for Nancy, but perhaps they could find one, or make someone swap – maybe that woman at the end who moaned all the time. Nancy moved in closer, enveloping Stella in her miasma of perfume and cigarettes. Her voice was low and urgent.

'I'm in trouble, Stell. Big trouble, and it's not Len's. I

thought he'd never know, but ...' She made a funny little sound that should have been a laugh but wasn't. 'How was I to know he'd had the mumps when he was a kid? I thought he'd kill me. I think he still might if he gets the chance.'

She made a jerky movement and the silk scarf around her neck – one of Len's many gifts – fell away enough for Stella to see the bruising on her throat, like fingerprints from a dirty hand. In its tomb of stone Stella's heart gave a feeble beat of pity and her faraway fingers tightened on Nancy's.

'You can stay here. It's safe.'

Nancy laughed properly then; a high, wild laugh like the one the red-haired woman in the bed opposite did whenever she saw anyone else crying. Nancy's hand flew up to touch her mouth, her eye, and Stella found her fingers were clutching at thin air.

'Bleeding 'ell, Stella – no! No. That's not what I meant.'

Stella was tired. Outside it was raining. She watched the water running down the glass, like it had run down Dan's face on the day he'd come back to find her. He'd held his jacket over her and Daisy, and sheltered them with his body.

'... I mean, it's just sitting there empty, ain't it? I could look after the place, keep it nice. And then, when you get out of here we could be there together – you and me, just like the old days.'

Nancy was looking at her expectantly, though Stella didn't know what for. Her face wobbled and stretched in front of her, as if it was trapped inside a soap bubble. Then, with a jolt, the meaning of what she was saying sank in and the bubble burst.

'My house. You want to have my house—'

'Not to *have* it, silly. Borrow it for a little while, until you've sorted things out with Charles and you're ready to live in it yourself. And then, just for a little while maybe we could live in it together, while you get your strength back. So you wouldn't have to be on your own.'

Nancy's hand was cool on her forehead, smoothing the hair away from her face. It was nice to be touched like that. No one ever touched her here. Her skin cried out for it. Stella closed her eyes so she could concentrate on the feeling, but something was needling at her, stopping her enjoying it, like a splinter lodged in her brain. Her eyes flew open as she located it and picked it out.

'A baby. You'll have a *baby*—'

'All right, all right,' Nancy hissed. 'No need to shout it out so everyone knows I'm in bother, is there?' She withdrew her hand and smoothed her skirt primly over her knees. Darting an uneasy glance around the ward she went on in a low voice. 'Anyway, I only said I'm *having* one. Never mentioned nothing about keeping it, did I? So can I stay in your little love nest or not?'

Stella turned her head away as tears drove their red hot needles into her eyeballs. A mini film reel played in her head, showing Nancy pushing a pram into a bomb crater. *I never said nothing about keeping it.*

'Stella?'

She was so tired. She just wanted Nancy to leave, and for the film in her head to finish. She nodded. 'My coat. At the Vicarage. The key's in the pocket.'

'Thanks darling, I knew I could count on you.' Nancy's kiss struck her on the cheek, and the chair scraped back as she stood up. 'I'll come back and see you soon.'

'Nancy!'

Stella stumbled out of bed. The floor was like ice beneath her feet as she ran after Nancy, who was walking briskly up the ward. She turned with an expression of alarm.

'What's the matter?'

'Not the violet room. I don't want you to have that one. I don't want you to go in there. Not at all – do you understand? *Not at all.*'

Nancy laughed, nervously. 'All right, keep your hair on. I'll lock the door and keep it locked until the day you move in, if it makes you feel better.'

'Promise?'

'I promise, all right? I promise.'

Even so, as Stella watched her walk away, knotting her silk scarf and settling her handbag on her arm, she felt like she'd lost the only thing she had left.

36

2011

Hi Dan, just a quick one to say sorry I haven't been in touch for a couple of days. I hope you're feeling lots better than you were on Wednesday and the cold didn't get any worse. It's my lunch hour now so I don't have very long, but I've been thinking of you a lot. Let me know that you're OK!

Well, I made it through my first week of work. I've got to say, working in a dry cleaner's wasn't top of my list of career choices but I actually like it. The people I work with are really nice. There's Mr Wahim, who owns it, and Samia who I work with mostly, and another lady I haven't met yet who does Saturdays. Samia and Mr Wahim are both a lot older than me, and they boss me around but in a really kind way. It reminds me of being back home in Leeds with my Gran. I told Mr Wahim about the Lunch Club and he says I can have an extra half hour's break on Mondays to sing for them. I thought that was pretty nice of him. He also gave me an advance on my first week's wages to get a proper haircut and buy some make-up. Yesterday after the shop shut I went along to the hairdressers down the road where they had a trainee night. I now look almost presentable! The last time my hair was cut it was by me, with some not very sharp scissors, so it was a total state.

I waited for the postman this morning but the certificates you ordered from the National Records Office didn't arrive. Hopefully they'll come tomorrow. I'll let you know.

You are all right, aren't you? The worst bit about my new job is not being able to email every morning, but I want you to know I haven't forgotten Stella or given up believing that we'll find her. I'm sure these certificates will show up something and we can pick up the search again with new information.

Look after yourself – for me, and for Stella.

Jess x

She pressed 'send' and waited a few moments, but the clock in the corner of the computer screen said six minutes to two and she had to get back to work. She refreshed her mailbox, but nothing came through so she logged off and left.

It was almost Easter and the shop windows were dressed with yellow and purple and green. Last month's snow had melted and you could almost feel the ground warming beneath your feet, the world waking up again. For the first time in ages Jess felt a sense of optimism, like something good was going to happen.

Which it did, as soon as she arrived back at the shop. Mr

Wahim called her into the back and held aloft a white box tied with gold ribbon.

'Is Friday afternoon – that deserves a celebration, no? You like baklava, Jess?'

She discovered she did like it, very much. Samia put the kettle on and they huddled in the little back room amongst all the plastic-shrouded garments awaiting collection, peering out for customers and licking honey from their fingers. 'You having fun this weekend, Jess? You out on the town dancing the night away now you have your smart new hairstyle?' Mr Wahim asked, his dark eyes twinkling. He was small and neat, with a fringe of snow-white hair at the sides of his head and a matching bristling moustache, from which he now brushed crumbs of pastry. He reminded Jess of the gnome that had stood beside the front door at Gran's house, welcoming visitors.

She shook her head. 'I haven't really made any friends down here to go out with.' There was a girl called Jazz in the hostel with whom she'd struck up a tentative friendship, but it was early days. 'Except you two. Don't suppose you fancy a bit of clubbing?'

Mr Wahim grinned. 'What do you say, Samia? We show these youngsters how it is done, yes?' In the confined space he lifted his arms and performed a sort of John Travolta tribute dance that made Jess shout with laughter and Samia roll her eyes. She was the Hardy to Mr Wahim's Laurel, the straight man to his clown. Samia's default setting was disapproval, but it was a poor disguise for her kindness.

'You wouldn't catch me in those places. All hot and crowded with intoxicated people making fools of themselves.' She pressed her finger into the corners of the box, picking up the last sticky crumbs of honeyed pistachio and almond, then hauled herself heavily to her feet. 'Right, are we ready to face the rush?' She eyed the row of garments lined up for Friday collection and frowned, pushing the hangers back from a dark suit. 'Mr Holt should have picked this up by now. I try to ring him this morning, but there is no reply. His brother's wedding is tomorrow – see? I wrote it here, on the ticket.'

Mr Wahim glanced at the label she showed him and shrugged. 'Maybe he has another suit?'

Samia looked sceptical. 'Maybe he has forgotten. You know what Mr Holt is like. Forgotten ticket, forgotten loyalty card, forgotten credit card.' She shook her head as she picked up the telephone. 'I will try ringing him again. Otherwise he will be banging on the door again when we have locked up, you mark my words.'

As Samia dialled, Jess waited for her heart to steady after the beat it had missed. *Mr Holt.* Hastily she checked the label attached to the suit's hanger: there was no first name or initial. Following Mr Wahim into the front she tried to sound casual.

'Holt? That wouldn't be Will Holt by any chance?'

'Mr Will Holt – yes! He comes in often, bringing his suits for work. You know him?'

'Yes. Yes, I know him. He's . . . he's nice,' Jess finished in a rush. 'He came to see me when I was in hospital with pneumonia. If he doesn't come in this afternoon I could always drop the suit round to him when I finish, if you like. I owe him a favour.'

Samia came through from the back, her forehead pleated with concern. 'Still no answer. I'm sure he has forgotten.'

Mr Wahim beamed. 'Not to worry – if he does not come our excellent new colleague has offered to deliver it to him. Thank you Jess – it's good to provide our regular customers with tip-top service. The address is in the book. You see, I knew you were going to be great asset to Team Wahim!'

The box containing the little foil blister packs of pills was on the mantelpiece. Will could see it from where he lay on the sofa and had been trying to summon the energy to get up and get it for the last four hours. Maybe longer. He had no idea what the time was.

The phone had rung again, but he hadn't even considered answering it. The drifts of paper from last night's research had settled around him, like week-old city snow, and the medical information leaflet that had come with the pills had fallen into it and become buried. Lost. Will stirred the lumpen porridge inside his head in search of what it had said about side effects. The list had been long and reading it had made him feel even more depressed. There was a certain black humour to be found in that, he supposed.

He stood up unsteadily, and waited for his head to stop spinning. In the glass of the picture hanging above the fireplace he could see his reflection, superimposed upon the landscape like a ghost. It was a photograph he'd taken in

Venice with Milla, standing under a bridge in a sudden summer shower. He'd had it blown up and framed because it was arty and cool, but now it seemed to release its toxic memories like the fetid, sulphurous smell of the canals. *A city for lovers,* he remembered her smirking as she read from some guide book. *How ironic.*

Sexual dysfunction. Of course — that was one of the side effects of antidepressants — how could he forget? At least he didn't have to worry about that this time, since the chance would be a miracle. Oh, and weight loss too — that was another one. Hallelujah, bring it on — except who cared? The determination he'd felt when the stupid wedding invitation had arrived was a distant memory now, impossible to recapture. He'd been going to turn his life around, but instead he'd crashed it into a fucking wall.

In a sudden burst of energy he crossed the room and yanked the picture down with such force that the hook was wrenched out of the plaster. It didn't make him feel better, but at least the pills were within reach now. *It'll take a little while before you feel the benefits,* the doctor's voice said again in his head. He picked up the box and stared at the label. Mr William Holt. One Tablet To Be Taken, Once A Day, Avoid Alcohol While Taking This Medicine.

Alcohol.

Now there was an idea.

He tossed the pills back where he'd found them and kicked his way through the mulch of paper to the kitchen. In the back of a cupboard he found a bottle of Southern

Comfort. Christ knew where it had come from; he didn't even like the stuff, but there it was. And here *he* was, a Southerner, very much in need of Comfort. It was a match made in heaven.

He took a glass from out of the cold water in the sink, wiping off the film of grease that rimed it like uneven margarita salt with a tea towel. Then he unscrewed the top, filled the smeared glass and began his descent into blissful anaesthesia.

Number 343 had steps up to a blue front door and three doorbells, two of them neatly labelled with names that weren't Holt. Jess pressed the third, anonymous one and stood back, heart jumping.

I brought your suit. No, no problem — they said you'd probably just forgotten. Yes, I work there now, so . . . yes, I'll probably see you next time you come in. Enjoy the wedding. That would be all there was to it. Thirty seconds at most. Friendly but completely casual, like she hadn't thought about him at least a hundred times a day for the last month. Like she hadn't been glad when he didn't turn up to collect the suit because it gave her a chance to go to his house, and hadn't rehearsed what she was going to say, over and over on the bus.

The suit was surprisingly heavy and difficult to carry in its slippery polythene wrapping. Her skin was damp where it was draped over her arm. She readjusted it and moistened her lips, wondering whether she'd got the right doorbell, and if she should press again. As she did so it struck her that it was

Friday evening; that the air was warm and sweet with spring and the pavements outside the pubs she'd passed had been crowded with early evening drinkers. Of course – he'd be out with friends, drinking expensive lager and deciding where to go on to eat.

Feeling stupid she turned to go down the steps again and almost collided with someone: a girl in jogging gear, her slim brown arms glistening with perspiration like an advert for something wholesome. Shit. His girlfriend?

'Can I help?'

'No. It's fine. I was just—'

'Will forgot his dry cleaning again, huh?' The girl stopped at the top of the steps, bending one leg and catching hold of her foot to stretch out her muscles. She had an Australian accent and the kind of figure Jess had only seen in magazines before.

'Er, yes. I'll just—'

But the girl had already opened the front door and walked into the hallway. 'He never answers his door,' she called over her shoulder as she unlocked the door of the ground-floor flat. 'He's down there, in the basement. If he's genuinely not in just leave it at the bottom of the stairs. It'll be safe.'

'Oh . . . OK. Thanks.' Clutching her slithery burden Jess hurried past to the stairs. The upstairs hall was wide and elegant, with fancy plasterwork like the icing on a wedding cake and polished wood banisters. The staircase that led down to the basement was narrow and dark. It ended in a space the size of a broom cupboard in which there was a single door.

She knocked, and was just looking around for somewhere to leave the suit when the door opened.

She almost didn't recognize him. His hair was dishevelled and the lower half of his face shadowed with what must have been several days' worth of growth. He was wearing a t-shirt and jeans and his feet were bare. Her first thought was that he looked ridiculously sexy. Her second, as he stood swaying slightly and squinting to bring her into focus, was that he was staggeringly drunk.

'I – I brought your suit. From the dry cleaner's.' The speech she had rehearsed on the bus was meaningless in the light of this unexpected turn of events. She began to back away, worried that she'd interrupted some kind of celebration. 'Sorry – they thought your brother's wedding might be tomorrow.'

He slumped heavily back against the wall, and then his knees buckled and he slid slowly down it until he was sitting on the floor with his head in his hands.

'Oh fuck,' he said.

37

He wasn't sure what had happened – a machete attack perhaps? All he knew was that it was OK as long as he didn't move his head. His mouth felt like it was filled with wallpaper paste.

A shard of memory drove itself into his throbbing brain: Jess Moran emptying the remains of a bottle of Southern Comfort down the sink. He gave a low moan, which ricocheted off the inside of his skull and made him clutch his head in agony. More fragments of the evening impaled his consciousness. Jess helping him to take off his t-shirt as he sat on the bed. Jess bringing him a glass of water and pulling the curtains closed. In a moment of dazzling optimism it occurred to him that he must have dreamed it, because why the hell would Jess Moran be in his flat? But then he heard the bedroom door open and a soft voice saying,

'You're awake then?'

He lay very still, his head buried beneath the pillows.

Maybe if he didn't move she'd think he was asleep. Or dead. In fact, if he lay there for long enough with the pillow over his face he might actually *be* dead. It took him a second to realize that, in spite of having a hangover that must register on the Richter scale, the thought didn't hold the same appeal it had yesterday.

'How are you feeling?'

He gathered his strength and excavated his head, then prised open one eye to look at her.

She laughed. 'I'll go and put some coffee on.'

The kitchen was small, basic and – now she'd washed up what must have been a week's worth of mugs and bowls – nice. The walls were white and there was an open shelf unit that seemed to house everything from crockery to curry spices. It was painted bright green, but it looked like it must have come from some big old house, or an antique shop or something because the paint was all chipped so you could see the blue colour underneath. She took a mug down from one of the hooks beneath it and spooned coffee into it as she waited for the kettle to boil.

Her neck ached from where she'd fallen asleep on the sofa in an odd position and her clothes felt crumpled and stale. Hastily she gulped down a glass of water, swilling the last mouthful around her teeth as a substitute for cleaning them. Then she poured water onto the coffee and carried it through to the bedroom.

Will had made an effort to sit up. He was fumbling to press

pills out of a foil packet when she went in. Paracetamol, not the ones she'd seen when she tidied up the living room last night. The antidepressants.

'So. How *are* you feeling?'

She set the mug down on the bedside table. In the semi-darkness she saw him grimace as he swallowed the pills.

'When you were a kid did you ever put salt on a slug, just to see what happened?' He gulped down water. 'That. That's what my brain feels like. I also feel pretty ashamed.'

'Don't be daft. It was your own private party – you didn't ask me to gatecrash it.'

She went over to the window and drew the curtain back a little. The new day's light was rosy and soft, but it made him wince. 'It's probably just as well you did. I'm not quite sure how it would have ended if you hadn't. But you didn't have to stay.'

'I wanted to. Just to be on the safe side.' She thought about mentioning Dodge's friend, who had gone to bed drunk like that one night and failed to wake up in the morning, but she didn't want to talk about Dodge. 'Besides, I owed you one. I'm not sure how things would have ended if you hadn't found me that time either.'

'Your illness wasn't caused by your own stupidity.' He sipped his coffee as if it was unpleasant medicine. 'Anyway – moving swiftly on, how are things for you now?'

She half-sat on the narrow windowsill. Despite everything that had happened between them it felt too intimate to sit on the bed, which took up most of the room. 'They're good, thanks. Unbelievably good compared to last time I saw you. I've got a place in a women's hostel, which isn't ideal, but I won't be there for long now I've got a job.'

'You've got a job? That's great – where?'

'At the dry cleaner's ...?' she prompted gently. 'Your suit ...?'

'Of course.' With a moan he fell back against the pillows and thrust his hands into his hair. 'Oh Christ alive, my suit. My brother's wedding ... Today is Saturday, isn't it?'

''Fraid so. I saw the invitation on the fridge. You have to be at some church in Oxfordshire by 11.30.'

'Actually, I was supposed to be at some swanky restaurant in Oxfordshire by seven last night for a pre-wedding dinner. Oh God ... I switched my phone off after my mother's sixth message.'

In spite of his predicament she was struggling not to smile, because, even hungover and harassed, Will Holt still managed to be sweet and funny. And because she was glad to have found him again. 'You're in big trouble. Why didn't you go?'

'Because I absolutely and completely couldn't be arsed. By which I mean I couldn't face it. You'd never guess it by look-ing at me, but my family is very polished. Very correct. Very clever and high-achieving and well-dressed and good looking. I'm the very odd one out.'

She thought of the pills and felt the smile dissolve. 'Your mother must be worried that you didn't show up.'

'I'm pretty sure my mother would secretly rather I stayed

away than turned up and embarrassed her with my crappy job, badly fitting suit, dreadful hair and trashed car.'

'So you're just not going to go? Won't that cause more trouble in the long run?'

'Probably.' He sighed. 'Who knows?' Putting his mug down he fell back against the pillows and she saw him wince again at the sudden movement. 'I'm tired of thinking about it, to be honest. I'm also tired of being treated like the village idiot. That might be exactly what I am but it would be nice not to be reminded of it at every verse end.'

'Don't say that.' Her voice sounded weirdly low. 'You're not.' She stared at the picture on the wall above his bed because she felt suddenly shy looking at him. It was a poster for some old French film. 'Last night . . . after you were asleep, I tidied up a bit. I hope you don't mind. I saw all the notes you'd made on Stella and Charles.'

'Ah. Yes. Notes are about all I've got, I'm afraid. I've hit a brick wall and I can't get any further.'

'But you *did* it. I . . . I thought . . .' she trailed off, realizing how bonkers it might sound if she said she thought he'd forgotten her, and how much it meant that he hadn't. 'Well, anyway, thanks. You've got loads further than I have, so it's definitely another one I owe you. I've made no progress,' she rushed on, 'but I've been in touch with Dan a lot. On the computer at the library.'

'Really? That's great.'

'Yeah, it is. He's amazing. It's easy to forget he's dying because he's so positive and, you know . . . alive, if that doesn't sound daft. I wish so much I could pull this off for him. I feel like I've let him down and wasted his time, not finding her.'

'How long has he got left?'

Will had propped himself up on one elbow, so she could see the contours of muscle beneath the smooth skin of his arm. She had a sudden flashback to last night, when he'd clumsily tried to take off his t-shirt and she'd helped him before he suffocated. She remembered the broadness of his shoulders, the hardness of his chest. And then she tried to un-remember them so she could talk to him like a normal person.

'I don't know. He doesn't talk about it much. I ask, but he always manages to skip over the question. They put him on a new drug, which seemed to work well, but then this week he thought he was getting a cold which could be really bad. He never complains, even though he must feel like crap most of the time.'

'OK, you convinced me.' With a sigh of resignation Will levered himself away from the pillows. 'If he can deal with a terminal illness without complaint, I can deal with a hang-over. Even though it is a pretty mammoth one.' He clutched his head, adjusting to gravity. 'Jesus Christ.'

She laughed. 'You don't have to get up yet. It's still early.'

'I do if I'm going to be in Oxfordshire by 11.30.'

'You're going?'

He gave a low moan and rubbed a hand across his face. 'I think you're right. If I don't it's just going to make things worse.'

'It might not be as bad as you're expecting.'

'I can absolutely guarantee it will be every bit as bad as I'm expecting.' He paused, his eyes narrowing. 'Unless . . .'

'Unless what?'

The air, which smelled of stale alcohol and warm male, seemed suddenly electrically charged. Their eyes locked over the expanse of crumpled bed.

'Are you doing anything today?'

Once the decision had been made – once he had overcome her objections about not having an invitation, a posh wedding outfit, the right accent, and once the paracetamol had started to loosen the steel jaws of his hangover – a mood of strange euphoria gripped them both.

There was no time to lose. While Jess showered, Will forced himself to tackle two fried eggs and half a packet of bacon in the hope of mopping up the remains of the Southern Comfort swilling around his system. He was thrusting the iron over his shirt front at breakneck speed when she emerged from the bathroom, swathed in his towelling robe with her dark hair slicked flat to her head. He opened his mouth to say something flippant, but found that his throat was too dry to speak.

Jess dressed in yesterday's clothes while he hastily threw on his morning suit and grabbed the first tie that came to hand.

'That suit looks like it fits well enough to me,' she said, glancing at him as they raced out of the door.

She was right, he realized. He'd felt so awful for the last couple of weeks that he'd completely lost his appetite, with the result that the trousers now did up comfortably and his waistcoat buttons weren't threatening to burst. Every cloud had a silver lining.

The roads were choked with Saturday traffic. Somewhere near Camden Town she told him to pull over outside a non-descript-looking building and was out of the car before he'd even stopped. If it wasn't for the persistent thud of his hang-over he'd have wondered if he was dreaming all this. Who would have thought it was possible to feel so physically wrecked and mentally exhilarated at the same time? She was back in about a quarter of the time he'd expected her to take, wearing a simple little flowered dress, carrying the same bag he'd taken into the hospital for her and a pair of red high-heeled shoes.

'Is this OK?' she asked breathlessly as she opened the door. 'It's the best I can do, so if you want to change your mind I won't be offended . . .'

'You look bloody gorgeous,' he said truthfully.

She got in. 'The charity shops around here are pretty amazing, but I didn't have any posh shoes. A girl down the corridor's lent me these.'

'Do they fit?' He concentrated on moving back into the stream of traffic, though it wasn't easy. Not with her slim legs splayed on the seat as she turned to sling her bag into the back and the scent of her clean hair and warm skin filling the small space.

'Not really, but I'll stuff the toes with tissue or something. Seriously, one day I'm going to go into a shop and buy some shoes that are actually my size. Anyway, you'll never guess what I've got.' Out of the corner of his eye he saw her hold up a large brown envelope. 'Certificates from the National Records Office. Dan ordered them. They must have arrived this morning.'

'Which ones?'

Jess had pulled the papers half out of the envelope and was studying them. 'Charles Thorne's death ... and Daisy Lillian Thorne, also death. I don't know how they'll help us trace Stella though.'

'They might give us a clue as to where she was living, though if it was a while ago the chances are she's moved. What do they say?'

She bent her head to study them. 'Blimey – the writing on Daisy's is impossible to read ... Charles was living in Herefordshire when he died. Cause of death was "misadventure" – whatever that means.'

'Hmm ... It's another way of saying accident.' Will was weaving between lanes, taking the fastest course through the traffic. 'Does it give any more detail?'

'Not that I can see.' She slid the certificates back into the envelope and leaned her head back on the seat. 'I'll feel sick if I read them in the car.'

He put his foot down to pass a bus and shot her a broken smile. 'That would make two of us.'

*

The mirror in the passenger sun visor was missing, so Jess had to wait to do her make-up until they left the motorway and Will didn't need the rear-view mirror so much. She was glad to have something to focus on, other than the grandeur of the houses they passed, nestling behind lush hedges and electrically operated gates, and the giant mistake she'd made in agreeing to come.

Will had got quieter since they left London and she wondered if he was regretting it too. Their manic mood had gradually deflated and they'd barely spoken for the last ten miles. As a beautiful honey-coloured church appeared around a bend in the road she glanced across at him. His face was ashen.

'This is it.'

A white vintage car decked with ribbons and flowers was parked outside. 'Oops,' Jess said as they passed it. 'Looks like we're late.'

'If it means we've missed having to talk to people outside the church I'd say it's perfect timing,' Will said through tight lips, pulling onto a grass verge beyond the gleaming rows of 4×4s, sports cars and top of the range executive saloons. As they got out, the sound of singing drifted out across the tranquil graveyard. Will leaned into the back to get his jacket while she put on the shoes Jazz had lent her. God, they were far too big. She felt like a little girl who'd raided her big sister's wardrobe as she tried to match his pace up the path to the church. But being slightly behind him allowed her to see exactly how gorgeous he looked in his wedding suit. She might have cursed the jacket with its long tails yesterday when she was lugging it off the bus, but she could certainly see its advantages now. With his newly washed hair falling over his forehead he looked like Mr Darcy. He slowed down to wait for her and held out his arm for her to lean on. Her stomach flipped.

'Here goes,' he muttered as they reached the door. His expression would have been more suited to a funeral than a wedding. The hymn was just coming to its rousing end as they slipped in, and an usher leapt up to give them an order of service.

'Sorry – I've only got one,' he whispered. 'Could you share? Are you bride or groom?'

'Groom.'

'Gosh, sorry.' The usher grinned. 'You're Si's brother, aren't you? Family's at the front.'

Will shook his head quickly as if to say he'd hate to cause a disturbance and steered Jess into a pew at the back. At some point between the door and the pew she'd stopped leaning on his arm and was holding his hand instead. She wasn't sure how it had happened, only that she liked it and that she was disappointed when he let go.

At the front the vicar was declaring that marriage was a gift of God, bringing husband and wife together in the delight and tenderness of sexual union. Bloody hell, thought Jess, get straight to the point, why don't you? She felt jittery and wired, acutely aware of Will's body, slumped in the pew beside her. She breathed in his citrusy scent, though since she'd used his shower gel and shampoo in the shower that morning she couldn't decide whether it was coming from her skin or his.

A massive stone pillar entirely obscured their view of the bride and groom and pretty much cut them off from the proceedings, which she guessed Will would consider a bonus, but was a bit of a disappointment to her. She hadn't admitted it, but she'd never been to a wedding before. Where she came from, marriage was about as outdated as bubble perms and giant shoulder pads; generally you showed your commitment as a couple by having a second, planned baby.

Looking around the church she worked out that the first rule of wedding attendance was that you wore a colour that would look insane in ordinary life; head-to-toe lilac, or coral, or yellow. Her dress was all wrong, she could see that, and she wasn't sure whether to be grateful to Will for not telling her before, or furious. But then remembered the warmth in his voice when he'd said she looked gorgeous and she realized she didn't care how wrong it was as long as he liked it.

The organ, swelling into the next hymn, drew them back in to the service. They stood up. Will sang deliberately off key, making her splutter with laughter. She elbowed him and sang louder to drown him out. It was a hymn she recognized from those distant Sundays watching *Songs of Praise* with Gran: *Dear Lord and Father of Mankind.* As she raised her voice above his their eyes met, and she watched the laughter in his give way to surprise and admiration.

'That is one *fine* pair of lungs you've got there, Ms Moran,' he murmured as the last note of the organ died away and the congregation sat down again. His gaze flickered briefly down to her chest, releasing a shower of sparks across her skin.

Afterwards they all spilled out into the bright afternoon, and people greeted each other in loud, nasal voices and tried to kiss beneath the brims of their hideous hats. Jess got her first proper look at the bride and groom as they posed for photographs under a cloud of pink cherry blossom with their gaggle of tiny bridesmaids. Blimey, she thought. I'm at the wedding of Barbie and Ken. The new Mrs Holt was delicate and slender in a narrow dress of ivory silk, her blonde hair held back from her face by a tiny tiara. Beside her Will's brother looked tall and manly and proud. He was a neater, more finished version of Will: an airbrushed, digitally remastered Disney cartoon to Will's impressionistic sketch of quick, impulsive lines. When he smiled at the camera Jess half expected to see a glittering star flash on his very white teeth.

A sharp gust of wind released a shower of pink petals onto the happy couple and the watching guests sighed with delight.

'Did you bring confetti?' Jess asked.

Will was leaning against a gravestone looking green again. 'Sadly not, but I find a handful of gravel makes a cheap and ecologically-sound alternative. Oh fuck, stand by for action. Enemy approaching at three o'clock.'

Jess looked round. A small, neat woman in a gold silk suit had broken away from the cluster of guests and was heading towards them, clutching the brim of her hat with one gloved hand. Jess had heard the term 'steely expression' but she'd never fully understood its meaning until that moment.

'Where. Have. You. Been?' She spoke to Will through a rigid jaw, without moving her glossed lips. 'Didn't you get my messages? I've been frantic. I was absolutely convinced you were dead in a ditch.'

'That explains why you look so grief-stricken. Ma, I'd like you to meet Jess Moran. Jess – my mother.'

Jess had no experience of meeting posh people, however some instinct told her that shaking hands was the correct thing to do. She held hers out.

'Pleased to meet you, Mrs Holt.'

Will's mother nodded at her curtly and ignored her hand, which remained stuck out like a shop dummy's. 'Is it too much to ask that for once you would just turn up at the right time, no surprises, no disasters?' she said, pinioning Will with eyes like sharpened icicles.

He took Jess's rejected hand, enfolding it in his and drawing her into his body. 'I've been ill. You really wouldn't have wanted me here last night, I can tell you. I wouldn't have made it today if it wasn't for Jess.'

A flicker of disgust passed over Mrs Holt's fine-boned, immaculately made-up face, though whether it was at the mention of illness or the sight of her son with his arms around a badly-dressed commoner, Jess couldn't be sure.

'Well. You're in luck, as it happens. Great Aunt Winifred cried off at the last minute.' (She actually pronounced it 'orf' Jess noticed incredulously.) 'Miss Moran can take her place on the seating plan, though I'm afraid you won't be together. You'll be next to Uncle Julius, as I recall, Miss Moran.' She gave Jess a Cruella De Vil smile. 'I do hope you enjoy the day.'

Surprisingly, she did.

Maybe it was the champagne, which she'd never so much as tasted before and now discovered was completely delicious. Maybe it was the fact that she was a stranger, her history unknown, even if her less than top-drawer background was probably obvious. Maybe it was the table she found herself on at lunch, which was the dumping ground for those guests who might spoil the pastel-flower, white-voile-bunting aesthetic of the wedding. 'Crocks corner,' Uncle Julius cheerfully declared it, since everyone apart from Jess was over seventy. As the only 'youngster' they all made a huge fuss of her and, thanks to her visits to the lunch club and the years she'd spent with Gran, she felt completely at ease amongst them. Uncle Julius's laugh rang loudly and frequently beneath the creamy canvas, until it became quite obvious that there was more fun being had on their table than any other.

But mostly it was Will. He was seated two tables away, next to a stunning girl in a lime green dress that showed off her expensive tan and blonde hair to perfection. She had one of those haughty, well-bred faces that looked permanently miserable, and although she talked a lot, she never got as far as breaking into a smile. Somehow Will managed to maintain a pretence of courteous attention while gazing at Jess across the space that divided them. At one point, while Lime Green girl was pushing her food around with her fork and talking he also mimed putting a gun to his head and pulling the trigger. Jess felt a great balloon of happiness rising inside her and took a swig of champagne to swallow it down again.

The only bad moment came just after lunch, before the speeches began. Jess's table was right by the door, on the path to the toilets, and Will had come over to talk to her when a tall man with silvery hair approached. 'Oh God, my father,' Will said with a grimace. 'I suppose I'd better introduce you.'

Fergus Holt shook her hand with elaborate courtesy, but Jess could feel his eyes sweeping over her like searchlights, exposing every cheap stitch and working-class atom of her. 'How nice to meet you, Jess. And what do you do for a living?'

She blinked, taken by surprise. 'I work in a dry cleaner's,' she said, and felt a beat of profound relief that she didn't have to say 'nothing'. Fergus Holt, however, did not seem impressed. His eyebrows shot up and the slick smile faltered, as if he wasn't sure if she was joking or not.

'A dry cleaner's? How . . . *useful.*'

He produced the word with a flourish, as if congratulating himself on managing to combine accuracy with disparagement. But Jess was temporarily distracted by the growing realization that he looked familiar. 'Actually, perhaps you know it,' she said, trying to work out where she'd seen him before. 'Wahim Clean, in Church End? I've only been there a week, but I'm sure I recognize you from somewhere . . .'

Fergus Holt's face hardened like concrete, his mouth

setting into a small, frigid smile. 'BBC Two, Wednesday evenings at nine o'clock. Now, if you'll excuse me, there are people I must speak to—'

As soon as he was out of earshot Jess turned to Will in horror. 'Oh God – he's some kind of TV celebrity? You should have told me! I've completely put my foot in it now. I knew I should never have come!'

Will was struggling to suppress his laughter, but his eyes were warm and deep and serious. 'I'm bloody glad you did.'

In the lapse between the afternoon reception and the evening one the guests drifted through the opulent reception rooms of the Holts' spectacular mansion and Will led Jess up the back stairs (back stairs!) to his bedroom. It was an oasis of clutter in the personality-desert of the rest of the house. She lay on his bed and tried to look at the photographs that crowded the walls, but they kept going round and round.

'Far be it for me to judge, but are you the tiniest bit tipsy, Ms Moran?' he said, smiling down on her.

There was an oar attached to the wall above his head that seemed to be rowing all by itself. 'I think I might be. Just the tiniest bit,' she said happily, wriggling over to make space on the bed. 'I'm also dead tired. I don't suppose you fancy a lie down, Mr Holt?'

He laughed, to disguise the fact that he'd just been impaled on a white-hot spear of lust. Her cheeks were flushed with the champagne and her lips were rosy and plump. Suddenly his suit trousers were too tight again.

'Better not, or I wouldn't wake up until ten o'clock tomorrow and my mother would pulverize me. You have a rest. I'll go down to the car and get the bags.'

He escaped with relief, his heart throbbing. Amongst other organs. Talk about emotional roller-coaster. This time yesterday he'd been in a trough of despair and now he was hurtling towards the stars with such speed he felt breathless. And terrified. What if he'd got it wrong? What if he was misreading the signs and what he thought was attraction was just her being friendly? But surely there was no mistaking chemistry like that? Every time they'd looked at each other over that interminable lunch the marquee had practically gone up in flames.

That was *lust,* he yelled silently at himself. Miraculous though it might seem, it appeared she actually found him attractive, but that didn't mean anything beyond a quick shag.

Outside it was raining, Will noticed with surprise. Dirty clouds had crowded into the blue sky and a stiff wind was making the marquee strain at its guy ropes like a hot air balloon. Unlocking the car he slid into the driver's seat and dropped his head into his hands. Of course, the truth was that he wanted more than casual sex. She was perfect: funny, beautiful and brave – brave enough to stand up to his father, even, who Will had never seen flounder like that – and he was in big danger of falling pathetically in love with her.

That was why he was terrified. The upwards swoop was exhilarating, but he wasn't sure that he could survive another downwards plunge right now. He had to be careful.

Gathering himself together, he got out of the car and collected the bags. Carrying them into the house through the back door he stood aside to let a procession of waiting staff pass with laden trays of smeared glasses, and heard the sound of tense voices coming from the boot room. He recognized Simon's, because when he was angry he spoke with the same withering impatience as their father. The other voice was a woman's; low and clearly tearful. He couldn't imagine Marina doing anything as messy as crying. Intrigued, he went to the door and pushed it open.

The happy couple were standing amid the jumble of coats and boots and shooting sticks, looking distinctly unhappy, while Wellington the Labrador cowered in his basket in the corner. He hated arguments, and parties. Marina's bridal make-up was in ruins, though she hastily tried to swipe away the rivers of black mascara streaming down her cheeks when Will appeared.

'Sorry, didn't mean to intrude. Don't suppose there's anything I can do to help?'

Simon's lip curled. 'I doubt it, unless you can stop the rain. Or bring Billie Holiday back to life.'

'Oh fucking shut up, Simon,' Marina hissed, with unbridal venom. 'The whole day is ruined and all you can do is make fucking sarcastic comments.'

'It's not ruined.' Simon sounded so exasperated Will found himself in the unprecedented position of almost feeling sorry for him. 'It's *April* – we knew there was a chance it might rain, but the singer getting stranded in Dublin is just bad luck.

There's no way we could have seen that coming, and there's not much we can do about it now. No one's going to mind dancing to a disco instead of a live band.'

'*I mind*. It's supposed to be a vintage-themed wedding. For fuck's sake, Simon, a year's worth of planning, *six months* of dancing lessons and we end up doing our first dance to a *disco* in the *pouring rain*—?'

Will was in the process of making a surreptitious exit, but the bit about the singer stopped him.

'Tell me it's none of my business if you like, but am I right in thinking you have a band but no singer? Because if that's the case I might just be able to help.'

38

As the light faded outside the marquee was transformed.

Little candles flickered in glasses on the tables and strings of fairy lights made the canvas glow warmly, even if the actual temperature was arctic. Standing on the stage above the square dance floor Jess shivered with nerves and the icy wind that found its way through the gaps in the sides.

But as soon as the band started up the nerves vanished, as they always did. The song Simon and Marina had chosen for their first dance was *The Way You Look Tonight*. It wasn't one she knew very well, but when she'd run through the song list with the band in Mrs Holt's Wembley-sized bedroom earlier they'd had time for a little rehearsal. Most of the songs were familiar, from Gran's collection of Sinatra and Elvis and Rod Stewart, and thanks to her Lunch Club ladies she was used to singing them. She sent out a silent prayer of gratitude to Vera, for keeping her voice from rusting away with lack of use in the past few weeks.

Simon and Marina circled the floor slowly, their movements perfectly synchronized. He held her expertly, his hand looking very big and tanned in the centre of her narrow back and probably the people standing around the dance floor and seated at the tables wouldn't notice the coldness in his eyes as he looked at her, or hear the instructions she muttered at him through a rigid jaw.

Above everyone's heads Jess's eyes sought Will. He was sitting at a table right at the back of the marquee, uninterested in the spectacle of the bride and groom and the charade of their first dance. His gaze was fixed on her, his face, in the light of the candle in front of him, full of something that looked like wonder.

The words were beautiful. She forgot the bride and groom and she sang them purely for him.

She was a goddess.

Song after song, the dance floor was full, the applause at the end surprisingly unrestrained from people whose usual definition of enthusiasm was cracking half a smile. Will was perfectly ready to accept that he was biased, but she seemed to bring something magical to the music. Warmth as well as technical skill. A sweetness of tone in addition to power. Hell, he knew nothing about music, but even his parents were enjoying it – dancing together with misty smiles on their faces, applauding heartily at the end of every song – and that had to be saying something.

He drained half his glass of champagne without tasting it.

The only downside to her being up on the stage singing was that it meant he couldn't dance with her. He wasn't the best of dancers, but music like this meant he could have held her and breathed in her scent. He finished the rest of the champagne and acknowledged that the time had passed for being careful. It was too late. He'd fallen in love with her. Ages ago probably, as she lay on the bed in the hospital and he'd glimpsed the fragile bones of her spine like pearls beneath her skin and known that he'd do anything to protect her.

The band struck up a new song – the last one of the evening, she announced to a chorus of muted disappointment. She bent to the microphone and for a moment the dancers stilled and the evening hung suspended as she opened her mouth to sing the first note.

'I–I–I'm—' She sought him out with her eyes. Staring straight at him from beneath her lashes, her delicious mouth curved into a wicked invitation of a smile. '*Mad . . . about the boy . . .*'

Oh Christ.

Thank God he hadn't taken those stupid pills.

Darkness had fallen while she'd been singing, creating an enclosed world beneath the softly lit dome of the marquee. As everyone drifted away from the dance floor and the babble of conversation rose again, Jess high-fived the pianist and accepted a brief, sweaty hug from the guy – Paul – on trumpet.

'Nice work, kid,' he said, reaching into the breast pocket of his dinner jacket and holding out an envelope. 'That's your cut. You've earned every penny.'

She shook her head. 'I couldn't, honestly. I was here anyway and . . . well, I enjoyed it. Thanks for having me.'

Paul looked doubtful. 'Well, if you're sure? But if you fancy a regular job we might just have one going – Suzy's unreliability is getting to be an issue. We'd have you like a shot. Let us know.'

'I might just do that . . .'

She turned round. Will was standing on the empty dance floor in front of the stage. He had his hands in his pockets and a look she couldn't read on his face. He shook his head, as if lost for words, and then took a step forward and held out his hands.

She took them and jumped down from the stage, stumbling slightly in her too big shoes. He caught her, steadied her, opened his mouth to speak, but whatever he had intended to say was lost as somehow their lips came together.

Oh God, the strength of him. Her legs, already shaky, virtually gave way beneath her but she gripped his shoulders, anchoring herself against him as the world dissolved away.

In the corner the DJ who would take the party into the small hours was setting up, and a sudden burst of music made them jump apart. 'I was going to save this one until the end of the night,' he murmured into the microphone, over the opening bars of the cheesiest slow dance song in the history of disco, 'but if you guys are ready for it now . . .'

They laughed, but it didn't extinguish the incandescent lust that glowed between them. His eyes were dark, the want in them impossible to misinterpret. He took her hand, slowly raising it to his lips and pressing a kiss into the centre of her palm.

'Shall we go?'

'Yes.'

He pulled her off the dance floor. She stopped at the edge of the marquee to take off the red shoes, and then they were running across the grass, holding hands and laughing breathlessly, a little dazed by the urgency of their need. As the damp earth soaked her tights she remembered how she'd run away from Dodge, in fear and desperation, and she wanted to shout back over her shoulder at the girl she had been that she was doing the right thing. That she wasn't just running away, she was running towards something. A better future.

A better man.

Hand in hand, they slipped through the legions of staff in the clattering, brightly lit kitchen and up the narrow staircase to his attic room. Kicking the door shut he reached for her, taking her face between his hands as he kissed her again.

It was quiet up here. The DJ started up in the marquee below, but the music was muted. Moonlight silvered the walls and threw precisely defined shadows across the bed and the floor. The molten excitement pulsing through her veins cooled a little, and she felt a shiver of doubt as old memories resurfaced. Memories of Dodge. Pain. Humiliation.

As if sensing her hesitation he pulled away.

'You. Are. *Incredible*,' he whispered. 'And there is nothing I want more than to take you to bed right now and make love to you for about the next twelve hours.' He kissed her lips, very lightly. 'But if it's too soon, or if it's not what you want, that's OK. To be perfectly honest, I'm not sure I can manage twelve hours anyway.'

His face was grave in the bluish light, his eyes dark and liquid. Looking into them was like stepping, naked, into a warm summer downpour; delicious, exciting, good. Her misgivings melted and she reached up to touch his lips.

'It is what I want,' she breathed. And then, moving away from him she peeled off her dress and walked across the moon-splashed floor to the bed.

The disco finished. Voices drifted up, shouting goodbyes. Car doors banged and engines started. And then, gradually, the quiet crept back in.

It was the familiar quiet of his childhood years, punctuated occasionally by the secretive call of an owl from the wood behind the house, but tonight Will listened to it with an unfamiliar feeling expanding in his chest.

Total contentment.

Jess lay curled around him, one leg thrown over his, her head on his arm and her hand resting on his chest. He couldn't see her face, but the soft, slow sigh of her breathing told him that she was deeply asleep.

She'd slipped into sleep quickly, tears still shimmering on her eyelashes, as if the intensity of her orgasm had exhausted her as much as it had taken her by surprise. Will couldn't stop himself from smiling like a fool as he went over it again. Not trusting himself to stay the distance he'd crushed down his own rampaging desire and focused on her first, stroking and kissing and licking until she was rigid and quivering. As she came she'd cried out with such rawness that for a second he thought he'd hurt her, but as he tried to move his hand away she'd seized it and pulled it back, then levered herself up and on top of him. He'd barely had time to tear the condom (ribbed, strawberry flavoured, and dating from the time when he'd thought such things the height of sexual sophistication) from its packet and roll it onto his throbbing erection before he was inside her. He'd only managed to last four earth-shattering thrusts.

Afterwards, when his heartbeat had almost returned to normal and she'd stopped trembling in his arms, she'd told him that she finally understood what all the fuss was about. 'I never got it before. I never . . . believed it could be like that.' Just thinking about it made him want to leap out of bed and do a naked victory dance, and stick two fingers up at Milla whose withering boredom in bed had been as much to blame as the pills for his inability to perform. It felt like the shadowy beast that had stalked him for five long years had finally been slain.

Her shoulder gleamed like pearl in the moonlight. He circled his finger around it, his stomach clenching with helpless love. He remembered the song she'd sung earlier – *The Way You Look Tonight* – and hummed it drowsily into the warm silk of her hair. She stirred, sighed, and sank back against him, her knee a little higher on his thigh. Too high for comfort, or relaxation. Bugger. He was never going to be able to sleep now.

The bags he'd brought up from the car were on the floor beside his desk, and from where he lay he could see the brown envelope sticking out of the top of hers. Very gently he disentangled himself and went over to get the certificates and took them back to bed. Propping himself right on the edge so he didn't disturb her, he tilted the paper up to catch the moonlight and began to read.

'Breakfast.'

Jess closed her eyes as he came in, to make it look like she'd still been asleep. Opening them a fraction she watched through her eyelashes as he set a tray down on the desk, acclimatizing herself gradually to how gorgeous he was so she didn't blush like a teenager when she looked at him properly. While he'd been downstairs she'd been looking at the photographs that lined the walls, mostly showing a younger, skinnier Will in a variety of settings – at parties, on white-sanded beaches, playing rugby – in all of them looking handsome and privileged and glamorous, and completely out of her league.

'There's coffee, and croissants. They're not warm, I'm afraid, but I wanted to escape as quickly as possible. Downstairs they're doing the whole silver cutlery and linen napkins in the dining room thing, but I thought I'd spare you that.'

She sat up, clutching the duvet awkwardly to her chest and

wondering whether he was embarrassed of her. One of the photographs showed him wearing a black suit and bow tie, with his arm around an exquisite blonde girl in a strapless dress. Had he taken her down to have breakfast with his family?

'If you want to go down I don't mind,' she muttered, trying to arrange the pillows against her back without letting go of the duvet. 'I'll stay here.'

'I'd rather have breakfast in the tiger enclosure at London zoo,' he said, opening a drawer and pulling out a t-shirt. 'Here – do you want to put this on?'

It was pale pink, with crossed oars and the words 'Leander Rowing Club' on the front. He turned away tactfully as she slipped it over her head. After the closeness they'd shared just a few hours ago – because of it, perhaps – it felt stilted and awkward. Last night she'd been utterly helpless with need; not just physically naked but emotionally too. As his hands and mouth had worked their magic she remembered crying out, and knew that the cry had come from the depths of her soul. Never before had she felt anything like what he'd made her feel, and it had changed her. In its aftermath she felt shaky and fragile, like she'd been broken apart and remade. Like the world had split open and she'd caught a glimpse of heaven.

He sat on the bed and passed her a mug of coffee. She took it without meeting his eye.

'Thanks.'

'You're very welcome. I'm afraid I have a confession to make.'

She sipped, determined not to let her emotions show on her face. So this was it; the bit when he told her it had been great but he didn't want a relationship. He was so nice, he was bound to add that they could still be friends, as if he hadn't noticed that she was the only person he knew who'd been to a comprehensive school. As if there was a possibility of bumping into her in a posh wine bar sometime.

'Last night I couldn't sleep. I have no idea why – I mean, it's not like I'm not used to having a fantastically beautiful and sexy girl in my bed or anything – and so I had a look at those certificates you brought. I know I should have waited and gone through them with you; I'm really sorry. Hey – I'm trying to apologize here. What's so funny?'

'Nothing.' Jess pressed her lips together, swallowing back the laughter, but it rose inside her anyway. She could feel it warming her cheeks, glowing in her eyes. 'There's absolutely nothing funny about doing something so . . . terrible. Did you find anything interesting?'

'Possibly. Stella's daughter died in a hospital called Leyton Manor.'

'That's not unusual is it? I mean, lots of people must die in hospitals – that's where you'd be if you were seriously ill.'

'Ah, but this isn't that kind of hospital.' He got up and went over to the desk, switching on the computer. 'I looked it up. It's on the outskirts of London, about fifty miles from here. It changed its name to Leyton Manor sometime in the 1930s, but it was built in the Victorian age and originally called The Imbeciles Asylum.'

'So it was like a psychiatric hospital or something?'

'Not quite. Listen to this . . .' He clicked on the screen and brought up a page of text. As he began to read, the expression on his face changed. The laughter of a moment ago evaporated and he looked troubled. Pained, almost. '"*The hospital was designed to accommodate one thousand, two hundred and fifty inmates in ten blocks, with separate laundries and workshops, a model farm and a kitchen garden. During the First World War its patients included those who had been removed from the front line suffering from 'battle fatigue' or shell shock. In the Second World War parts of the hospital were given over to civilian air-raid casualties and the treatment of venereal disease, though the majority of its patients were still those termed 'mentally defective' or 'ineducable'. Many of these were children, given into the care of the hospital by families who were unable or unwilling to support them at a time when both mental illness and learning disability carried huge stigma.*"'*

'I don't understand.' Jess put her cup down, trying to assimilate this new information into her picture of Stella. 'It sounds . . . horrible.'

'Oh yes, you can bet it would have been.' There was an edge to Will's voice that she hadn't heard before. 'This article doesn't go into detail, but it goes on to say that "*. . . conditions in the hospital were exposed by a campaign group made up of patients' families in the 1970s and '80s, and this led to gradual improvements being made. In 1990 it was finally closed, and the old, barrack-like Victorian blocks demolished to make way for small, modern units providing 'family' houses*". That would have been too late for Daisy Thorne, though,' he finished bitterly.

'But why . . . ?' Jess shook her head in confusion. 'Stella gave up . . . *everything* for Daisy. It makes no sense – why would she abandon her in a place like that?'

Will sighed heavily and slumped into the chair in front of the desk. His lips were oddly pale, his eyes black and unreadable. 'It says it right there. It was a time when mental illness and learning disability carried huge stigma – even more so than they do now.' He gave a scornful laugh. 'Which believe me, is saying something.'

Her heart gave an almighty jolt, like it was trying to break out of her chest, as she began to understand. 'Will . . . ?'

'Sorry.' He dropped his head into his hands for a second, then raked his fingers through his hair. 'I should've told you, but it's not the kind of thing you can easily slip into conversation. Not unless you actually want to make someone run away from you screaming, in which case announcing that you're a former inmate of Readesmere Hospital for Complete Nut-Jobs is a rather neat way of doing it. Six months I was there, much to the horror and embarrassment of my parents. There is just no socially acceptable way of saying in the annual festive round-robin that your son has entirely lost the plot and is in a secure unit, medicated into oblivion and—'

He didn't get any further. She got out of bed and went to him, taking his face between her hands and stopping the flow of words with her mouth. Her heart felt swollen with compassion, too big for her chest. She kissed him gently, emphatically, lovingly, again and again, until she felt the tension leave his body and his arms go around her.

'I wouldn't have run away. I won't,' she said fiercely. Her forehead was pressed against his and she looked into the dark, troubled pools of his eyes. 'Come back to bed and tell me. Tell me everything.'

Neither of them spoke much as they drove home.

Earlier, the words had come spilling out of him as he'd told her how the shiny mirror of his life had cracked, then shattered into tiny, lethal fragments. About the laborious process of putting the pieces back together again. She had listened, holding him and stroking his hair until the well of words had run dry again. And then she'd shown him, with shivering tenderness, that what he'd just told her made no difference to how she felt about him, and that he was no longer alone.

When they finally surfaced and went to say goodbye to his parents he'd been able to do it without the symphony of negative emotions that was the usual signature tune to the end of his visits. But, as the Spitfire swallowed up the miles and London got closer he found himself trying to think of ways to make the journey last. There was so much he wanted to say to her, like 'thank you for turning my potential worst nightmare into the best twenty-four hours of my life', and 'when can I see you again?', but he couldn't think of how to say any of them without sounding needy. Actually, he couldn't really think of anything at all, because her hand was warm on his thigh.

'I still don't get it.' Her face was turned away from him, her voice drowsy as she looked out at the featureless grass bank of the motorway. 'Dan said Stella stayed with Charles because of the baby. She wouldn't leave her, and yet, that's exactly what she ended up doing. I can imagine that there was a stigma, but when you love someone that means nothing. *Nothing*. It doesn't make sense.'

She turned towards him then, and their eyes met briefly before he had to tear his away and look back at the road. A motorway sign loomed suddenly in front of them, like – well, a sign. He flicked his indicator.

'Where are we going?'

'To Leyton Manor. I think we should have a look at the place where Daisy Thorne lived and died, don't you?'

The hospital was on the outskirts of the town, signposted from the main road. All that remained of the original building was an imposing Victorian block, three storeys tall, with a bell tower in the centre which looked somehow sinister, even on a bright spring day with the daffodils in bloom and cherry trees like sticks of candyfloss in the landscaped gardens around it.

Will left the Spitfire in a little car park beneath a huge oak tree that must have stood there since a time when there was nothing but fields around it. They walked around the Victorian building, which had been renamed The Manor and converted into offices for a healthcare trust. Behind it were several single-storey buildings, which Will guessed was the new accommodation for former residents mentioned on the website. They looked neat and homely enough, if not exactly beautiful. Bird tables stood in their front gardens, and brightly coloured windmills spiralled in the brisk breeze. It wasn't yet warm enough for people to be outside on a Sunday afternoon, but you could see that they would be, when the summer came.

At the front of the old hospital building a more formal garden had been laid out in a large rectangle. It was slightly sunken, and edged with thick, square hedges that provided shelter from the wind. Gravel paths ran between flowerbeds in which tulips swayed and staggered.

They came to a bench, beneath an arbour that in a few months would be smothered with roses, and sat down. The old hospital was straight ahead of them, a black shape against the clean spring sky.

'It still looks bleak,' Jess said, with a shudder. She was wearing a shirt of his, a checked one from his wardrobe at home, and she looked so clean and wholesome and beautiful that he felt his heart expand in his chest. 'Can buildings absorb feelings, do you think? Like the house on Greenfields Lane. Even though it's damp and neglected and full of Nancy's stuff, it still feels happy somehow. And safe—' She stopped as something behind him caught her attention. 'Hello there. Are we sitting in your seat by any chance?'

Will turned to follow her gaze. A stout little figure had appeared from behind the hedge and was standing a small distance from them on the path, staring at them with bright, curious eyes. Her short grey hair put her at about fifty, he guessed, though there was something distinctly childlike about her open expression and the way she was shyly shifting from foot to foot.

She shook her head abruptly, darting out her tongue and running it over her lips. 'Not my seat. Daisy's.'

The words were spoken quickly and indistinctly, so that for a moment Will wasn't sure he'd heard properly. But he felt the little tremor that passed through Jess's body. She sat up, leaning forward.

'Who's Daisy? Is she your friend?'

Encouraged by the warmth in Jess's voice the woman came closer, though she was still too shy to look directly at them. 'She was my friend, a long time ago. She died.'

'I'm really sorry to hear that.'

Staring down at the path, the woman nodded solemnly. 'Mrs Daniels put the seat there, so we wouldn't forget her. It's got her name on it.'

Will and Jess turned to look. Neither of them had noticed the little plaque on the back of the bench that said: *In memory of Daisy Thorne, who loved flowers.*

'Mrs Daniels?' Will asked.

'Yes. She was Daisy's mum, but she's my friend now. She comes to see me on Monday afternoons. In the winter we go out to a café and have cake, but in the summer we sit here and have ice cream.'

Realization exploded inside Will's head, dazzling him. Daniels. *Of course.* It was perfectly legal to call yourself what you liked without any kind of official paperwork being done. No wonder Stella Thorne hadn't shown up in any of the usual places. It was all he could do not to let out a shout of triumph and astonishment, and to hold back the flood of questions, but beside him Jess's voice was perfectly calm, her manner completely relaxed as she moved along to make room on the bench. 'Which do you like best?'

'Ice cream.'

'Me too – especially if it has a flake in it. I'm Jess, by the way, and this is Will. What's your name?'

'Georgina.'

'It's very nice to meet you, Georgina. Do you want to sit down?'

The woman came forward, an expression of hesitant pleasure on her face. She sat in the space Jess had made between them, and smoothed her skirt over her knees, studying the buttons down its front intently.

'I don't suppose,' Jess asked gently, 'you'd happen to know if Mrs Daniels's first name is Stella?'

Georgina looked up, bright-eyed. 'Yes, Stella. Do you know her?'

Over her head Jess's eyes met Will's, and she smiled.

'Not exactly. But I have a friend in America who knew her very well once, and he's been trying to find her for a long, long time.' She turned her sun-filled smile to the woman sitting between them. 'I'm so glad that we met you, Georgina. Will you help us?'

39

As Jess rushed to get ready for work on Monday morning Jazz knocked on her door and handed her a letter.

'Postman's just been. Looks official. Maybe you're being called to give evidence in the trial or somefink . . .'

When she'd got back late yesterday afternoon Jess had returned the red shoes and ended up drinking coffee in Jazz's room until after dark. They'd sketched in for each other the outlines of their lives, the events that had brought them to the hostel. She'd told her about Dodge, and about the story she'd read in the newspaper. She looked down at the envelope. *Furnivall Ramsay Pemberton Solicitors* was stamped on the front, in red ink. With trembling hands she tore it open and scanned the contents of the letter quickly, while Jazz looked on.

'Well?'

'It's not about Dodge. It's about a house.'

The words pulsed meaninglessly before her eyes, and she started again from the beginning to try to make sense of them. There was a line at the top of the letter that was printed in bold. **Transfer of ownership of 4 Greenfields Lane, Church End** it said.

'Whose house?' Jazz demanded impatiently.

Jess finished reading, then looked up at her in disbelief. 'Mine.'

At lunchtime she ran to the library. There was someone on her favourite computer by the window, so she went to the one at the opposite end of the row.

Hi Dan

I can't believe it – there's so much to say I don't know where to start! First of all, a letter came this morning from a firm of solicitors, asking me to go to their offices to sign some papers. It's something about transferring the house in Greenfields Lane from your name into mine. Is it a scam? My Gran always used to say that if something seemed too good to be true then it most likely was. The name of the firm was Furnivall Ramsay Pemberton. I'm going to look them up in a minute to find out if they're even real and not just a name made up by some creepy geek in a bedsit to take advantage of daft people like me.

Anyway, even more importantly – are you actually ready for this? – I THINK WE MAY HAVE FOUND STELLA. I really don't want to get your hopes up, and I wouldn't say anything unless I was pretty sure, but we've definitely found out that she's alive and well, and a regular visitor to a residential care

centre for people with learning difficulties, just outside
London. Stella's daughter had been a patient there, years
ago – it appeared on the death certificate that you ordered.
When we went to check it out we met a friend of hers,
someone she visits every week. It seems that Stella changed
her surname after she cut her ties with her husband, which
was why she's been so hard to trace. Will left his mobile
number with this friend, and a message to call.

I don't think I told you about Will, did I?

She'd been typing quickly (as quickly as she could with two
fingers and the necessary time taken up with correcting the
multiple mistakes she made in every sentence) but she broke
off there, feeling her heart lurch a little and her cheeks heat
up. What could she say about Will that was suitable for a
ninety-year-old to read, even one as wise and open-minded as
Dan Rosinski?

*I don't know him that well, but I slept with him on Saturday
night and it was the most incredible experience of my whole life? I'm
nuts about him. I can't think about anything else, and I'm worried
sick that he'll go off me now. Because he's totally out of my league,
in just about every way you could think of . . .*

She stopped herself before her thoughts spiralled out of
control again, as they had during the sleepless night. You
could only beat yourself up so much about something you
couldn't actually regret because it was so good. She forced her
fingers back to the keyboard.

Well, I don't really know where to start with that either, so I'll
just say that he's decent and kind and honourable, and
definitely someone you'd want to have on your side for —
well, for anything, really. He was the one who found me when
I was ill, and he visited me in hospital. He discovered your
letters back at the house and brought them in to me, so I told
him about your search for Stella. It's completely thanks to
him that we've got this far.

Anyway, all we have to do now is wait and hope she calls.
She will, I just feel it. I'll let you know as soon as it happens.

Take care

Jess xx

P S. – I didn't tell you what she changed her name to, did I?
It's Daniels. Stella Daniels. I wonder how she came up with
that?!

It was only as she pressed 'send' that she felt a prickle of
unease. Quickly she clicked back to her inbox. No new messages. She checked Sent Items, to make sure her last email had
gone. It had, on Friday lunchtime.

In an instant her elation evaporated and her blood ran cold.
Three days, and he hadn't sent a reply. And she'd been so
wrapped up in Will and the wedding and her own news that
she hadn't even noticed.

'Please, no,' she murmured aloud, then pressed her hand to
her mouth and prayed silently instead, to whoever might be
listening. *Please don't let us have found Stella too late.*

*

501

The offices of Furnivall Ramsay Pemberton were in a building that looked old-fashioned from the front. Jess climbed the stone steps to a front door that looked exactly like the Prime Minister's, but which opened into a space that was all bleached wood and glass walls.

The girl on the front desk glanced up from her screen as Jess approached. A look of distaste settled on her pretty, bland face at the sight of her orange nylon 'Wahim Clean' tabard.

'Can I help you?'

Jess pulled the letter from her jacket pocket and put it on the desk, where it looked dirty and crumpled.

'This came this morning. It says I should come in as soon as convenient.'

The girl picked up the letter as if it might be contaminated with the plague, or something that might damage her immaculate manicure. She looked at it sceptically.

'It says to *make an appointment* as soon as convenient. Let me see when I can fit you in . . .' She turned her attention back to her screen and began tapping her white-tipped fingers on her keyboard. 'How about next Tuesday at 10 a.m.?'

'Tomorrow?' In contrast to the receptionist's steely composure Jess's voice sounded shrill and hysterical. She'd hoped to get to the bottom of it today. Seeing the state in which she'd returned from lunch Mr Wahim had been kind enough to let her go an hour early today, but she couldn't ask for more time off tomorrow. And besides, she needed to *know*.

'No, not tomorrow,' Little Miss Superior said. '*Next* Tuesday. It's a cancellation; Mr Ramsay is our most senior partner, and he's very busy. Would you like me to book the appointment for you or not?'

'Next week? But I need to see someone before then! I don't care if it's the senior partner or the cleaner, I just want to know about the house and ... and about Dan. I haven't heard from him, and he's ill and I've got no way of getting in touch with him apart from by email, and he's not answering . . .'

The tears took her by surprise. One minute she was angry, frustrated by Miss Superior's apparent determination to be as unhelpful as possible, and the next moment her throat had closed up and she felt her face crumple. Miss Superior regarded her coldly.

'I'm very sorry, Miss —' there was a tiny hesitation while she read her name from the letter, 'Moran, but it's completely impossible to arrange an appointment with a senior partner at such short notice.'

As she spoke a door at the top of a short flight of pale wooden stairs opened, and a very elderly lady in a glossy fur coat emerged, followed by a dark-suited, balding man with narrow, rimless glasses. He took the lady's arm to help her down the stairs, amid much polite, posh-people's banter about how she'd outlive the lot of them, then addressed the superior secretary.

'Natalia, please arrange a taxi for Mrs Ambrus.'

The frosty mask melted into a simper. 'Of course, Mr Ramsay.'

Ramsay? Jess spun round, her mouth opening before she

could think. 'Mr Ramsay! You're the person I need to see about Dan's house—'

The girl behind the desk leapt to her feet. 'Miss Moran, I've explained that you have to make an appointment! I do apologize, Mr Ramsay. I've tried to tell her—'

But the man in the dark suit wasn't looking at her. His pale gaze was directed at Jess. 'And which house would this be, young lady?'

'4 Greenfields Lane. Dan Rosinski's house. I got a letter —' she snatched it from the desk and held it up, 'and I don't know what it means, and I'm worried because he's not answering my emails.'

'Ah, you're Mr Rosinski's friend.' Instantly his manner became solicitous. 'Mr Rosinski is a very special client. Why don't you come into my office? Natalia here will make us some tea just as soon as she's arranged Mrs Ambrus's taxi.'

He shot the girl behind the desk a chilling glance, and Jess had the satisfaction of seeing a tide of angry pink wash into her cheeks before she was ushered up the steps into Mr Ramsay's office.

'I'm afraid it's not terribly good news.'

Mr Ramsay had just put the phone down following his second call to America. Jess, sitting opposite him and drinking the tea that a frosty Natalia had brought, had pretty much worked that out from listening to his carefully veiled comments and watching his grave expression. Her heart was beating painfully, fear thickening her blood.

'What's happened?'

'Mr Rosinski has been admitted to hospital. Up until now he'd been being cared for at home, but it seems his condition has taken a turn for the worse and he was taken into intensive care on Friday.' Mr Ramsay's pale eyes were full of awful compassion as he looked at her over his glasses. 'He's not really conscious, from what I can make out from Mr Goldberg, his American lawyer. I'm afraid to say that they don't really expect him to recover.'

The tears had started again, only this time they were silent and defeated. They slid down Jess's cheeks and dripped off her chin, sinking into the orange nylon of her overall. Mr Ramsay pushed a box of expensive tissues, thick as restaurant napkins, across the glass desk towards her.

'But he *can't* die. Not now. We've just found her.'

'Mr Rosinski has been ill for some time: he knew he wasn't going to get better. And he's old, don't forget; over ninety. He's been exceptionally thorough in putting his affairs in order. The house in Greenfields Lane was really the final piece in the jigsaw, and Mr Goldberg has told me how pleased Mr Rosinski was to be able to fit it into place after all these years, with your help. He spoke very highly of you, Miss Moran. That's why he wanted to give the house to you, along with a sum of money for its renovation. It's a very . . . *generous* gift, as I'm sure you know. A property like that will raise a considerable sum, should you decide to sell it. He was most keen to stress that it should be yours to do with whatever you choose.'

He was being kind, she understood that, and yet with every gently spoken word she felt the pressure inside her head mount. She scrubbed fresh tears away with the tissue. 'Please don't talk about him as if he's already dead,' she said through clenched teeth. 'It's not the end yet. It can't be.'

A shadow of impatience fell across Mr Ramsay's compassionate expression for a second. 'Miss Moran, tragic though it may be, we have to know when to let go of those we love. Mr Rosinski is a very old, very sick man. It's time to—'

'No!' She got to her feet, splashing tea from her cup onto the glossy bleached wood floor. 'It's not time yet! Look – please – ring them back and tell them we've found Stella. Even if he's unconscious, tell them to make sure he knows. We've found Stella Thorne. *Please.*'

For a moment she thought he was going to argue, but after a second's hesitation and some visible effort he produced a rather taut smile. 'Very well, Miss Moran.' He picked up the phone. 'Natalia, Mr Goldberg's office ... *again*, if you will.'

She walked to Will's house, through suburban streets that smelled of freshly cut grass. In the gardens she passed, cherry trees bore their pale blossom like fragrant clouds, and the evening was blue and luminous with the promise of summer. A summer that Dan wouldn't see.

Her head was too full, so that twice she lost her way and had to retrace her steps. It was only when she finally found herself within sight of Will's car parked on the road outside his flat that she realized what a sight she must look, in her orange uniform with her make-up all cried off and her nose red. It wasn't as if he hadn't seen her in a worse state, but that was *before* ... She felt suddenly self-conscious, and wished she'd slipped into one of the pubs she'd passed to repair some of the damage.

But she was there now. Heart jumping, she rang the bell. A light was on in the basement and few moments later he opened the door, and all her misgivings vanished as he stepped forward and pulled her straight into his arms.

'I hoped it was you. I've missed you. It's just as well you don't have a phone or I'd have left fifty pathetic and annoying messages throughout the day.' He released her enough to kiss her, and then pulled back, frowning. 'Hey, what's the matter? Jess? Fuck — come in.'

She followed him down the dark stairs to his flat, where he disappeared into the kitchen and emerged again carrying a bottle of red wine and two glasses.

'Sorry. Look, I shouldn't have said that about texting.' He splashed wine into her glass and onto the table. 'It was just a joke — honestly. If you've come to say that you don't want to see me again—'

She gave a watery smile and pulled the letter from her pocket. 'This came this morning. It's about the house.'

He picked it up and read it. She watched as his expression changed from anxiety to confusion to astonishment. He looked up at her, a slow smile spreading across his face. 'Does this mean what I think it means? That he's given you the house? Oh my God, that's fantastic — isn't it?'

She nodded. 'It's the most amazing, generous thing imaginable. I couldn't believe it at first – I thought it was one of those scams you hear about – but I've just been to see the solicitor who sent the letter and it's all official. The house is mine. I'll be able to get the keys from the council within the next couple of days. But—'

Tears swept in like a sudden storm, and there was nothing to do but submit to them. He moved to her side, folded her into his body and held her as it spent its fury, rocking her gently, his breath warm in her hair. And then, as she sniffed and spluttered in its aftermath he reached into the pocket of his jeans and pulled out a white cotton handkerchief. Jess laughed.

'I can't blow my nose on that.'

'Why not?'

'It's too clean. I'll ruin it.'

'I'll do it then.' Gently he blotted the tears from her cheeks and wiped her nose. His face was serious, and full of a kind of tenderness that made her want to cry again. 'There. Look, I know I'm an insensitive idiot sometimes, but I think I'm missing something here. You're the new owner of an extremely desirable property in a top London location. What's to cry about?' Realization suddenly dawned and his expression changed to one of horror. 'Unless – Oh Christ, Jess – is he—?'

She shook her head. 'Not yet. But it won't be long. He's been taken into hospital and they don't think he'll be coming out. He's unconscious.' Her voice wavered, and she swallowed.

'And I feel like I've cheated him. He's changed my life, and given me the most amazing gift, and what did I do to deserve it? Nothing. He never found Stella. He's going to die not knowing what happened to her and I – I—'

She broke off as the phone began to ring, making them both jump. She felt Will hesitate, as though he was going to ignore it and then changed his mind.

'Perhaps I should – just in case—' He got up, keeping his eyes fixed on Jess's as he answered. 'Will Holt.'

He went curiously still as the person on the other end of the line spoke. Then he mouthed, *It's her.*

Jess leapt to her feet and went to stand beside him. He angled the phone so she could hear. From the other end of the line the voice that reached them was reedy with age, but calm and crisp.

'My very good friend Georgina has passed your number on to me. I must say, I was rather reluctant to telephone you. I can't think what it could concern, but at my age I suspect any news is likely to be of the depressing kind.'

'Mrs Daniels, I'm so glad you did telephone.' Will's tone was grave; gentle, and respectful. Jess thought fleetingly how much better he was at all this than she would have been, and was profoundly grateful to him. 'It is rather a personal matter, but not, I hope, depressing. It's concerning an old . . . friend of yours; a gentleman by the name of Dan Rosinski.'

There was silence. A silence that stretched and crackled with the weight of the years while Jess and Will gazed at each other and time stopped.

'Mrs Daniels? Are you still there?'

'Yes. Yes, I'm still here.' The crispness had gone now. The voice was low and hoarse and full of yearning. 'Dan ... Is he ... still alive?'

'Yes, though he's not very well. He's been trying to find you. He'd like very much to make contact again, if you'd allow him to.'

Her reply was a tiny indrawn breath, barely audible; and then, 'Yes. Oh ... *yes*, please.'

40

Stella Daniels lived in a small village about eight miles from Leyton Manor Hospital. It was the kind of place that appeared on Agatha Christie adaptations, with houses clustered around a village green and a picturesque pub. However, the woman who answered the door of the wisteria-draped cottage was a little too smart for the part of Miss Marple, with her softly swept-back silvery hair and neat grey cashmere cardigan.

Will wasn't sure what he'd expected, but it certainly wasn't such composure, such grace. Stella Daniels wore her years well. Her figure was fragile but upright, her skin deeply scored with lines, but her eyes were clear and blue and brimming with the emotions she had banished from her face. Wordlessly she ushered them inside, and in a small hallway filled with slanting evening sunlight and the scent of lavender, took both of Jess's hands in hers.

'Thank you for coming,' she said softly, looking from Jess to Will. 'How is he? Have you heard anything?'

Jess moistened her lips nervously. 'He's still unconscious, but apparently that's not necessarily a bad thing. He's under the care of the top doctors in the field, and they're doing all they can. They say we mustn't give up hope.'

Stella's eyes closed for a brief moment, then she gave Jess's hands a squeeze. 'Quite right. If there's one thing I've learned, it's that we must never give up hope. Now, come through and let me put the kettle on.'

They followed her into a light, pretty kitchen, on the end of which a conservatory jutted out into the garden. There was a sofa and a chair, and a coffee table bearing a tray, neatly laid with china cups and a milk jug. Will and Jess sat stiffly on the sofa while they waited for the water to boil. It seemed too soon to talk about serious matters, so Will filled the gap by admiring the house.

'I bought it to be near to the hospital,' Stella said. Her voice still held a flavour of her London roots, faint but unmistakable. 'Georgina will have told you that my daughter Daisy was also a patient there, when Georgina was quite tiny? Now Jess, would you be a love and carry this teapot? Arthritis has made me a liability with things like that.'

While Jess got up, Will studied the photographs that stood on the little white table beside the chair. The newspaper and magnifying glass as well as the well-worn cushions proclaimed that it was Stella's favourite sitting place, and the photographs were placed where she could see them easily. One was a grainy shot of a young woman smiling broadly at the camera, her slanting eyes creased with infectious happiness. In another a faded bride and groom stood side by side, the bride's blonde hair swept up into a style that seemed so dated now that it had a distinct retro-cool.

'Ah, my daughters – Daisy and Vivien,' Stella said, catching the direction of his gaze as she lowered herself carefully into her chair. 'Chalk and cheese, aren't they? Daisy was so sweet, so loving, so happy, even though most people would say she didn't have much to be happy about. But the simplest things – watching the birds on the bird table, or buying an ice cream from the van would make her brim over with delight. It was such a precious gift, that, and especially wonderful to me when I'd been used to Vivien's high standards. Even as a child, if you bought Vivien a dress she'd pout because she wanted a skirt as well. She was just like her mother in that respect.'

'Her mother?' Will asked, thoroughly puzzled.

'Forgive me – I'm confusing you. Vivien was Nancy's child. Nancy Price. When Georgina said you had news of an old friend I thought it must be Nancy. We lost touch a long time ago, but it would be just like her to reappear as if nothing had happened.'

Will leaned forward, lowering his voice respectfully. 'As a matter of fact, I do have some news of her. I'm afraid she died, a couple of years ago. She'd been living in a nursing home for some time before that, and the house on Greenfields Lane was empty. No one knew who owned it.'

Reaching across to hand out cups, Stella stilled for a moment. 'I'm sorry to hear that. We were close once, Nancy and I. As close as sisters.'

Iona Grey

'What happened?'

Stella's smile was sad and soft, hinting at hurts suffered long ago but never quite forgotten. 'That's a rather long story.'

Beside him, Jess straightened up. She had been sitting with her bag on her knee, clutched to her chest, but she unfolded it now and took out the bundle of letters. 'I'd love to hear it, but can I give you these first? It doesn't seem right, me holding on to them a second longer when they belong to you. You've read all of them, except the top one. The one that arrived a couple of months ago and started the search.'

'Oh ...' Stella took the letters and stared at them for a second, her hand flying to her mouth. Then she closed her eyes and held the tattered bundle against her heart. The lines on her forehead had deepened, and two grooves of pain were scored between her brows, giving her face an expression of intense private suffering.

Will got quietly to his feet and held out his hand to Jess. 'Mrs Daniels, you have a beautiful garden. Perhaps we could go outside for five minutes and admire it properly?'

'I'm so sorry, do forgive me. It was seeing his writing again, after all these years. It brought it all back, I suppose.'

Will and Jess had come in from the garden and they were all drinking tea that was just a little too strong and too cool. The letters were in a neat pile on the table beside Stella. She hadn't read them: she would do that slowly, luxuriously, when she was alone and could immerse herself completely in the memories. Except for the newest one – that one she had read.

514

She held it in her hands now, touching the paper that he had touched, hearing his voice in her head saying the words he'd so recently written.

Darling girl . . .

She managed a smile. She felt their curiosity, and was touched by their courteous attempts to conceal it. 'We were so in love,' she said, and laughed at the wistfulness in her own voice. 'We truly believed it would conquer everything. Except death perhaps: we thought that was the only thing that could separate us.'

'But it didn't turn out like that,' Jess said, reaching across to put her teacup back in its saucer. She had slipped one foot out of her little ballerina pump and tucked it up beneath her on the sofa and her body was angled so she could lean against Will beside her. Stella remembered that imperative to touch. Almost like a magnetic force.

'No. No, it didn't. Not for us. It wasn't a foreign enemy that tore us apart in the end, but something much closer to home.' Stella traced her fingertips over Dan's writing on the envelope, and wondered how to explain to these young people, who had grown up in a world of equal opportunities and emancipation, the situation she had found herself in. 'Things were very different back then. Women were out there, doing men's jobs in factories and on farms, but we were still the property of our husbands. We bore children, took sole responsibility for caring for them, and yet the law gave us few rights to them.' She took a sip of cold tea, and grimaced. 'And a woman like me had none at all.'

'A woman like you?'

'An adulteress. A disgraced wife. An unfit mother. Back then there was no such thing as a blameless divorce. To end my marriage I would have had to admit to being unfaithful, which would have instantly removed any chance I might have had of being allowed to keep Daisy.'

Jess sat upright, bristling with indignation. 'But that's so unfair!'

'Especially as Charles had been unfaithful too.' Seeing surprise flit across their faces Stella went on with a wry smile, 'Oh yes, Charles was in love with someone else when we married, though I was too naïve to see it. In fact, his lover was actually best man at our wedding.'

Will stopped, his teacup halfway to his mouth. 'Charles was gay?'

'Yes, though no one would ever have suspected it, or believed me if I'd told them – he was a vicar, and a family man, and he had all the parish ladies eating out of his hand. Nor would they have believed that he'd hit me, or forced himself on me. For years afterwards I would go over and over the afternoon when Dan came back, trying to work out how I could have done it differently – should I have been braver and shouted out the truth? But by then it was already much too late. I'd been silent for too long. I hid away with my bruises when Charles hit me. I let everyone treat me like an incompetent mother. I didn't even tell Nancy the truth about our marriage. I thought I was being good and loyal, but really I was sealing my own fate. I—'

516

She stopped.

For years it had felt like she was tiptoeing along a cliff edge, stumbling sometimes and losing her footing, focusing all her energy on not looking down onto the jagged rocks and churning sea below. Gradually it had become easier; the ground had become firmer and her steps more assured. Now it was as if she had just opened her eyes and found herself right on the edge of the precipice again, looking down.

'It's OK,' Jess said gently. 'You don't have to talk about it if you don't want to.'

Stella nodded. She'd never spoken about what had happened. As far as possible she'd tried to avoid thinking about it. The memories were sealed in an airtight box that she'd pushed to the back of her head. Perhaps it was best — safest — to leave it there, unopened. She looked down at the letter she held, and her heart clenched at the sight of the familiar, beloved handwriting. *Pretty soon none of this will matter, and our story will be history . . .*

But it did matter. It mattered so much.

She took a breath in and let it out slowly. And then she began.

As she talked, the shadows stole in from the garden, blurring the edges between the present and the past. The birds finished evensong and the world settled and stilled.

Stella told the story about how Dan had come back, just as she'd prayed and longed for, and how Charles had stolen their hope and turned it to ashes. She told them about the choice he'd forced her to make and the agony of watching Dan leave; about Dr Walsh and the pills that had eased that pain a little, but cost her her daughter.

'That was the summer the V1s started,' she said softly. 'Just after D-Day, when things seemed to be going so well for the Allied forces, a new terror began at home. We'd been bombed before, of course, in the Blitz of '40 and '41, and it was awful, but you almost got used to the nightly ritual of the sirens and going to the shelter. This was different. They came out of nowhere – just a dot in a clear blue sky – and you didn't know where they were going to land. I'd taken Daisy to the shops in her pram one day. It was hot. The pills had made everything . . . blurry and I couldn't think. I heard that noise – the buzzing. I thought it was inside my head, that I was going mad, and I had to get out of the shop and try to get away from it. I . . . I left her. And then the explosion came.'

'But she was all right? The bomb didn't hit her?'

Will's gentle prompting brought her back, and she opened her eyes. She hadn't even realized they were closed.

'I know. I know that now, but not then. I tried to get back to her, you see, but it was impossible. Everywhere was in chaos. A house had been hit, and a bus full of people, and I couldn't get through. If I'd have been thinking clearly I would have realized that the shops where I'd left her were in a different direction, but I couldn't think at all. It was dark by the time they found me, down by the canal. I don't remember how I got there or what happened, but I was soaking wet and covered in mud. I remember being so cold, and Dr Walsh giving me an injection. I could feel it going into my blood, warming it up.' She listened to her own voice, and was vaguely surprised by how matter-of-fact it sounded. 'I was taken to a hospital. An asylum. I was locked up, just as if I was a prisoner, and I was glad because it was what I deserved for killing my daughter.'

'But did no one tell you that she was safe?' Jess said, horrified.

'No one mentioned her at all. And I didn't ask, because I was afraid of having to listen to someone tell me what I'd done. They kept me heavily sedated so for weeks I was barely awake. I wanted to die, and I think I probably would have if it hadn't been for Nancy.'

It was almost dark now. Stella leaned across and turned on the lamp beside her. Its glow fell on Jess's face and showed up the anguish written on it.

'What did Nancy do?' she asked.

'She came to see me one day. She was in trouble; the oldest kind of trouble a girl can find herself in,' Stella said ruefully. 'She had no one else to turn to and she needed my help. She knew about the house, you see; the one at Greenfields Lane that Dan had bought for me. She wanted to go there. At first I didn't want to let her – the house was my last connection with Dan, and the time we'd spent there together was so precious – but I think I felt that if I helped her with her child it would be the first tiny step in atoning for what I'd done to my own.'

Understanding lit up Jess's face. 'So *that*'s how Nancy came to live there.'

'It was only supposed to be for a little while in the beginning, until she'd had the baby. In fact, the original idea was that we'd live there together, but of course, that never happened.' Stella laughed softly. 'I'd just about been strong enough to get out of hospital, but I couldn't begin to work out how to get out of my marriage. So I went back to that miserable Vicarage.'

'And Daisy was . . . gone?'

'Yes. Her room was empty, her things packed into a tea chest in the attic, her cot all folded up. There was so much I longed to know – had they found a body, had there been a funeral? – but Charles wouldn't discuss it. I thought it was because he was too upset and I didn't press it because it was all my fault. I got through the days by focusing on the arrival of Nancy's child, and . . . Well, I suppose what started out as a penance gradually became a lifeline . . .'

Ruby the cat appeared, stretching up and plucking her claws into the arm of the chair with the delicacy of a harpist before jumping up onto Stella's knee. She put Dan's letter on the table with the others and began to stroke her, as she told Jess and Will how Nancy had given birth to her daughter in the front bedroom at Greenfields Lane, and about her indifference to the baby, her revulsion with the physical realities of motherhood.

'The whole process disgusted her from the start. I had to go to the welfare clinic to get milk and bottles because she wouldn't entertain the idea of feeding her herself. About a week after Vivien was born it was VE day and Nancy bitterly resented missing out on all the fun. She wouldn't pick the baby up and couldn't stand to hear her cry, and of course she had nothing for her – no clothes, or nappies or anything. It made sense for me to get out Daisy's things. And then, as it became apparent that Nancy was set on giving the baby up, it made sense for me to take her, too. London was overflowing with abandoned children in those days – refugees, orphans of the Blitz, GIs' accidental babies – and the welfare bodies could barely cope.'

'Didn't Charles object to the idea of taking care of her permanently?' Jess asked.

'No, actually. It was the perfect solution for him too.' Beneath Stella's rhythmic stroking the cat had started up her rattling purr. 'Appearances were everything to Charles. They gave him something to hide behind.' She rolled her eyes. 'He wanted a family, but he certainly didn't want to do what was necessary to create one. Nancy's baby gave him a chance to appear charitable – giving a home to an innocent victim of war – and like a conventional family man. And so that was that; the deal was made. I gave Nancy my house and she gave me her child. Nothing signed, nothing official, but there it was . . .' She paused. Those had been the years when she had been closest to the cliff edge. When sometimes the idea of just giving in and tumbling over had been horribly seductive. 'I had a daughter. She wasn't *my* daughter, but . . . we did our best.'

'And all that time, Daisy was in Leyton Manor,' Will said. He was leaning back, so that his face was in shadow and impossible to read, but his voice was low and slightly hoarse. 'Charles betrayed you in so many ways, didn't he? He wouldn't let you leave with Daisy, and yet he . . . got rid of her like that. And he let you go on thinking that she was dead, and that it was your fault.'

Stella nodded, silenced for a second as emotion thickened in her throat. 'He thought he knew what he wanted, and then he got it and found he didn't want it after all. Dr Walsh had suspected there was something wrong with Daisy for a little while, but Charles had always refused to accept it. After he found out about Dan I think it planted the seed in his mind that she might not be his daughter, and so the suggestion that she wasn't "normal" gave him the perfect excuse to get rid of her.'

'And you had no idea.'

'Not then. Not for a long time. I found out later, of course, but for twenty years I carried around the pain of losing her and the burden of my guilt. And you see, that was why I couldn't go to Dan. I had my freedom, but because of what I'd done I knew I didn't deserve it. I certainly didn't deserve to be happy.'

She trailed off, remembering what he'd said in his letter at the start of it all. *Stella, I don't want you to feel guilty . . . It poisons happiness and makes us believe that we're not good enough . . .* She'd read that letter a hundred times, and then she'd put it in the box with all the other ones and given them to Nancy. For safekeeping, but also so she couldn't read them any more. He was offering her a forgiveness to which she believed she had no right.

'How did you find out what Charles had done?'

'When he died. He had left all the paperwork – the forms he and Dr Walsh had signed originally, and all the letters he'd received from the hospital over the years, requesting money for new clothes, informing him that she'd had measles, that sort of thing – in an envelope with my name on it. I suppose it was his one act of kindness that he didn't destroy them as well as himself.'

'Himself?'

'Oh yes. You see, for all those years he had been carrying his burden of guilt too, though he kept it hidden from me. Eventually the burden got too great for him to bear. The coroner was very kind – kinder perhaps than Charles deserved. He said it could possibly have been an accident that Charles took too many of his sleeping tablets. An oversight perhaps.'

'Death by Misadventure,' Will said softly.

'Exactly. Charitable of him, since suicide is an abomination in the eyes of God.'

If Stella had had her way it would have said 'death by poisoning' on the certificate: twenty sleeping pills and as many years of toxic guilt.

'And so you were finally reunited with Daisy,' Jess said, bringing her gently back to the story. 'What was it like?'

'Heartbreaking.'

Stella had talked about this before. In fact, during the long years of campaigning she seemed to talk about little else, to anyone who would listen, waving the truth in front of unseeing eyes like a banner. 'Putting children into places like that was considered to be the right thing to do at the time, but the conditions they lived in were dreadful. You can't imagine . . . They were treated like animals, tied up or left in bed because no one bothered to get them up.'

It was familiar territory, but it had never stopped being painful. 'Of course, I wanted to gather her up and take her as far away as possible, but I couldn't. I was a stranger to her. She'd grown up without knowing warmth or affection, and it had turned her in on herself. It took a whole year to get her to trust me enough to hug her, and two years to get her to talk. She had simply forgotten how to because no one ever spoke to her. I did what I could – for all of the patients there. I spent as much time as I could with the children, playing with them and talking to them; it became the focus of my life. And when I went home I wrote letters to the authorities, asked questions, made demands, and generally made a thorough nuisance of myself. Gradually things began to improve. Daisy died when she was just thirty-six – she had a heart condition, you see – and the hospital was an altogether different place by then. A happy place. There were so many others that weren't, though, and so the work didn't stop there. I set up a charity, and became a consultant for the government on policy – things I'd never dreamed I could do.'

'You got an OBE,' Will said gravely. 'I couldn't find any

information on the internet about Stella Thorne, but there was plenty about Stella Daniels, including some great pictures of you at the Palace.'

Stella laughed, touched by his admiration. 'I changed my name after Charles died. I didn't feel like that same timid, powerless girl any more. I felt a terrible fraud accepting the OBE, though. I did what I did for such selfish reasons. For Daisy, to make up for being such a poor mother to her for all that time, and to fill the huge hole left by Dan.'

'You're amazing,' Jess said quietly, getting up to put her arms around Stella. 'Honestly. Amazing.'

Stella returned the hug, blinking back the sudden sting of tears. 'No. I started off being ordinary and in the end I was *lucky*. I found my daughter, and I discovered my voice.' As Jess released her she brushed her cheeks quickly and laughed. 'Now, let me make you some more tea. A hot cup this time . . .'

She gathered her strength to get up, but Will was too quick for her. 'Let me do it. We've tired you out enough already.'

The lamplight reflected on the glass, sealing them into a golden bubble, holding the darkness beyond at bay. Over freshly brewed tea they moved on to other subjects, and Jess told Stella about the mother who, like Nancy, had opted out of her daughter's life, the boyfriend who, like Charles, had abused her. So many similarities, and a world and two generations of difference, but Stella was grateful that she shared her story. When the teapot was empty Will and Jess carried the cups across to the sink. She washed while he picked up a tea towel and dried.

'Dan told me that he wrote to you often, after the war,' Jess said above the noise of running water. 'He wanted you to know that he was waiting for you and he still loved you, but Nancy must have thrown the letters away. Why would she do that?'

Stella was tired now. She had been talking for a long time; her voice had worn thin with use and there was a faint throbbing at her temples. 'Nancy was a survivor. She could be ruthless, and she always did what was necessary to protect herself. I imagine she was worried that if I heard from Dan I'd leave Charles to go to him, and Vivien would be sent back to her. Or that Dan would come over here to be with me and we'd want the house back . . .'

Or maybe she was thinking of me. The idea came out of nowhere, like the pale moth that emerged suddenly from the darkness to batter delicately at the windowpane, then settle there in the lampglow. Nancy had seen her in the hospital and witnessed her painful journey back into the outside world. In her brisk, no-nonsense way she'd encouraged it – partly for her own sake, perhaps, but there was little doubt that she'd saved Stella's life. Maybe she'd believed that letters from Dan would undo all those months of laborious progress and drag her back to the cliff edge?

She would never know now. Nancy was gone, like so many of the other people whose names she'd spoken tonight for the first time in half a lifetime.

The glass in front of her reflected the bright kitchen behind, where the shapes of Will and Jess moved around each other, speaking in soft murmurs. Beyond the windows layers of dusk deepened into night. Stella felt herself suspended between the present and the past, the lit-up room and the dark garden.

Talking had exhausted her, but she was glad she had done it. She felt calm; lighter somehow, as if she'd shrugged off a heavy overcoat on a hot day. Speaking those things out loud had given her a different perspective on them: she could see them now simply as a series of events, like beads in a necklace, distinct from each other but joined together in an unchangeable sequence. Bad ones, but good ones too. In locking the past away she'd forgotten about the good things.

The cat was warm on her lap and her eyelids were heavy. She let them drop. In the comforting blackout she began to take out memories and examine them one by one. It was like unwrapping precious tissue-swathed treasures. There was Nancy, with her fierce, grudging kindness and her raucous laugh; hitching up her blue satin bridesmaid's dress to get a cigarette from her garter, eating tinned peaches at the church fete, showing off her smart new trench coat. The colours of each image were fresh and unfaded. She saw Ada wearing her flowered pinny, and recalled her miraculous ability to defy rationing and produce a hat, a bread pudding, a pretty dress. Ernest Stokes came next, with his insatiable appetite, and Fred Collins with his Box Brownie. Marjorie and her scones. Hilda Goodall dispensing milky advice in the maternity ward. Dan.

Dan . . .

And there the flickering film reel behind her eyes stuttered and ended.

She didn't want to relive the old moments with Dan. She wanted more than memories, no matter how precious and perfect they were.

She wanted *more*.

She picked up his letter and held it to her cheek. Even after all these years she wasn't on good enough terms with God to ask Him anything, so she squeezed her eyes shut again and sent a whispered message straight to Dan.

I'm here, hold on . . . Forever isn't over yet.

The Spitfire's headlamps gilded the pale froth of cow parsley in the hedgerows and made the cats' eyes gleam. The night's breath was cool.

'What if we're too late?'

Jess spoke in a low voice, through clenched teeth, as if she was cold and trying to stop them from chattering. Will switched on the ineffectual heater and turned it up to high.

'Remember what he said in the letter. He hadn't given up hope, and neither should we.'

He stopped at a junction. Turning to check for cars coming from the left he could see her face in profile, palely silhouetted against the dark blue beyond. The headlights of a passing car showed up the glitter of tears on her cheeks.

'Oh Jess, sweetheart . . .'

She scrubbed quickly at her face with the sleeve of her

shirt. His shirt, the one he'd given her from his wardrobe at home. 'We tried to help, but I'm scared we've only made things worse. Isn't hope a bad thing when it comes to nothing? Isn't it better to accept less and not be disappointed?'

He turned out of the junction, out of the village. Only darkness lay ahead of them. 'We've done our best. We've done everything we can.'

As he spoke he felt the inadequacy of the words, their smallness. The smallness of themselves, too. The car was a tiny boat, afloat on a black sea beneath the vast dome of night.

'But what if it's not enough?' she said. 'What if he dies without knowing that we found her?'

A gateway loomed ahead in the beam of the lights. He pulled into it and turned off the engine. The silence was sudden and complete.

'Then he'll still have known that you tried,' Will said quietly, angling his body towards her awkwardly in the tiny space. 'He'll still have known that over in England a wonderful girl cared enough to listen to his story and take up his search. And Stella will know that he never forgot her.' He reached out and stroked the backs of his fingers down her cheek. 'All these years, through all she's suffered, she's been loved. Isn't that the most important thing, in the end? To know that you're loved?'

41

'But the stain is still there.' The woman jabbed at the fabric with a finger that was barnacled with diamonds, and gave an exasperated little laugh. 'Look, perhaps you don't understand, but this is a four-hundred-pound dress. I brought it to be cleaned, and you're returning it in exactly the same state and expecting me to pay?'

'I'm really sorry,' Jess said, completely untruthfully. 'We did explain when you dropped it off that removing red wine from raw silk was unlikely. The solvents we use are the most effective available, but even so—'

The woman hitched her handbag onto her shoulder. It was the size of a tennis bag and hung about with gold padlocks and chains that no doubt signified its exclusive brand heritage to those in the know. 'Yes, of course,' she snapped. 'I understand that. But I didn't think I'd be expected to pay when it's no better than when I brought it in.'

'Well, it's because we still had to do the work on it, you

see.' Jess's patience was pretty much at an end. Anyone, she reckoned, who parked their gleaming black-windowed Chelsea tractor on the double yellow lines outside and came in lugging a handbag like that, wearing sunglasses with a designer logo big enough to see from space and bragging about how much their dress had cost could probably afford the £6.95 for dry cleaning. 'It's the cost of materials, and the labour involved—'

The shop door opened, letting in a blast of traffic noise and a tall man in a suit. Samia came through from the back and went to serve him, and Jess watched out of the corner of her eye as they both looked in her direction.

'I don't care,' the woman was saying coldly. 'The fact is that you expect me to pay for a service that has not been carried out to a sufficiently high standard. I'll pay, but I'll be taking it further, I can tell you—'

'Do excuse me, madam,' Samia interrupted, flawlessly courteous as always. 'This gentleman would like a word with my young colleague here. Perhaps I can help?'

Jess's immediate relief became a lurch of foreboding as she looked properly at the man for the first time and recognized him.

'Mr Ramsay?'

'Forgive me for bothering you at work, but I was passing and I thought I might as well drop this off. The council's Empty Homes Officer delivered it yesterday.'

He placed a key on the counter. Jess picked it up and held it in her hand. It felt very small, considering everything it represented. She made an attempt to look happy. 'Thanks. It's good of you to bring it. Does that mean I can go into the house now?'

'It does indeed. The electricity and gas have both been reconnected and the council have done an initial tidy up, but I don't need to tell you that there's still a lot to be done.'

At the other end of the counter the woman with the hideous handbag was speaking very slowly and loudly to Samia. 'It's the Supply of Goods and Services Act,' she was saying, as if Samia was deaf, or stupid, or both.

Jess pressed the key into the palm of her hand, feeling the metal warm up against her skin. 'I don't suppose ... You haven't heard how Dan is, have you?'

'As a matter of fact, I have.' Mr Ramsay's smile made hope fizz in the pit of her stomach. 'There was a message on my machine this morning, from Mr Goldberg. He phoned before he left the office yesterday evening, which would have been about ten o'clock our time, to say that Mr Rosinski was awake and talking.'

At Jess's squeal of excitement Ms Hideous-Handbag stopped talking and stared, outrage turning to disgust as Jess clambered onto the counter to throw her arms around Mr Ramsay's neck. '*Talking*? So he knows? He knows about Stella?'

'Oh yes, he knows,' Mr Ramsay said dryly, straightening his glasses as Jess released him. 'Apparently he's been trying to pull strings and call in favours to get a flight to London.' His smile slipped a little. 'But he's not well enough for that. He's asked to come home, and they're arranging that as soon as possible, probably tomorrow or Friday. But don't get your hopes up, Jess. It might seem like he's getting better, but Mr Goldberg says it could be quite the opposite. It's not uncommon for people to . . . rally a little, near the end.'

'I get that.' She bit her lip, eyes stinging. 'But it's like . . . I don't know, like a gift. A gift of time. We mustn't waste it. Thanks, Mr Ramsay. Thanks for letting me know.'

'You're welcome. Don't hesitate to get in touch if there's anything else I can help you with.' As he turned to leave he gave the handbag woman a frosty glance over the top of his glasses. 'Excuse me, madam, I couldn't help overhearing. I'm a solicitor, and I'd advise you that, since the work on your garment has been carried out with reasonable care and skill, you have no redress from the law for your accident with the red wine. I'd hate you to waste your money on a claim you couldn't win.' Turning, he gave Jess the ghost of a wink, and was gone.

My Dear Jess

Sorry for the radio silence. I wasn't feeling so good last week and they took me into the hospital. I guess everyone thought it was the end – me included. And then they told me that you'd found Stella and although I was pretty far out of it and I don't remember hearing anything, I must have. Because here I am. The docs said it was quite a dramatic comeback.

Jess, I know I don't have long; miracles, like lightning,

don't strike twice in the same place. I wanted to say <u>thank you</u>, though those words sure are inadequate to express my gratitude towards you. These last few months you've given me hope and friendship and something to look forward to. Your emails brightened my days, and – even if we'd never got close to finding Stella – I knew that the search had turned up someone pretty darn special in her place. I'm glad I was able to get the transfer of the house organized in time. I hope that it, or the money that it raises, will give you the things you deserve in life. Security. Independence. A place to be happy.

It seems like I have been old for a long, long time; so long that I forgot what it was like to feel young. You made me remember, and allowed me to relive those days. I can't think of a more precious gift.

Thank you.

Take care of yourself for me.

Dan xx

She'd picked up the email on Will's laptop. It was Friday evening and they were at the house, the doors and windows thrown open to allow the green-scented air to flow through and dry the walls and surfaces and paintwork she'd scrubbed. Will had been there all day, and all of yesterday too, clearing out rubbish, sweeping away cobwebs and hacking into the overgrown garden, getting ready for tomorrow when Stella came.

She read Dan's email again, swiping at tears with the hem of Will's rowing club t-shirt. Before this week how long had it been since she'd cried? Years; when Gran died, probably, but it was like she'd inadvertently drilled into some kind of spring, hidden deep inside herself. All her emotions kept gushing out.

Leaving the laptop open, she got up from the lumpy sofa and went through to the back of the house. Through the open door she could hear Will's voice, the staccato rhythm of his words spoken in time with the swing of his axe. Or Albert Greaves's axe, to be precise, and Albert himself was sitting on a kitchen chair by the back door, one elbow propped on his walking frame, a can of beer in his hand, supervising.

They both looked up as she went out. Will straightened up, letting the axe fall to his side. The evening sun made a halo around his head and gilded the hairs on his forearms. After two days outside they were already turning brown.

'Everything all right?' he said, watching her face.

She nodded. 'The connection's working fine.'

He looked relieved. 'That's good.'

Albert took a sip from his can. 'You get it up and running, then, your inter-whathaveyou?'

Jess went to perch on the windowsill beside his chair. The rose clambering up the wall would soon be in flower, she noticed. Creamy yellow petals were just visible where the green buds were splitting open. A drop of pure happiness expanded inside her at the prospect of what lay ahead; the summer, and a garden of her own, Dan's priceless gifts of security and independence. And Will.

'The internet. Yes. Karina next door has very kindly let us

use her wireless connection, just until we get our own. We'll need it tomorrow, you see.'

Albert shook his head, puzzled but content. 'I don't know. In my day, the wireless was something you listened to. Tommy Handley, now he was a funny man. Vera Lynn – The Forces' Sweetheart. What was that song she used to sing ? Let me think . . .'

Will and Jess looked at each other. Smiled. An aeroplane droned distantly, a white trail fluffing up in its wake across the lavender sky. Albert started to sing creakily, like a gate opening on rusty hinges.

'*It's a Lovely Day Tomorrow* . . .'

'Yes,' Will said, still looking at Jess, holding her in the sunlit warmth of his gaze, 'I think it probably will be.'

Of course, it would have changed. It was silly to expect it to be the same after seventy years. New houses might have been built around it, a mini-estate, perhaps. The forget-me-not blue front door would probably have been replaced by one of those low-maintenance UPVC ones. Nancy might have taken out the fireplaces and installed radiators, and put in a modern bath of moulded plastic in place of the cast-iron one in which Dan had soaked on that long-ago summer evening. The violet wallpaper would be gone, for certain.

'Nearly there,' Will said gently beside her. 'Are you all right?'

'Yes . . . thank you.' The shops along the main street were all different. Unrecognizable. In fact, most of them weren't shops at all but restaurants and cafés and takeaways. There was a bowling alley in the old picture house, a burger bar where the fried fish shop used to be. The pub was still there, and the corner shop where Dan had seen the card advertising a house for sale, though its old wooden front had been stripped away and replaced with glass and garish hoardings.

And then the car was slowing and turning into Greenfields Lane and she couldn't look any more. How silly Will must think her, sitting there with her eyes closed, though he was far too sweet to say anything. She felt the car stop, heard the engine stutter into silence and Will open his door to get out. Inside her head she relived the moment when Dan had first brought her here, and she had stood with his hands covering her eyes and his breath warm on her neck.

Dan, where are we?

Home.

She opened her eyes, and saw that it was all just exactly the same.

Jess and Will stayed in the front room as she made her slow pilgrimage through the ground-floor rooms, gathering memories, greeting ghosts, touching the places where Dan's hand had rested, all those years ago.

'I hope you're not shocked by the state of the place,' Jess said as she came back through from the dining room. 'We've cleaned it up as best we could, but it can't have been touched for years.'

'It hasn't.' Stella let out a breath of laughter, her gaze falling on the crumbling velvet sofa. 'It's all just exactly the same. Nancy never was the domesticated type.'

'The council had cleared out a lot of her belongings when they took charge of the place, but they kept the things they thought might be of personal value. There wasn't an awful lot here, to be honest. A lot of it had been taken when she moved into the home, but we thought that maybe you might like to take what was left. For Vivien . . . ?'

'Yes. I'll ask her.' It was a thoughtful offer, though Vivien had never shown any interest in her real mother and, given her taste for designer trappings and expensive décor, Stella couldn't think that there would be anything from here that would find a place in her carefully styled home. 'How kind of you to think of that.'

'Would you like to go upstairs?' Will asked.

'Oh . . . I'm not sure . . . Really, there's no need.' Now the time had come, her chest felt tight, as if the thin walls that held her emotions in check might suddenly break. The violet-strewn room was so vivid in her memory, she wasn't sure she could bear to have the image overlaid by something different. But Jess was taking her arm, leading her gently towards the stairs.

'Actually, there is really. Some of the things they kept were yours. One of the rooms was locked. We didn't know what was behind the door, but the council must have opened it when they took over. They found the missing letters in there, lots and lots of them. They'd been pushed under the door – that's what Nancy must have done whenever one arrived. They're up here, waiting for you. Come and see.'

And so, slowly, carefully, they filed up the stairs. Jess led the way and opened the door into the bedroom that had been shut and locked for almost seventy years.

'Oh . . .' Stella pressed her hands to her mouth as she turned to take it all in, though there was really no need. All was as it had been. The afternoon sun sloped across walls strewn with faded violets and lay in honeyed pools on the old brass bed. On the bedside table the pile of letters waited for her.

'It was a bit of a mess, as you can imagine, having been shut up for so long,' Will was explaining from the doorway. 'Lots of soot had fallen down the chimney and there were cobwebs like ships' rigging. We think a bird must have built a nest in the chimney because the floor was covered in straw.'

Packing straw, she thought, remembering Mrs Nichols' gift and stifling a gasp of laughter. The bed creaked as she lowered herself onto it, stroking her hand wonderingly over the sheets she had brought from the Vicarage in her suitcase. Dazedly she shook her head.

'I feel like I've come home. Like he's here.'

There was the tiniest pause. And then, taking in a breath Will stepped forwards and opened the laptop computer he was carrying.

'Well, actually . . . in a manner of speaking . . . he is.'

*

The sun slipped down the wall to the floor. The violets in the corners of the room retreated into the shadows. They talked.

In the corner of the computer screen there was a small box in which she could see herself, the image that Dan would see on his screen. She looked old, but she didn't feel it. The years rolled back and she was the girl she'd been back then; shy, a little uncertain, enchanted by him.

Illness and age had altered her golden boy. The unruly mane of tawny hair was almost gone and his skin had the pallor of sickness, but he was there in the gestures she remembered so well, the quirk of his smile and the pitch of his voice. The things he said. The way he made her feel.

He was there.

He had married, he told her. He had married Louis Johnson's widow, Jean, when her boy was fourteen years old and beginning to be a handful. 'She figured he needed a father, and I figured I owed it to Louis. It was a happy enough marriage. We didn't have any babies of our own, which I guess she would have liked, but Jimmy was a good kid. He has a son called Joe, who fixed this whole thing up with your Will. He's great. He works as a stunt driver in the movies.'

'Is he married?'

'No ... but he has a great partner. Called Ryan.'

Across the thousands of miles that separated them their eyes met and held and they smiled, both thinking of Charles. 'Things have changed,' she said softly. 'The world is a better, more tolerant place these days. Did we help to make it better, do you think?'

He sighed and shifted his position on the bank of pillows. Pain flickered across his face and she felt her heart twist. 'I'd like to think we did, because otherwise what was it all for? What did those men die for – Louis and Joey Harper and all the others? Wasn't it so people could live the lives they wanted to have and be the people they were meant to be?'

'Sometimes I think we were unlucky, being born at the time we were,' Stella said. 'I look out there and see Jess and Will, and it seems so simple for them. They love each other. They'll have a life together; a home and children – simple, wonderful things. I envy them that. But then I remember how lucky we were too, to have met at all. If it hadn't been for the war I would never have known you. I could never have become the person you made me. I would have lived a smaller, narrower life if I hadn't loved you.'

'Jeez, Stella . . .' She had heard him say those words before, in that exact same weary, ragged way, as if he was drawing them right out from his soul. The deliciousness of hearing them again made her shiver. 'Just one more time. What I wouldn't give to see you one more time; properly, so I could touch you. They won't let me fly, you know. I've tried every airline and not a single one will have me on board.' He shook his head. 'Insurance risk, they say; I might die in the air. It would be funny if it wasn't so goddamned infuriating. We died in our thousands in the skies over Europe back then. They sent us up there to die. No one ever mentioned insurance risk.'

She was laughing, and crying, and melting inside. 'I'll come. To you. I'll get a flight as soon as I can.'

He was tired now, she could see it in every line of his face, in the opaqueness of his eyes. Tired and in pain. His smile was slow and sad and relieved and beautiful.

'Good. I'll wait for you.'

She sat, for a little while after the screen had reverted to its view of an improbably featureless hill, and thought. Her head was full of his voice and the things that he'd said. She wanted time to just hold those things there, and cherish them.

In the garden below the window Will was working, hacking into the overgrown shrubbery that had swallowed up the lawn. It had been hot before, and he had taken his shirt off. She watched him now, noticing how the muscles moved beneath his skin, remembering how it felt to be quick and strong and young. And suddenly it was as if she had fallen through time, and she was walking across the garden to Dan, who was pushing a lawnmower, a sheen of sweat like gold-dust on his sun-warmed skin, a cigarette wedged in the corner of his mouth.

Time. It stretched and contracted. Jess appeared and the boy on the lawn turned and was Will again. She watched him loop his arm around her and kiss the top of her head. They looked beautiful together, she thought with a sharp lurch of emotion. Not only because they were both young and attractive, but because they were so transparently in love. It transformed them; set them slightly apart and made them seem invincible. She wondered if they knew how precious it was, to have the whole joyous adventure of their life together ahead of them? And then she caught a glimpse of the rapt expression on Will's face as he smiled at Jess, and she knew that they did, and that they would be all right.

She took a step back from the window, but the movement must have caught his eye and he looked up. Seeing her there he raised his hand, questions written across his open face.

She smiled and raised a hand in return. Then she gathered up her precious letters and left the violet-scattered bedroom to go and ask if they would be so good as to help her book a flight to America.

Epilogue

The wide sky is a deep, glowing indigo. The stars are beginning to fade and there is a thread of pinky gold where it meets the more opaque blue of the sea, showing that a new day will soon begin.

The house is on the beach, exactly as he said it would be. The rooms are big and airy, one leading into the other, in a way that makes you feel like you can breathe and spread and relax, and there are whole walls of glass looking out over the sweep of pale sand and the ocean. In the living room, huge sofas are placed around the fireplace.

On the floor there is a white fur rug.

Dan's family had been there to greet her, to welcome this elderly English stranger who knew their father and grandfather even before they did, and who has flown across the Atlantic to be with him at the end. For a while the house had been filled with people, and voices, and a curious atmosphere of tender joy that was almost like a celebration. Then, with infinite kindness and tact, everyone melted away and left the two of them alone. Again. The circle is complete.

Photographs lie scattered across the bed, like bleached autumn leaves. Last night she lay beside him and they studied them together, marvelling at their own youthful beauty, gilded and warmed back into being in the soft glow of the lamp. The photograph he'd taken of her in the ruins of St Clements is creased and torn at the edges, but it brought the moment back with a clarity that made her feel breathless; the throbbing thirst of her first hangover, the anguish over a lost watch (whatever happened to that? She hasn't seen it for years), the uncomfortable awareness of the American stranger. The expression on that girl's face is closed and self-absorbed. She can't see what lies ahead.

How different it would all have been if she could. How many different choices she would have made.

But it is over now. The time for choosing is past.

The pale strip of sky on the horizon is spreading upwards; water bleeding into ink, diluting the darkness. The chest against which her cheek rests is still, and the hand she holds beginning to lose its warmth.

But she holds on.

In a little while she will let go. She will get up, alert the hovering nurses and find Joe and Ryan. In a little while. But for now the sun is rising and the sky is turning pink and gold, and she is with him. And they are both at peace.

Acknowledgements

There are many people who helped *Letters to the Lost* on its journey from head to printed page and to whom I owe thanks for the encouragement and support they gave me as I wrote it. Chief amongst these are my fabulous friends Abby Green (whose perfectly timed parcel in the post provided a spark of inspiration and gave me the boost I needed to start the story), Sally Bowden, Sharon Kendrick, Heidi Rice, Fiona Harper, Scarlet Wilson and Julie Cohen (with thanks for her invaluable research assistance). Before I started writing the book I was lucky enough to get to know the wonderful Lucinda Riley, and I am indebted to her for her advice and friendship: the former made it easier to write, and the latter made the process much more enjoyable.

I couldn't send this book out into the world without saying a special thank you to the inestimable, irreplaceable Penny Jordan, without whom I may never have written a word, and whom I think of with gratitude and love every time I sit down at my computer. Heartfelt thanks also go to Lucy Gilmour, whose wisdom and insight have guided me on the road from aspiring to published writer, and to Susanna Kearsley, whose generosity played a big part in the book's journey to publication when she introduced me to Becky Ritchie of Curtis Brown at an RNA party (thank you, RNA!). Becky was its first reader and its greatest champion, and I'm incredibly fortunate to have her as my agent. I feel honoured to be a CB author, and sincere thanks go to Rachel Clements, Sophie Harris and Alice Lutyens for all they've done to send *Letters* out into the world. And to Deborah Schneider of Gelfman Schneider, who wrote me an email that actually made me shout with happiness. Thank you!

After the solitary months of writing, one of the best bits about actually selling a book is suddenly becoming part of a team. I'm hugely grateful to the warm, wonderful and welcoming people at Simon & Schuster UK and St Martins Press in the US; especially to Clare Hey and Anne Brewer for their thorough but sensitive editing, their patience and positivity, and for long email exchanges in which we discussed Dan and Stella, Will and Jess like they were people we all knew.

Final thanks go to my family. To my mum, Helen, who proved an excellent research assistant, calling upon her more senior friends for first-hand information about whether hotels did room service in the early 1940s and how houses were bought and sold in wartime. To my husband, John, for always, *always* believing it was just a matter of time until the book got published and never minding how long it took, and my daughters, Poppy, Rosie and Ella, for being patient about research trips thinly disguised as family holidays, and understanding that wearing pyjamas all day and messing about on the internet is work when I do it, but not when they do. (Sorrythanksloveyou xxx.)

An Interview with Iona Grey

Letters to the Lost **is a big sweeping love story. What came first: the characters or the storyline?**

Actually, the title came first! For some time I had been working on a completely different novel, set in the early years of the twentieth century, and one day after lunch I was making my way upstairs to my study in the attic (reluctantly: to say it wasn't going well would be an understatement) when I passed my daughter's room and glimpsed a letter lying open on her desk. Instantly curious as to whom it could be from, I continued on my way but as I sat down at my keyboard the phrase 'Letters from the Lost' drifted into my head.

I still have the piece of paper that I began to make notes on that afternoon. At the top it says (ungrammatically) 'Who are the letters to? Who are they from?' In the dusty filing cabinet at the back of my mind I had an idea about an ordinary house, empty and long-abandoned, and I knew that the letters would arrive there. I think all the chaos and upheaval of London in wartime made it feel very possible that the house could have belonged to someone from that time who had planned a future there. A future that, for whatever reason, hadn't happened as hoped. Those were the seeds from which the present and the past storylines grew.

What is it about letters that so appealed to you?

There's just something immediately intriguing about a letter – as the one on my daughter's desk proved! Especially in the twenty-first century when communication is mostly done by text and email, a handwritten letter is inescapably significant: special, and suggestive of words and emotions too important to be trusted to technology. Texts are dashed off in seconds, emails in minutes, whereas a letter takes time and involves planning; the purchase of paper, envelopes, stamps, and the unhurried ritual of setting out the address and date at the top of the page. A letter bears the personality of the sender in every stroke of ink, and it can be folded away and kept somewhere secret, to be rediscovered a lifetime later.

We switch between 1943 and seventy years later. What was is about those periods that drew you to write about them?

I feel helplessly drawn towards the Second World War as a setting, I think because I grew up with wartime stories. Born in the 1970s, mine is the generation whose parents and grandparents had lived through it and were beginning to filter their memories and experiences into children's fiction. I remember the scramble to be next in line for Judith Kerr's *When Hitler Stole Pink Rabbit* and Noel Streatfeild's *When The Siren Wailed* from the library cupboard in my primary school, and my great excitement when *Carrie's War* by Nina Bawden (my favourite book) was adapted for a TV series. As I got older I continued to seek out books set in this era, so it was instinctive to place my own story during the war.

The 2011 bit was a balancing act: I knew I had to have a modern enough setting to make all the technology the story uses to be possible (there's much internet searching for historical records, as well as email and skype) but I was aware of Dan and Stella's advancing years!

If you could travel back in time to London during the Blitz what would you most want to see? Do you think you would recognise the city from your research, given how much it has changed?

What a great question! I think more than anything, I'd like to experience the atmosphere and the mood of the people. Today we use the term 'Blitz Spirit' quite casually to refer to cheerfulness in adversity if the train we're travelling on breaks down, or when one of those rare heavy snowfalls makes everything grind to a halt, but I don't think anyone who wasn't alive during the war can possibly appreciate its true meaning: the relentless, understated courage required by everyone to simply keep going, through privations and separations and fear. I was captivated and moved by all the photographs I came across during my research, of people picking their way through rubble to go about their everyday business, smiling as they bedded down with their children on the platforms in the underground for the night, drinking tea amidst smouldering ruins. It's humbling to remember that they weren't just coping with such conditions for a few inconvenient days or weeks, but indefinitely, all the time.

In twenty-first-century Britain the threat to our lives from enemy attack is – in real terms – relatively low, and yet we live in an atmosphere of anxiety and high alert. I'm fascinated by the way the country, and in the Blitzed cities in particular, continued to function with apparent normality during those six long years between 1939 and 1945. To us Keep Calm and Carry On is a slogan that appears on mugs and tea towels, but to millions of ordinary people it was a basic principle of survival, when they didn't know when – or how – the war would end.

The Second World War was a time of increased opportunity for women with many working outside the home for the first time, yet Stella remains very much within the domestic sphere. Was that a deliberate decision?

I've read – and loved – lots of novels set in the war in which women take on the new roles the conflict afforded them;

delivering aeroplanes, working in government departments or for the S.O.E. doing terrifying and dangerous missions in occupied territory. The bravery shown by those pioneering women (who must have faced a degree of prejudice from their male colleagues in addition to everything else they had to deal with!) is fascinating and inspiring. However, I wanted a heroine who absolutely wasn't heroic. Stella is shy and mousy and painfully self-effacing. She infuriates Nancy and at times she infuriated me. Wearing red lipstick on a night out is the closest she gets to daring, until she meets Dan.

I wanted to write about a woman like that because I think there must have been a lot of them, and history (understandably) doesn't record their experiences as much as those of the pilots and ATS girls and secret agents. I think I was influenced by the stories I heard so often growing up, from my grandmother and godmother, about the challenges of feeding a baby in an air raid, or getting a new dress for a dance. Stella starts out being afraid of everything, wanting to bury herself in domesticity and almost pretend that the war isn't happening, but when that becomes impossible she has to draw on inner reserves of courage to face the situation she finds herself in. It was this quiet, ordinary brand of bravery that interested me.

Which part was easier to write – the past or the present?

I wrote the past story, in its entirety, first, so in a sense that was the easiest. It was the core of the book, and its spirit – the spirit of the 40s – was the one that I wanted to evoke most strongly. I think of it now as being an absolute breeze to write, though I recently opened up my first draft document and saw all the scenes that were slashed and abandoned, so I think I've slightly deluded myself about that! The first scene I wrote was Stella and Charles's wedding, which is initially seen through the eyes of

Ada, and her voice came into my head with absolute clarity and really led me into the period. She's only a fairly minor character but for me she was the lynchpin.

The present-day storyline was trickier in that it needed to be fitted around the past one, so I had to keep half my mind on structure. At the start, with Stella and Dan's story still so vivid in my mind, Jess and Will were very much secondary characters whose main purpose was to discover and reveal what had happened seventy years ago, but as time went on they really sprang off the page for me and their story took on a life of its own.

If you could write a letter to anyone from the past who would it be?

My grandmother; my mother's mother. My mum was only ten when she died so I never knew her, but I've always felt her presence in my life, I think because her absence had such a huge impact on my mum's. She was a remarkable woman: a doctor, who graduated from Glasgow University with her degree in medicine in 1933 (and was awarded a gold medal for her thesis) and spent her career working in public health. I'd like to write to her and ask about the challenges she must have faced as a female medical student in the 1920s and 30s (Were there many other women in her year? What was the attitude of the men in her classes?) and, of course, about her experiences of being a doctor during the war, as well as a first-time mother. My mum was born at the end of 1940 and her mother went back to work almost immediately, partly because there was a shortage of doctors to look after the civilian population, but also because she loved her work and (unlike Stella!) wanted a life outside the home, in a time when this was relatively uncommon. She sounds like such an interesting person. How wonderful it would be if, somehow, I could receive a letter from her in return . . .

You have a pinterest board with loads of great photos on it, including some of film stars who inspired you while you were writing the novel. Who would you love to see playing the leads if *Letters to the Lost* was made into a film?

I'd be a Casting Director's nightmare as I tend to take my inspiration from actors from all different eras. So, I'd need Richard Gere in his *Yanks* incarnation (circa 1978) for Dan, and *Four Weddings*-vintage Hugh Grant (1994) for Will. Gene Tierney, the 1940s actress, would have to be Stella (if she could do a good English accent), but I've never come across anyone who looks or sounds like the Jess of my imagination. (If anyone has any suggestions I'd love to hear them – and add them to my Pinterest board!)

What novels inspired you as you were writing?

Completely by coincidence, the day after I started writing the book the postman delivered a signed copy of Kate Atkinson's *Life After Life*, sent by my lovely friend Abby Green. I don't think any writer could help but be inspired by Atkinson's effortlessly vivid writing. She makes it seem so easy and natural; having her voice in my head as I plunged into those first few chapters gave me a big boost of confidence.

I'm also a huge fan E.M. Delafield's *Diary of a Provincial Lady* and its sequels, and love the way she juxtaposes gravely serious events with small domestic detail. And I can't help but be influenced by books I first fell in love with as a teenager – the big, sprawling stories of Rosamunde Pilcher, Jilly Cooper, Maeve Binchy. Books you would fall into and lose yourself for days, emerging to find that reality was a pale and faded imitation of the world you'd discovered between the covers. I learned so much from those books – including what I wanted to do for a living when I was older!